JANE DE LA VAUDÈRE

SYTA'S HAREM
AND
PHARAOH'S LOVER

TRANSLATED AND WITH AN INTRODUCTION BY
BRIAN STABLEFORD

SYTA'S HAREM AND PHARAOH'S LOVER

JANE DE LA VAUDÈRE was baptized Jeanne Scrive and was married to Camille Gaston Crapez, who began styling himself Crapez de La Vaudère after inheriting the Château de La Vaudère from his mother. Her prolific literary work is very various but she was assimilated to the Decadent Movement firstly because of two scandalously scabrous Parisian novels, *Les Demi-Sexes* (1897) and *Les Andrognyes* (1903), and, more pertinently, because of a series of accounts of *moeurs antiques*, some of which—notably *Le Mystère de Kama* (1901)—set new standards of excess in their exotic eroticism and fascination with torture.

BRIAN STABLEFORD'S scholarly work includes *New Atlantis: A Narrative History of Scientific Romance* (Wildside Press, 2016), *The Plurality of Imaginary Worlds: The Evolution of French roman scientifique* (Black Coat Press, 2017) and *Tales of Enchantment and Disenchantment: A History of Faerie* (Black Coat Press, 2019). In support of the latter projects he has translated more than a hundred volumes of *roman scientifique* and more than twenty volumes of *contes de fées* into English. He has edited *Decadence and Symbolism: A Showcase Anthology* (Snuggly Books, 2018), and is busy translating more Symbolist and Decadent fiction.

His recent fiction, in the genre of metaphysical fantasy, includes a trilogy of novels set in West Wales, consisting of *Spirits of the Vasty Deep* (2018), *The Insubstantial Pageant* (2018) and *The Truths of Darkness* (2019), published by Snuggly Books, and a trilogy set in Paris and the south of France, consisting of *The Painter of Spirits*, *The Quiet Dead* and *Living with the Dead*, all published by Black Coat Press in 2019.

CONTENTS

Introduction / *vii*

Syta's Harem / 3
Pharaoh's Lover / 139

INTRODUCTION

This is the fifth of six projected volumes translating fiction by Jane de La Vaudère (15 April 1857-26 July 1908). Five of those volumes each contain two of her short novels, while the second in the series, *The Double Star and Other Occult Fantasies*, contains a selection of her short fiction. The first volume, *The Demi-Sexes and The Androgynes*, contained translations of *Les Demi-Sexes*, originally published by Paul Ollendorff in 1897, and *Les Androgynes, roman passionel*, published by Albert Méricant in 1903. The third volume contains translations of *Le Mystère de Kama, roman magique indou* (Ernest Flammarion, 1901) and *Les Courtisanes de Brahma* (Flammarion, 1903). The fourth volume, *Three Flowers and The King of Siam's Amazon*, contains translations of *Trois fleurs de volupté, roman javanais* (Flammarion, 1900) and *L'Amazone du roi de Siam* (Flammarion, 1902). The present volume contains translations of *Le Harem de Syta, roman passionel* (Méricant, 1904) and *L'Amante du Pharaon, moeurs antiques* (Jules Tallandier, 1905). The sixth volume, *The Witch of Ecbatana and The Virgin of Israel*, contains translations *of La Sorcière d'Ecbatane, roman fantastique* (Flammarion, 1906) and *La Vierge d'Israel, roman de moeurs antiques* (Méricant 1906).

Jane de La Vaudère was baptized Jeanne Scrive; both her parents died when she was still a child, and in the social class to which her family belonged, which might be described as the "upper bourgeoisie," the standard practice when a young girl was orphaned at an early age was to put her in a convent, where she would be educated until her teens, and then marry her off as soon as possible. That appears to be what happened to Jeanne Scrive and her elder sister Marie. It is necessary to say "appears" because almost nothing is known for sure about Jane de La Vaudère's personal life and death, which is now covered by an obscurity that remains virtually impenetrable save for the statements she made in a few newspaper interviews and a few objectively determinable facts.

In one such interview La Vaudère said that while in the convent of Notre-Dame de Sion she seriously considered remaining there permanently, the idea of living as a nun having a certain romantic attraction, but soon abandoned the idea. In fact, shortly after leaving the institution, when she stayed for a while with Marie, by then married to a military surgeon, she was married herself to Camille Gaston Crapez (1848-1912), who inherited the Château de La Vaudère in Parigné-l'Éveque (Sarthe) from his mother and styled himself thereafter Crapez de La Vaudère. The name with which she signed her books was not, as many sources report, a pseudonym, although she deleted the Crapez and anglicized her forename.

The Crapez de La Vaudères had one child, Fernand, who apparently stayed with his father when his mother went to live in Paris, where she seems to have lived alone. Although she was never divorced, and her body was taken back to Parigné-l'Éveque for burial after her death in Paris, the separation appears to have been complete; no newspaper reports of her appearances at social events or interviews conducted at her home ever mention the presence of her husband. Nothing was reported about the circumstances of her death, and neither her husband nor her son appear to have been with her at the time; the unusual brevity of the death notices and the conspicuous absence of the customary post-mortem eulogies suggest a diplomatic silence, but we can only speculate as to what it was that was deliberately not being said about her sudden death at a relatively young age.

The circumstances of Jane de La Vaudère's early life evidently had a profound impact on her literary work, to which she turned a trifle late in her career. Before she began writing, she attempted to make a career as an artist and exhibited at the Paris Salon; when she decided that her real vocation was literary she first began writing poetry, and then wrote for the stage. Her first collection of poetry, *Les Heures perdues* [The Lost Hours] (1889) appeared in the same year as the production of her one-act comedy *Le Modèle* [The Model]. Her verse is Romantic and might have seemed a trifle old-fashioned at the time of its publication; she was certainly not unaware of contemporary trends in Symbolist poetry, as she was a very voracious reader and her influences were eclectic. *Le Modèle* was the first of many frothy one-act comedies, usually in verse and often performed with musical accompaniment—fifteen of them were collected in *Pour le Flirt! Saynètes modernes* [approximately, Just For Fun, modern satirettes] (1905)—but she also wrote longer comedies and dramas.

She continued to write poetry and plays alongside her prose fiction, but there are striking differences between her work in the three genres, and her prose work also shows sharp generic divisions. It is not unusual for writers to manifest seemingly different personalities in their prose fiction and work for the stage, especially if the latter mostly consists of vaudevilles written as pure entertainment while the former is more earnest and intense, but in La Vaudère's case the difference is extreme, even in her contemporary Paris-set novels, which often feature female characters not unlike those routinely featured in her stage comedies—young socialites, actresses and artists' models—and even more markedly in the remarkable series of exotic novels set in far-flung places and times that make up the last four volumes of the present series of translations.

La Vaudère's first novel, *Mortelle étreinte* [Mortal Embrace] (1891) is the story of a young orphan brought up in a convent, who then goes to live with a relative, where she continues to live in virtual seclusion, in the psychological environment of her vivid imagination and the books she reads in abundance. She knows nothing about the real world and is utterly unready to cope with her own hectic emotions when she is first attracted to a man—a man who is also greatly attracted to her, but who is, from every other viewpoint, quite unsuitable and incapable of providing her with the existential anchorage and security that she needs and desires.

The basic features of that story-line were to recur again and again in the author's work, almost to the exclusion of any other, even in the most bizarre décor. Its melodramatic intensity is inevitably restrained in *Mortelle étreinte* by the conventions of the society in which it is set, but when it is removed to ancient India or ancient Babylon, in the author's accounts of *moeurs antiques*, such shackles no longer apply and the pitch of that intensity is turned up to a level unequaled in the work of any other writer of the era. The sensation of having been brought up in an artificial environment, with little or no parental guidance, and then thrust into a world equipped with hopes and expectations that are certain to be betrayed, is developed in story after story, in variants that are extraordinarily wide-ranging, often wildly exaggerated, and almost always brutally tragic.

Following the publication of her second novel, *Rien qu'amante* [Only a Lover] (1893), La Vaudère devoted her principal effort to novels, although she contributed weekly articles to *La Presse* between 1897 and 1901 and then went on to supply a long sequence of unreprinted short stories to the weekly supplement of the daily newspaper *La Lanterne* in 1901-3. She published a good deal of poetry in the same newspaper, and several further poetry collections. As well as her solo work for the theater she adapted a short story by Émile Zola for the Grand Guignol and collaborated with a number of other writers on theatrical work, including Félicien Champsaur and Aurélian Scholl.

Once begun, her literary production rapidly became unusually prolific, and she published more than twenty novels between 1894 and her death in 1908. Seven more appeared posthumously under her name. It is unclear why she wrote in such profusion, but she seems to have been avid for success, trying out several popular formulae in her varied fiction, as well as deliberately plowing new literary ground in order to fish for interested attention. The direction that La Vaudère's later work took seems to have been largely determined by the success of her first best-seller, the highly controversial *Les Demi-Sexes*, whose *succès de scandale* she tried hard to repeat in one of the strands of her subsequent work, to considerable effect. Equally important, however, was the evident inspiration she took from the novel that was the great best-seller of the era, Pierre Louÿs; *Aphrodite, moeurs antiques* (1896), which sold three hundred thousand copies and, inevitably, launched a bandwagon chased by many Parisian publishers, including Ernest Flammarion and especially Albert Méricant, who became La Vaudère's second major publisher in the last few years of her life, and the publisher of most of the posthumous works signed with her name.

Aphrodite carried forward a rich tradition of feverish antiquarian erotic fantasies begun with Théophile Gautier's "Une nuit de Cléopâtre" (1838; tr. as "One of Cleopatra's Nights") and continued by Gustave Flaubert's *Salammbô* (1862; tr. as *Salammbo*) and Anatole France's *Thaïs* (1890; tr. as *Thaïs*), and demonstrated in no uncertain terms that erotic extremism seemed more acceptable and more plausible to the contemporary French literary audience if its exemplars were set long ago and far away, in the context of a culture where moral standards and expectations could be presumed to be very different.

La Vaudère's first venture into exotic erotica, the Java-set *Trois fleurs de volupté* (1900; tr. as "Three Flowers of Sensuality") is not set in the distant past, and owes something to the French genre of "travelogue fiction," but its successor, *Le Mystère de Kama* (1901) pulled out all the stops in a flamboyant extravaganza of eroticism—Kama is the Hindu god of amour—which is also remarkable for some gruesome scenes of torture. *Le Mystère de Kama* was the first of La Vaudère's novels to sell thirty thousand copies, and it set a pattern that she continued in a series of novels, initially issued at the rate of one a year, all featuring the same garish eroticism, and many of them displaying the same fascination with gruesome physical torture.

Le Harem de Syta is La Vaudère's third India-set novel, and seems to have been planned, in part, as a calculated attempt to reproduce the effect of *Le Mystère de Kama*, featuring a similar fakir, who refers at one point to the Nassudamy of the earlier novel as a predecessor, although that seems chronologically unlikely, as *Le Harem de Syta* is a prehistoric novel set ten thousand years in the past, while *Le Mystère de Kama*, although carefully undated, does not seem to be so remote. However, although Salassim seduces Syta in the same supernatural fashion that Nassudamy had employed to seduce Viamalah, his reason for doing so is never very clear; his character seems to change markedly as the novel progresses, while the author tries to keep the storyline—of which she has clearly lost the direction—in motion. The novel also carries forward, very deliberately, the descriptions of religiously-impelled orgies introduced, a trifle tentatively, in *Les Courtisanes de Brahma*. In the rest of its narrative materials, however, *Le Harem de Syta* is quite different from its predecessors.

What is most distinctive—and hence, perhaps, most interesting—about *Le Harem de Syta* is a component unique within La Vaudère's work and highly unusual in the context of the French fiction of the era. Among the proto-anthropological fantasies of which La Vaudère made use in *Les Courtesans de Brahma* is the notion that polyandrous societies once existed in India. The hero of *Les Courtesans de Brahma* claims to belong to one such society, although he hastens to assure the heroine that he has no intention of sharing her with other men of his tribe, and the matter is then forgotten. The early chapters of *Le Harem de Syta*, however, take up that notion again, robustly and elaborately, establishing Syta is the queen of a long-vanished earthly paradise, already isolated in an India where polyandry has been replaced in other regions by brutal male rule and the virtual enslavement of women; the story then attempts to develop the corollaries and possibilities inherent in the notion.

In fact, there is no necessary logical connection between polyandry and matriarchy, but in the hypothetical society of the novel, women are not only able to have several husbands, but to exercise tyrannical authority over them. The early chapters thus become a kind of feminist satire, in which Syta's six senior husbands and her "concubins" make all the efforts to please her that the wives and concubines of sultans must make, and instead of her capital being abundantly supplied with *filles de joie* it has brothels staffed by *fils de joie*. As those themes are tentatively developed, the story sometimes teeters on the edge of farce, but as it is supposed to be an exercise in erotic exotica, not a vaudeville, its development is obliged to steer clear of that edge, and that requires some rather peculiar narrative moves, of dubious plausibility.

Few of La Vaudère's plots stand up to rigorous rational analysis, and *Le Harem de Syta* is one of the worst offenders in that regard, but as with her other novels, logical consistency is not really a significant issue in what is, in essence, a nightmare of helplessness in the face of arbitrary, inexorable, self-destructive passion. Many of her works fit that description, but it is in *Le Harem de Syta* that the motif attains its greatest exemplary clarity, and its logical incoherencies are best viewed as intrinsic aspects of the nightmare. Seen from that angle, the novel becomes a surreal phantasmagoria, closely akin to both *La Sorcière d'Ecbatane* and *La Vierge d'Israel*, although both of those later novels, doubtless benefiting from the lessons learned by the author in writing *Le Harem de Syta*, are more tightly focused on their nightmarish core.

Before progressing from the supernatural fantasy of *Le Harem de Syta* to the supernatural fantasy of *La Sorcière d'Ecbatane*, however, La Vaudère produced *L'Amante du Pharaon*, which, although still an account of *moeurs antiques*, contrasts sharply in several ways with the Indian and Assyrian novels, representing a thematic and imaginative leap akin to the one that separated the strangely sentimental *Trois fleurs de volupté* from the brutally violent *L'Amazone du roi de Siam*. In this case the change might reflect the fact that *L'Amante du Pharaon* was the only one of La Vaudère's exotic novels to be published by Jules Tallandier rather than Ernest Flammarion or Albert Méricant; Tallandier might well have commissioned it, and imposed certain recommendations on the commission that the author did not have to follow elsewhere. On the other hand, La Vaudère explicitly makes the point in *La Vierge d'Israel* that the mores of Babylonian society, in her estimation, were very different from those of ancient Egyptian society, the brutal institutionalized torture that she considers so natural in the societies of ancient India and Assyria, as well as relatively modern Siam, having no place in the Third Empire of Thutmose I.

Another factor that might have played some part in her decision to abandon India for ancient Egypt—although this is pure speculation—is that she might have taken some inspiration from one of the other novels produced in the rush to take advantage of the marketing opportunities opened by *Aphrodite*'s bestsellerdom, *Les Femmes de Setnê* (1903; tr. as "Setne's Women" in *Pan's Flute and Other Stories*), signed "Enacryos" [J. H. Rosny aîné], which also features Thutmose II and the queen whose name La Vaudère renders as Atasu, but at a much later stage in their lives, and which also features an unusual troilistic relationship. Even if there was no direct influence, the juxtaposition of the two novels makes an interesting comparison and contrast.

Although certainly not without its nightmarish aspects in the emotional sufferings of its separated lovers, the story-line of *L'Amante du Pharaon* is much more robust and coherent than that of *Le Harem de Syta*—again, perhaps the result of the lesson learned while floundering in the writing of the former—and is, in fact, so coherent that its narrative logic virtually specifies its climax and its culmination, in a fashion quite atypical of La Vaudère's fiction. It is one of the few works in her canon that not only borrows the feverish narrative pitch of generic melodrama but also pays lip service to the standard plot-formula of popular melodrama. Typically of La Vaudère, however, the story perverts that formula flamboyantly in its descriptions of the sexual components of the misadventures of Zelinis and Hary-Thé in the aftermath of their sudden loss of their perfect amour. The troilistic relationship that develops between Zelinis, Atasu and Thutmose, on the one hand, and Hary-Thé's quasi-necrophlic relationship with what he believes mistakenly to be Zelinis' mummy on the other, are striking examples of the author's peculiar Decadent artistry and her invariable sympathy for unusual expressions of passionate distress.

Although *La Sorcière d'Ecbatane*, in reverting to the supernatural seductions of *Le Harem de Syta* and restoring gruesome tortures to its story-line, makes *L'Amante du Pharaon* look like something of a momentary sidestep in the sequence of her exotic novels, *L'Amante du Pharaon* was not without a sequel of sorts. Several of its passages of background description are reproduced verbatim in the novelette *Le Rêve de Mysès* (1908; tr. as "The Dream of Myses" in *The Double Star and Other Occult Fantasies*), which develops the necrophilic theme of Hary-Thé's obsession with greater intensity. That was the last book that La Vaudère published during her lifetime, although not necessarily the last one she wrote; if the seven novels published posthumously under her name really are all her work—and some of them certainly are—one or more of them might well have been written in the months preceding her death, and the first of them to be published, *Sapho, dompteuse* [Sapho the Animal-Tamer] (1908) might well have been in press when she died. Perhaps, had she lived longer, she might have returned imaginatively to ancient Egypt again, although the pattern of her work as a whole suggests, perverse and paradoxical as it might seem, that she felt more at home in more brutal imaginary environments.

The translation of *Le Harem de Syta* was made from the copy of the text of the Méricant edition reproduced (without the illustrations) in the Internet Archive Digital Library at archive.org. The translation of *L'Amante du Pharaon* was made from a copy of the Tallandier edition.

—Brian Stableford

SYTA'S HAREM

PART ONE

I
For Timorous Readers

Humans, who have invented nothing, have sometimes, like nature, put the remedy alongside the ill. Although countries exist in India where wives are burned on the pyres of their beloved husbands, in other provinces, numerous husbands devote themselves to the felicity of a unique wife, bringing her, with a jealous urgency, the tribute of their homage and their caresses. Malabar, which saw so many conjugal torches, so many tearful lovers offering their charming bodies to the kisses of the monster in a supreme spasm of amour, also saw many husbands sacrifice themselves for the happiness of one alone.

In some parts of that strange country, the women enjoyed an entire liberty, and polyandry is in general usage there. Thus, in one family, several brothers only had one companion, whose children called all the collaborators of equal merit "papa." But the woman, insatiable and fickle, often added strangers to those husbands of the same blood. The richest provided themselves with a carefully selected harem, the poorest supplied themselves at the hazard of encounters.

Does not that custom, which we would qualify as immoral, raise an obstacle to the division of heritages, to poverty and to famine, by preventing the population from increasing in a country where there is little land to cultivate and where the importation of food can only be operated in difficult conditions?

The first fiancé put around the neck of the young woman a necklace made of enchanted seeds, which she retained in all embraces and which even death did not unfasten. After a few

3

days, however, which had the sweetness of honey, that first lord was dismissed with an honest recompense, and had to give way to numerous successors.

The young wife had become the property, not of the entire tribe, as in the primitive family, but a large number of members, whom she chose at her whim among the most robust and the most docile. Each of them, after the initial caress, planted his dagger in the door of the beloved to indicate that he had shown himself worthy of that great favor.

The children that resulted from these temporary unions could only bear the name of their mother, since the father generally remained unknown. The drone of sensuality quit the active hive as soon as his duty was accomplished, and the bee continued to collect pollen in all the fields of amour.

That polyandry, so shocking for our modern ideas, is a very ancient institution in India, and the "Kill her!" of our passionate comedies would have plunged those pacific peoples into a profound amazement. Does one not see, in the Mahabharata, the five Pandava brothers espousing the beautiful Draupadi "with eyes the color of the lotus"? Does one not see in the sacred poems, the Tantras and the Sutras of the Backti, sixty lovers, and even more, consecrating themselves to the happiness of one alone?[1]

From the limitless promiscuity of savage tribes to the absolute prohibition of the work of the flesh, outside of certain ceremonies that change in accordance with the country, how many different degrees there are in the liberty granted to sexual relationships by public opinion and social law! In certain peoples monogamy is obligatory, among others polygamy is permissible in all refined and brutal forms. In a distant epoch the women who had, in certain countries of India, the advantage over men, enjoyed prerogatives that the new religions refuse them today. Sovereign

---

1 This is true, but in none of these instances is it implied that polyandry is a social institution rather than a rare exception. The story of the Pandavas was the basis for a novelette by the Symbolist writer André-Ferdinand Herold, "L'Ascension des Pandavas" (1896; tr. as "The Ascension of the Pandavas"), which La Vaudère might well have read.

mistresses of the household, and authorized advisers in affairs of State, nothing was done independently of them, and the State was no worse for it.

But the "devil" had not been invented then, and the apple of discord remained on the tree in a Terrestrial Paradise that contained, in any case, tastier fruit . . . The Rakshasas, Beelzebub, Iblis, Satan, demons and evil spirits that all the prophets and all the pastors of men called to their aid in order to maintain the oppressed under the yoke of religions had not yet appeared officially in the world, and, the work of the flesh not being a work of shame, woman remained respected and powerful.

In some parts of the Deccan, the ancient customs would persist, in spite of Buddhism and Islam. The Nairs of the Malabar coast still conserve the primitive institutions that no longer exist in the Occident, except in a vestigial state.[1] One can study among them the maternal family such as it was in remote times.

The woman, then, was the veritable head of the association and exercised an authority over it that no one ever sought to contest. She had as many husbands as she desired, only taking care to choose healthy and handsome subjects among the men of her caste. Brahmin women, above all, by reason of their sacred character and their ancient prestige, went from house to house offering themselves for the work of amour.

The sovereigns consecrated a part of their palace to young and seductive men that were brought to them from all countries. When a husband died, it was not his children that inherited his wealth but the children of his eldest sister. The matrimony passed from daughter to daughter—in the same way as royal power—and it is the story of one of those gracious queens with the skin of a ripe lemon, the large eyes of a gazelle, and arms as satiny as the trunk of a young elephant, that we are going to tell.

---

1 Anthropological evidence, although vague and slightly dubious, does suggests that in some sectors of Nair society both polyandry and polygamy were simultaneously permissible. The Naurs appear to have had a matrilineal system of inheritance at one time, but that does not imply that the society was ever matriarchal.

II

Princess Syta

Princess Syta lived in a city now dead, the glorious palaces of which seemed to be rising to the conquest of the stars, and which twenty thousand elephants harnessed in gold guarded day and night against the whim of invaders.

It is necessary to undertake the voyage from Ellora to Bombay, traversing a picturesque region of the Deccan, and to see the admirable claim of the Vindhya mountains, in order to comprehend all the seductions of that ardent and eccentric nature, which renews itself incessantly while always remaining the same. Fatiguing stages are compensated by stations of unusual splendor, of which our pale vegetation and our anemic sun cannot give any idea. Sometimes the forest combines its lianas to frame the tomb of Salabab Khan,[1] to embrace it with a thousand supple arms, knotted by flowery hands, sometimes angry cataracts sweep the ruins of the temple of Shiva, spitting their wild irony in the face of the perverse god.

On the horizon of a desiccated plain, ringed by russet mountains and sharp rocky crests, stands the silhouette of Ahmehnagara, today a desolate city, ruins full of mute and frightful apparitions, once the capital of the State of the same name, which was governed by Queen Syta. In contemplating the ravages of time and the melancholy of the stones that collide with the feet of the traveler, one would scarcely suspect that that disquieting necropolis, which was fecundated by the thousand tributary

---

1 The author might well have the tomb of Salabat II in mind, although it is not in a forest. It is near the town of Ahmednagar, but that is of recent foundation and has no possible connection with the fictitious prehistoric Ahmehnagara. It was, however, once famously defended against Muslim forces by the female regent Chand-Bibi (1550-1599), whose name is co-opted as an alternative name for Syta.

streams of the Krishna and the Godavari, was covered with crops of crimson and gold, and that nature had nothing but smiles for it! That is because the earth has its revenges, and the good fortune of a city fades away, like the felicity of a people and the glory of conquerors. The most beautiful lands were the most tested, and history relates to us the vicissitudes of ridiculed heroes.

Once, a long time ago, Timur the Lame and his sons had not yet paraded anarchy through India from the banks of the Indus to the banks of the Ganges when the young Rani, Syta or Chand-Bibi—which is to say, the lady of election—received power from the hands of her mother, Salabatki, and raised her adorable scepter over Ahmehnagara.

This is how the king of Oude celebrated her in vehement verses:

"The hair of the princess caresses her bare feet, putting heavy rings around her slender ankles, and her entire charming body has the appearance of a star in the mantle of the night.

"The eyebrows of the princess rise to a point, like the enchanted bow of Kama, and her immense eyes have the velvet profundity of the Himalayan lakes where reflections of moonlight dance.

"The teeth of the princess, purer than jasmine petals, attract kisses as flowers attract bees.

"The ears of the princess, as finely rolled as the tender buds of the lotus, are open to all words of amour, and the song of the waves comes to kiss them when she reposes on her bed of ivory and nacre, believing that it is penetrating once again the delicate shells of beaches.

"The loincloth of the princess could be held in a child's hand, and her loins are softly rounded for the desire of man, like a corolla swollen with pollen.

"How many times, O Splendor, seated on your throne under the awning constellated with diamonds and opals, or passing with the undulating stride of an Asparasa alongside pools of alabaster and onyx, you must have felt yourself imprisoned in the quivering wings of moths attracted by the perfume of your mouth! How many times you must have palpitated under the metallic mesh of dragonflies asleep in the cradling algae of your hair!

"O adorable sovereign, divine Syta, whom only the hand of genius of Vicrakarna, the eternal sculptor, could have modeled in unalloyed gold, who would not have been proud to die for you?"

Syta was beloved but did not love, bored by so many homages and so many embraces, which were unable to satisfy her soul or exhaust her body.

However, the princes and the aristocrats of the realm avidly sought the favor of entering her palace and consecrating themselves to her pleasures; her guard of honor was composed of eight hundred ardent, young and well-built husbands, among whom she only had to choose the elect of one night, the passionate lover of a few hours of intoxication.

The Sultana of a harem of lovers, she listened, yawning, to adulatory voices enfevered by desire, and sometimes, with the tip of her scepter of precious stones, she indicated a preference.

The husband then prostrated himself three times before Syta, kissed the diamond on her toe, and the queen, lifting her dainty foot, placed it on the favorite's head. After further actions of grace, the latter went to the temple of Durga, immolated a ram to the goddess, and delivered himself to the Brahmins, who rubbed him with mysterious balms, braided his hair, which he had to wear long, and, by means of savant artifices, made him more beautiful than Smara, the god of supreme joys.

On the threshold of the nuptial chamber, the husband had to kneel and thus travel the path that separated him from the bed of the Most High, and then, lifting her veil of gold and silver, plunge himself in the contemplation of her splendor. Closing her eyes, she allowed herself to be adored, with a smile in the corners of her delicate lips. Without moving, she listened to the prayers and sighs of that lover of an evening, and often, changing her mind, only permitted him meager caresses.

III
The Snake

In the luminous and embalmed morning, Syta was hunting antelope. The entire court of Ahmehnagara, in carts drawn by buffalo, in palanquins or on the backs of elephants and dromedaries, was following the Rani, whose white horse, covered with a net of pearls, was galloping through the long grass. Panthers and leopards, in chains, their eye blindfolded with half-masks of green velvet, appeared on chariots, two by two. As soon as a herd of antelopes appeared, they sought to scatter them, and then the carnivores, released, leapt on the hindquarters of the animals or seized them by the neck, and brought them down.

Syta, clad in light veils that kissed and gave a nacreous sheen to her flesh, alternately covering and uncovering her legs, loved hectic races through forests full of mysterious shadows. Sometimes, she went astray deliberately, remaining for long hours in the soft shade of the branches intersecting above her head. When the sun went down, a dust of light, in tones of copper and rust, bloodied the calices that opened like mouths, avid to inhale the first breezes.

Syta set off again, her spear supported on her high, ready to defend herself against the assaults of wild beasts. She rode through the chaos of landslides, through the tangles of giant ferns sown with delicate leprosies of golden yellow or silvery gray. The clamors of birds of prey with somber wings, the moans of pink turtle-doves and the appeals of crested parrots, great eaters of honey, struck her ears. She shivered when a giant moth brushed her cheek or the silken thread of a blue spider suspended itself from the golden ornaments of her temples. The gilded hooves of her horse crushed the phyllias leaves that ran through the moss, and living corollas, gorged on insects, whose petals contracted.

Descending from her horse, she went forward on foot in the violet shadow, brushing the foliage of poisonous bushes, which agitated diamantine needles and russet pods suspended like the clappers of bells under the rounded leaves, fleshy cups with pale buds reminiscent of virgin breasts.

The Rani's thin nostrils palpitated gently; she went toward the unknown, toward life or death, and the fearful whinnying of Ackbe, tethered at the edge of the wood, filled her with a delicious dread.

The plants often affected the fantastic forms of Hindu gods; they raised menacing arms, livid and sticky tentacles in the hues of rotting flesh; poisonous translucent corollas darted their stamens like bewitching eyes, and opened in the depths of the calyx a bloody mouth armed with a fleshy needle. On the branches, other flowers were lurking, as flaccid and gelatinous as medusae, and poisonous tears fell from them at the slightest contact.

But Syta, on that beautiful, luminous and embalmed morning, listened to a distant grave voice intoning the stanzas to Para Purusha, and the sounds descended within her like waves of honey.

"O god of supreme caresses, deign to accept my invocation! May your breath penetrate me, like that of a young lover swooning under the first kisses of his mistress!

"Adoration to Brahma!"

"Adoration to Brahma," repeated the Rani, in a sigh; and suddenly, only showing the whites of her eyes, she uttered a loud cry and fell to the ground.

A snake marbled with livid patches, of the most dangerous species, was swaying above her head, softly, like a liana agitated by the breeze. Slithering voluptuously, it drew nearer to the charming visage, darting its tongue toward her mouth, redder and more fondant than the fruit of the bimba.

At the moment when it was about to drink from that cup of felicity, a strange man clad entirely in white parted the bushes and extended his hand rapidly toward the Rani. The reptile uttered an audible hiss, coiled up, crawled toward the Charmer and nestled under his bare foot.

Syta had opened her eyes again, and her astonished gaze was fixed on the motionless man.

"Thank you," she said. "I would like to know your name, in order to recompense you."

He raised his head proudly. "Recompense me for what? Here, the snakes and the wild beasts obey me."

"You're similar to the gods, then?"

"The gods are favorable to me; they have revealed many mysteries to me."

"Ah! You know who I am, then?"

He reflected momentarily. "No. For that, it would be necessary for me to read the lines of your hand. I can see in the backti[1] and I spread the good word everywhere. But I have come from far away, and I shall quit this forest tomorrow, never to return."

The Rani shivered; it seemed to her that darkness suddenly enveloped her.

"I don't want you to go!"

"By what right would you prevent me from following my destiny?" The man darted a luminous gaze at her, more terrible than that of an eagle.

"I don't want you to go!"

He laughed ironically, took a step back and revealed the snake still coiled up before her. "All creatures obey me," he said, "but I obey no one except the Supreme Being."

"Perhaps you would submit to my will if you knew me . . ."

"I don't desire to know you. I have excluded women from my life, for I dread suffering through them. I belong to Indra, god of the air, and Varuna, god of the waters. I travel perpetually, with beneficent mantras on my lips. What would I do with a

---

1 I have left this word as it is in the original, because it has at least one idiosyncratic meaning in the course of the story, referring to the forest, although it is later rendered as "bakti" with that apparent meaning as well as another. It is probably derived from the Hindu term *bhakti* (devotion to a single deity, usually Vishnu or Shiva), but the duality of its meaning in the present text does not license a substitution.

companion in the midst of the dangers that surround me and the struggles that I have to sustain?"

"Do you know who the sovereign is who governs this realm?"

"Her name is Syta; she is charming and her people remain submissive to her."

"Would you not like to live in her court? You could show your magical power there, and you could consult the stars for the good of all. People would only have admiration and respect for you."

The Rani tested on the unknown the fascination of her large moist eyes and her voluptuously smiling lips. She attempted to seize his hand between her caressant and voluptuous fingers.

"Come—you won't have to repent of it."

Gently, he pushed her away.

"In touching your flesh," he said, "I divined that you are the Rani. I thank you for having deigned to choose me for such a high favor, and I will consult the gods before responding."

"But you will respond to me?"

The Charmer smiled enigmatically, and his eyes became veiled, as if to conceal his thought.

"I will present myself at your palace tomorrow, and whatever the decision of the Para Purusha is, I shall make it known to you."

He whistled three times, and Ackbe, the Rani's great white horse, came, prancing, to stand beside her. The animal even bent his knees under the network of pearls that beat his breast, and Syta leapt lightly into the saddle, sitting astride in the fashion of the amazons of Ahmehnagara.

"May the spirits of water and fire be favorable to you, and may Indra guide you to your palace!"

She turned round before disappearing under the flowery branches.

"Your name? Will you tell me your name?"

He hesitated momentarily.

"You shall know tomorrow."

"Until tomorrow, then," she murmured. "Until tomorrow."

And the man of tall stature with the strange fiery pupils went back into the backti, protected by the thousands of reptiles whose ocher and cinnabar rings were flowing through the branches.

IV
Ahmehnagara

Ackbe, the great white stallion, steered with surety between the ferns and the falling garlands of the lianas. The rattle of pearls accompanied the song of bees drunk on honey, and bushes of gold, copper and silver sometimes enveloped the little queen, who resembled a frail Valkyrie on the flames of some vengeful god. Here and there, colossi died of old age or struck by lightning inclined their aged heads, in which pink doves and chirping songbirds dotted with topaz and ruby were nesting. A dust of seeds enveloped the barks, projecting diamantine sprays, crests of glittering powder traversed by sunlight.

Syta was dreaming of sweet things, very distant, to be sure, from her eight hundred husbands, whose kneeling adoration importuned her. In the same way as tyrants with gynaecea populated by white, yellow and black wives, she aspired to other caresses, freely offered and received, in some delightfully hidden solitude.

The dainty Rani reentered her city, and everyone, after having thrown a little sand under the feet of her great stallion, inclined their heads to touch the ground as a sign of submission and respect. Syta had gathered her veils, torn by the lianas, around her torso, and her legs, bare under rings of gems, pressed Ackbe's flanks nervously; he whinnied with contentment.

Women and children threw flowers, adolescent girls ran behind her, in the hope of placing their lips on a corner of her flesh and carrying away a little of her beauty and her perfume.

All those women were charming, with their delicate green or mauve tattoos and the great metal rings that traversed their nostrils. Only the most beautiful were retained, in any case, all of whom had several husbands. The disgraceful, the paltry and the infirm were sealed at birth in large vases that were buried at the threshold of the dwelling, the dead child having to protect the crops and attract the benefits of Durga to the maternal household.

Thus, all the inhabitants of Ahmehnagara were rich, not having to nourish too numerous a progeniture; and the wives distributed the quotidian tasks with wisdom and justice to their husbands.

At the age of ten or twelve years, every young girl thought about choosing a first radogk. Each one had the right to unite herself legitimately and consecutively with four suitors; she could, moreover, maintain, in accordance with her wealth and caprice, an unlimited number of cohabitants. When one of them had ceased to please or had not fulfilled to his honor the engagements made on the day of the first interview, he was sent back to cultivate his field, with a remuneration proportionate to his merits. The husband market was held in a large square in the city, where the young women, carefully veiled, made their choice without betraying the incognito of their actions. Some, more timorous, preferred to trust in the sagacity of a procurer, whose only function, well known in Ahmehnagara, consisted of going from house to house, frequenting the baths and examining the secret charms of youths destined for the joys of the gynaecea-in-reverse.

In very good families, however, the young women would not accept any other intermediary than their own mother, whose reliable experience was not fallible. Coiffed in a sort of bonnet with metal ear-flaps, which gave them a vague resemblance to bats, they informed themselves conscientiously as to the beauty and the health of the suitor, combed his hair, which he had to wear long, inspected his teeth and the grain of his skin, and settled the question of the reciprocal contribution. The bride, in fact, paid her radogk a certain sum of money, which he took away with his coiffures and his jewels in the case of divorce.

There was no more important affair than a marriage in Ahmehnagaran high society. The ceremonies, the preliminary feasts, and the processions on the backs of camels and elephants, followed by the golden lingams of the temples, crowned with flowers, amid the songs and dances of a joyful people, lasted for several days. On the eve of the marriage, the friends of the fiancé depilated him carefully, anointed his body with balms with aphrodisiac effluences, and put the seven hollow pearls of the "perfect union" around his neck—one for each of the night's kisses! The bride received no less care, but, accustomed to such ceremonies, which were renewed frequently for her, she did not feel such a vivid emotion. If, during the wedding night, the radogk showed any indecision, she could send him back to his family, and the marriage was thus annulled without any other formal procedure.

Sheltered by their rampart of mountains, which extended to the north in a double line, and were fortified by the profound ditch hollowed out by the Nerbudda, those regions of the Deccan had resisted better than the plains the flood of successive invasions and conserved their original physiognomy. Is it not to the south of the Vindhyas that one finds the remains of the most ancient populations of India?

In that ardent earth, eruptive mouths opened in those days, which, from time to time, launched their floods of lava over the cities. But the abundant rains gave new birth to vegetations, and a singular momentum to agonizing energies. The sea covered a large part of the Indo-Gangetic plain again, and the waves, ever angry, beat with unusual violence the feet of the mountains that surrounded the land like a girdle bristling with menacing spikes.

Thus, the Rani was the mistress of her city, circled by thick walls and covered with temples edified to the glory of the redoubtable trimurti. Almost all the constructions presented facades of granite in which were sculpted fantastic animals and the enlaced figures of gods and goddesses. Yajasala, places of sacrifices, were found at many crossroads, and Ackbe carefully avoided those sites of carnage, where the blood of rams and great white stallions ran.

The Rani descended from the horse in the courtyard of the palace, encumbered with slaves and guards, and then passed through an initial portico, which sheltered a colossal bull in red marble, ornamented with golden horns. Large niches all round protected sacred persons, terrible or smiling, in various postures. The vast esplanade that followed was formed on the sides by galleries sustained by monolithic pillars, and at intervals, giant lingams rose up, crowned with roses. Each of them was a testament to an incarnation of Shiva. In wood or in marble, disposed on pedestals incrusted with ivory and precious stones, they allowed perfumed oil and water to flow through slight entails, with which they were sprinkled every day to honor the omnipotent deity.

Behind those galleries a further wall rose, sustained by crouching granite oxen. Sacred elephants wandered at liberty in the courtyards. They were paler in hue than others and bore superb rings of peridots and chrysoberyls on their tusks.

Having accepted the aid of her women, Syta went into her apartments through doorways composed of seven successive frames, each behind another. The first was in gold and bore marvelously sculpted lotus flowers, the second was in jade, the third in ivory, the fourth in black iron with opal nails, surcharged with clusters of amethysts and olivines, the sixth in copper ablaze with ruby suns and the seventh in faceted crystal studded with moonstones.

The key to those doors was handed, in great pomp, to the husband of an hour or a night, and he only crossed the threshold with a violent heartbeat.

Syta's bedroom was divided into two parts: one, at a higher level, contained the bed, borne by four silver lions under a diamantine awning more fulgurant than a summer firmament.

Marvelous ivory sculptures ran along the walls, and a network of precious stones in broad diamond shapes covered them without hiding them, putting astral and firefly gleams everywhere. The second part of the room, into which one descended by means of a staircase of six steps, formed a large bath into which almond, jasmine and rose water sprang from the trunks of twelve silver elephants, intersecting, mingling and spreading an exquisite freshness. Syta loved to bathe in the embalmed basin, under the gaze of her women, and sometimes summoned one of them to share in her games.

That evening, distracted and weary, she allowed herself to be massaged with balms after the customary ablutions, and permitted Lackmama, her favorite, to mingle pearls with her long hair and braid over her forehead a garland of pink saligrams, the perfume of which was agreeable to her. A gauze more fluid than a wave of the Hadamur, the sacred spring, was draped round her loins, and songbirds were released around her couch in order to lull her slumber.

Meanwhile, Lackmama obtained her sovereign's orders.

"Which of the Great Husbands do you deign to honor with your favors? The six primary Granichy have asked for news. Will they be admitted to your august table?"

Lackmama only asked that question for form's sake, for the six primary husbands, or grandees of the realm, were always present at the Rani's meals, took part in the council and gave her their advice regarding difficult questions.

What Solomon wrote as a proverb on papyrus for the edification of the Hebrew people, Syta had engraved on a golden lingam in the temple of Kanda-Swamy. Inscriptions of it, fairly well preserved, have been found. That little Rani was an artist and a sovereign full of wisdom. She was also a sensualist, but is that not also a reflection of the bounty of Brahma, who wanted the Yoni-Lingam to be the finest ornament of his sanctuaries? The religion of Brahma, as no one is unaware, is the most ancient in the known world, and Syta knew no other.

She wanted, above all, a morality favorable to weak and suffering humanity. That morality had tolerance; it protected the life of everyone, imposed generosity, gratitude, benevolence, mutual aid and the alms of amour—all virtues that ought to elevate the human race, created in the image of Brahma, the Supreme Being, but too often forgetful of its origin.

The little sovereign was even more eloquent than pretty, so the inscriptions on her golden lingam were honored throughout the realm. But as she had written at the base of the symbolic cone that the rights of the six legitimate husbands were imprescriptible, she dared not contradict Lackmama, and elected to share the six times conjugal meal, in accordance with custom.

V

The Six Great Husbands

Those fortunate lords were named:
    Soulabatka, or the Flavorsome Fruit;
    Ruman-Bibi, the Perfect Science;
    Biskourmi, the Column of Felicity;
    Nandamu, the Golden Ram;
    Paraçou, the Incomparable;
    and Doudouma-Lovi, Above All!
When the Rani, adorned by her headband with twelve inverted hearts, more dazzling than the twelve snowy peaks of the Vindhya Mountains, appeared in the banqueting hall, the six husbands rose to their feet simultaneously. Supple and gracious, she passed before them, applying the tips of her tapering fingers to her lips, which signified that she was addressing the kiss of welcome to them all. They responded by putting the palm of their left hand on their breast, and, as if the gesture were a signal, twenty barbaric instruments became audible all at once, while the shrill voices of a battalion of young boys hidden in the galleries of the immense hall rose up.

Syta installed herself on a throne of ivory and gold, while the husbands crouched at her feet in order to serve her by turns, passing her dishes vehement with turmeric and curry, and pouring her lotus wine speckled with precious stones.

Apart from the ladies-in-waiting of the royal bedchamber under the orders of Lackmama there were no women in the palace. Young boys, admirably made with charming faces, circulated among the diners with velvet footfalls. They were scantily clad, but their pale bronze arms and legs were scintillating with jewels, and fresh flowers ornamented their hair at every hour of the day.

Soulabatka, who had an amber-brown visage and eyes with the glaucous gleam of peridots, interrogated the Rani in a tender voice, vibrant with emotion.

"Why did you quit the hunt, Blue Lotus of the sacred pools? Nothing unfortunate happened, at least?"

And Ruman-Bibi, the Perfect Science, added: "What an imprudence to distance yourself like that, when there are so many wild beasts and reptiles in the woods!"

"We have languished, far from your beauty," sighed Paraçou, the Incomparable.

As for Nandamu and Biskourmi, they dared not direct their gaze toward the adorable majesty of the sovereign, but quivered with impatience,

Doudouma-Lovi, more audacious, posed his lips on the sapphire-fringed veil of the Very August. "Reassure us, Star of Glory and Amour!"

The Rani dipped the tips of her slender fingers in the perfumed water that a young slave offered her in a precious cup, and passed on to a new dish, not without having drunk a few sips of rose wine powdered with rubies, which had the scent of the flower and pepper.

"My dear husbands," she said, in a voice softer than the sigh of an owl, "I was almost bitten by a snake, but I was saved by a Charmer."

The Radogks opened their eyes wide.

"A Charmer! Pehaps a yogi from the temple of Shiva?"

And Ruman-Bibi the Perfect Science asked: "Doubtless you will open your couch to him?"

"That would be an honor for us," remarked Nandamu the Golden Ram.

"The man has made a vow of chastity," sighed Syta.

"He does not know, then, that you are the sovereign!" roared Paraçou, the Incomparable

"He knows."

Doudouma clenched his fists. "What! He dared to refuse the divine favor of your kiss!"

"He did not collect the dust of your footfalls in order to rub his lips with it?"

"He did not confess his unworthiness by striking the ground three times with his forehead?"

"He did not address vehement actions of grace to the Para Purusha?"

"No," said Syta, humiliated. "And I don't even know his name."

"It's necessary," said Biskourmi, the Column of Felicity, "that this Charmer gives you satisfaction, and we shall take measures to render you happy!"

The little Rani, whose expert fingers were peeling the tail of a suhsunia—a sort of blue shrimp—cooked in Himalayan honey, shrugged her shoulders,

"I'll be able to see him again on my own, and I hope I'll succeed in persuading him to cross the threshold of the august temple."

Ruman-Bibi and Nandamu approved of the sovereign for wanting to act without assistance, but Paraçou, Doudouma-Lovi, Soulabatka and Biskourmi were of the contrary opinion. They even showed a little ill humor at the scant credit that was being given to their zeal and sagacity. In their capacity as Great Husbands, did they not have the right to choose Syta's cohabitants and assure themselves of their merits? To want to do without them was, in sum, almost an insult addressed to them, for they had always shown themselves worthy of the princess' confidence, fulfilling their delicate function with tact and dignity.

Nandamu the Golden Ram had already furnished a considerable number of secondary husbands, and Syta had generally shown herself to be satisfied with his choice. Why, on this delicate occasion, was she refusing his services?

"My dear lords," the sovereign said, while eating the eggs of a scobati—a kind of large lizard—in almond milk, "I'm desolate to have caused you any pain. Believe that I had no intention of offending you, and, if I desire to choose a lover without your assistance it is because the case is very particular. This Charmer, whose name I don't know, comes from distant shores where women only have one husband and husbands as many wives as they wish; he doesn't understand the wisdom of our laws."

"Oh!" said Nandamu, with a disdainful smile. "How can a man, who is so rarely sufficient to content one wife, possibly have several?"

"How can a husband, who has such difficulty in offering in a single night the seven regulation discourses, accept to speak to so many insatiable wives?" said Paraçou, supportively.

"Those wives," said Soulabatka, "must hardly ever hear the word of truth."

"How elementary their science must be!"

"How artificial their meager felicity!"

"How much rancor must accumulate in their heart against the man, presumptuous and insufficient, who only knows how to strut in the sunlight like a peacock, proud of his feathers!"

"Ah!" sighed the princess. "The poor things have little joy in this world—not to mention that they're employed in the hardest labors and have scarcely more esteem than beasts of burden!"

"Certainly," said Doudouma-Lovi, "It would be better to kill their daughters at birth, as we do, than to condemn them to such a miserable life. Their little elect souls would flutter over the houses and spread happiness in the woods and the meadows. Better to immolate a woman than to misunderstand her sacred nature! These sacrilegious countries will perish by the fire of heaven!"

"Out there," Nandamu affirmed, "the husband only approaches the wife in order to fecundate her. She knows nothing of amour but the sufferings of childbirth and nursing."

Biskourmi sniffed scornfully. "Peoples that act thus are peoples consigned to all divine vengeances. War, conflagration, pillage, epidemics, revolutions and all the cataclysms of nature will decimate them gradually. They will not be able to nourish all the individuals issued from their criminal fornications and they will devour one another like wild beasts in the jungle!"

Syta, having dipped her hands one last time in a cup perfumed with jasmine and rose, leaned on the shoulders of Soulabatka and Paraçou in order to mount a flowery throne that had been set up at the entrance to the hall, in an immense garden planted with the rarest trees. Light luminous garlands intersected above the head of the young Queen; cushions of saligrams and tuberoses were beneath her feet; lotuses with pistils of flame emerged from the waves of a pool. To either side of the throne, and all around the garden, elephants bore pyramids of little lamps of all colors, and at each of their movements the great pachyderms resembled mobile mountains of fire.

VI
A Singular Ballet

"Let the dances begin!"

Syta's six Great Husbands have sat down beside her, and lords of lesser importance have taken their places randomly in pathways covered in golden sand, in the bushes and on the lawns, Macabou flutes make shrill stridulations heard, while snakeskin tchilas resonate under closed fists.

Charming creatures in gauzes fringed with pearls, with diamantine wings of their shoulders and heels, enter, holding hands, and surround the Rani's throne. They are little boys about twelve years old, with long hair gathered on the head and large eyes circles with kohl. They are prettier than girls; their flesh, steeped in balms and special essences that discolor the pigments of their skin and communicate a new complexion, shines like gold. They are delicate and plump, only nourished on certain aliments, expertly dosed.

The Queen's little dancers know all the sensuous steps; they disarticulate themselves and twirl for the greater pleasure of the eyes; they attempt a thousand charming games, incessantly renewed. Some have elytra, antennae and long, quivering stings; others are metamorphosed into flowers, with tunics that are veritable corollas of petals, fixed one by one to golden silk confounded with the skin. The smallest carry snail shells or the pink carapaces of ladybirds. They glide between the dancers and assemble to form living obstacles, above which the winged artistes seem to fly, so gracefully do they leap up.

These first exercises are succeeded by a round dance of wild beasts. Lions, tigers and panthers, linked by chains of roses, circle around Syta. Their cord tightening more and more, they stop at the foot of the sovereign's throne, and she places her dainty foot on the head of Yassoub, her favorite lion.

All the wild beasts are directed by the children; no more than the people of Ahmehnagara had they ever attempted, in that era, to revolt. Very submissive and well-cared-for, they are plump and grateful; they sleep in the shadow of porticoes and do not regret the lionesses of the desert, which hunt all day in order to calm their hunger.

Syta also loves the game of the great pachyderms, which lend themselves to a hundred complex exercises. She laughs on seeing them displace themselves heavily and place their enormous feet carefully on metal balls or sway in cadence to the sound of barbaric instruments.

The tigers and the lions bear bonds of flowers, but the elephants are covered in metal plates studded with gems and more radiant than stars. They have rings in their tusks and shake a multitude of little tinkling bells and pompoms. It is a frightful thing when two elephants armed for war charge one another; one might think it the impact of two mountains crowned with flames. The ground oscillates beneath their feet, and the two menacing towers project death. The enormous beasts brace themselves on their massive legs as powerful as buttresses, arching their backs, swelling their flanks, enlacing their supple trunks, and become animated in their rage to such a degree that the struggle only ends with the death of one of the combatants, and perhaps both. Sometimes, too, they are intoxicated by opium or arak before rendering the most momentous combat. The tottering beasts falter in their attacks, stagger, fall and get up again, but they are generally separated before the fatal denouement, in order to serve for other games.

There are also combats of vultures, which are starved, and above which a morsel of living flesh is attached. Their chains leave the birds of prey a field of flight; they attack one another furiously, or try, by means of a thousand ruses, to take possession of their prey.

That evening, Syta did not obtain any pleasure from these habitual tourneys. Pensive on her flowery throne, she saw the yogi Charmer again, and told herself that the next day, he might perhaps be in her arms, and might teach her caresses and kisses that his magical power could render more profound.

More little boys entered with stallions whose long tails were sweeping the ground. The white coat of the animals was so fine that their skin was transparent and they seemed roseate. Nothing was as harmonious as their movements, and their gilded hooves, in their turbulent leaps, merely brushed the soil. They had gems mingled with their silky manes; a small glittering saddle covered their backs, and their heads were coiffed with a long diamantine crest.

The roseate stallions trampled roses, they played amid the verdant interlacements and iron hoops, rose up on their hind legs and fell back more lightly than the flowery balls that were thrown to them. The children ran behind them, leapt on to their rumps and bounded from one to another with cries of laughter. And the great pink horses carried away the golden statuettes in the mutilated corollas, perfumes and flames . . .

Syta had saluted the six Great Husbands and she passed, indifferently, before the radogks of lesser importance, who had not ceased to devour her which their eyes since the commencement of the performance. That night belonged to her; she only desired to give herself to her dream, weary of excessively similar embraces and kisses.

Lackmama, very arrogant, had gazed at the six great lords in a discreetly ironic fashion, and favored the others with a mocking smile. In the same way that a sultan cannot listen to all the lamentations of the women of his gynaeceum, a queen could not submit to the discourses of all her husbands. Syta certainly showed more courtesy and vivacity than the majority of turbaned tyrants, so she could accord herself a few hours of pleasant solitary reverie without remorse.

VII
Lackmama

"Tell me the secret of temples, Lackmama. You have lived in the favor of priests and you have discovered some of their mysteries. Personally, I have scarcely quit the court, and although I reign over men I have no power over the gods."

In fact, Lackmama had spent a few years of her life at the foot of a redoubtable altar. Devoted to the worship of Parvati, she had witnessed the bloody sacrifices and the orgies of the Shakti Puja. She had also, in accordance with her duty, contented the Brahmins and the yogis, sacrificing to the goddess as much as she could. She retained from those excessive fêtes a languor full of charm, which shaded her eyelids and rendered her gold-spangled irises more brilliant.

Syta, extended in her royal chamber in the silver basins, suddenly showed herself full of curiosity for the strange practices of the temples, and Lackmama, nestled at her feet, told her what she knew with an eloquent mildness.

"Is it the Shakti that you want to know, divine Flower of the Sacred pools?"

"Yes. Isn't it said that the Brahmins have a science of sensuality unknown to other men"

"Certainly, for their fêtes have been instituted in honor of universal fecundation."

"Do the yogis take part in them?"

"The yogis and all the assistants. But the Rani cannot show herself at those saturnalias."

"Alas! Perhaps I'd find the remedy for my ennui there and I'd discover new sensations?"

"However, adorable Rani, what do you lack? Do you not have the most handsome husbands of Ahmehnagara? Do you not know the most ardent caresses?"

"I would like," said Syta, her gaze remote and her hand clasped, "to savor mystical amour, to experience tremors of the soul that owe nothing to the flesh and do not leave either fatigue or disgust. That Charmer, whose name I do not know, affirmed to me that he feared women and that his body was as chaste as his heart . . ."

"He is not of your realm, then, divine Syta," Lackmama declared, "for here, the Brahmins and the yogis are more avid for women than all your husbands put together! It is lucky that the gods have given us so much strength of resistance! But who is this Charmer of whom you speak?"

Having put her arm around her confidante's neck, Syta recounted her adventure in the forest, and begged her to tell her what she knew about the life of the servants of the redoubtable trimurti, Brahma, Vishnu and Shiva.

"By the pancha-amrita, the five divine perfumes, and by the tortures of the unaraca, I will tell you all that I know about the yogis, but that will be very little, for those singular men scarcely converse except with the spirits of the dead, and even the Brahmins do not know their mantras. Those wandering solitaries have escaped feminine omnipotence; they are incorruptible."

"No celestial grandeur, even that of the mysterious Swayambhuva, can resist an invocation made appropriately, and every morning, at the sacrifice of the aswamedha, the officiating priest caused the god Vishnu, incarnated in Krishna, to descend upon the altar by the virtue of mantras. I should be able to bend the will of an obscure Charmer in the same fashion!"

"I hope, O Divine One, that your desire is realized, since this unknown yogi has been able to capture your heart. When will you see him again?"

"He promised me to come to the palace, for he knows that I'm the Queen."

"He won't come."

"He wouldn't dare not to come!"

"Yes, August Majesty, for he will fear your grace and your beauty . . ."

"Oh, Lackmama, I hope that your habitual perspicacity is misled! I'd be so unhappy not to be able to converse, if only for a minute, with that envoy of the gods. If you knew how little he resembles other men! He's a being of strength and mildness. His beauty is truly supernatural."

"Listen," said Lackmama, lowering her voice. "It's necessary to suspend from your neck the seven hollow pearls of the karma yoga, the sacred veda, and to dress yourself like a Kuruba of the Blue Mountains. Thus the Charmer will feel more reassured. When he appears, say to him the single word AUM, and he will prostrate himself before you."

"AUM?"

"It's the oldest of all the Brahmanic invocations, the most irresistible. If the yogi is not an envoy of Naraca he will accomplish your wishes. Repose, Divine Flower, August Torch of the Temple of Smara! It is necessary that anxiety does not contract your features, nor the fever of desire desiccate your lips. Our greatest power comes to us from our beauty."

VIII
The Sons of Joy[1]

Syta fell asleep on the bosom of her confidante, and the image of the six Great Husbands did not come to trouble her sleep. Those fortunate lords were similar to all men, ardent for the accomplishment of their desires and devoid of eloquence after their realization. They showed themselves, in the exercise of their rights, abrupt and willful, and went to sleep irresistibly after a few slight satisfactions. Although their faces changed, their soul and their instincts were the same. Syta found them so similar to one another that she no longer took the trouble to choose, offering them the favor of her royal couch by turns.

All were delighted, except for the little sovereign, whose heart remained deplorably empty. Oh, how she would have liked to give herself differently, and better, to caress her soul with a little veritable amour, to experience in the union of bodies not only the physical caress but the exchange of two divine aspirations, the communion of two spirits emanated from the Swarga of which the Vedantasara speaks.

The day after her encounter with the Charmer she got up later than she usually did, more feverish and exhausted than after the visit of one of her spouses. Clad in a gaudy golden simarre

____

1 As with some other words and phrases in the story this is a masculinization of a term that is normally used only to refer to women: *filles de joie*, which is a common euphemism for "prostitutes."

embroidered with large fantastic birds, she passed her royal guard in review in the courtyard of the palace and distributed the customary treats to the sacred elephants and wild beasts of which she was fond.

Yassoub, the handsome domesticated lion came to run his enormous head on the sovereign's legs, and in his pensive eye a spark of vague desire was ignited, as if so much grace and feminine bounty had touched his bestial heart.

Lackmama presented Syta with a basket full of choice morsels, surrounded by flowers, in order that the Queen's fingers need not by reddened by the bloody flesh; and the little boys of the "Choir of Angels" intoned the hymn of "Salute to the Queen" in the upper galleries, accompanied by the hoarse sounds of the vina and the tchila.

> *"Are you the lightning that furrows space, the rainbow the shines softly, the Ganges of the sacred waves or the mysterious Ocean? Are you the voice of amour that speaks to the gods of the summits of the Himalaya?*
>
> *"O woman, we love you!*
>
> *"Are you the burning sand that lifts the golden sands of the land of Madyadesa? Are you the nocturnal breeze that moans over the lake of Kama and murmurs in the velvet kusha grass?*
>
> *"O woman, we desire you!*
>
> *"Are you the Swarga that the devas inhabit, and which the accursed regard as the land of exile? Are you the earth, are you the waters, are you the fire that devours, are you the benevolent sun?*
>
> *"O woman, we possess you!*
>
> *"Are you life, the source of all lives, the soul of all souls, the principle of all principles? Are you the amorous force that unites all beings, the force that conserves, destroys or renews? Are you the goddess of all joys and all magnificence?*
>
> *"O woman, we prostrate ourselves before you!"*

"Alas," sighed the Rani, kissing the prominent forehead of the affectionate great lion, Yassoub, "I'm only a petty creature whom the gods have abandoned!"

"Courage," whispered Lackmama. "Doubtless the Charmer will respond to your desire, since he is the cause of your torments! Who could resist your divine grace?"

However, the yogi did not come. Neither that day nor on the following days did the mysterious man of the forest deign to present himself at the palace.

Syta, who was consumed with ennui, had sent the six Great Husbands to search for the holy man, but neither the Brahmins of the temple of Kanda-Swamy nor those of Bhavani, Lakmi and Shakti had been able to furnish the slightest information.

The sovereign, accompanied by Lackmama, had decided to set forth on campaign herself. Covered in somber garments that only allowed the glint in her eyes and the rhythmic gait of her stride to be divined, she had visited the place of sacrifices, the husband market, the crossroads, the back streets and the cul-de-sacs of Ahmehnagara.

Dusk filled the city, blurring the erections of the lingams placed at every street corner, and even against many of the houses, as a presage of good fortune. In front of the doorways, men were stopping matrons, begging them to choose them for a husband, boasting of their zeal and docility. Young boys lying on florid couches, their bodies rubbed with balms and carefully depilated, sang hymns to woman sweetly while plucking the strings of a vina.

The queen and her servant went along the walls, covered in inscriptions and bas-reliefs. Here, a sort of altar bore traces of blood, still fresh; woolen pompoms and fluffy paper balls ran in a garland around the pedestal of an amiable god, naively and coarsely carved in the trunk of a tree. Based on the legend of the Avadhana Sastra, it was the statue of Krishna, the divine son of the virgin Canya.[1] That tree-trunk had collected the prince Devindra, who was about to drown, and Indra-Mana, the grateful father, had had the image of the god reproduced in the wood, for that providential raft, said the legend, had descended from heaven just in time to save the young prince, who was struggling against the angry elements. The temple of Djaggernat, in the province of Orixa, possessed the same statue.

Alongside Krishna, a black goddess was displayed with rings in her nose and ears, a diadem of human phalanges and strange turquoise green eyes. According to some, that image represented Canya, the twenty-five-thousand-year-old virgin, the mother of the god of amour; according to others, she was only the disquieting wife of Shiva, the black ghoul, who bathed in blood and made a fuming loincloth out of entrails torn from victims of torture.

Further away was the temple of Aluvihara, in which the troop of copyists was assembled charged with transcribing the religious doctrine on palm leaves. Over the portal, punctured like precious lace, ran the stone stanzas of a poem recounting the adventures of Vishnu and all the divinities of the Hindu heaven. Parts of the wall and vaults were ornamented with paintings and precious mosaics.

The princess also wanted to interrogate the Brahmins of the temple of Sat Mahal Prasada, the temple of seven stages, and those of Raknot Dagoba, who were reputed to know the future and the great science of bewitchments, but those holy men were unable to tell her what had become of the Charmer.

---

1 This is odd; Krishna's mother is usually said to have been Devaki. *Christna et le Christ* (1874) by the French occultist Louis Jacolliot, which tries to associate the myth of Krishna and Christ, has a chapter on "Canya (la Vierge)," and also waxes lyrical about "le culte du Nahamam," from which La Vaudère appears to have borrowed that term, subsequently cited in the present chapter before becoming an important theme in the novel. *Christna et le Christ* is obviously an important source for the novel, although Jacolliot does not gave "Canya" as the name of Krishna's mother.

"Oh, Lackmama," the little sovereign sighed, "I sense my desire increased by so many difficulties to overcome! In the beginning, the yogi simply interested me; now it appears to me that he is necessary to my life. I've never experienced anything similar! But where shall we direct our steps? We won't learn anything, alas."

"Perhaps the Sons of Joy are better informed than the Brahmins."

"The Sons of Joy?"

"They see so many women!"

"Let's go and consult them, then."

Syta and Lackmama took a broad avenue, in the elegant quarter of the city, which led to the temple of Kanda-Swamy. Shops opened to the right and the left, selling ointments flowers, fruits, barbaric jewelry, and statuettes representing idols with faces of jade, ivory and wood.

And men always solicited them, offering their abode and their cares, boasting of their ardor and the modesty of their prices. A few followed them, trying to part their veils, to judge by their jewelry what they might expect of their munificence.

Elegant women were going into beautiful houses filled with songs, laughter and dancing. Others were perceived through windows, surrounded by a swarm of devedas—sons of joy—sumptuously adorned, their eyes painted, their hair braided beneath a mesh of pearls. Many women came there with the sole design of distracting themselves, of hearing a little music in fragrant gardens, beneath the illusory flight of golden flies.

The devedas rarely married; they belonged to everyone, and employed their lives adorning themselves, composing hymns of amour, and learning the art of singing and dancing. They were highly considered and pampered by the great ladies of the realm. Weary of their husbands, doubtless full of good will but deprived of the gifts that charm and retain, they came to spend the best moments of the day with the Sons of Joy. Those painted walls, those gardens filled with murmurous waves and prestigious flowers, larger than parasols, those discreet overtures, which muffled a quiver of kisses, pleased their insatiable imagination. They let themselves go in the arms of the devedas and returned from those embraces calmed and satisfied.

In front of a florid portico adorned with the double image of the lingam and the nahamam, Lackmama stopped the Rani.

"Why not go in here, divine Majesty, to seek, if not forgetfulness, at least repose? Your veils hide you sufficiently that no one will recognize you. Perhaps, too, someone can give us news of the Charmer. The Sons of Joy are informed about everything!"

"Go on ahead, Lackmama; it seems to me that I'm committing a bad action in penetrating into this house of pleasure!"

"O August Princess, the action that you're committing is agreeable to the gods, and Krishna himself informs us that we have only been created for amour, that amour is the reason and goal of our life, and that those who misunderstand that divine law are consecrated to the harshest punishments!"

The two women opened an orbicular door, on which fateful symbols were distributed, and penetrated into a large hall with a ceiling in a cupola, open to the stars in order to permit the nocturnal breeze to circulate freely among the flowers, the lanterns, the pennants and the sumptuous fabrics of silver and gold suspended almost everywhere in a charming disorder. In the center, on a small stone pedestal, colonnettes of lapis-lazuli supported a gigantic solid silver lingam-yoni, or nahamam. On the entablatures, statuettes of the three goddesses Bhavani, Lakmi and Shakti, alternated with enlaced mortal couples and fuming incense burners that were never extinguished.

Around the hall, on low divans and silky cushions, Sons of Joy of various origin were chatting, lying or smoking, none of whom were more than twenty-five years old.

Those devedas possessed a gripping beauty, and their virile grace was shown to good effect by the ingenuity of the ornaments with which they excelled in decorating themselves.

The men of the land of Andhra had slender limbs and a soft skin shinier than gold; they showed a very keen liking for spangled gauze, and turquoises and moonstones mounted in amulets with religious inscriptions.

The men of the Oude, with more powerful muscles, curly hair and thick lips, had their left shoulders decked in tiger skin, and wore tufts of pink feathers over their ears.

The men of Aparatika and Lat showed themselves more passionate than the others, and only adorned themselves with a scarlet loincloth retained at the hip by a gemmed clasp.

The men of Malva, more supple and seductive, adorned their wrists and ankles with strings of pearls of the purest luster. Their noses were slightly upturned, their eyes glaucous and their hair very long with ruddy glints.

The devedas of Vanasi, Avanti and the Punjab had high-pitched and well-timbred voices. They cultivated music and all the arts of giving pleasure.

The Dravidians were more specialized poets. As for the youths of Pataliputra, Avantika and Maharashtra, they were trained in dancing from a very young age. They were so delicate and charming that they might have passed for girls when they glided voluptuously to the sound of dhols and tambourahs. Many of them had tinted their bodies yellow with saffron and shaded their eyelids with antimony. All the artifices of beauty were known to them, at any rate.

In perverse families with abundant children, the most learned and well-formed sons were sent to Ahmehnagara, knowing that their merits would be appreciated there, and returned to their homeland with a fortune honestly acquired.

IX

Soumati

Syta, who had not gone into the house of the devedas in order to receive and give caresses, but in order to try to obtain information about the yogi Charmer, chose a young poet who was playing his vina, and sat down beside him.

"Sing me the stanzas of the Sun," she said to him, "for my soul is sad."

He moved closer on the cushions and attempted to penetrate the mystery of her veils.

"Let's love one another first; I'll sing afterwards."

She pushed him away.

"No, I repeat that I don't want to sacrifice to Kama this evening; but I'll recompense your good will generously if you consent to dissipate my sadness with your harmonious verses."

He still hesitated. "You seem beautiful, and the sight of the treasures that you are hiding from me would have inspired my heart . . ."

"Leave your heart out of it," she said, impatiently. "You know as well as I do that it cannot be mingled in these matters. You're here to obey your mistresses of hazard, and I have the right to command the Sons of Joy. Sing!"

"So be it. I will sing the hymn to Surya that you have been kind enough to ask of me."

He raised his large eyes toward the starry vault, and played a few sweet chords as a prelude.

"Surya, god of the world and the sky, when your resplendent face parts the clouds, nature entire shivers with delight . . ."

The song was long, but the singer sighed it with so much charm that the little princess did not weary of hearing it.

Around them, couples fell silent in order to take advantage of the unexpected interlude, and a little tender poetry cradled the ephemeral embraces, accompanying the kisses devoid of any aftermath of the buyers and sellers of amour.

When the devedas had allowed the last note of the sacred song to die on his lips, Syta detached the pearls from her neck and gave them to him.

"Oh, that's too much!" he said, refusing the royal necklace.

But she attached it to his breast. "No, no, keep it in memory of this beautiful night, and, in order that I can also conserve something of you, tell me your name."

"My name is Soumati. I would have liked, however, to prove my gratitude to you differently . . ."

"You can also give me some information that would be a great help to me. Has anyone mentioned a yogi, more seductive than Smara, who must have stopped in Kanda-Swamy? The Brahmins that I have interrogated did not want to reply. But you see so many women who emerge from the temples, that you might perhaps be able to get me out of difficulty . . ."

"This yogi was doubtless a Charmer?"

"Yes, a Charmer who came from far away, for he was wearing the white sala of wandering holy men. Oh, tell me what you know!"

"I don't know anything. Many yogis pass through the city. However, as the Shakti Puja is tomorrow, you can go to the temple yourself tomorrow, and look among the officiants for the one that interests you. Pilgrims from all lands come here, twice a year, to take part in those festivals of fecundation."

The Shakti Puja to which Soumati referred had been instituted in honor of the incarnation of the trinity of Brahma, Vishnu and Shiva: an incarnation that, according to the vulgar worship of the Hindus, operated by the ordinary act of generation. Nature, in its union with the divinity, is represented by the three goddesses Bhavani, Lakmi and Shakti. As the trinity does not affect the unity, the three goddesses are only one, just as the three gods are only one, and the work of generation was accomplished by a single lingam and a single nahamam. Nature, thus fecundated, has produced everything that exists. Once creation was achieved, the custody of the lingam was confided to Shiva and that of the golden womb to Shakti. It is for that reason that temples consecrated to the black god and his wife present so many insignia of the generative organs.

It was said, however, that monstrosities occurred at the fête of Shakti Puja, and the princess shivered merely at the idea of going to it.

"Isn't there any other means of obtaining information?" she murmured.

"No," Soumati affirmed, "and if you don't attempt that step, it's probable that you'll never see your yogi Charmer again."

The Son of Joy drew closer, seductively. "You've given me your necklace, but I'd like more . . ."

"What?"

"Your kiss. It's the first time that anyone has scorned my caresses, and I'd be so glad to demonstrate my science. Your husbands certainly can't compete with me!"

"Oh," she said, "I'm weary of amour, weary of embraces and sensuality. I want to know intoxications that you can't give me. Bless my indifference, which permits you, this evening, to content other desires. The reign of the Sons of Joy is brief; the old age that is the commencement of death soon arrives for them. Take advantage, Soumati, of the glorious hours that the gods grant you!"

Lackmama was asleep between two devedas who had given her the pleasure that she wanted. Syta shook the servant, who opened eyes clouded by dreams.

Couples were reposing on cushions at the hazard of embraces. After the ardor of caresses, it was time for games and dances. Clamors fused, accompanying the stridulations of flutes and the enthusiasm of tchilas. A deveda was plucking a vina with lascivious movements of the buttocks and hips, raising up a yellow gauze spangled with gold over the supple lines of his body. He was handsome thus, with the beauty of fine polished bronze, amid the flames of his floating garment, the gems of his hair, bracelets and necklaces of translucent little bells.

Other Sons of Joy surged forth from all directions, scantily covered in diaphanous muslins, and their movements accelerated under a rain of flowers, and a drizzle of perfumes, which fell from the vaults.

More spectatrices were coming in sometimes in joyful bands, and some, having undressed, mingled with the dancers and sang, in high voices, verses to Kama. Arms enlaced, black female tresses overlapped with male tresses; protruding breasts were crushed against round shoulders, hands sought one another and were joined, and lips forgot themselves in an infinity of kisses.

X
The Council

Syta and Lackmama had emerged from the white house. In front of them the city was resplendent in the first rays of the sun, with its monuments whose golden roofs were ablaze, its columns, its minarets and its green and blue palaces, with the radiance of peacocks' tails. The dust of the streets rose up in light swirls under the morning breeze, and a rumor emerged from the houses, like the buzzing of a swarm of insects.

"Have you learned anything?" the princess asked Lackmama.

"No, nothing, alas. The Sons of Joy only advised me to go to the Shakti Puja."

"I received the same advice."

"What are you going to do?"

"I don't know yet. I feel a certain repugnance at the thought of going to that festival of the material, in spite of the symbolic lies with which the Brahmins try to adorn it. I fear being recognized and criticized for that curiosity."

"We can go down into the crypt. No one will see us, and, through an opening adapted for that purpose, we wouldn't miss any of the ceremony."

"That's true, you know all the secrets of the temple, and you've doubtless figured among the vestals of lust?"

Lackmama lowered her eyes. "I confess it. The duty of a priestess of Shiva is to offer herself to all, to Brahmins and yogis alike. Oh, the servants of the black god are more expert than our husbands, and even the Sons of Joy! Nothing can give any idea of those saturnalias! However, the wandering holy men keep themselves apart; a grille even separates them from the other fakirs, and they never deliver themselves to the debauchery of the Shakti."

The two women adjusted their veils over their faces, and traversed the tortuous back streets of the city at a rapid pace, choosing the most deserted quarters in order to return to the palace.

In front of the houses, merchants of fruits and vegetables were beginning to install themselves, proclaiming their wares. There were handsome youths there who smiled and young women, ever ready to quit their displays in order to satisfy a random caprice or to enlist in the battalion of serving husbands. Children carrying bronze vases on their shoulders accumulated the day's provisions in light baskets. They were pretty and sprightly, with necklaces of turquoises and coral, and bright muffs over their ears. Naked, for the most part, they only had thin leather loincloths or a metal leaf retained at the hips by a slender chain.

Only the boys came out in the morning for the household chores, the girls remaining at home, adorning and perfuming themselves, ever occupied with the care of their beauty. They were, in any case, in a minority, custom dictating that the paltry and malformed be immolated at birth, so there was scarcely a dwelling whose threshold did not have the tombstone of a number of nagallas—victims of amour—destined to watch over people and things.

Those little angels returned at a fixed date, in certain villages, they were seen emerging from the earth, brighter than the rays of Ma, the moon, and they formed strange aerial rounds until the hour when the morning breeze opened the heart of the lotus.

The nagallas were as venerated as the benevolent spirits of water, air and fire; there were even temples consecrated to them in the solitudes of the Blue Mountains.

The Rani, on her return to the palace, put on the headband with the twelve diamond hearts, dressed in gold-embroidered gauze and, in the company of the six Great Husbands, went, as usual, to review her royal guard and feed the wild beasts. Then she went to the Council Hall.

There was no question, that day, of public concern or the interests of the State. Syta, feverish and nostalgic, told her husbands what she had done during the night, and how her sacrifice to Kama, in the house of lust, had been futile.

The six lords shared her pain. Ruman-Bibi, the Perfect Science, was especially chagrined at being unable to furnish any preponderant advice. Biskourmi, the Column of Felicity, being jealous, criticized the Sons of Joy slightly, and Nandamu, the Golden Ram, warned Syta about the dangers of the Shakti Puja.

"With your permission, Divine Light, we will accompany you on that expedition," Soulabatka proposed.

"Well-armed men are always useful in such brawls!"

"And if your Charmer resists, we can abduct him!" concluded Paraçou, the Incomparable.

Syta remained anxious. It did not please her to associate the six lords with her affairs of the heart. Certainly, they were ardent and tender, in accord with etiquette, and fulfilled their duties loyally, but they lacked that which is everything for a woman: the charm of the unexpected and the unknown. What happens in broad daylight, without difficulty, without debate and without contest, is of meager interest. How banal amour would be if no one obfuscated it! It is for that reason, doubtless, that the little princess could not love her six Great Husbands, much less the pretty satellites that gravitated around those important planets.

"I'll go alone, with Lackmama," she declared, curtly.

"As you please, August Queen!" sighed Ruman-Bibi. "You're free in your actions."

"And we can only incline before your desire," agreed Paraçou, with a hint of bitterness.

"All men belong to you," added Biskourmi, in a honeyed tone, "so you would do well, after having satisfied your desire, to send that yogi to a better world."

"We'll immolate him in a beautiful ceremony in honor of Shiva," concluded the six lords, serenely. "It will be an occasion for limitless rejoicing."

"And the Brahmins will assist us," said Ruman-Bibi. "Deep down, they detest these wandering holy men, who steal a little of their influence and prestige. We'll leave them the fakir's heart for the altar of Bhavani."

Syta laughed, lightly.

"At least wait until my mouth has known the savor of his kisses! I don't know his name, I don't know where he comes from or where he's going, and you've already disposed of his life. What if he's an envoy of the gods?"

"You would have seen the aureole of glory around his head."

"Before the sun he would have seemed another sun, and the forest would have been illuminated by him."

"Did he work any miracles?"

"He saved me from the snake's sting."

"Any charmer could have done that."

"After all," declared the princess, impatiently, "if he weren't superior to other men, he wouldn't have been able to produce a supernatural effect on me, and I'm grateful to him for having revealed to me that I'm not a doll devoid of a heart and soul!"

Disdainful and haughty, she stood up in the midst of the consternated silence of the six radogks; then, having readjusted the golden gauze over her breast, which had been slightly disturbed by the heat of the argument, she quit the Council Hall at a rapid pace.

The Mystery of the Temple

"Lackmama, I want to resemble Rathi, the goddess of infinite joy! I want my body to appear slimmer than a Siricha tree, Put under my breast that gold ornamented siouba, with the straight spike. My skin is softer to the kiss than the trunk of a young elephant; glaze it with gold, and touch my lips, nostrils, nipples and the crease of my loins with an agile brush. Leave my hair, soaked in balms, beat my heels like a wet cloak and make my dark eyebrows stand up the Kama's bow!"

The servant hastened to obey.

"Your mouth, O Divine One, resembles a bimba fruit steeped in dew! Your arms are ashoka branches and your breasts are as supple as a cobra coiling around a Charmer."

But the Rani was saddened by her terrestrial splendor.

"What does it matter, Lackmama? I don't want the caress of the flesh; that of the soul must be far more adorable. I want to be resplendent with a superhuman beauty that troubles the spirit of the Beloved! Envelop me in long veils the color of a misty sky, and let my eyes resemble two stars piercing the clouds!"

Since the previous day there had been a noisy crowd outside the palace, and pilgrims making their way toward the temple of Kanda-Swamy to witness the sacerdotal orgy of the Shakti Puja. The perfume of cassolettes was added to those of sandalwood, rose acacias and amatlis wrapped in the flexible stems of young bamboos.

A light breeze also brought the distant aromas of fields of cuscus grass and forests of cinnamon trees.

Syta, feverish and irritated, had not been able to savor a moment's repose. Her mind skimmed multiple subjects, like the frail hummingbirds that only quit the calyx of one flower in order to plunge into the heart of another. It seemed to her that her destiny depended on her conversation with the Charmer, and a secret voice affirmed to her that she would encounter him at the festival of fecundation, of which the mere idea made her blush.

"Lackmama, enable me to drink the wine of the pink lotus speckled with gold, in order that my tottering reason will no longer permit me to be frightened by the imminent orgy. Will I have the strength to support such a singular spectacle?"

Lackmama shrugged her shoulders. "Men are similar everywhere when their senses are stimulated, and nothing that they imagine ought to surprise you any longer."

"I'm the sovereign, and men adore me on their knees, knowing that I have the right of life or death over them," Syta sighed, dipping her lips into the prestigious liquid that the servant offered her. "I don't know their veritable nature."

The streets were illuminated; every house had its primitive orchestra and sometimes, the breeze, which was beginning to slacken, brought to the ears of the princess high-pitched songs accompanied by the dhol and the vina. In the depths of the city, the temple of Kanda stood out, increasingly somber against the starry sky. Nothing betrayed the preparations for the fête, although they must have been in full activity. What had become of the day's pilgrims, and the crowd avid with emotion whose clamors had only ceased a few hours ago? Doubtless the vast building concealed in its flanks all that human livestock, flesh for the tortures and pleasures in which the Brahmins were about to delight.

"Give me my flask of saligram, Lackmama, and put essence of tuberose on a flap of my veil, in order that those vehement odors can preserve me from disgust and weakness. And then . . . understand me well . . . as soon as I have found the Charmer, you'll insinuate yourself to his side and inform him of my desires."

"What if he refuses to follow me?"

"Tell him that Shiva is inspiring you and that it's his will that you're expressing. Have you not served the black god, and are you not still submissive to his power?"

"I'll do as you order, but the yogis are in constant communication with the divinity of the temple, and it's difficult to deceive them."

"Have yourself assisted by a Brahmin. What is the point of this dangerous step if I can't satisfy my will? Oh, Lackmama, how long time seems to me!"

"Don't you want to take your leave of your husbands, August Princess?"

"No, leave me to my dream! My husbands importune me, and cannot find the road to my heart. They're like multicolored parrots arguing in the trees. Although the plumage of the birds is agreeable, their voices cannot charm the ear of a poet. I know obscure birds whose song is as melodious as the murmur of springs. One can't see them, for they hide in the utmost depths of the woods, but one cherishes them for their virtuoso talent and the mystery with which they surround themselves. The speech of my Charmer is even more adorable than the song of those divine birds!"

Sitting on the malachite balustrade of the great terrace that overlooked the landscape, Syta uttered a little cry. As if by enchantment, the temple of Kanda had just lit up from the base to the summit; a formidable clamor, coming from who knows where, dominated all the sounds of the city.

"Let's go, Lackmama."

And, like a girl running to her first rendezvous, the Rani, trembling and all white in her long veils, went down toward the Mystery of the temple.

PART TWO

I
The Sacred Orgy

"*Devadinam djagat sarvam*," said the princess, in the language customary in such circumstances, to the Brahmin who opened the door of an obscure redoubt for her, into which she slipped in company with Lackmama.

"*Mantradinam ta devata*," he replied.

He guided the two women through a series of interior corridors, all of which contained giant lingams and statues of Shiva in different transformations. Sometimes, a pool of water offered its freshness near altars still red with the blood of victims. Little lamps of horn or jade illuminated the horror of sacrifices that certain Brahmins were finishing in honor of the Shakti.

Syta slipped in a sticky puddle and had to hold on to the arm of the servant, whose stride was more assured.

An acrid odor of old oil, blood and rotting grease dominated the perfume of flowers of cassolettes. A heart, already blue-tinted, reposed in a golden vase, and a gelatinous parcel of entrails was dirtying the pedestal of a statue with three heads representing the sacred trimurti.

The guide, who had not pronounced a word since the entrance, had the two women pass between two granite lions with flamboyant eyes, and descended with them into the subterranean parts of the edifice by means of a narrow and slippery staircase of a hundred steps. At intervals, a small lamp with a sizzling wick filled the air with smoke.

Having reached the bottom of the stairs they turned to the left in the darkness, advancing over elastic, spongy soil, like that of ancient peat bogs. At certain turnings, gleams were reddening in horn recipients that had a color of sanguine orange and troubled gold. The cellar spread a singular perfume of damp earth gorged with blood, with the reek of hot wax, oil and melted butter. It was an exhalation, simultaneously painful and intoxicating, that the nerves felt. Granite altars bore grimacing images, brutal and terrible, dirtied by the gifts of fakirs. The vault sometimes lowered almost to touch the heads of the visitors; it was calcined by the heat of candles that were burned on days of sacrifice.

Syta preferred to those lairs of fear the gardens up above, with tomb-like pathways, agonizing flowers drowned in blood. Over those funereal enclosures, where sacred basins opened like the mouths of wells, at least the turquoise eye of a sunlit sky opened, a reminder of life. Here, everything was motionless and deserted. One could not even hear the hive-like buzz that was perceptible through the windows of closed houses.

Syta sat down on the overturned stump of a stone bench. It seemed that her soul had divested itself of her and was floating, indecisively, like the yellow light of distant little lamps. A Sanskrit script was engraved on the salagrama that she was contemplating with dreaming eyes that did not see. Lackmama murmured the distich, which she knew by heart:

> *"Tan mantram brahmanadinam*
> *"Brakmana mana devata."*

The Brahmins possess the prayers, so the Brahmins possess the gods!

"Not a word," breathed the priest. "Here, you will be able to see without being seen. You are under the pedestal of the colossal statue of Shiva that dominates the altar. It is before your eyes that the sacrifice of the three virgins will be accomplished, and you will not lose anything of the ceremony that will follow . . ."

"But this cellar is darker than Nacara!" sighed the princess.

"Patience! Everything will be illuminated for you when the moment comes. It will seem to you that the Swarga is opening before your dazzled eyes."

There was a slithering in the darkness, and then everything became silent. Syta was shivering with impatience and dread. She had never felt anything similar. The dismal, damp obscurity that surrounded her must be populated with ghosts, like that of tombs; her feet were certainly reposing on the dust of the dead; specters were wandering under the vaults of that frightful crypt.

"Let's go, Lackmama! I'll never have the courage to remain immobile in this darkness. Anguish is making my heart race!"

But the servant was familiar with the terror of the place.

"Have no fear, Divine One; I'm beside you and watching over you. No danger is threatening us. Soon, you'll know the mystery of the golden womb fecundated by Brahma, the sole god in three persons. When the universe is plunged again into the chaotic Pralaya it is by means of a new union of the lingam and the nahamam that the movement of life will descend once again on to the earth."

Vague whispers were now coming from the darkness; one might have thought that a swarm of buzzing bees was beating its wings against the walls. There were also rapid frictions, the scrape of shifting vases, and something like the ripping of silk.

"The priestesses are preparing the altar," said Lackmama. "They're putting shredded roses on the steps, in order that the naked bodies of the women who are offering themselves to the Shakti will repose more softly. You can't imagine, Divine One, the quantity of roses that are collected for this ceremony! So much perfume is also poured on to the steps that it's necessary to scrub them for days to restore their gleam."

"I can't see anything yet."

"That's because the women are circulating with little lamps, in order not to wake the pitris, who must not be troubled before the hour of the sacrifice. Otherwise, there won't be enough of them to chase away the evil demons. Patience, now; Parvati will soon make herself manifest."

Parvati is the redoubtable goddess, the wife of Shiva. She often changes her name, but her function, alternately benevolent and maleficent, is almost always the same.

Shiva was the efficient cause who, by means of his energy or his Shakti, as the instrument, produces or destroys the world. Gradually, however, by the predominance of the role of the Golden Womb in the universal fecundation, the power of the male element is diminished. According to the Vayu Purana, Shiva possessed a dual male and female nature. In the white nature, in the quality of bounty, the benevolent Shaktis are attached to him, in the black nature, the redoubtable goddesses. As several of those divinities are notoriously aboriginal, however, it is probable that the ensemble was constituted by the grouping of female powers to form a sort of feminine polytheism, which the Brahmins accepted as a popular religion, introducing mortal women into it at the last degree, after the Brahmins. Thus, the beliefs, until then hidden from the masses in their essence, became accessible to all, by virtue of the sensuality and passion that were added to them.

The bakta, or worshipers of the Bakti,[1] were divided into several branches, but those of Shivaism addressed their devotion preferentially to female energies and divinities, to the union of the sexes and to the magical powers. The Tantras, in particular, are books of eroticism, bewitchment and occultism.

The rites of the Shivaist Bakti unite the two sexes, without distinction of caste, and in the secret gatherings of the temple, consecrated to Shiva and Parvati, the intoxicated affiliates rush upon one another, after a few preparatory ceremonies, delivering themselves to the strangest orgies under the benevolent gaze of the priests of the black god.

Given these manifestations, it is not astonishing that the cult of the woman has developed, in those countries worshiping the

---

1 This is the fashion in which this word is rendered here in the original, which seems to differentiate it from the earlier term "backti," and is apparently closer in meaning to the Hindu term, *bhakti*. Hoever, the spelling "bakti" is subsequently used in a way that seems to refer to the forest, as the term "backti" did. The problem of whether La Vaudère really wishes to distinguish between the two terms is confused by the fact that she sometimes uses two different spellings of the same term (e.g. trimurti and trimurty) in other instances, with no discernible pattern.

Backti, in the form of the sacred union of the sexes: lingam and yoni, or nahamam.

Syta was no longer speaking, lost in her reveries, anguished and curious at the same time.

Suddenly, a faint light appeared; then a firework burst, as if by enchantment, illuminating all the corners of the temple. The two women had an opening before them large enough to permit their eyes to lose nothing of what was about to occur.

While a multitude of little multicolored lamps lit up simultaneously, a strange and mysterious music emerged from the depths of the immense hall, which no window put in communication with the outside. There were gurgles of swooning women, the sad and monotonous cooing of turtle-doves, which sustained a masculine buzz. Sometimes, the song mutated into a very soft plaint, which seemed to be the piercing note of a crystal flute; then a sob replied, and unity was restored, in a brisker mode. But the desolate melody returned, as if issued from the depths of the earth, underlining the horror of the murder of flesh and soul that was about to be accomplished, the frightful poem, taken from the sacred books, depicted the story of the punishments and pains of the Naracra. In the end, when, mingled, the voices had carried away on the waves of the chilamchi, all the wrecks of human dolors, they fell back into amorous sighs, and the invincible desires of possession.

Thousands of scented candles darted their lances of flame into the air blue with incense; everywhere, light garlands of tinted glass ran, in the forms of flowers, also enclosing a luminous pistil that was steeped in the sacred oils.

Thus illuminated, the temple displayed the marvels of its vaults, covered in bas-reliefs and sustained at intervals by elephants with upraised trunks and tusks circled by enamels. Hindu art, which inspired the ancient art of Greece and Egypt, was deployed there in all its incomparable magnificence. Aerial columns of onyx and porphyry, capitals more indented than expensive guipures, lotus flowers wrapped around the bodies of goddesses, enlaced with gods, ruby tongues and eyes, glittering in the convulsed faces of rutting monsters: it was an unusual vision, by which the little queen, although accustomed to all its splendors, was surprised and charmed.

Three undressed women were superhumanized on a very high throne, and behind them, the white robes of the officiating Brahmins spread out. At a precise moment of the ceremony, the three virgins, chosen from among the most beautiful and most powerful Brahmines of the temple, would lie down on the roses, and the priests would possess them before the gazes of everyone, while the sacred melody faded away into sighs of ecstasy, and the thousand cassolettes of the altar spread aphrodisiac fragrances.

The three young women, entirely naked, their hair mingled with gold and diamond powder, knelt down before a lingam crowned with flowers. They responded with a soft note, held in unison, to the lapidary and fluid note of a flute, as indestructible thus as the artifices of the symbol itself, conqueror of the universe.

Syta felt as if she were being lifted up. *It's impossible*, she said to herself, *that the amour inspired by those celestial voices should not be the great rule of life, the unique goal of creation, the supreme will of nature. And yet, individuals like that Charmer remain chaste through the temptations and the deliria of the flesh. What is the god or demon that haunts them?*

The musical liturgy, naïve and tender, of the mass of sensuality, entered into the ecstasized soul and excessively vibrant nerves of the Rani with the shrill and willful voices of women and the ardent clamors of men exasperated by desires.

Syta ended up being gripped to the marrow, suffocated by everything that the assembly emitted, intoxicated by carnal emotions and lascivious transports. Before her, the nave was magnified, ornamented with extraordinary imprints and fabulous images, in which couples rushed at one another beneath the inverted cradle of the vaults. Centuries were united there in order to bring to Brahma, the powerful god, in three distinct persons and yet unified, the superhuman effort of their superb art.

The three gods, androgynous in nature, which only made one god, represented in Zyaus, Swayambhuva or Brahma, had inspired the first artists of India marvelously. They had also exercised themselves in the personification of the three female principles, Bhavani-Lakmi-Shakti, which they had combined on the pedestal of the Nahamam or Nari. Poetry and general worship had made three goddesses of them, the wives of the three gods of the trimurty, and they also formed a virgin trinity under the name of the Kanyake trimurty.[1]

The naïve invocations that had once only had for a temple the vault of the skies and or an altar the sacred herbs and mosses, were replaced by sacrifices offered on stone tripods in temples of marble and bronze. All the genesic and fabulous legends of India originated from that.

It was then that the first workmen of the world had carved those squat pillars, covered with precious ornaments, the curiously indented capitals crowned with nympheas and foliage in volutes, those columns with trusses, sustained by monsters with ruby tongues, and other monsters united at the bases of pillars that alternated with golden lingams. All that religion had the flesh for a trampoline. Logically, humanly, it triumphed in its wild power, for it permitted men and women to satisfy their passions, even encouraged them, by assuring them that all sensuality was holy and agreeable to God.

The three Brahmin pujaris, or sacrificers, had knelt down in their turn to adore the eternal symbol of eternal force and eternal youth. They raised their pale hands and then struck their foreheads on the stone slabs.

---

1 "Zyaus" and "Nari" are both employed by Jacolliot in meanings similar to those employed here, but "Kanyake" is not; it is probably a misrendering of Kanyakumari, which is one of the names attributed to Shiva's consort, but I am not sufficiently sure of that simply to make the substitution. The thesis expressed here is an obvious modification of Jacolliot's, but it is a significant modification, and hence partly original.

<h1 style="text-align:center">II</h1>
<h2 style="text-align:center">Brahma's Caress</h2>

Around the altar, erected in the middle of the nave, similarly entirely nude, and in voluptuous poses, stood the sacred dancers of the temple, with triangular bracelets on their ankles and arms.

At intervals they prostrated themselves, all at the same time, their hands extended, and then kissed the ground three times, and got up again with a guttural cry. They turned on their axis, their breasts erect, their backs arched, and with a slow torsion of the upper body they swept the steps with their long hair, their lips parted and their pupils dilated. Then they stood up straight again, in a harmonious ensemble, and raised their arms with a new plaint, to which the tremulous voice of the officiants responded.

"We want amour, the only good on earth! We want the pleasure of gods and humans! Let the divine ecstasy penetrate us!

"Brahma is great!

"We want, until morning, to offer ourselves to all desires, for we were created for voluptuous joys. The bounty of the Almighty made us in his image. Let the divine ecstasy penetrate us!

"Brahma is great!

"We want to annihilate ourselves in amour, until we only form, with our brothers, one body and one soul! Nature only wants the union of beings in order to renew herself incessantly: be born, love, die; everything is summarized in three sighs. Let divine ecstasy penetrate us!

"Brahma is great!"

The three officiating priests had drunk the wine of forgetfulness in golden cups; they had thrown themselves on the three Brahmines and had laid them on the altar offering them to the fecund trimurty. In them, they worshiped the creative force of the universe, anointed their svelte bodies with balm in order to purify them one last time and render them entirely worthy of the favor of the gods.

"Let the flowers of amour open to the kiss of the breezes in order to receive the sacred pollen! Nothing exists outside of amour! Let those who are no longer capable of loving return to death, for they are taking the place of blissful lovers! Let divine ecstasy penetrate us!

"Brahma is great!"

The priestesses agitated censers around the three virgins laid on the altar and rang crystal bells.

Slowly, the Brahmins climbed and descended the steps of the altar, seeming to hesitate before the solemnity of the sacrifice. At each step their tremulous voice resumed a couplet of the hymn to Brahma.

Finally, they stopped before the young women, mute and motionless, embraced them, and the divine offering took place before the eyes of all.

"Brahma is great!"

Syta squeezed Lackmama's hand feverishly, and her heart beat forcefully. "Oh!" she said. "I can't see the man I love! Why isn't he beside me?"

"The yogis who have made a vow of chastity remain apart, behind the Brahmins and the sacred dancers. You'll recognize them by the bandlets surrounding their heads. Their voice is sad; they disdain carnal joys, and only live for prayer. Soon they'll quit the temple, in order not to witness the scenes of orgy that follow the Shakti . . ."

Syta looked ardently in the direction indicated by Lackmama. Suddenly, she uttered a cry.

"I see him! I see him! He's leaning against the last column, and closing his eyes."

"He's the tall yogi whose face is similar to that of Kama, the god of holy sensuality?"

"Yes, no one is as handsome! He's as resplendent as the luminous lotus of the temple of the coast of Orixa! Go fetch him . . ."

"What shall I say to him?"

"Tell him that it's a matter of saving a soul. Go!"

A great movement had begun in the temple. At a signal given by the chief of the pujaris, the women were lying down in the midst of flowers, entangled with one another, mingling the gems of their ankles and their arms. A garland of naked bodies now surrounded the altar, living, quivering, lascivious corollas offered in a flood of spread hair, in the exasperated fragrance of roses and tuberoses. Slowly, the human crown rotated around the pedestal, tightening the embrace of moist flesh, offered to the desires of all.

The poses of ecstasy and adoration became precise, addressing the senses more directly before the Brahmin pujaris, the namadaris and the fakirs with ascetic faces, who, in the last ranks, were holding vast amphorae full of cantharide liquors.

The women now remained motionless, after having embraced one another's arms and legs more narrowly. The priests were shredding new flowers over their breasts and swinging balls of perfume contained in golden censers, pronouncing mysterious mantras.

The pujari sacrificer made a sign, summoning the holy men and the guests to the adoration of the three goddesses, mothers of the universe. They approached, clad in saffron salas, crowned with foliage, and prostrated themselves before the altar of the Lingam-nahamam, without yet crossing the rampart of supine women.

At that moment, vehemently spiced dishes, forbidden at ordinary times, and thick and heavy wines, were circulating among the audience, while the Brahmin sacrificers cut the throats of seven kids and a seven-month-old child nourished on the same milk as the kids, over the altar. The warm blood, collected in precious cups, was offered first to the three goddesses, and then to all those who desired to render themselves worthy of the benefits of the nahamam.

The invocations now concluded, men and women threw themselves on the dishes that were offered to them and drank arak, lotus- and palm-wine, sprinkled with curry and cinnamon, from leather bottles. In very little time, the drunkenness was complete. The dancers, their eyes languid and their lips dry, writhed on their flowery couch; the priests staggering, dragged themselves along the pillars, uttering raucous gasps.

Three times the Brahmin pujaris accomplished publicly, on the red altar, amid the blood of the sacrificial victims, the work of generation, and then collapsed, exhausted.

Finally, the links broke and there was a general melee. With cries and sighs, couples slid to the ground, mingling sexes, desires and kisses. How can one describe that immense saturnalia of frightful ruts, often unnatural, surrounded by all the pomp of Hindu ceremonies, which is called the fêtes of the Shakti Puja, or the mysteries of universal fecundation?

The guests no longer formed anything but a herd of crazed wild beasts. No other choice than hazard presided over the embraces, and the kisses sometimes languished in the blood on the lips of gaping wounds, which feverish fingers enlarged.

Syta had veiled her face in order no longer to see those scenes of passion and murder, sobs contracting her throat.

What could Lackmama be doing? Had she yielded to the frightful temptation?

But at that moment the confidante reappeared, and in the demi-obscurity of the cellar, the tall silhouette of the yogi loomed up.

III
Salassim

With a glad sigh, Syta let herself fall at her savior's feet.

"Finally, you have come! I see you! I can press my lips against the hem of your sala, and your eyes are enveloping me with their astral fluid! Oh, tell me your name, in order that I can murmur it endlessly, until the supreme spasm!"

"It is not my name that it is necessary to pronounce."

Then Syta, remembering Lackmama's recommendation, said with fervor: "AUM! Adoration to the Sun! Yes, I know that in coming into the world you have been placed in the first rank on the earth. Sovereign lord of all beings, and better than me—whom my sisters call queen of this land—you must watch over the conservation of civil and religious laws."

"That is my duty."

"Everything that the world contains is your property. By your primogeniture and by birth you have a right to everything that exists. I beg you, tell me your name."

"Get up," said the holy man. "It is Salassim who is watching over you."

"Salassim!"

"You know my name. Pronounce it sometimes after that of the Supreme Being, who alone is great, AUM! Adoration to the Sun!"

Again, she wanted to prostrate herself, but by the power of his gaze alone, Salassim maintained her motionless.

"What do you desire of me?"

"I want you to dwell in the palace," she said, "In order that I can listen to your divine word at every moment of the day, and caress my soul with the flame of your strange eyes, which seem two hearths in the night. No man is as strangely beautiful as you. None has ever penetrated me with such a delectable languor . . . However, Salassim, I do not want the possession of your flesh, nor the burn of your kiss. You are too far above me for my amour not to respect you infinitely.

"I have all the men that I designate to Lackmama. Some drag themselves on their knees to my palace in order to kiss the diamond on my toe and let themselves die of the excess of their joy. I love the games of adolescents, and many, after the initiation, condemn themselves to the worst tortures in order no longer to know other transports that those that I have taught them. I could, therefore, remain beside you without desiring anything but the balm of your speech. Come to the palace."

But the yogi shook his head sadly. "It's impossible."

"Impossible? Why? Am I not the Queen?"

"Above the Queen there is Swayambhuva, king of the world and of the known and unknown stars. There is the great Mystery that has created us and will destroy us."

Syla made herself plaintive and cajoling.

"Next to you I would be more timid than the asparasa of the distant bakti, and I would obey you as the Master of my heart and the universe. For me, you are no longer a man like the others, you are the equal of Vicrakarma."

"No, adorable little princess, I cannot follow you and live at your side like Yassoub, your favorite lion. My mission is to wander the profound forest, where my brothers live. We possess subterranean shelters there, and yajasalas that the pitris visit. In addition, we die and we are reincarnated at will; we would be eternal if our desire to live were sufficiently powerful. Unfortunately, we weary of humans, who are vulgar and cruel; of our own free will we quit the earth after having tried to sow the good seed here. We depart pure, and worthy of Issouara, the Supreme Being, who is nothing but a marvelous Spirit of Light."

"And you never love?"

"We love in soul and in thought. Do you know the story of my brother Nassudamy, who damned himself for having possessed a woman?"

"Yes," said Syta, trembling. "He abducted Viamalah, the most beautiful of the daughters of Benares, and died poisoned by the sacred naga."[1]

"You see that woman is deadly to us."

"I am not similar to the others, for I have exhausted human enjoyments; I have assuaged all my desires and all my tempta-

---

1 The author inserts a reference here to her own novel *Le Mystère de Kama* (tr. as *The Mystery of Kama*), which is slightly odd, as this is not what happens in the novel in question, and raises the possibility that *Le Harem de Syta* might have been written before *Le Mystère de Kama* and went to Méricant belatedly after Ernest Flammarion had declined to publish it.

tions, and my being aspires to higher felicities. You would have nothing to fear from my sex, Salassim; my body would be as icy as if it were covered by the snows of the Himalaya."

"It seems so to you, O Divine One, O Perfume, but in reality, it burns like the yajasala of the Blue Mountains before the sacrifices. You would doom me, without saving yourself."

Syta wept softly on Lackmama's breast.

"Then you're rejecting me," she said, desolate.

"I'm refusing to follow you."

She straightened up, grimly.

"Oh! In spite of your speech, you're similar to the Brahmins, who only take pleasure in dolorous scenes of passion and murder. The priest has always been the evil genius of our race. Everywhere, he has made alliance with evil spirits in order to proscribe all independence, all verity, all justice and all science. He does not want humans to conceive a sane and rational idea of the Supreme Being, for he can only reign by terrorizing consciences and stifling the noble aspirations of the soul."

"You are angry," said Salassim. "I shall withdraw, and I shall pray for you in my solitude."

But she clung on to the yogi's sala, sobbing. "No, no, don't abandon me."

"It's necessary. And then, these scenes of orgy sicken me."

She darted a distracted glance at the sanctuary, which the velakous,[1] the sacred lamps, were illuminating with green-tinted jets. Enlaced couples were agitating on the mutilated roses, in puddles of wine and blood, drunk on kisses, cries, blasphemies and murders.

Children destined for the Brahmins were lying with their throats cut; young women with slashed breasts were lying on their bloody veils, agitating feverishly, their faces earthen and their hair stuck to their cheeks. Many guests were sleeping

____

1 Another term taken from Jacolliot.

heavily, hiccups and snores mingling with the gasps of lust and death.

Salassim raised his gaze higher than the scene of the monstrous orgy, contemplating the marvels of Hindu art that would later inspire the art of Egypt and Greece. The ancestors of those men who were sprawling pell-mell in their abjection had sculpted in those aerial columns, with their chisels, the frail goddesses of grace and amour that adorned the capitals like a precious necklace. They had invented the lotuses, the acanthuses and the ivy that wound around the keys of the friezes, preceding the pure Greek, the Dorian, the Egyptian, the Gothic, the Roman, the Arab, imagining a thousand masterpieces five thousand years before Egypt had laid the foundations of Thebes, Greece had raised the Parthenon and the Arabs had carved the Alhambra.

And all the marvels of that marvelous place only rendered more odious the scenes of rut, murder and drunkenness that unfurled at the fêtes of the Shakti.

"Come," murmured the little princess, trying to draw the yogi away. "Come with me. I will make you greater than my six husbands, greater than myself, you will be the most beloved, the most venerated."

But he pushed her away and recoiled into the darkness of the gallery.

Already, she could no longer see him, but she could hear his distant voice.

"If you want to abandon your palace, your children, your husbands and your people, if you want to live, like the most humble of the Kuruba, on roots and honey, you will find me in the depths of the bakti, where I dwell with my brothers. 'Know, want, dare, be silent.' Such is the occult quaternary of those who govern the world."

IV
Return to the Palace

He had disappeared, and Syta sobbed more forcefully on Lackmama's bosom.

"Abandon my people! Renounce power! Flee like a criminal! Is that possible?"

"It's necessary to forget the insensate words of the yogi; holy men as handsome and as eloquent will console you, O Divine One, for the blindness of that man. What other would be mad enough and disdainful enough of the sensualities of life to resist you?"

"Let's go back to the palace, Lackmama. I can scarcely sustain myself."

Groping in the long, dark gallery, they tried to find the door that opened to the courtyard of sacrifices, between the two granite lions with flamboyant eyes.

The smoky little lamps were extinct, and the spongy ground made walking more difficult. The blood of the Shakti had flowed through invisible fissures, and stuck to their feet; the charnel house odor grabbed the throat, and the Rani's anguish was augmented in that place of agony. She would have fallen but for the solicitude of Lackmama, who had been familiarized with the nightmares of the temple long ago.

Finally, they reached the gardens, with the tomb-like pathways, the heavy flowers gorged with blood, the perfume of which rose violently in the night. Syta breathed more freely, satisfied with seeing the sky again, hearing the distant noises of the city, and escaping the morbid suggestions of the red orgy.

"*Saranay aya!*" murmured the Brahmin who opened the door for them.

Rapidly, she responded: "*Assirvadham!*"

The temple of Kanda, seen from outside, was still radiant from the base to the summit, as if celebrating, by the thousand fires of its façade, the frightful drama that it sheltered.

Rapidly, the Rani resumed the route to the palace through the deserted back streets, effacing herself alongside the houses and covering her face with the pleats of the gold-hemmed saffron veil with which she enveloped herself for her nocturnal excursions.

The other temples of Ahmehnagara remained plunged in darkness; only the fantastic animals that guarded the entrances stood out against the granite walls, between lingams and nahamams ornamented with flowers. At the crossroads, the yajasalas were still smoking, encumbered by the bones of animals immolated in honor of the Shakti.

Syta finally reached the portico of her palace and passed furtively under the gigantic red marble bull that guarded the entrance. Perhaps she was recognized, but no one dared testify astonishment. Was she not the adorable sovereign whom everyone respected, all of whose desires were sacred?

It was with a happy sigh that she delivered herself to the care of her women, whose light hands glided over her body in perfumed caresses, pouring essences and balms, and when she was ready for repose, she closed her eyes delightedly on her solitary couch.

V

Bewitchment

But sleep did not come.

The astral body of Salassim, disengaged from its terrestrial envelope, manifested itself to the dazzled eyes of the princess in the form of a luminous disk, which moved with an extreme rapidity. It brushed her forehead and her lips, and its fluidic essence penetrated her, sometimes shaking her ardently from her nape to her heels, voluptuously. She heard a divine murmur, although no voice was perceptible in the night. The whispers wandered over her face, between her breasts, descending along her charming body and causing her to weaken indefinably.

She had never experienced anything similar and she repeated, passionately:

"O my beloved, O my Master, descend within me again, always, that I may feel the flame of your kiss! No other felicity on earth is comparable to this divine ecstasy!"

"Open your arms," he said, and he posed on her heart. "Open your lips"—and he enveloped her tongue with an expert caress. "Open your knees"—and he forgot himself within her, recklessly.

The blue disk sometimes disappeared, seemingly traversing the walls. Then she recalled it, unable to weary of its sight, always wanting to possess it more fully.

The chamber was entirely illuminated by its presence; it traversed it like a beautiful bird of light with rapid wings, often presenting the melted hues of the rainbow.

That night was exquisite for Syta. She would have liked to remain under the hypnotic charm forever, without mingling with the vulgar sensations of life.

So, when her women came into her apartment, she refused to get out of bed, giving the pretext of a sudden fever.

Her six Great Husbands, admitted to her presence, became very anxious on seeing her so plaintive. The eyes of their little sovereign had never had such strange gleams; she seemed marvelously seductive to them, in the disorder of her long hair, with her quivering breasts with the gilded nipples and the still-ecstatic smile of her mouth.

Ruman-Bibi, the Perfect Science, took possession of her hand with a sudden ardor, while Biskourmi, the Column of Felicity, slid a kiss a little above the elbow. Paraçou, the Incomparable, had already knelt down with Nandamu the Golden Ram and Soulabatka the Flavorsome Fruit, while Doudouma-Lovi, above them all, stammered indistinct words in his disturbance.

But the Rani pushed them away with a weary gesture.

"Oh no! Not today!"

"However . . ." hazarded Ruman-Bibi.

"We didn't rendered you any homage yesterday," observed Nandamu, sadly.

"And all your secondary husbands, whom you're disdaining like us, are in desolation!" sighed Biskouri.

"O admirable Lotus, flower of flesh worthy of Vicrakarma, the eternal artist, let us intoxicate ourselves with the perfume of your body, and drink from your lips the wine of forgetfulness, sweeter than the sacred water of the spring Hadamur!"

Soulabatka was weeping with admiration and covetousness.

"Only let us weave you a veil of kisses! Let your adorable body be covered entirely by them, and let each stitch caress a tiny corner of your perfect beauty!"

"No," she said. "You don't know the true sensualities."

"We don't know them!" moaned Nandamu. "Teach us the supreme science, then. Are we not your prostrated slaves?"

"You cannot know the divine joys of luminous spirits! You are of earth, and unusual felicities have transported my soul to the isle of Raunak,[1] the isle of sensuality. Krishna alone would be welcome today, for he alone would be able to set me ablaze with the fire of his astral love!"

Consternated, the six Great Husbands looked at one another with astonishment.

"What is the matter with our little princess?" whispered Paraçou.

And each lord, in his turn, offered his opinion.

"Maleficent pitris have visited her last night!"

"They've taken her to the adda-loca and robbed her of her reason."[2]

---

1 "L'île de Raunak" [isle of Raunak] is featured in an 1893 French translation of Lallu Lal's early-19th-century version of the story of Krishna, *Prem Sagar*, but does not seem to appear anywhere else.

2 The adda-loca can be found in Jacolliot but was not original to him, having previously been employed by Jean-Antoine Dubois in his account of India, published in 1825; it is difficult to locate elsewhere. Maha-Merou is also featured in Dubois and Jacolliot, but is much more widespread.

"She's icier than the Maha-Merou of the eternal snows."

"The most irresistible caresses disgust her."

"Our kisses seem more redoubtable to her than a wasp's sting!"

"Woe betide us!" wept the six Radogks, veiling their faces; and they summoned the old Brahmin of the court, whose experience and sage advice they appreciated very particularly.

VI
The Slaves of Amour

The holy man, on learning of the fears of the great Radogks, experienced a joyful shudder, rather bizarre in the circumstances, and rendered to the part of the palace reserved for Syta's husbands. That construction resembled a fortress, for, as in the gynaecea of women, everything had been suppressed that might permit the young men contained therein to look outside and to be seen. With high walls, towers and interior courtyards of the lodgment, framed within edifices, the slaves of the Most High's amour had no communication with other men. At sunset, they were permitted to go up on to the terraces, to sing, accompanying themselves on various instruments, and to recite erotic poems, the most ardent of which sometimes had the gift of touching the sovereign's heart.

Those handsome slaves, occupied all day in depilating themselves, perfuming themselves and adorning themselves with precious fabrics, were, like almost all the men of Ahmehnagara, extremely ignorant. Apart from the amorous rules of the Kama-Shastra, they only knew the usage of the various objects necessary to their existence, and even then, only appreciated them under the transformations to which their industry had submitted them.

The rooms they occupied were sumptuously furnished, in the Hindu manner, with carpets, mats, and broad, soft divans upholstered in silk and gold. The walls, in white and green marble, sculpted with chisels and more uneven than lace, presented nails of precious stones assembled in diamond- and star-shapes.

Heavy draperies, mingled with silver and gold, separated the rooms, which were illuminated from above, through green stained glass, the mild hue of which calmed the gaze.

The Rani's secondary spouses were smoking nonchalantly, extended on cushions, all accomplished and irritating in their grace, their long eyes blurred by kohl, their hair carefully braided or spread over the shoulders, dazzling smiles on their fleshy lips. They displayed the forms of young gods, simultaneously svelte, wiry and robust, with hands whose fingernails were more polished than agate, and delicately arched feet studded with gems all the way to the ankle. A network of precious stones covered their loins, and delicate tattoos in various colors ran over their breasts and arms.

The six Great Husbands chose them with care, wanting them to be as well endowed morally as they were physically, of cheerful humor and perfect health. They were the sovereign's true luxury, and she often came to sit in their midst in order to rest from the worries of power.

When the Six Great Radogks and the Brahmin came in, all the husbands stood up respectfully for the customary salutation. They each put their hand to the breast, bowing with grace and dignity.

"May the Supreme Being be with you, husbands of the Divine One, and with you, Aracknai, servant of the beloved temple of Issouara," they said, gravely.

The granichy made a slight protective and benevolent sign to the slaves of amour, and they sat down on the precious cushions that had been reserved for them. Aracknai, sitting slightly apart, invited the Radogks to express themselves freely on the subject of their anxieties.

"This is it," said Paraçou. "Our adorable Syta is in a strange humor this morning. She had refused our homages and did not want to accord us the usual audience. She is alone in her room, where she is reposing on her large bed like a victim destined for the sacrifice of the ashwamedha."

"She went to the Shakti yesterday," said the Brahmin, hypocritically. "It's doubtless fatigue that is overwhelming her today."

"No," said Soulabatka. "We have experience of the Very Beloved's fatigues. Her eyes express something other than you think. We know the Rani's happy fevers. They have never prevented her from visiting the sacred elephants and taking treats to her favorite lion Yassoub. Clad in her simarre decorated with gold and her pearly belt, with the great sash of sapphires across her breast, she passes her Royal Guard in review every day, and occupies herself with the interests of the State, for she shows herself to be wise and informed in all matters. We can affirm to you, Aracknai, that our Divine One is singular this morning."

The Brahmin uttered a shrill laugh, which surprised the Great Radogks, in spite of their painful preoccupation.

"Has she talked to some fakir during the Shakti?"

"We don't know," sighed Nandamu. "We only know that one of those enchanters has cast a spell on her."

"Yes," said Doudouma-Lovi, supportively, "the evil has been in her heart since the last antelope hunt."

After seeming to plunge himself in long reflection, the Brahmin said: "It is necessary to give her this holy man that she loves and desires for a husband."

"We'd like nothing better," cried the six Radogks, "but the yogi is undiscoverable and no one knows his name."

"Oh," said Soulabatka, "be persuaded, Aracknai, that we only want the happiness of the Incomparable Syta, and that there is no effort that we would not attempt in order to put the lover she has chosen in her arms. Ought not husbands worthy of the name devote themselves entirely to the satisfaction of the Very Beloved? But we have visited all the temples of Ahmehnagara, all the flowery houses where the Sons of Joy live and all the yajasalas where the sacred animals are immolated. Neither the Brahmins of Kanda-Swamy, who are informed of all things, nor the men of lust, nor the sacrificers, have been able to give us the slightest information. This yogi Charmer is doubtless a solitary of the backti, and it will be difficult to discover his traces."

Doudouma-Lovi uttered a profound sigh; he was greatly infatuated with the princess, and suffered from her rigors more than the other husbands.

"Might not a holy man be able to destroy the charm that envelops our Divine One?" he asked.

Aracknai shook his head sadly, but a gleam passed through his yellow cat-like eyes. "Fakirs sometimes reach an understanding with maleficent spirits to bewitch the victims they have chosen. But attacking the princess is a great audacity!"

"We would need a perfectly beautiful and virginal subject to console and distract Syta from her caprice," said Nandamu.

"Alas," sighed Biskouri, "we have the most accomplished young men of Ahmehnagara and distant countries here. Few have not yet approached the Rani, and only know of amour what we have taught them."

"It would be good, I think," declared the Brahmin, "to bring the bewitched soul to an intimate union with the Supreme Being. She would arrive at that by means of contemplation, ecstasy and knowledge of the sacred Mystery. Woman, as you know, is superior to man; she possesses, throughout our beautiful realm, an unparalleled authority, for the maternal attributes of the divinity are venerated in her. The virgins of the temples instituted in honor of the female trimurty, Bhavani-Lakmi-Shakti, conserve the supreme dignity. It would be easy to choose among them a creature of charm and tenderness capable of caring for and curing our sovereign. But what man, even raised in the mystery of the temple, would have enough science, passionate eloquence and persuasion to make himself heard? We have to struggle against the malign spirit of the nacara, and the Charmer they have chosen in the accomplishment of their perverse design is doubtless an androgyne, a supernatural being."

"The situation is grave," sighed Ruman-Bibi. "You cannot see any remedy, then, Venerated One?"

"I'm offering you the virgins of the trimurty."

But the Great Husbands seemed hostile to the Brahmin's project.

"No," said Soulabatka. "If our Very Beloved savors the felicities that the priestesses of the trimurty teach, she will no longer want to know others, and the remedy will be worse than the disease!

"Send us, Aracknai, one of those handsome young men destined for the temple who are nourished on milk and honey, steeped in balms, and virgin in soul and body. We'll put him in Syta's bed after having instructed him in accordance with the books of holy sensuality."

Aracknai crossed his stiff hands over his breast. "What you're asking of me is grave, for that victim of amour must be immolated after the initiation, and our young disciples, as you know, are becoming increasingly rare. A wind of folly is blowing over all those frail consciences, who only aspire to deliver themselves to woman. We only possess six men of perfect purity and beauty."

"Show them to us. But are they really as immaculate as you assure us?"

"Oh, they're completely ignorant of life, and only know the sacred mysteries that the yogis transmit in the silence of temples."

"That's what we need. Doubtless the disciple will be able to combat the bewitchment that is weighing upon the faculties of our Divine One."

The Brahmin did not reply, but a satisfied smile passed over his features, furrowed by occult storms.

In the depths of his heart, Aracknai detested the Rani and all the women of the realm. In accord with the Brahmins of the temples of Kanda-Swamy, Bahvani, Lakmi and Aluwihara, he was only seeking an opportunity to vanquish the power of the Golden Womb in order to substitute that of the male symbol. The occult practices of the Charmer were known to him, and if he was feigning ignorance it was in order to strike more effectively when the time came. Already, in certain religious ceremonies, the worship of the nahamam was neglected, no longer celebrated with the pomp of old. Aracknai groaned and struck his breast as a sign of desolation, but joy was sparkling in his eyes in spite of everything.

The slaves of amour inclined again as the six Great Radogks passed by.

The sovereign's husbands were so affected that they had not wanted to touch the Lotus wine and the scobati eggs preserved in honey that the youths had offered them on trays of amber and jade.

Hastily, they lifted the silky door-curtains and were engulfed in the shelters of sensuality where cushions, thrown at hazard, obstructed progress. Without stopping, they traversed the hall of celebrations and the banqueting hall, where immense tables supported fruits and sugar flowers artfully arranged on precious trays, wines with amethyst and emerald hues, and lilies in gold and silver vases delicately studded with gems. Jets of rose, jasmine and tuberose water sprang from the walls through the mouths of twenty metal lions, and slaves in the upper galleries stood ready to swing immense reed fans over the heads of guests.

A golden throne laden with soft fabrics with fine embroideries awaited the pleasure of the Rani, who sometimes shared her secondary spouses' meal. Children with pure voices celebrated her adorable qualities then; there were sweet harmonies of which certain very high notes expired like the sighs of lutes. The musical instruments were of three kinds: string, wind and percussion; they offered a fairly considerable range of form. A few harps were fitted with thirteen strings; they were played with two hands, sometimes while walking, for they were light and affected the form of a bow. There were lyres of a sort in tortoiseshell or coconut shell, cymbals, snakeskin rums and tambourahs. The men cultivated singing particularly, and some of them, castrated in childhood, possessed extraordinary voices, more extensive and more splendid than the most beautiful female voices.

Syta forbade her secondary husbands to talk to her about amour; little boys celebrated the ecstasies of possession during her embraces with seraphic trills, and the melody rose or weakened, thunderously unleashed or expiring in crystal droplets, following all the phases of the mysterious act.

The enlaced couple savored the ineffable poem in itself, without any cerebral effort coming to spoil the savant rhythm, and the dream was thus alloyed ineffably with the reality.

Only the Great Radogks, more learned and more cultivated, had the right to express their sentiments, but Syta preferred, without saying so, her silent lovers.

VII
The Nahamam

The Brahmin Aracknai and the Radogks had reached the part of the temple of Issouara in which the aspirant yogis entered into meditation and prayer. The most important act, for them, consisted of the celebration of the sacred Mysteries, and they awaited the revelation of tenuous verities hidden in the tragic secrecy of sanctuaries and tombs. Those adorers of the gardawabahya, or white lotus,[1] celebrated the nahamam in particular, the attributes of which were found sculpted in profusion on the columns and the walls.

The stone and the marble have still conserved that symbol, which originally had an importance far greater than that of the lingam in the Brahmanic religion. It was only later that belief in the beneficent qualities of the nahamam gave way to the obscene practices of the cult of Shiva. According to Hindu mythology, the universe was born from a seed that Being, existing alone, cast into the water after having created it first, in order to occupy infinite space and to remain the reservoir of organic life.

---

1 The term and its supposed definition are taken from Louis Jacolliot, yet again, as is most of the argument that follows, in this instance from the book first published as *La Genèse de l'Humanité* (1875).

Having resolved, in its thought, to make the various creatures emanate from its substance, it first produced the waters in which it deposited a seed. That seed became an egg as shiny as gold, etc . . . (The Genesis of Manu.)

That seed was produced by the union of the lingam and the nahamam, the two principles, male and female, of the creative power of Brahma. Legendary and religious poetry represents those two organs of generation under the features of a young man and a young woman, the god Nara and the goddess Nari.

"One kiss of Nara on the lips of Nari," says the poet VinaSnati, "and nature entire awoke!"

It is certain, however, that Nari did far more than Nara, for the latter only had the pleasure of the act without the pain. It was just that the goddess of amour was honored very particularly, since she gave birth in tears, while her divine lover only made a voluptuous gesture. Nari is the veritable creator of the world, of which Nara only had the first idea, and the Hindus acted with equity in devoting an unalloyed amour to her.

Less sage and more arrogant, the priests of Egypt and Greece only took from the primordial religions of India the cult of the lingam, the male cult, which became that of the phallus and Priapus, of which the symbols can be found sculpted even in our Medieval cathedrals, unconscious works that the naïve workman continued, without suspecting that he was following a part of Indo-Brahmanic tradition.

The nahamam, or feminine attribute, is still shown on the walls of the oldest pagodas, Elephanta, Chelambrun, Djaggernat and others, although people had ceased to render it the homage that was its due.

"Every seed that falls into the Golden Womb," says Soumati, "contains in germ the gods, the heaven, the worlds and the universality of things. Glory to Nahamam!"

Covered in long white veils, like virgins, the disciples of Vicra-Karma, in a low, dimly lit room, were reciting mantras round the object of their adoration. Three among them, displaying their naked flesh, were dancing slowly, their eyes revulsed and their lips parted, as if in ecstasy.

"See," said the Brahmin to the Great Radogks, "these are our sons of election, the six white pearls of Ahmehnagara, the most perfect things under the sun and the stars!"

The young men of the temple were, in fact, of a rare beauty, with expressive features, dark sparkling eyes, long and lustrous hair mingled with cords, over skin of a marvelous delicacy and polish. Their easy, noble and gracious movements had an unparalleled harmony.

"Oh," said Ruman-Bibi, "none of the sovereign's husbands possess as many attractions as these servants of the temple, and our Divine One will have reason to be satisfied."

"None of the lovers that we have given her," said Paraçou, supportively, "has this supreme distinction."

"She'll forget her yogi Charmer," declared Nandamu, "and become again the adorable princess that she was before."

"May Brahma hear you!" concluded Aracknai, with an equivocal smile.

The handsome disciples, protested, intoned a hymn to the nahamam, taken from the Nitya Karma:

"O Nahamam!

"You are a calyx of the immaculate lotus, and you receive the divine seed of Brahma in a profound caress! You are the ancestor of all beings! You are purity and chastity, the Golden Womb in which the power of the supreme god resides!

"O Nahamam!

"You are as fragile and strong as the prayer that an ardent soul exhales, the perfume to which the flower gives birth, the kiss that expires on the lips of lovers! You are the sacred Ganges, honey and amrita, the essence of Zyaus, the mother of the vedas and Brahmins! It is from your womb that everything that exists emerged!

"O Nahamam!"

"O Nahamam!" sighed the six Great Husbands, prostrating themselves in their turn before the symbol of supreme felicity and eternal fecundity.

The disciples, still feverish in their passionate mantras, had risen to their feet and were standing motionless before the Brahmin. The latter named them in turn, praising their skill, their fervor and their obedience.

"Make your choice," he concluded. "The disciples of Vicra-Karma belong to the sovereign. They will be glad to offer her the Gardawabahya of their adoration and their chastity."

VIII
The Virgin Lover

The Great Husbands, after having conferred, declared unanimously that Prismama seemed to them to be worthy of sharing the august couch of the Rani.

Prismama fell to his knees, for he knew that after his voluptuous night he would be immolated to the gods in the temple of Kanda-Swany. He knew, too, that the Brahmins were seeking to doom Syta, and his heart was constricted dolorously.

The young man had a troubling beauty, with his oval face, his velvet and nacre eyes, shaded by long curly lashes, and his supple and wiry body, with perfect proportions. The pale gold complexion of his skin had paled further in the sanctuary, and its texture was so uniform, so lustrous and so mild that he seemed a flower rather than a human face. An anatomist, a painter and a sculptor combined would not have been able to find the slightest flaw in that charming ephebe. A few meters of light gauze enveloped his loins and his torso; his tresses, braided in cords, flowed over his shoulders like serpents.

"Follow us, Prismama," Ruman-Bibi ordered. "We have chosen you among your brothers to deliver our Divine One from the amorous bewitchment from which he has been suffering for weeks. A Charmer of the backti has cast a spell on her while she was hunting antelope, and since then, nothing has been able to cure her malaise."

"You know the sacred mysteries," added Naudamu, "and the strange practices of fakirs are doubtless familiar to you?"

Prismama, his eyes lowered, made no reply. A terrible combat must have been engaged in his soul, and the Brahmin, more perspicacious than the Radogks, was following its development with interest.

Aracknai, revolutionary and ambitious, in spite of his functions as the high priest of the palace, was quietly irritated by the privileges of women in the realm of Ahmehnagara. He would gladly have approved the example of other provinces that had chosen a master, and he thought that, sooner or later, feminine domination would yield the upper hand to male potency.

In fact, the Brahmins were already the masters of the country almost everywhere. They had divided it into districts, which they governed by means of an assembly, a council of four and a chief, elected for a number of years, who fulfilled all the responsibilities of executive power. They coveted the realm of Ahmehnagara, which an exceptional situation and a divine climate rendered enviable among all.

Although the geography of the world was still confined within narrow limits and knowledge was scarcely more than Asiatic, the religion of Brahma already flourished like a lotus of infinite and mysterious pools. India, the flower and queen of Asia, was the source of Egyptian, Greek and Latin theology; it was the civilizer and the governor of the regions of the Occident, and it possessed as many colonies as it furnishes colonizations today.

All the other religions pillaged Brahma, and Brahma, without Brahmins, has remained the master of the universe.

But the priests, who were too ambitious, killed the religion of forgiveness and amour in waning to take possession of human wealth, after being content to reign over hearts. The Brahmins still claim today that their ancestors were the kings of the land,

and that the murder of a Brahmin ought to lead immediately to the supreme punishment. The most absolute papacy cannot give an idea of their spiritual authority, and they still enjoy such a great multitude of temporal advantages that no sovereign can be compared with them. They speak to the great men of the kingdom and even the king without rendering them the customary homages; freer than the grandees of Spain, who have the right to remain covered before the very Catholic monarch, they abstain from putting their hand to their face for fear of sketching a salute.

Those priests are, for the most part, voluntary martyrs who, by means of sacrifices, subjugate weak minds paralyzed by the sight of blood. The spectacle of Brahmanic mortifications renders all Indians respectful and enchains them to a fanatical devotion. Some have themselves buried alive and condemn themselves to remain, until definitive death, lying in a narrow cave almost devoid of air and devoid of light; others, buried to the waist, leave their faces and breasts exposed to the burning sun. Sometimes they even coat themselves in honey in order to attract flies and insects whose bites draw blood. One of those madmen lived for years with his legs crossed over his thighs and his hands joined behind his head. He subsisted on alms from Brahmin women who nourished him on milk and crushed seeds.

Prismama, like his fellow disciples of Issouara, was destined for the torture of fire at Karbi, in the temple of elephants, so named because every pillar of the vault is surmounted by an elephant bearing a figure of a man and a figure of a woman, narrowly united, in its back. The galleries of the sanctuary are more lugubrious in appearance than those of Elephanta and Ellora. One encounters a host of Brahmins and fakirs there who have come from all parts of India in order to recite mantras in the cellar of evocations. Many establish a dwelling in the vicinity of the temple, mortifying their flesh, and only existing henceforth in the most absolute contemplation, Sitting day and night in front of large braziers carefully maintained by the faithful, with a bandage over the mouth to avoid respiring the slightest pollution, only eating a few grains of grilled rice, moistened by water filtered through a cloth, they gradually arrive at an almost skeletal state, having nothing alive any longer but their eyes, turned inward in the ecstasy of the dream. In that game, mental strength also weakens with rapidity, and when those fanatics attain their final end, they have lost the consciousness of things a long time before, by virtue of that slow suicide.

All the yogis who desire to attain the most elevated transformations in the superior worlds must submit their bodies to these frightful ordeals.

Prismama, placed between two braziers in order to celebrate the decomposition of his organs, had been due to die thus, after the perfect initiation; but the possession of the Rani would spare him that destiny by consecrating him to immediate torture.

The Brahmin priests claim that phenomena and exterior manifestations are the means that the pitris, or sanctified manes of the ancestors, employ to prove their existence and to communicate with humans.

By sacrificing Prismama, Aracknai hoped to doom the sovereign conclusively, whom that night of intoxication ought to bewitch more profoundly. Syta, incapable of reigning, would flee, abandoning power, and the Brahmins would become the veritable masters of the realm.

In the temples there were symptoms by means of which it was easy to divine a certain discontentment. However, although malady and mendacity remained almost unknown in that charming country, India was choking under the exactions of invaders, the thefts of supreme stewards, exorbitant taxes that did not leave enough to live on, plague and famine, which imposed their domination by turns.

Thus far, Syta had governed with mildness and wisdom, and everyone, except for the priests, testified the most profound respect and the most submissive affection for her. But in India, the religious element is the one that has the most weight and consistency, and is the most widespread, the most active and the most influential. It possesses ramifications in all the castes and all the provinces, and eventually triumphs over the greatest obstacles and the most combative energies.

The little princess therefore had much to dread in the hostility of the temples, and the Radogks were very imprudent in choosing a virgin lover for her among the initiates of Issoura.

The Brahmin murmured a few recommendations in Prismama's ear; the latter finally replied that the will of the gods was his own and that he would do his best to fulfill the amorous mission that the Great Husbands had deigned to confide to him. Perhaps the disciple was already carrying the image of the sovereign in his heart and devoting an ecstatic worship to her.

After a final prayer to the nahamam and an affectionate farewell to his brothers of election, he emerged from the temple, carefully veiled, and allowed himself to be led into one of the chambers of the palace reserved for the toilette of the newly elected.

In her large bed, Syta was still appealing, with a sort of delirium, for the occult kisses of Salassim.

All day long she had sensed the luminous and serene astral form fluttering around her, brushing her hair, melting over her lips and in her feverish intimacy. The fluidic essence penetrated her passionately, causing her to faint with a very gentle death, or shaking her vertiginously from the nape of her neck to her heels.

And Syta repeated, with intoxication: "O my Adored, descend into me again, always! No other ecstasy is comparable to your divine possession!"

The blue disk, like a great sidereal butterfly, settled on that flower of flesh, that divine lotus with the perfume of sandalwood and honey.

"Descend into me! Penetrate me with your invincible caress! O my Lover! O my Master! O my All!"

"She has a fever," said Ruman-Bibi, who was standing next to the bed of the four silver lions, contemplating the sovereign.

"May the disciple of Issouara come to her aid!" sobbed Biskourmi, veiling his face with desolation.

As for Doudouma-Lovi, the most infatuated of the great Radogks, he could no longer find words vehement enough to express his pain, and he contented himself with uttering deep sighs, which made the beads of his necklaces dance on his breast.

Lackmama, the maidservant, shook her head with a sad smile. "It's the yogi's bewitchment; we can't do anything about it."

"Yes," said Paraçou, "the Initiate of Issouara will destroy the Charmer's work. He knows the secrets of life and death; he knows how to read in the stars, and his power equals that of the most powerful, for he's a virgin."

IX
The Unexpected Event

Combed, depilated, perfumed, more beautiful than Kama, the god of amour, Prismama was introduced into the royal bedchamber. His hands were full of roses, which he shredded over the couch; then, kneeling in the shadow, he murmured mysterious mantras.

And the great Radogks, with felted footfalls, went away in order to permit the immaculate lover to deliver the princess.

"Is that you, Salassim?" Syta asked, tenderly.

"No," said Prismama, "but I have come on his behalf, for he knew that the husbands would choose me to render you the peace of the soul."

She sat up on her cushions abruptly.

"Is that really true?"

"Look," he said, in a melancholy tone, "and no longer doubt."

The great butterfly of flame had reappeared, and it settled on the young man's head, flapping its wings lightly.

"You see?"

"Oh, yes! Salassim is with you! Tell me what it is necessary to do in order to be agreeable to him?"

"Would you like to quit the palace and accompany me into the depths of the backti?"

Syta, indecisive, did not reply.

"You're hesitating out of pride; you're proud of being the sovereign, and receiving the homages of a prostrate people. Perhaps you're right. Only follow your desire, O Divine One, for the words that I pronounce are dictated to me by the Charmer."

"Yes," she said. "I ought not to abandon the people who love me and have confidence in me. A deserter is an ingrate and disloyal heart."

"The reign of woman is terminated; revolt is lying in wait. But it's necessary to stay in spite of everything."

Syta opened her eyes wide. "Revolt? My subjects have never been more submissive."

"The Brahmins are against you."

"What have I done to them?"

"Nothing, but you're a woman. The priests of Ahmehnagara no longer want to submit to the symbol of eternal fecundity. They are beginning to prefer the male principle that is honored in other countries."

"I'll expel the Brahmins from my realm!"

"Could you? They're the masters of India. They are *gurubrahmatma dwidjaha*—which is to say, invincible."

Syta was now trembling on her royal bed with the great silver lions.

"Perhaps you're right. I sense that I'm lost, because, for the first time in my life, amour has penetrated into me."

"Nothing is sweeter than amour, O Divine One. Allow yourself to be cradled by the caresses of dream, and let the occult kiss of Salassim enable you to forget forever the vile demonstrations of your terrestrial husbands . . . And yet, Salassim is also in danger."

Syta slid her dainty foot constellated with precious stones out of the bed.

"Take me to the yogi. I no longer want another spouse down here."

"And you're renouncing power?"

Prismama would have given his life to retain the sovereign, but a force superior to his own paralyzed his will.

"I renounce the wealth of this world and everything that is not the divine caress from which I am still fainting!" Syta exclaimed. "But tell me, who are you, whose face seems more beautiful to me than the visage of Ma, the moon? Is it the Beloved who sent you?"

"The great Radogks and the Brahmin Aracknai have ordered me to cure you by means of the transport of my virgin amour; in doing that they were only obeying the will of Salassim, who has confidence in me. I shall not be a lover for you, but a faithful servant."

As he said that, the young man sighed, and his eyes filled with tears.

The Rani had put her most precious gems in a silk scarf, and the headband with the twelve diamond crowns on her head. Prismama took her jewels away from her.

"Don't forget, O Felicity, that you must be humbler than the least Kuruba of the Blue Mountains, and that nothing that enables splendor can exist any longer for you."

"You're right," murmured Syta; and before going away she darted a last glance at the marvelous chamber where so many sighs of sensual pleasure had been exhaled.

The diamantine awning of her couch scintillated again above her head, while the admirable sculptures of ivory and jade became more precise under the network of gems arranged in broad diamond shapes that covered the walls.

The second part of the room, to which one descended by a staircase of six steps, sent her the freshness of its large bath with singing jets of water. And the waves of almond, jasmine and rose that ran from the twelve silver elephants sent her the pleasures of the bath. She went into the perfumed water one last time in order to wash herself clean of the pollution of sin, but she did not summon Lackmama to rub her with balms and mingle pearls with her long wet hair.

"Quickly," she said, "let's flee while the night envelops people and things. The great Radogks must be watching the golden door, quivering with desire, only waiting for your departure in order to overwhelm me with their amour."

"Reflect again, O Divine One! Perhaps the amour of the husbands is preferable to that of the troublesome spirit that is haunting you."

But she shook her mutinous head.

"No, no. I'm abandoning myself to the adorable mystery! The soul of Salassim possesses me entirely! Come, let's flee. Detach Ackbe, my great white horse, and take another stallion with slender and muscular legs for yourself; no one will be able to overtake us."

"So be it," said the disciple, "let it be done in accordance with your wishes."

Syta descended into the courtyard of the palace, and leapt on to the back of the superb animal, which uttered a joyful whinny. Prismama chose another mount almost as admirable in form and suppleness; then the two fugitives, as rapid as Pavana, the god of the wind, set forth for the backti.

X
The Guru

The true *gurubrahmatma dwidjaha*, or man who knows everything, scorns other men. He is fond of savage places, in the chaos of landslides and the enchantment of unknown plants with monstrous flowers, open like mouths ever avid for prey to seize.

To all the inventions of human genius he prefers the inexhaustible marvels of nature, which builds for herself alone cathedrals of verdure with tangled domes of lianas, and mossy trunks adorned with ferns more delicate than gold and silver lace.

The true Guru understands the clamor of birds of prey and the roar of wild beasts whose eyes are phosphorescent in the night. He travels, powerful and gentle, with pink turtle-doves in his hair and reptiles asleep on his breast. He can charm tigers and the blue spiders that suspend their threads of silk from one branch to another. He talks to calices, stones and trees; he is the king of the world, for all creatures are submissive to him.

Syta rode through the disquieting solitudes at the gallop of her great white stallion, guided by Prismama, whose expression darkened increasingly. Sometimes, the disciple darted a glance of pity and profound adoration at the princess.

They always went further forward into the violet night, brushing the foliage of poisonous trees that shed ocher and cinnabar powder as they passed. Immense moths with wings stabbed with red fluttered before them, and bats slapped them with their viscous membranes

Sometimes, the skeleton of a carnivore swung from the branches, and in certain places, heaps of white bones crackled under the hooves of their horses.

"Where are you taking me?" sobbed Syta. "I'm afraid!"

But Prismama reassured her in a tremulous voice.

"We'll reach our goal soon. Life, you see, accompanies death everywhere . . . but death is necessary to life. Everything is renewed and everything collaborates in the universal splendor."

They were now traversing terrains abandoned by the sea, hills of mobile sand that gave certain desolate regions the arid aspects of Arabia and Africa. In the midst of yellow clumps of mimosas and the sharp blades of cacti there were marine incrustations, nacreous shells in bizarre and charming forms.

"Nature," said Prismama, "is more powerful than humans; she plays with their efforts, absorbs them, swallows them and devours them. That bamboo, springing forth in the ardent atmosphere and projecting its rigid stem and metallic leaves irresistibly toward the clouds; those plants, as passionate as lovers, join one another, seize one another, embrace one another and cling to one another until death. The rut of feverish vegetation would stop an army! A tree can make a forest under the inevitable action of its exasperated productive forces. Twenty feet from the ground, like the ribs of an impenetrable vault, the branches enlace, drunk on sap, only allowing a crepuscular light to pass; they form a temple with a thousand columns and florid arches under a dome of moving foliage."

"Yes," said Syta, "everything on earth is nothing but amour; amour alone, which drives the reproduction of beings and plants, is necessary. We are only sexes that engender incessantly, for the universal splendor."

"Above sexes there are the spirits of light, and it is toward divine knowledge that I'm guiding you."

The queen sighed, suddenly chilled and indecisive.

"Have you abandoned me then, Salassim, that I will no longer savor your kiss of flame within me?"

"The Guru is waiting for us. His astral fluid will soon circulate in your veins like a flow of honey. He wanted to let you come to him freely in order to test your faith. Soon, you will know the supreme ecstasy."

"Yes, I know that it's him who is inspiring you. You're accomplishing a mission, and you're no more enlightened than I am."

Life, once again, was seething around them under the impenetrable and burning shelter of jungles, while the dust of cadavers was crushed under the hooves of the horses. Everywhere, entire skeletons barred the path, but it was sufficient to brush them to make them fall into ashes. In certain places the plants plunged into greasy mud in which viscous forms swarmed, the backs of unknown beasts covered in pustules, medusal spiders with the hues of precious stones, and water snakes. Under the gigantic trees, fantastic orchids opened their dazzling parasols, or seemed to be hiding like malevolent beasts against the leprosy of the bark. A few, crouched on their stems, attracted impudent insects, inhaled life and death, bathing voluptuously in putrid miasmas, and translated the cruel intoxication of nature by means of their unusual colors.

In places, everything was mystery, crime and torture, while a hundred feet higher, above the darkness of the accursed regions, noble and powerful corollas mirrored themselves in the hot sunlight.

And in the clearing there was an eternal buzz of emerald beetles, velvet moths, hummingbirds smaller than certain insects, and giant bees drunk on dew.

The princess and Prismama had arrived next to a lake, around which the admirable flora of those ardent regions loosened its belt. In the distance, the great chain of the Vindhyas was visible, forming a series of plateaux almost parallel to the course of the Nerbudda. From each of its extremities, other chains departed: the occidental Ghats that extended along the shore of Malabar and the oriental Ghats that of Coromandel.

"Brahma be praised," said the disciple, "we've arrived."

Ackbe pricked up his ears, and feverish waves ran along his flanks. Suddenly, he made a violent sidestep and stopped.

On every side, in the grass, on the branches and the giant lianas, crawling, undulating and rearing up, hundreds of reptiles appeared. They seemed to surge forth from the ground, forbidding entry to some mysterious shelter.

"Have no fear," said Prismama. "Salassim's snakes won't do you any harm."

While he was still speaking, the Guru appeared in a resplendent aureole, and the Rani, bewildered, let herself slide to the feet of the Beloved.

PART THREE

I
Dangerous Intoxication

The yogi, confident in his power, knew that his hour had come to subjugate and to possess the heart of a woman. That woman was the sovereign whom an entire people adored on their knees. The Charmer's pride was ineffably flattered by that precious victory, and although he hid his joy, Syta nevertheless followed the scintillating reflection of it in his eyes.

"You see," she said, humbly, "I've come and I'm abandoning myself to your power. Consider me, henceforth, as a docile slave, and do with me what you please."

She kissed his knees, and seemed a flower scythed down by the torment.

The reptiles surrounded them, forming a barrier between their amour and the rest of the world. Coiling around one another, they hissed softly, their little triangular heads raised toward the Charmer.

"Do you love me as I love you?" sobbed Syta. "You see that I have abandoned everything to follow you, and no woman, I believe, has ever offered her lover a tenderness as great. And yet, you are nothing to me but a pure spirit, an inaccessible form of glory, power and splendor! What, then, is the god that has given you that frightful will and that occult power?"

"You have done what I expected of you. I'm satisfied. You shall know the secrets of life and death, the monstrous and grim rites that make Initiates the masters of the world. Splendors as surprising as visions of refined and grandiose beatitudes will be unveiled to you. But the key to the mysteries, of which our religion is full, can only be found in the ruins of ancient temples, the icy plateaux of the Himalaya, and the feverish forests of your land, where dazzling and formidable nature hides unknown vestiges. It is in those books of granite, which cannot lie, that the thought of Brahma is conserved."

"Instruct me, in accordance with the holy books, since I am no longer anything but your humble servant."

"Come," he said.

She got up, kissed a flap of his sala, and followed him again into the depths of the backti, escorted by the reptiles, which undulated gently in the long grass.

Prismama had remained in prayer on the edge of the lake, and Ackbe, reassured, was browsing plants and aromatic herbs, of which he appreciated the flavor.

The heat was overwhelming, but the intersecting branches filtered the light, which was decanted with violet tints. In spite of her fatigue, everything was an enchantment for the sovereign.

Salassim stopped on a sort of platform dissimulated amid the lianas, went down a staircase hollowed out in the rock, and arrived at the entrance of a marvelous temple illuminated by an infinity of little lamps. Pillars surmounted by fantastic animals sustained the vault. Their bases were covered with inscriptions in mysterious characters, which defied any attempt to read them.

A large vestibule preceded the temple. Artfully sculpted in haut-relief, the united figures of men and goddesses could be seen there. Two elephants of colossal dimensions were placed to either side, supporting travelers in their howdahs. The arched vault, above the bulging chevrons, was sustained by ranks of columns surmounted alternately by a human figure and a royal tiger.

Without the lamps that cast their glaucous light everywhere the interior of the temple would have been plunged in darkness.

Initiates, or yogi charmers, remained prostrate at the foot of a gigantic altar supporting an image of Shiva, man on one side, woman on the other. Black blood was escaping by means of grooves excavated to each side of the pedestal. Flowers, rice, honey and precious vases full of balms and perfumes ornamented the altar. The odor that reigned in the place was both insipid and acrid, sickening and intoxicating.

"This is the cellar of evocations," said Salassim. "Prostrate yourself and pray, if you want the spirits to manifest themselves."

Syta trembled.

"I'm only a creature of amour! I'll obey you, without knowing the frightful practices of your cult. Spare me."

But already, a strange melody was filing the immense nave, and the little lamps, like fire follets, seemed to be running around the pillars or hovering in the air, like luminous flowers or moths; a phosphorescent cloud had formed above the Rani, and on every side, severed heads with large enamel eyes were emerging from the cloud and reentering it rapidly. Hands appeared, sustaining the heads like cups, from which blood was still flowing in vermilion streams. One of those hands traversed the cloud and came to pose on the heart of the queen, who uttered a cry.

"The spirit is here," said Salassim. "You can confide your desire to it."

"My desire is to stay with you."

"Until death?"

"Until death."

The Prophet pronounced vague incantations, extending his arms toward the red vision—but suddenly, he threw himself backwards, in terror.

"What's the matter?"

He did not reply, his pupils revulsed by fear.

"Speak," she said. "It would be sweet for me to die for you, if the powers that govern us demand it. Is it the announcement of my death that is making you querulous?"

"Yes," he groaned, "the future is somber for you. I see revolt, murder, desolation everywhere in your realm."

She shrugged her shoulders.

"I have made the sacrifice of my frail existence. Is it a woman who will succeed me?"

"The reign of woman is ended."

"Yes," she said. "It's the Brahmins who have decided to take possession of power. Prismama has already told me that. And doubtless you are the instrument of which their ambition is making use?"

"I am the envoy of the gods."

"Oh, don't defend yourself!" she sighed. "I remain weaker in your hands than a naraya stem. If my doom has been decided by the Brahmins and the initiates, I forgive them for having chosen you for the accomplishment of their designs. A woman in love does not know rancor or ambition."

Salassim had a melancholy smile.

"But don't deprive me of your dear presence," said Syta. "Let me feel your kisses of flame on my lips again, and let your fluid penetrate me until the supreme intoxication. The caresses of men have never enabled me to feel such transports. Oh, Salassim, I love you!"

II
Curses and Spells

Yogis, ascetics, prophets and sacrificers are certainly the most skillful sorcerers in the world. Their magnetic power is exercised even on inanimate objects, and they support all tortures rather than renounce their marvelous reputation.

Syta knew the intoxications of possession again. A delicious languor invaded her limbs and unusual effluvia penetrated her invincibly. For her, Salassim made unknown flowers bloom with corollas of silk and spun glass; strange fruits, sweeter than honey, were suspended from branches, and all of nature sang an adorable hymn to Kama.

One day, from a vat filled with the blood of a dozen sheep whose throats had been cut, Salassim caused a monstrous orchid to emerge, with a hairy calyx and nightmarish tentacles, which extended toward the young woman, who fell backwards, terrified. Gradually, the bloody flow increased its intensity at the foot of the plant, burst forth in all directions, as if it had been subjected by heat to a violent ebullition, and the princess was covered by a murderous rain.

These phenomena left her exhausted and tottering, but even more submissive to the power of the Charmer. Even the torture of victims of the altar of Shiva, the black god, ceased to fill her with horror; she lent herself to the fantasies of the Master, listened to his magical conjurations, and delivered herself to the Spirits. When the sacred elephants struck the bronze goings of the pagoda, the Charmer penetrated into her, or, at least, his astral form communed ineffably with her passionate being.

She no longer saw, as in the royal chamber, the blue disk emerging from the walls and fluttering around her like a great moth of flame. She only felt its presence, and appealed to Salassim the conjurer to manifest himself again by means of adorable caresses.

"O my Beloved! O my Master! Nothing equals the intoxication of your kiss! Descend into me! Penetrate me until death!"

When she awoke, however, she was sad, for the ancient images of the cult had been removed from the temple of Shiva, to make way for the lingam, whose power was augmenting every day. The ascetics no longer wore the nahamam on the left arm, suspended from a silver chain, and even Prismama no longer sang the adorable hymn to Nari, the mother of the world.

"Oh, I sense clearly," sighed Syta, "that amour will subjugate woman! I was unable to resist amour, and amour has doomed me! The woman who listens to the lying words of a man or a god is destined to perish. How I curse the charm that took away my self-possession!"

But Salassim reassured her.

"Nothing is accomplished except by the will of Issouara; regret nothing, O Divine One! You will be venerated among all, through the ages."

"No," she said, "men are slaves or executioners. I have ceded to a slave, I have raised him up as far as me, and already, he is showing his hateful instincts, biting the hand that caresses him. The Brahmins are beginning to substitute the arrogant and cruel male principle for the principle of bounty, fecundity and forgiveness. The redoubtable symbols are being erected everywhere in the temples and human sacrifices have succeeded the admirable ceremonies of the primordial worship. The priests will debase men, and carnage and famine will desolate the world."

The Charmer smiled sadly.

"You don't know what you're saying. Being as weak and fickle as any human creature, how can you judge the divine will?"

"I judge in accordance with my reason and my heart. If my appearance is frail, my soul is great and strong."

The Charmer considered the sovereign with pity. He would have liked, then, to set her free, for he understood, too late, that he had only been an instrument in the hands of the ambitious and cruel priests, unremitting enemies of woman.

"Go!" he said to her, sometimes. "Return to your realm. Perhaps your people will still recognize you."

Systa wept softly, extending her imploring hands toward Salassim.

"Oh, you know full well that I love you, and that it's no longer in my power to tear this strange passion out of my being. If you want me to go away, order me to leave. I will obey your occult power and my people will forgive me. Save me from others and myself!"

Shivering, she dragged herself to her lover's feet, kissed the hem of his sala and tore her breast, sobbing. But he still kept her with him, fulfilling his redoubtable mission in spite of everything.

III

Fear

The Rani remained prostrate for long hours at the foot of the black and white, male and female idol that no sacrifice contented and which bathed in blood night and day.

Prismama, clad in the immaculate sala of an ascetic, still devoted to the worship of the Nahamam, exhorted her to patience.

"Have your wishes not been accomplished, O Divine One? What more do you desire, since you are with the man you love? Did you not want to join him, at the price of all sacrifices?"

Syta shivered, more clear-sighted and more dolorous.

"Is the strange disturbance that I feel in the company of that supernatural being truly love? Certainly, Salassim dominates me entirely, bending me to his will like a fragile stem; however, I do not have with regard to him the confidence of lovers, the adorable abandonment of sacred spouses. It is rather a sentiment of terror that dominates me, now that I am in this frightful temple of torture and death. The silence is only troubled by the cries and gasps of victims. Look, my knees are red, and my breasts also; everywhere that I rest my hands the dew of murder flows. This sanctuary is a charnel-house and the god to whom one prays here nothing but a cruel executioner."

"Alas, I suffer as you do from these futile hecatombs."

"Why have I quit my palace?"

"You'd like to savor homages and glory?"

"Oh, glory! You can't know how scornful I am of it. Our existence is nothing in the ensemble of existences. We pass, we pass, and when death has taken us, what remains of our paltry personality? A little mud, a little ash—even less! Who, then, will honor the great among us in future times? In any case, the veneration of men is addressed to anonymous cadavers. Are we not all similar in the horror of sepulchers? The gazelle whose throat you cut, Prismama, is as glorious as me, and when I am dead and my body buried, embalmed, burned or devoured by the vultures, it will count for no more. My name, if it remains in memory, will no longer be applied to any visible being. What is the point, then? Nothing exists, you see, but the present hour."

"Have you repudiated all belief, then?"

"Yes, Prismama; since I witness so many crimes, I cannot believe in the bounty or the justice of Issouara. Insensate are those who work for the good of humanity and the respect of future races. There is nothing but life and death: the animate body that makes people, the icy body that makes plants. Nature only wants reproduction, incessantly, in tears and blood. It is the blind force that nothing stops in its ever-victorious effort. Even amour cannot shine for us. What we mistake for tenderness is only sexual desire, the invincible law of the world that drives us to unite in order to perpetuate the species."

"You're ignoring, or pretending to ignore, your august mission. Everything does not end in this world, you know that very well."

Syta laughed bitterly.

"Perhaps there is, in fact, something that escapes us, something that we cannot comprehend, for our intelligence is only relative. We have the human science that enables suffering, we do not have the divine science that would elevate us and truly console us. You see, Prismama, whatever efforts we make, we remain incomplete beings consecrated to eternal tortures."

"It's necessary to believe without understanding."

"I can't. Oh, certainly, the unknown power that governs us has been crueler to us than the other creatures, whose obscure brains are ignorant of reflection, reasoning, the combat of good and evil, sin and punishment. We are feeble beings, physically and morally, beings tortured by futile aspirations toward an ideal of justice and goodness. We devour one another and are more bitterly unrelenting in harassing our prey than the predators of the jungle. It would be better to cease to engender, to seek the total destruction of the human race. Yes, yes: only the end of humanity, freely consented by humanity itself, would prove a veritable intelligence."

"That is dementia, O Divine One."

"All, all of us, are languishing, from the humblest to the most powerful. Nothing can dissipate our feverish anxiety, our morbid desire for a happiness that never arrives. What, then, is this ungraspable something that tortures us relentlessly? The efforts of science, the so-called benefits of civilization only serve to render us even more miserable. Every animal finds its pittance down here without the help of others. Only the human being cannot do without other humans. The human being is the eternal slave, the pariah, the accursed who tears her own breast and devours the children that she cannot nourish."

"Your country is prosperous, your people are not complaining . . ."

"I see further than my own country and I know that people are unhappy. In any case, Salassim has told me that the reign of woman is reaching its end."

The Charmer had slipped behind the altar a moment before and was listening in silence. He emerged from the shadow and put his icy hand on the princess' forehead.

"You no longer believe in anything, then?" he said.

"No, for even amour has betrayed me."

"I love you."

She revolted, and did not dare look at his great dark eyes, in which an indignant flame was burning.

"You only love the abominable sect that you represent, and you drew me into a trap in order that it might triumph."

Salassim made a vague gesture of negation, but remained silent.

"Oh," she sighed, "you certainly didn't come in search of me, but I've obeyed your deadly influence since the day I encountered you in the backti. You knew, when you touched my flesh, that I would belong to you body and soul. I have been subjugated by your astral influence, the irresistible bewitchment of your accursed power. I crawled to you like the reptiles that you charm, and I remain quivering in the dust."

The yogi, his thought lost in a distant dream, did not reply. After a pause, the Rani went on in a clear voice.

"The peoples will become the prey, the livestock, of the priest, who will plunge them into the most vulgar superstition. He has made gods of capricious and sanguinary monsters, scarecrows destined to protect the idle and debauched life of the initiates. The stories of the sacred books are merely vulgar fables invented to strike the imagination of the weak and seat your domination solidly. And you, in accord with the Brahmins, jealous of my power, have drawn me here in order to give me death."

Salassim had picked up the heart of an antelope from the paving stones, and he offered it to Shiva, asking him to pardon the blasphemies that the sovereign had proffered. Between the columns of the temple the vehement mantras of pilgrims rose and fell like the wind in the branches.

"Bring me Ackbe, the great white stallion," said the Charmer.

Syta uttred a scream. "Ackbe! Why?"

"To immolate him to the gods, in order that they might deign to forget your sacrilegious words."

She seized Salassim's arm, in terror.

"You won't do that! I forbid you to!"

"That sacrifice might efface your crime, and perhaps save you."

"That sacrifice is iniquitous! Ackbe, my companion in exile! My only friend! I love him! I no longer have anything but him in the world!"

"Shiva will take account of that precious gift."

"No, no, Salassim, you can't be cruel to that extent! Let Ackbe wander among the florid lianas and drink the water of the sacred pool between the rushes. What harm has he done the gods? He's so docile and so handsome! I had him as a child and I brought him grain in the hollow of my hand. He followed me everywhere in the gardens of the palace. Lackmama decorated his mane with ribbons and flowers, and he was more ornate than the Sons of Joy of the amorous quarters."

The Charmer repeated:

"Bring me Ackbe, the great white stallion."

IV
The Torture of Ackbe

Outside, the delicate hooves of the horse glided over the steps, the network of pearls that beat his flanks rattling faintly . . .

"He's coming," said Salassim.

"Drive him away, I beg you."

"What's the point? He wouldn't go. He hasn't put up any resistance, since he knows that you're here."

"Oh, I don't want it! I don't want you to immolate him!"

She was already at the entrance to the temple, raising her arms to frighten the animal, but Ackbe considered her with his great soft eyes, not understanding that welcome, to which he was not accustomed. He came down the last steps of his own cord, and came to present his intelligent head to the Rani's caress.

Syta began to weep then.

"Salassim," she begged, "don't do any harm to my gentle Ackbe! I'll give you, to decorate the temple, all the jewels of the crown, my gold, my tigers, my elephants, my royal headband with the seven diamond hearts, and even the seven hollow pearls of the Karamy-yega, the sacred fetish! I'll give you my lion Yassoub, which I also love with a very keen affection; in addition, you can dispose of my six Great Husbands for the cult of Issouara."

"No," said the Charmer. "It's necessary, to appease the gods, that I accomplish the great sacrifice of the Ekiam, which is, as you're not unaware, particularly agreeable to them. Ackbe will have his throat cut, in honor of the trimurty, and it will be a very great honor for him and for you."

A profound sadness was legible in the limpid eyes of the beautiful white stallion, as if he had understood the Charmer's design. However, he allowed himself to be led to the altar of Shiva, and did not struggle when the ascetics bound him to the pedestal of the idol.

All the pilgrims, gathered together, clad in immaculate salas, recited the Shaktanga of the Ekiam fervently.

The sacrifice of the Ekiam, or white stallion, was then as much in favor as the Shakti puja, or mystery of universal fecundation, but it remained chaste, and only initiates could participate in its celebration.

At a signal from Salassim, the hundreds of little lamps suspended under the vaults of the temple were lit, and spread a streak of green gleams, while a firework of minuscule stars burst behind the pedestal of Shiva, whose double male and female nature was irradiated in apotheosis.

The glaucous rockets were gradually extinguished, and the subterranean crypt, hollowed out in granite, remained in a half-light more anguishing than darkness. In the midst of all the marvels of architecture and sculpture of the ancient Brahmins, dominators of India, in the heart of that subterranean temple full of beauty and horror, Ackbe, the innocent victim, awaited the exterminator's knife.

Prismama, being the youngest of the assistants, was chosen by Salassim to strike the mortal blow. The virgin lover turned his saddened gaze toward the princess, as if to beg her pardon for the crime that he was about to commit.

Other ascetics, similarly virgins, were standing in the lateral naves, with one hand on the attributes of the lingam reproduced on all the columns of the temple. The charmers, in poses of ecstasy and adoration, reciting their mantras, awaited the decision of the pujari sacrificer. Namadarys—initiates—emerged from who knows where, had filled the immense nave almost entirely.

Syta caressed Ackbe, imploring Salassim and Prismama by turns, in an invincible hope of clemency. Her red eyes had no more tears, but her hands were trembling feverishly.

"Take that woman away," said the Charmer.

Immediately, twenty arms were extended toward the sovereign, who, losing consciousness, abandoned herself.

Prismama had plunged the blade into Ackbe's throat. A flood of vermilion blood sprang impetuously from the wound, flowing into the thick layer of congealed blood that already covered the flagstones. The beautiful animal convulsed, lifted his head two or three times, seemingly seeking a loving caress. Then his eye gradually became vitreous, entirely extinguished; his lips, white with foam, contracted, exposing his teeth; his long, silky tail beat the ground feebly, and his hobbled feet made a final effort, as if to escape Death, whose cold breath he felt on his back.

He remained lying on his side, still covered with his mesh of pearls, which had become, in places, a net of rubies. His head, so nobly and so purely sculpted, seemed, in its melancholy mildness, to have been inhabited by a human thought, and all the jewels with which he was still adorned only rendered his meager cadaver more lamentable.

The heart and liver of the victim were offered to Shiva; then other killings followed. The charmers cut the hamstrings of large animals that were brought to them, in order to be able to bleed them without resistance.

It was no longer a sacrifice but a repulsive butchery. The dagger sometimes encountered bone or rebounded; it was necessary to search for the right place, to make the blood flow in great seething gouts, prolonging the agony in order to permit the urns to be filled before death.

The fakirs, intoxicated to the point of stupidity, drew themselves along the pillars uttering the howls of wild beasts. It was no longer the formidable rut of the Shakti puja, mingling the sexes, but the inebriation of opium and blood, perhaps more redoubtable.

There were few peoples among the ancients who did not erect altars to debauchery and unnatural passions, in imitation of the Indians, in order to render worship to creation and the fecundity of nature, but nowhere was fanaticism pushed as far. We know, however, what excesses still soiled the temples of Jupiter, Bacchus and Venus in Greece, Osiris among the hierophants of Egypt and Mithra among the magi of Persia.

The cult of Shiva was, in ancient India, a sign of slavery. All the voluptuous and lascivious art of the pagodas was born from that: the bas-reliefs of united figures of men and animals, the monstrous sculptures of chariots celebrating the symbol of the androgynous god. Those images, of an unusual liberty, all had for their object the worship of the lingam, or male organ, and its representation in infinitely varied positions.

Every temple of Shiva shows, at its entrance, that attribute of marble or white granite, which the Brahmin anoints with rare essences and purificatory balms every morning, after having made an oblation of honey and milk. Every visitor, on entering the sanctuary, offers it, in his turn, bunches of flowers, garlands of gilded paper, grains of rice or fruits of the neem tree. In some countries, virgins give themselves to the lingam before belonging to their husbands.

The cult of the male organ gradually dethroned that of the Nahamam, or female organ, and the Brahmins became the masters of India.

V
The Male Principle

Too late, Syta understood the nullity of all affection, even mystical. She had abandoned her people, and her people had been doomed in consequence. She had loved Salassim to the point of dementia, and Salassim did not love her.

The Charmer now became disinterested in her; it was in vain that she wished for the voluptuous ecstasy that had once set her senses ablaze and paralyzed her will. An infinite sadness and a great discouragement curbed her near the horrible altar of Shiva. Devoid of hope, almost devoid of thought, she remained in the sanctuary for long hours, waiting for the Charmer, who extracted her from her torpor.

The priests had completely effaced from the walls the representations of the feminine attribute, in order to forget the original worship; the strophes of the Nahamam had been replaced by those of the male god. Shiva was only adored any longer in one of his faces.

The princess sometimes begged the disciple to take her back to her realm.

"Perhaps my people have not forgotten me," she sighed. "Let us flee, Prismama; you can become one of my Great Husbands, the most loved and the most powerful."

The virgin lover smiled sadly. "Salassim is alert," he replied, "and we would not be able to escape him."

"The astral influence of the yogi has ceased to weigh upon me. I feel liberated from his deadly bewitchment."

"It appears so to you, O Felicity, because the Charmer knows that you are in his power, and disdains to subjugate you by means of further manifestations."

"Let us flee!" Syta repeated, as she had once cried in the midst of the splendors of her palace; but a superhuman force still enchained her, against her will. And when her rebellion became too active, new magnetic influences came, as if miraculously, to paralyze her. As soon as her light feet trod the threshold of the temple, ready to take their course, while her entire soul aspired to liberty, a sudden weakness nailed her to the ground. The great luminous bird of her insomnias fluttered around her, brushing her hair, her shoulders and her breast; hands emerged from the shadows to caress her, to embrace her, to run over her body like medusae of flames. Sometimes, an occult kiss, delightful and profound, drilled into her lips, and the fluidic current penetrated her irresistibly.

At those instants she cherished the Charmer again with all the force of her being, and appealed to him passionately for a direct communion that was never accomplished.

Meanwhile, Prismama scarcely quit her, praying and weeping with her. The adorable beauty of the sovereign had produced on the virgin lover the effect that it produced on everyone. In order to conquer her he was ready to betray his own people, to submit to the torture of fire reserved for infidel disciples. Already, in the temple of Issouara, he had accepted death in exchange for one night of amour; it would have been sweet for him to succumb for such a joy.

The last worshiper of the gardawabhya, or white lotus, he remained faithful to the cult of the nahamam, not admitting the triumph of the male principle. On his wrists and round his neck trembled amulets of rubies and peridots representing the feminine symbol of eternal fecundity, and Prismama did not want any other.

"Forgive me, O Splendor," he repeated, contritely, "for having delivered you to your enemies, and for having, on their orders, killed the great white stallion. At least I tried to abridge his agony by the profundity of the wound. That was, alas, all that I could do."

"Oh, I forgive you," the princess sighed, "and I will give you the first rank among my husbands if you succeed in protecting my flight."

Prismama shook his head.

"Let's wait. At the moment, I can do nothing for you, and even my death would be useless to you."

"But we'll go, won't we? We'll quit this place of terror?"

"Yes, soon. Perhaps Salassim will liberate you himself. His designs are mysterious."

"I still can't understand by what accursed spell I abandoned my husbands, my children and my people, everything that I loved, everything that constituted my power and my glory."

"The magnetic influence of the Charmer vanquished your energy. By means of its resistance, Salassim was able to exasperate your desire and accomplish the will of the priests, enemies of the feminine principle. Alas, the evil is even more profound than you suspect."

"What do you mean?"

"May I be mistaken?"

"Go on, Prismama, I implore you. You've learned some bad news?"

"Tonight, during the dance of the gandharvas and apsaras, a pitri announced to me the revolt of your people. Your beautiful country has been delivered to fire and blood. The Brahmins, led by Aracknai, have sacrificed virgins in the squares where the husband markets were once held. The six Great Husbands are governing in your stead. They have murdered Lackmama, whom they accused of having favored your flight and having commerce in the temple with evil spirits."

"Lackmama is dead!"

"Yes, and other women of the city with her. The Sons of Joy have deserted the white houses and have pillaged the houses of the rich."

Syta, trembling, still tried to doubt what the disciple was saying.

"Perhaps you've had a bad dream, Prismama?"

"Perhaps, O Felicity. Like you, I hope so."

VI
The Revolt of the Men of Joy

Meanwhile, the Brahmins had resolved to bring the queen back to Ahmehnagara and burn her alive in front of the temple of Kanda-Swamy, in order to impress the minds of the people. The Men of Joy, having become the masters of the city, invented new tortures every day to punish those they had served on their knees before. Fifty, sixty, sometimes a hundred women per day were strangled, quartered or delivered to the erotic fury of males, suddenly unleashed.

The terror produced by these executions led to further reprisals. Convinced that their complete extermination had been resolved, and that they would all pass that way, one after another, the women abandoned themselves to a perfectly natural panic, disarmed by the stronger sex and certain of being tracked like beasts of prey by slaves attracted by the lure of gain—for there was a price of every woman's head. In that frightful hunt the Sons of Joy played the role of bloodhounds employed in the pursuit of criminals, and the pursuit was continued day and night in order that no victim could pass over the frontier.

The Sons of Joy, led by the priests, avenged themselves for their servitude, and nothing was as terrible and cowardly as their wrath of former slaves.

The revolution had established the power of the great Radogks, a rather unpopular measure that was intended to distance the Hindus from a cause judged purely religious, for, in reality, it was not the husbands of dethroned sovereign who governed but the Brahmins led by Aracknai.

The women were disarmed, and when they were defenseless, they were exterminated in the public squares before the altars of Shiva, one of whose sexes had been veiled. The black god was only worshiped any longer under one of his faces; here, as elsewhere, the lingam replaced the symbol of eternal fecundity.

One morning, at sunrise, six hundred condemned women were taken to the main square of Ahmehnagara; it was the fiftieth batch in ten days. The elephants of the royal garden were waiting behind the altar, adorned with lotuses and roses; that day they were to fill the office of executioners, and under their powerful feet, skulls were crushed and brains made to spurt forth.

The place of execution was surrounded by garlands of foliage, and the victims, prostrated three by three, waited with their foreheads on the paving stones for their final minute to sound.

The elephants, whose feet were already red with blood, seemed only to be obeying their cornacs reluctantly; the tigers, which finished the bloody work, turned away from the repast that was offered to them. It was necessary to build immense pyres in order to complete the work of death.

There was a routine massacre of almost all the women of the realm. Not one house was spared, not one female child, whatever her age, was granted mercy. Little girls were raped and disemboweled. Drunk on sunlight, opium and blood, the Sons of Joy tore the fetuses from the wombs of women and sometimes left the agonizing to linger for hours in frightful suffering, without finishing them off.

Meanwhile, the six Great Husbands had put themselves at the head of a little troop recruited from among the priests and the Sons of Joy, in order to search for their sovereign. Ruman-Bibi, Biskourmi and Nandamu were inclined toward clemency; Paraçou and Doudouma-Lovi remained neutral; only Soulabatka, in accord with the Brahmins of the temple of Kanda-Swamy, demanded her death.

The six Husbands, mounted on elephants whose painted trunks offered allegorical subjects related to the significance of their name, therefore set forth through the backti along the route that Prismama and the fugitive Rani had followed.

The ferocious sun filled the sky, but only fell in a fine rain of radiance through the sieve of the branches; the vault of shadows was only broken in places, letting the brilliant arrows pass through a thousand wounds to sting the hearts of the trees.

From the summits of hills, in the smoke of the conflagration, the admirable city appeared, put to fire and blood. During rare calms, however, it seemed peaceful, with its narrow streets, its marble palaces, its houses painted in cheerful colors, its temples with walls jagged with precious sculptures, its main courtyards with galleries and colonnades, its stairways with bas-reliefs, its ramparts, and its square roofs over which tiger-cats ran.

All that impressed the gaze like a prodigious poetic dream realized, the apparition of a fantastic city rising toward the stars.

The great Radogks, after a long and painful march, rested on a platform hollowed out in the granite a short distance from the temple of Shiva.

The Brahmins, familiar with the mysteries of the backti, had led them without hesitation to the Charmer's abode, but Salassim's reptiles, crawling at their feet, seemed to be forbidding them to profane the august dwelling.

Soulabakta, the Flavorsome Fruit, spoke first.

"Man," he said, "is not made for peace. Since the women have been governing us, we have not had any dispute with other powers; we have lived, it is true, in abundance, but that physical and moral quietude is beginning to weigh upon us."

"Woman," said Nandamu, the Golden Ram, supportively, "only thinks about the sensuality of amour and of reigning pacifically, when fighting is beneficial to the gods."

"Oh," Soulabathka continued, "we have fists in order to strike, arms in order to embrace and teeth in order to bite. We are the stronger, and we ought to prove it! We ought to vanquish the feeble, amorous, sensual beings unhinged by reveries and enjoyments, to whom we have been submissive for too long. We should cut into their very flesh; we should shed the blood of the weak, for blood is necessary to the triumph of Liberty! We should complete the brutal holocaust, the living sacrifice, in the midst of the purifying fire. Henceforth, woman will be our slave!"

"Yes," said Paraçou, the Incomparable, "and we will have harems of women as women had harems of men."

"We would not be sufficient for them," remarked Biskouri, the Column of Felicity. "Each of us can scarcely furnish the six regulation discourses in a single night . . ."

But Ruman-Bibi shrugged his shoulders insouciantly. "The women will do without amour, that's all."

Doudouma-Lovi, Above All, remained thoughtful. When he was pressed to give his opinion, he eventually said: "The new laws will certainly give satisfaction to our vanity, for we will be the sole masters of the land; however, it will be necessary to labor, to toil and to think, when it would be truly agreeable to receive, every day, as something due, everything that makes the charm of life: luxurious shelter, abundant nourishment and sensuality. And then, a woman with all the husbands in the world can only have one child every nine months, whereas with our feminine harem we could have as many children as wives. It would therefore be necessary to toil relentlessly and perform prodigies of economy for that frightful progeniture."

"Oh," said Soulabakta, "our children will get out of difficulty as best they can."

"It will be poverty for them," Doudouma-Lovi continued. "Our country did not have a single vagabond. The shelters and the hospitals were empty. Our wife sufficed for everything, and her ingenuity was only equaled by her munificence . . ."

"Well," said Soulabatka, impatiently, "our country will be similar to others. Man is the master almost everywhere; it would be humiliating for us to persist in ancient errors."

Aracknai, the high priest of Kanda-Swany, who was listening to the words of the six Radogks, smiling, completed the victory by citing the Holy Scriptures.

"We ought to have respect for everything that is attached to the religious idea," he said, authoritatively. "It is necessary that the conquering male principle should not appear to be the tributary of the enemy principle on any point. We must scythe down the evil weed at the root. Avid for truth, science wants light to be cast on all things, especially the religious dogmas that reign over humanity.

"Hindu books, as you know, are palm-leaves on which one writes with a little iron spike. It is easy to add, to retrench or to destroy the manuscript; our detached leaves, without any link between them, conserved preciously in the temple of Kanda-Swamy, concluded the triumph of the feminine principle, of Nari over Nara, of the Golden Womb, in sum, the creatrix of the world.

"Now, our Brahmins, who, by the will of Issouara, possess divine infallibility, are going to change all that. The lingam alone will govern the world, and Shiva, who possessed the two male and female natures, will only show one of his faces in future. Our temples already contain only that glorious image. Vulgar worship only sees in the lingam and the nahamam the apparatus of the ordinary union of the sexes. Only the male divinity Purusha will be honored henceforth, under the form of the attributes of virility.

"Elephanta, Chelambrun and Djaggernat will, in their turn, efface from their walls the lascivious images of woman, which we will cease to worship. She has accomplished her work and will only regain some authority in the awakening of nature succeeding another pralaya, or periodic dissolution of everything that exists, for every seed that falls into the Golden Womb contains, Soumati affirms, the germ of the gods, the heavens and the worlds."

"You do realize," said Doudouma-Lovi, the most infatuated of Syta's Great Husbands, "that we can do nothing without the principle of eternal fecundity?"

Aracknai laughed scornfully.

"For the moment, we are the stronger, and that is sufficient. When universal chaos comes again, things down here will not interest us much, for we shall be in the bosom of Brahma, who survives annihilation.

"And let no one come to contest our writings, for no authority has ever made itself the guardian of primitive texts and sacred orthodoxies. In our beautiful country, every religion, every sect and every school wanted to have its own text of Vedas and Puranas. Already, more than a thousand different texts exist of our Holy Writings, and Maya, Illusion, rules the world! Let the worship of the Nahamam return, therefore, to the domain of fabulous chronologies! Henceforth, woman will be the servant of man!"

The six great Radogks, penetrated by the wisdom of those words, approved them with enthusiastic, admiring demonstrations.

Soulabatka, having plucked three corollas of pink lotus, threw them into the air in honor of the holy Trimurty.

"Brahma is with you!" said Aracknai, striking his breast three times with his closed fist.

And all of them murmured: "AUM! Let his will be done!"

106

VII
The Domain of the Dead

The Great Husbands had decided to knock on the door of the temple, and Salassim, dragging the sovereign, had taken her into a secret crypt where, for centuries, the remains had been kept of Charmers whom torture, fire and the vultures had spared.

It did not please the yogi that his property might be stolen, and, although he did not love Syta, in accordance with human laws, at least he still had the interest in her that any hypnotizer, even astral, retains for the subject that he magnetizes. She belonged to him, as a little bird belongs to the vulture; he retained the right of life and death over her, and he deemed that, since he had obeyed the Brahmins in making her his, he no longer owed them any submission.

In addition, Salassim, after having passed through the twelve degrees of contemplation, had become Nirvany—which is to say, free of any terrestrial authority. Other men, however elevated their rank might be, no longer inspired him with anything but an immense scorn. His inclinations, his affections and his thoughts were invariably fixed on the divinity to which he believed that he was getting closer every day. By virtue of penitence and contemplation, the material part of his being was gradually melting away like Kapura—camphor, in Sanskrit—when thrown on a fire.

Handsome, with a supernatural beauty, he no longer had anything living but his immense eyes of flame, whose glare no one could support, and his magnetic power, which was even greater over those he desired to submit.

The tremulous Rani had descended numerous steps in the darkness, and her feet were now treading the dust of the dead. But Salassim, with a gesture, had commanded light, and hundreds of little lamps had lit up in the subterrain.

By their vermicular light, she distinguished the arched vault supported by bulging chevrons, sustained themselves by two rows of granite pillars. A scaffolding of teak wood had been added, all around, in order to avoid collapses and fissures in the walls of rock.

That crypt, which was very deep, was only known to a few rare initiates, and no one except Salassim ever went into it.

"What are you going to do to me?" asked Syta, her pupils dilated by fear. "Haven't I suffered enough?"

"I want to save you," the Charmer murmured.

"Save me? You want to save me now?"

"Yes."

"Oh, anything is preferable to this place of horror!"

And the little Rani veiled her face, in order no longer to see the lugubrious guests of the cellar. To the left and the right, in front of her and behind her, an entire population of skeletons was standing upright. White salas were stuck to their sides, and the frontal cords of fakirs were hanging down to either side of the bare skulls, in which the gaping orbits seemed still to have menacing gazes. All the jaws were open in a strange rictus, and the arms and legs were sometimes raised, as if for some *danse macabre*. And enormous blue rats with phosphorescent eyes were running through that mass of blackened bones, uttering shrill cries reminiscent of the ululations of owls.

Syta shuddered, but her anguish became almost intolerable when, Salassim having made a mysterious gesture, all the orbits and jaws were illuminated, projecting jets of green-tinted flame into the furthest corners of the cellar. Like frightful marionettes, the dislocated bodies started to shake, advancing and recoiling, causing the bones of the feet and hands, the disjointed kneecaps and the eroded bones of the neck to rattle; often, a poorly attached head fell to the floor, and then went of its own accord to replace itself on the shoulders of the corpse.

"You see," said Salassim, "the defunct obey me as the living do, and I can accomplish miracles. If I wished, these skeletons would resume their previous form of muscles and flesh; they would emerge from their sepulcher in order to accomplish my will."

But the princess had run out of energy. "Make me similar to them," she begged. "At least I wouldn't be suffering any longer."

"Your hour has not yet come, O Divine One. You shall return among the living to reconquer your royalty."

"What! I can still do that?"

"Yes, one chance remains to you . . ."

And Salassim, kneeling before Syta, spoke to her as he had never done before.

"Forgive me for having drawn you into this trap. I obeyed the Brahmins, believing that they wanted to get rid of you in order to reign in your stead, without violence, in all conscience and all justice. But the massacres of recent times have filled me with indignation, and I am abandoning their cause. I know that you wanted to flee with Prismama, for I can read in souls. Well, woman, let your desire be accomplished! Prismama, the virgin lover, is waiting for you in a secret crypt that I have indicated to him. By means of a passage known to me alone, you can reach the backti; you can return to your capital, show yourself to your supporters, harangue your people, and perhaps your sublime beauty will be able to reconquer their hearts. To augment your power I am going to render you more beautiful than any human creature; you will act on the senses better than on minds, and the man who covets a woman is almost always vanquished by her."

The Charmer passed his feverish hands over the queen's face as she leaned toward him. Immediately, a kind of sidereal light seemed to penetrate her flesh; her eyes had the profundity of Himalayan lakes in which reflected moonlight was dancing, her eyebrows took on the form of Kama's enchanted bow, and her entire divine body was modeled for amour: the impetuous, crazy, irresistible amour that tames the male and leads him to the abyss. She was an adorable and sublime creature of lust, a celestial Magicienne, a Sataness of perverse temptations whom the gods had designed in order to avenge themselves on men.

"Now you're armed for the struggle," said Salassim, tracing in the air the sign of the holy trimurty, while the crypt's macabre guests twirled, and flowers, falling softly from the vault, formed an embalmed carpet beneath the sovereign's feet.

"The force that brought you here," the Charmer went on, "will act in the contrary direction, and you will feel yourself attracted to all human joys as you have been by celestial joys. You were, without knowing it, the docile servant of priests; henceforth, you will be their enemy. Go, and may your destiny be accomplished!"

He immobilized the mob of the dead with a gesture, and guided his companion through the avenues and the intersections of the sinister place, parting with his foot the skulls, tibias and femurs that impeded their march.

"Ah!" Salassim continued, angrily. "Evil priests, those eternal rogues who live on the exploitation of the sacred mysteries, care little about soiling the great image of Brahma by their sacrilegious action, for they try all means of demoralization and despotism on people. Everywhere they show themselves to be relentless adversaries of the instruction of peoples, and if they forbid the examination of their doctrines, it is in order better to govern by means of lies and terror. They have made use of me to bring about your fall, but my science will vanquish theirs!"

"Thank you, Salassim," murmured the princess, with a profound gratitude. Involuntarily, she felt that she was still under the Charmer's domination. Not only did she not retain any rancor for the extraordinary bewitchment to which she had been subjected, but she venerated and admired him.

"You are great among the greatest," she said.

The ascetic shook his head sadly.

"I am only the servant of Issoura, and I hate imposture! The Brahmins were able to subjugate me momentarily, but I am raising my head like the divine serpent that only obeys Shiva. I am of the Djeina sect,[1] and I protest against the vulgar polytheism of idolaters."

They had arrived at the entrance to the secret cellar, a long way from the part of the temple to which the six great Radogks were laying siege under the guidance of Aracknai.

The Virgin Lover, draped in the pleats of an ample sala, one of whose flaps hid his face, was waiting for the sovereign.

"I confide her to you," said Salassim. "May you guide her with amour and take her back to her realm safe and sound."

Prismama prostrated himself and put his lips to the slight trace that Syta's feet had imprinted on the sand.

"O Divine One! O Felicity! O Perfume!" he sighed. "My virgin body and soul belong to you. I will serve you faithfully until death."

The backti, full of murmurs and enchantments, opened before them. Enlaced, they launched themselves into the plants and flowers, which closed their curtain behind them.

Pensively, Salassim retraced the route that he had followed with his adorable companion through the midst of the Dead. Melancholy clouded the august features of the Charmer. Perhaps he regretted not having drunk, once in his life, from the cup of human joys and known the veritable ecstasy of the heart and the senses.

His sparkling eyes contemplated the animated skeletons that were shivering under his gaze: all that lugubrious dust that his magnetic force had caused to quiver. *Undoubtedly*, he said to himself, *I command the dead, and I can, at my whim, raise the stones of sepulchers, but no living and voluptuous lips have ever been placed on mine, and perhaps the supreme happiness simply consists in forgetting the world and the gods in the arms of a woman.*

---

1 The term *djeina* is found in both Dubois and Jacolliot, referring to an individual who has renounced the manner in which other people live; it has nothing to do with Jainism, a religion of much more recent origin than the supposed date of the present story.

VIII
Black Mass and Red Mass

In front of the temple, at the bottom of the steps, the great Radogks were still waiting. The royal troops and the Sons of Joy occupied the surroundings of the edifice; no one could escape.

"Enter," said Salassim, letting the heavy battens of the door swing on their hinges. "No one is hiding here. Visit the halls, the chapels and every corner of the Temple. The pilgrims and the yogis will guide you, if you do not trust me. We are about to sacrifice two rams on Shiva's altar. The throats of those animals will be cut in your honor, and you can collect the blood."

"It isn't the sacrifice of two rams that we desire, but that of a woman."

"Women do not enter here," said Salassim. "We do not worship, it is true, the Nahamam or the Golden Womb, but we refuse to fill the office of executioners. To you, Brahmin of Kanda-Swamy, the shame of human sacrifices; here, we have only ever immolated animals."

Aracknai trembled with anger, but he knew that the Charmer was invincible, and that his dominating will would break against his.

"We are the stronger," he said, however, "and we shall immolate a woman on Shiva's altar."

Salassim smiled scornfully.

"Seek, then," he said, "to offer to the gods a body of amour and beauty. Here, you will only find servants of the male principle."

The Sons of Joy had traveled the temple, searching the slightest corners of the holy place, without discovering the person for whom they were searching. When they were all assembled before the sacrificial altar, Aracknai enveloped them with a somber gaze.

"The divinity requires a splendid homage," he said, "and only human blood can attract the beneficence of Shiva to us. Let one of you be sacrificed."

All of them recoiled fearfully. Then Soubatka pointed at one of the young men.

"That one," he said, "possessed the princess in the white house of the quarter of amour. His name is Soumati and, by immolating him, we would be immolating a little of the one who is escaping us. By his death we shall surely pick up the fugitive's trail."

Soumati started to weep. "In fact," he said, "the Rani came to the house of the Devedas, but she only asked for poems. I sang the stanzas to the Sun for her and she gave me her pearl necklace as a recompense. I swear by the sacred Trimurty that we did not exchange any kiss, and that we did not even talk about amour."

"What did she come into the white houses to do, then?" asked Paraçou, surprised.

"She came in search of information regarding the Charmer, to whose bewitchment she was subject. Only mystical sensualities attracted her, for, she said, she was weary of her legitimate spouses and all the slaves of amour in her harem of men."

Deeply humiliated, the Radogks exchanged angry glances.

"She disdained us to that degree!" sighed Doudouma-Lovi, the most infatuated of the Great Husbands.

"And on my advice," Soumati continued, "the Divine One went to the Shakti puja, the festival of fecundation. It was doubtless there that she found the Charmer."

"Yes," said Salassim, "it was there that I saw the person for whom you are searching for the second time. But I shall not surrender her, for I disapprove of the violent measures you have employed to subjugate the people. I am not in favor of the reign of woman, but it is not necessary to immolate her in order to vanquish her. Treat her with mildness and tenderness, love her, protect her, make an existence of quietude and felicity for her. Be good to her, as she has been good to you."

"Ah!" said Aracknai, furiously. "You and your accursed sect will reduce us to the utmost degree of abasement. We will overturn your temples, destroy the objects of your worship and deprive you of all religious and political liberty!"

Salassim turned toward the altar. "I scorn human anger," he said.

"Divine anger will pursue you as well!" howled Aracknai. "And in order that that will weigh upon your damnable sect, we will offer the blood of a Son of Joy to the black god."

The Devedas immediately fell upon Soumati, stripped him of his garments, and bound his hands and feet, while he rolled his bewildered eyes and begged for mercy.

On the altar ornamented with flowers, the sacrifice of amour and murder was accomplished under the equivocal gaze of the male and female idol. The Great Husbands, confounding the sexes, thought that they were avenging themselves, once, for the long humiliation of their servitude.

Soumati's agony lasted for a long time; then, when he was finally motionless, in the blood and the mutilated flowers, a great orgy burst forth, as in the Shakti puja of the temple of Swamy.

The Sons of Joy, the great Radogks and the pujari Brahmins, devoid of women henceforth, gave themselves the illusion, in a frightful intoxication, while the djeina fakirs, with ascetic faces and bodies thinned by privations, ran away in fear.

The Brahmanic saturnalias were renewed before the altar of Shiva; the men, like tigers in rut, precipitated themselves on one another, embracing one another, biting one another and rolling pell-mell on the filthy pavement soiled by thousands of sacrifices. A few got to their feet, even drinking spiced liquors from flasks they had found under the pedestal of the god.

The Sons of Joy had adorned themselves with the sacred ornaments and had put flowers in their long hair. Thus, they resembled women, and the priests, after having caressed them, killed them furiously. Gasps of amour and agony mingled, and from the heights of the columns and along the walls, the fixed faces of the idols contemplated them gravely.

Then the great Radogks, Aracknai and the initiates, sated, went to sleep next to the cadavers, which some were still embracing in an unconscious desire. A great silence descended.

Salassim, upright, contemplated the streams of black blood, the bodies pierced by stab-wounds, the flowers and the jewels that were strewing the floor. With his glittering eyes of an illuminate, he perceived the hatreds, hopes, red tears, dolors and conjurations that were in preparation, and the abyss that was being hollowed out under the feet of those imprudent individuals.

The future was somber, and the victors would soon be the vanquished. He understood that India, with its grandeurs and its weaknesses, India, the most admirable hearth of civilization, would be doomed by its own excesses, and would one day cease to count in the great human family.

IX
The Adoration in the Backti

The Rani, too long weaned from tenderness, had given herself to Prismama in the grass and the flowers. She began to live again, delectably, forgetful of the imminent dangers, hatred and treasons. She intoxicated herself on the lips of the young man, and initiated him slowly into all the mysteries of amour.

Prismama, the virgin lover, let himself go, bewildered by joy, grateful and insatiable. He saw the golden irises of the sovereign shining on his own and veiling themselves in ardent ecstasy; he felt his breast beating tumultuously, and fainted in a felicity of which he had never dared to dream.

Lying on the moss, happy and free, they gazed at the leaves quivering above their heads. Breezes carried away the perfumed soul of flowers. Before the sun, a curtain made of a thousand hermetically enlaced branches fell softly, and the glaucous daylight, nuanced by every shade of green, enveloped them with a mysterious tint. Evening was approaching; the exhalations of swooning corollas became sharper. There was the incense of aromatics, the honey of greasy plants, the odor of earth, shady woods and warm mosses: an entire potent bouquet that intoxicated to the point of vertigo.

Prismama did not weary of drinking from the voluptuous cup, and he composed exquisite poems for the Adored, which he sang aloud.

"Your tresses are somber wings that palpitate in the light, and your mouth is steeped in volcanic fire. Your eyes are iridescent and changing moonstones; they have the unfathomable depth and the mystery of the skies!

"Your ear is the rosy shell into which the ineffable confession of Smara slides. It opens to the amorous kiss like the shell to the kiss of the waves!

"Your breasts are golden calices in which the pollen-collecting bee goes to sleep.

"I want to drink from the cups of your breasts, I want to know the ardor of your lips. I am the wood-pigeon that sighs, the moth that catches fire, the drone that is intoxicated, I want . . . I want . . . I want . . ."

And she interrupted the adoring melody with further kisses. Her lips posed upon Prismama's like living flowers drunk on dew, and the latter immediately felt the profound sting of the hornet of amour, which was recklessly intoxicating him for the first time with terrestrial joys.

"O Divine One! O adorable Felicity," the initiate sighed, "why return to the capital? Let us flee toward the Himalaya, where no one knows us and no one will occupy themselves with our happiness. Why tempt Destiny? I've understood, by virtue of the mysterious revelations of the pitris, that your life is threatened. The Brahmins will sacrifice you to their ambition; you will not be able to fight, for almost all the women of Ahmehnagara have already perished!"

"I must avenge them," Syta declared, sadly. "I must make one last effort to save the crown. It's necessary, Prismama, that I expiate the inconceivable folly that drew me toward Salassim, to the scorn of all my duties. It's necessary that I reestablish order and peace in my realm, and that I punish the guilty."

"You will be devoid of strength against them, for they reign over the people by means of lies and superstition. All the tortures of the Naraca, they say, will overwhelm the rebels in the other life, and the account of the atrocities to which they will be subjected here frightens simple hearts."

"What does it matter?" said Syta. "I am fighting for good and justice. My Great Husbands will sustain me!"

Prismama, who had been visited by the spirits of the dead, was in despair at his sovereign's resistance, for he could read the book of the gods clearly.

"Your Great Husbands," he said, "have abandoned you, like the slaves of amour. Their masculine pride has reawakened under the instigation of the Brahmins of Kanda-Swany. You probably have no enemies more determined."

But the Rani shut her eyes and put her forehead on the young man's shoulder.

"Oh, let's not think about the future. Let's live for the present moment, which seems ineffably sweet, by contrast with past sufferings. If you truly love me, Prismama, we shall die together, and you shall have my last kiss."

"I belong to you, O Splendor! My existence is very little, and I offer it to you with joy. Let it be done in accordance with your desire."

Again, without any longer thinking about anything, they lost themselves in their ecstasy, in the midst of the magical vegetation that surrounded them.

Prismama, leaning over the Beloved, caressed with his burning lips her closed eyelids, as soft as silk, the amber skin of her cheeks, her slender and willful chin, and her breasts, rounded like fruits of sensual pleasure. He traveled the divine body offered to him, madly, all the way to the tapering legs and the slender feet.

"If you have ceased to reign over your people," he said, "you will reign over me. I want to put into your frail hands, until death, my ardent heart, which only beats for you. I will drag myself over the ground, kissing the imprints of your footfalls, and your slightest desires will be orders. You will be able to give yourself, become my sacred wife, or refuse yourself, as you desire. You will be everything for the slave that you have subjugated with your splendor."

Again his lips strayed over the feverish flesh of the Rani, making her a veil of caresses, tremulous and soft. She let herself go, avidly, and it seemed to her that a new blood was circulating in her veins, alternately burning and fresh.

How had she been able, for a morbid dream of pride and false science, to scorn the benefits of the union of beings in terrestrial amour, which alone permits real assuagement? Following Prismama's mouth, her sensibility was displaced, ardent between her breasts, in the hollows of her raised arms, the undulating circumlocutions of her torso, and the ridges of her hips, creeping over the curve of her loins, and flowing like a jet of fire along her trembling legs.

And as he paused, out of breath, she uttered a profound sigh and fainted.

Dusk had arrived now, without them being conscious of the flight of time. The ululation of owls and the brief calls of chameleons burst forth in a concert of voices impatiently soliciting sensuality. Luminous flies formed complicated arabesques in the air, an expertly woven lacework dotted with precious stones. Then there was a galactic scarf, a stream of insects, so tiny that they only formed a sheet of undulating light over the guipure of the trees, clinging to the asperities of bushes and tumbling into the moss in prestigious ribbons.

Syta was haloed by light; she resembled an Asparasa of the Blue Mountains. Her veils parted over an admirable body and she had put a glaucous crown of glow-worms in her hair, in order to affirm her melancholy royalty.

Her velvet eyes filled with the magical reflection of her dream; she pressed her pale lover against her breast more forcefully.

"Oh," he sighed, "how I admire all your metamorphoses, in accordance with the disposition of our souls. I was not alive before knowing you, nothing interested me of that which charms men, for I was ignorant of amour . . ."

"Yes," said Syta, "there is only amour; it alone governs the world. Men, you see, want to suppress amour, and they will die of no longer loving . . ."

They went to sleep in one another's arms in the magical nature, forgetful of the reptiles that brushed them in the grass and mingled their pale bellies patched with yellow and blue, and their glaucous backs with somber stripes, with the warm colors of the vegetation. Pink monkeys with black and gray beards let themselves fall from the trees beside them; wild beasts brushed them; but none of those guests of the Bakti did them any harm, for beasts, less cruel than humans, only seek to defend themselves, and a sleeping human is almost always sacred to them.

<h2 style="text-align:center">X</h2>

<h3 style="text-align:center">The Rani Speaks to the People</h3>

"I need a stallion," said Syta, "pure of form and immaculate in its coat, in order to reenter my capital. The people knew Ackbe and fêted him. Ackbe is no more, alas. Find me, Prismama, an animal beautiful enough and noble enough to replace him."

"Wait for me here, Divine One!" cried the disciple. "I will go to search for what you desire."

He had made her a nest of foliage and flowers, an exquisite and amorous retreat that lianas veiled with a silky curtain. Half-naked on the embalmed couch, she was even more adorable than during her night of amour, and nothing in nature equaled her splendor.

"Go," she said, "and may Brahma accompany you."

He left, sending her a final kiss, while she gathered corollas from an entire charming flora that blossomed around her. There were tulip-trees, mimosas and dragon-trees speckled with metallic green leaves, beneath golden bells opened by a light clapper laden with pollen. White and pink tuberoses covered all the other scents with their ardent exhalations, and that perfume was so intense that even the soil was impregnated with it.

Syta suddenly felt the weakness of the entire being that excessively violent emotions bring in their wake, a vertigo of the mind and the senses. Her solitude, the gravity of the mission that she was about to undertake, in the midst of the wreckage of her former splendor, left her tremulous, overwhelmed by an occult sensation of danger, before which her soul was suddenly frightened.

She remained breathless and torpid, experiencing a kind of anguish in her side, which flowed all the way to her legs, which had become unsteady and limp. She ate a little of the honey and fruits that Prismama had bought her in large leaves, and then she started to reflect.

Her glorious life, her husbands, prostrated before her until now, her submissive people, the incredible festivities of the court, her liberty and her indisputable influence, the fervent worship of her beauty, and a thousand memories whirled in her head in tumultuous and distant visions. Yesterday, still, she had been the adored Queen of one of the most beautiful provinces of India, and now a menacing barrier suddenly loomed up between the past and the present, and even her life, once surrounded by all tenderness, was threatened!

How had so many changes been produced in a matter of days? By virtue of what frightful evil spell was she being tracked and pursued today like a harmful beast?

She headed toward a nearby spring, and commenced her ablutions, methodically, in accordance with the sacred rites.

The limpid water sent back the image of her splendor, and she was astonished herself by such a marvelous radiance. Certainly, Salassim had granted her the most generous gift that an individual endowed with supernatural powers could bestow on a woman, for he had augmented her beauty to the extent that it was dazzling.

A tiger, which had approached the spring in order to drink, stopped in surprise, and its predatory eyes took on a caressant gleam in contemplating the exquisite creature that its presence had not caused to flee.

Syta had scattered over her shoulders the warm tangle of her immense tresses, which kissed her heels. With a gentle swaying of the arms she was chanting prayers, and her veils were coiled up at her feet like silky lianas. She was naked, supple and gilded, as if a luminous clarity had traversed her flesh. Perfumes floated around her, forming an aureole around her and evaporating in the distance, in gusts that were sometimes agile and sometimes heavy.

The tiger had lain down in the grass, and its topaz eyes no longer quit her.

Meanwhile, Prismama bought back a white stallion almost as noble as Ackbe. On his saddle, peridots and olivines were shining, and a pearly crest was swaying on his head.

Syta clapped her hands.

"Oh, how charming he is!" she said. "But I don't have any adornment in order to present myself before my people."

Prismama smiled sadly.

"No adornment is worth as much as your beauty. It is necessary that not a single jewel should break the admirable line of your body. Remain naked, O Divine One, and all men will kneel before you."

"You think so?"

"Yes, you will triumph more surely by showing yourself thus. Only let your hair of darkness form a screen for the pure diamond of your skin, and you will radiate like a sun over the profound blue of the sky."

Lightly, she leapt on to the beautiful stallion, while Prismama bent the branches before her, in order that she should only be touched by amorous corollas.

A musky breath rose from the ardent Bakti, a breath that intoxicated the mind and troubled the senses. The desire of beings and plants floated, indefinably and maddeningly, around the Rani.

The city of Ahmehnagara was surrounded by the forest; it extended like a tawny fleece to the foot of the pink, blue and mauve mountains that seemed iridescent with all the fires of the sky. A thousand streams, tributaries of the Krishna and the Godavari, ran like reptiles through the golden moss; above them flew immense dragonflies with nacreous and quivering glassy wings, and horned moths perched on the plants of the ground and the black reeds of the water.

Syta recalled her return from the hunt after her first encounter with Salassim. Men and women, as she passed by, had inclined their heads all the way to kiss the ground as a sign of submission and respect, children had thrown flowers and adolescent girls had run behind her in the hope of placing their lips on a corner of her flesh, in order to carry away a little of her grace and her perfume! Her Great Husbands were waiting for her, with words of adoration; her slaves of amour were rubbing themselves with balms, depilating themselves and ornamenting themselves in order to welcome her and contemplate her adorable smile for a moment. How far away all that was!

Here is the city, with its temples, edified to the glory of Issouara, its monuments with granite facades covered with fantastic animals and the enlaced figures of gods and goddesses, curiously sculpted. The yajasala, places of sacrifice, are still fuming, and the sacred elephants have feet red with blood. A few hours ago they were crushing heads and causing the brains to spurt. All the buildings around the accursed place, the walls, the trees, the flowers and the spectators have been splashed. Immense carts are filled with headless corpses to be delivered to the fire, because the sated wild beasts no longer want them.

Here is the husband market, once full of joyous animation, now deserted; here is the quarter of the Sons of Joy, similarly empty, for the granichy are directing the massacre and haranguing the people.

Syta has entered the outlying districts of the city. All those who have seen her have cried miracle and have prostrated themselves in the dust, for she is similar, on the great white stallion, to a luminous idol.

Surrounded by a superstitious respect, she heads toward the yajasala, where the crowd is massed, behind the Sons of Joy. People look at her with a surprise mingled with terror; no one dares touch her, but more than one man feels a tumultuous blood flowing in his veins and the seething of a mysterious desire sets faces ablaze.

Syta stops her horse, directs her flamboyant gaze over her people, and speaks, in a voice as clear as crystal, which everyone can hear:

"I am your sovereign," she said, "and I have returned among you. I have engraved my will on the golden lingam of the temple of Shiva. It is therefore sacred, and you must obey me as the god himself. For what do you have to reproach me? I have wanted laws favorable to weak and suffering humanity; I have only ever sought your moral and physical wellbeing. With me you have been happy in a prosperous country. Apart from the Brahmins' sacrifices, which I was unable to prevent, blood has not been shed during my reign. I have protected the life of everyone, preached gratitude, pity, charity, mutual aid and the alms of amour: all the virtues that are agreeable to the Supreme Being, who is presently being outraged by frightful crimes.

"For as long as I have reigned, all the combined forces of industry and agriculture have been applied to augment the fortune of everyone, to favor the study of the sciences and the development of the arts. The regime of favoritism, hatred and compression that crushes people everywhere else, has never existed here. In consequence of the diminution of the population, you have never known poverty, and you blessed me as a benefactor. What wind of folly, then, has blown over you?"

The people, in ecstasy, remained silent. Only the Sons of Joy had scornful smiles and malevolent gazes. With their clean-shaven faces and the gems that still covered their arms and ankles they resembled women somewhat, and their rage was all the greater for that.

"To death!" one of them shouted.

Syta went on, sadly:

"What have I done to you? Never I swear, have I ever wanted anything but your happiness, and the yoke of woman was mild to you. You seek equality? But human equality does not exist. There will always be the powerful and the weak, the rich and the poor. We have for you pity, tenderness, devotion and abnegation, all virtues that you scarcely know. When you have overturned feminine power, which governed you with bounty and justice, you will choose masters who will exploit you and deceive you. Ambitious and perverse minds will triumph over simple natures, the malign will supplant the naïve and the honest. There will be, henceforth, oppressors and oppressed, a relentless struggle will decimate men, and you will fight for the women that you wanted to vanquish.

"By destroying that which exists, you will not arrive at perfection, which is not of this world. You will, alas, create new evils and greater crimes, which will only profit the Brahmins, your hidden enemies. Oh, how far we are from the ancient and pure religion, which even prohibited the sacrifice of animals and only wanted laws of amour! All your efforts will tend to make as much blood flow as possible, and it is not with remorse for your criminal follies that you will arrive at the peace of mind and soul."

"Why did you leave us?" sobbed a young boy who was in the front rank of the spectators.

"How do I know? The servants of Kanda-Swany subjected me to the bewitchment of a Charmer, and I have been in his power, devoid of strength as of will. The occult and maleficent power drew me to the worst follies, and I remain the victim of a damned sect."

A great rumor rose up in the crowd. The Brahmins emerged from the temple, preceded by a troop of dancers arrived from neighboring provinces where masculine influence already reigned.

An old prophet, whose sala was ornamented with silver cords knotted around his waist and his wrists, began to speak with fire, while the princess, trembling, looked at all those young women, humble and pretty, ornamented in their turn for the pleasure of the male.

"What that woman has just said," declared the angry Brahmin, "is nothing but stupidity and lies. For too long you have curbed your heads under her humiliating domination, whereas in other countries, the lingam dethroned the symbol of weakness and cunning a long time ago. You will not have to regret your former existence of luxury, your days of idleness in brothels. Nothing will have changed, fundamentally, for you, for you will make your wives work and you will profit from their labor. Your wives will be your servants; you will have the right of life or death over them; widows will be burned on the bodies of their husbands and virgins will await your desire in solitude . . ."

Syta tried to interrupt the Brahmin, but the cries of the Sons of Joy drowned her protestations.

"Certainly," continued the old soothsayer, "that creature is very beautiful, but other women, from the provinces that we have conquered, promise us a true feast of flesh; they are slaves, already fashioned to respect and obedience. All of us can choose from their amorous flock."

The young women had advanced on to the place of sacrifice. The devedas had thrown pink and blue flowers under their feet, and freshly cut branches, in order to hide the blood that was still flowing in sticky streams. But they did not seem surprised; their large moist eyes only reflected the lascivious emotion of the senses.

They had taken one another by the waist, tilting to the right and the left, uttering a sort of languorous plaint. The veils of their cleavage, coming apart, allowed the sight of their superb breasts, which stood up like lotus corollas outside the water.

Syta made a supreme effort. Upright on the great white stallion, with the splendor of her flesh, which effaced all others, she spoke in the tumult, and silence gradually fell again.

"You want," she said, "to follow the example of other peoples, simultaneously so ferocious and so corrupt. You are appealing to revolutionary energies to overthrow a woman, a woman whose soul of benevolence and forgiveness has only wanted your good. The seizure of our possessions, the expropriation of that which belongs to us will therefore be accomplished by anarchic communism. You will destroy the government, repudiate its morality and its laws in order to follow the initiative of the Brahmins, to serve their cause and their interests!"

"Yes, yes!" howled the prophet. "It is after that overthrow of the former power that the freed slaves will be able to deliver themselves to the attractive occupations of freely chosen labor and proceed scientifically in the cultivation of the soil and commercial production. It is the ancient civilization, in its entirety, that we see concluding. Henceforth, we shall reign by the right of strength and male authority. The tradition of the Golden Womb, mother of the world, no longer dominates us; we profess a new faith, and as soon as that faith, which is also the consciousness of our value, has become that of all those who seek the truth, it will acquire substance in the world of realizations."

Syta, her eyes closed, seemed to abandon herself to a mysterious dream; a proud and melancholy smile creased her lips. Around her, the lascivious dancers caused their hips and buttocks to shake, raising their arms, charged with rings, limply.

The Brahmin continued, in a shrill voice:

"Certainly, the imminent revolution, important as it might be in the development of humanity, will not differ from previous evolutions in accomplishing an abrupt leap; nature is not made that way. But one can say, by virtue of a thousand conclusive symptoms, a thousand profound modifications, that the rights of man have been constituted for a long time. They are becoming evident everywhere; they are bursting forth in cities as in the country; they reign over the earth, which belongs to the strongest. To continue to misunderstand the laws of nature would be pure folly."

In a pose of irresistible sensuality, the dancers seemed to be offering themselves to the crowd. There was an immense clamor of triumph and desire.

Syta understood that her cause was lost. While the Brahmins seized the bridle of the great stallion, in spite of Prismama's resistance, she said, scornfully: "Insensates! All your efforts, henceforth, will do evil for evil's sake, kill for the sake of killing, and it is not with the remorse of your crimes that you can be happy! Humanity, henceforth, is irresponsible, and I forgive you for your dementia. But believe me, our institutions of mildness, pity and tenderness are far better than the sanguinary rage that will lead you to despair and ruination!"

Stones were now raining down on the sovereign, who remained upright and proud in the admirable nimbus of her beauty. She made no further gesture, and allowed herself to be taken away by the Brahmins, while the people, roaring like wild beasts, threw themselves on the courtesans extended in the mud and the blood.

XI
The Supreme Possession

Syta was taken to her palace and the seven doors of her chamber—the golden door, the jade door, the ivory door, the iron door, the silver door, the bronze door and the crystal door—were locked upon her.

It was decided that she would be burned, in great pomp, in front of the temple of Kanda-Swany, after having belonged to the six great Radogks and all her slaves of amour.

In her turn, she would have to obey the caprices of men and submit to their desires. She would be attached, on her ivory couch, to the four silver lions, and the torture of amour would precede the torture of death.

Syta had listened to the sentence calmly, resigned henceforth to all tortures. Only the sobs of Prismama, whom the Brahmins brought, still awoke some pity in her heart.

Then the clamors were lost in the distance, and she remained alone in her grand bedchamber with the mysterious gleams and the voluptuous memories, where she had lived surrounded by adorations and homages.

She thought that it requires very little to overturn an existence and overthrow an empire. A few paces too far had led her to the Charmer. Was that hazard or fatality? The weakness of a sovereign for a vagabond fakir had changed human destiny, vanquished woman forever, made her glorious reign into a humiliating slavery. Woman, henceforth, would be lost for amour, lost for the liberty and dignity of her sex, and happiness. She would no longer be anything but an instrument of pleasure, a performer, a raiser of children or a servant. She would be ornamented for the pride of men, she would be exhibited, like a precious trinket, or locked up in the dwelling in a humiliating servitude. A creature of lust or a creature of sacrifice, scorned in every fashion, she would only have the bitterness of life without knowing its joys.

Syta, collapsed at the foot of her bed, and remained motionless, buried in the mists of dream. However, the flight of the minutes was heavy and dolorous for her. Her thought, like a wounded bird, returned incessantly to its point of departure, the broken, painful wing. Her silent despair clasped her everywhere like a suit of armor, paralyzing the beating of her heart. She seemed to see shadows agitating nearby, to feel hands brushing her and hear voices cursing her. The specters of the women who had perished in infinite tortures because of her flight were certainly wandering in the dark room, and their menacing flock surrounded her, crowding her, augmenting by the minute.

Her nerves were vibrating painfully; she sought with her eyes, widened by horror, for anything that might give her death rapidly, without suffering. The large bath, with its jasmine-, almond- and rose-water springing forth, showed a blue-tinted reflection in the shadow. The Rani went down the six steps that led to it, but she judged that the pool was not deep enough, and that she would not have the energy to wait for deliverance there.

Everything became terrible and fantastic for her; everything was a subject of anguish. The weakest of creatures, a domestic animal or a child, would have been a support for her heart if not a defender of her life, but she was quite alone, irremissibly alone, and she became torpid in her nightmare, with the sweat of fear on her brow. She listened to the distant bells of Kanda-Swamy, Bahvani and Aluwihara, the temples of hatred in which the Brahmins were doubtless rejoicing in her agony.

A pink lizard sometimes ran over the bas-reliefs of the walls, and she remained with her eyes fixed, not daring to turn them away from the point at which she was staring, in the dread that they might encounter some greater cause of stupor.

A night and a day passed in that anguish, and then, in the evening, her former slaves offered her delicate dishes, spiced and frothy wines, perfumes and flowers. She was adorned with pearly gauzes and the headband with the dozen diamond hearts, more scintillant than the twelve snowy peaks of the Vindhya Mountains.

As before, the orchestra of barbaric instruments was heard, while the high-pitched voices of a battalion of little boys hidden in the upper galleries celebrated the cult of Smara.

On the great bed of the silver lions the sovereign was attached, with knots of roses dissimulating the solid bonds, and the six great Radogks slid next to her.

"O Divinity! O Light!" said Soulabatka, the Flavorsome Fruit, putting his hand to his forehead and his breast, "permit us to render you one final homage."

"Before dying, you will deign to make us the gift of your beauty," added Ruman-Bibi, the Perfect Science, with a very gentle irony.

"We are your foremost spouses, and we have always fulfilled our duties gloriously," declared Biskouri, the Column of Felicity. "This time, again, we shall show ourselves at the height of our reputation. You will see that the occult practices of a Charmer are not worth as much as the amorous transports of a veritable lover."

Nandamu, the Golden Ram, added that Syta's dazzling beauty awoke burning desires in him, and that although the sovereign had fallen, woman had the right to reign over souls, for none, among terrestrial creatures, seemed as perfect as her.

Doudouma-Lovi, Above All, who had always shown himself more infatuated, could not say a word, so great was his emotion, and Paraçou the Incomparable limited himself to approving the discourse of his companions.

Syta, her eyes closed, nailed to her great bed, remained silent. Her veils were parted over her young nudity, and the adorable harmony of her body burst forth for all gazes. From her breasts, softly rounded in cups of intoxication, to her abdomen, more polished than Kama's buckler, everything was poetry, light and enchantment in that divine flesh, made for the adoration of a world.

The Radogks were crouching at the foot of the bed, and the slaves passed them vehement dishes spiced with turmeric and curry, and poured lotus wine speckled with precious stones.

Young boys, the same ones that had once circulated among the guests with felted footsteps, showed their slender forms under scarves of flowers. Macabou flutes made shrill stridulations heard, while snakeskin tchilas resonated under closed fists.

Here come the performers of the *corps de ballet*, charming creatures about twelve years old with long hair brought up on to the head and large eyes circled with kohl. Their flesh, steeped in balms that discolor the pigments of the skin, shines like gold.

They are delicate and plump, and know all the steps of sensuality, which they dance for that infinite and final enjoyment. Some have skirts staged like petals, representing flowers, while their companions, provided with antennae, elytra and long, quivering stings, pursue them in the throb of snakeskin tambourahs. There are larvae covered in silver and gold gauze, which remain motionless under the assault of audacious insects. The smallest wear the carapaces of pink ladybirds and bronze cantharides; they pursue one another and deliver themselves to a thousand games, as in the fine times of royal glory.

Syta, on her feverish couch, witnesses all those games, but her thought is distant, already lost in the beyond of dream.

Finally. Soulabatka approaches, and while the orchestra redoubles its harmony and the choir of little boys lets rip triumphantly, the great Radogk possesses the sovereign. Then come the turns of the other five primary husbands and all the secondary husbands . . .

The princess has lost consciousness on the great ravaged bed, into which her tresses, in the mutilated flowers and the blood, put their wave of darkness . . . She seems dead already, with her pinched nostrils and the dolorous bruising that rings her eyelids.

The silence of the night falls around her; only Aracknai, the Brahmin of Issouara, remains, in order to recite the mantras of the agonizing. He has brought a little of the water of the Hadamur spring to anoint the Rani's hands and feet, and to give her the strength to see herself brought to the yajasala of the torture. The supreme anguish of victims is agreeable to the gods; it is necessary that they are not unaware of what awaits them, and that they suffer in their soul as in their body.

With a cruel smile at the corners of his lips, Aracknai leans over the ravaged couch, and by means of occult invocations, and all the magnetic force that he possesses, he attempts to extract Syta from her lethargy.

Already, rapid frissons are passing through the young woman's exhausted limbs, running over her skin like reptiles, and knotting themselves over her throat, from which gasps emerge. Her eyelids are raised slowly over the nacre of the eyes; she seems to be suffering more. The Brahmin redoubles his passes and incantations; he is about to triumph when a panel of the woodwork moves aside soundlessly and gives passage to Prismama, who, by virtue of an extraordinary effort of audacity and will, has been able to overcome all the obstacles and reach the presence of the woman he loves.

The two holy men are together, and consider one another with a grim hatred.

"Priest of false, unjust and wicked gods, I order you to quit this chamber, which you are soiling with your presence."

And the young disciple, his eyes glittering, advances toward the consternated old man, whose hands are trembling and legs vacillating.

"It is because of you and the evil spirits of the temple that the most adorable of creatures has been calumniated, insulted and subjected to the most abominable tortures. It is because of you and the infamous servants of the black god that the ancient religions of clemency and pity have been abolished. May the vengeful anger of Brahma weigh upon your lying sect and this accursed earth!"

Prismama has drawn a dagger from his belt, and Aracknai, frightened, has raced to the first door of the royal bedroom, which is closed again.

"Cowardly, hypocritical and perfidious priest!" the ascetic goes on, vehemently. "You can see that my power is triumphing over yours and that the celestial powers are with me. I command inanimate objects as well as inferior beings, and I have the occult force of prophets, for Salassim has initiated me into the sacred mysteries. Brahma is the supreme god, Vishnu and Shiva are his deputies and form the holy trimurty, but you only worship Shiva, the god of death, and, like a filthy animal, you bathe in the blood of sacrifices. You are no longer a propagator of divine verity, but a wild beast unleashed by hunger."

Aracknai had taken refuge near the bath. By running around the basin he tried to evade the disciple's attack, but his uncertain feet became entangled in his sala; he fell and his forehead struck the marble with a dull sound.

Prismama pushed the twitching body into the water and maintained it there until the immersion had done its work. The last bubbles of air, under the effort of the lungs, broke the surface of the water; then Aracknai remained motionless.

"Glory to Nari, mother of the world," said the disciple, and having approached the couch where the queen lay, still inanimate, he prostrated himself and annihilated himself in an ecstatic adoration. His lips, however, were moving; very softly, he was intoning the stanzas to Nahamam.

"You are a calyx of immaculate lotus and you receive the divine seed of Brahma in a profound caress! You are the ancestor of all beings! You are purity and chastity, the Golden Womb in which the power of the supreme god reposes!

"O Nahamam!"

XII
Death

Outside, the heavy tread of elephants could be heard, which the cornacs were arranging for the cortege and the march to the pyre. There was a turbulent sea of rumps and heads, swaying under heavy bronze ornaments. Little boys, still adorned for lascivious dances, were lifting gold and silver idols on to their shoulders. Some had baskets full of rose, jasmine and tuberose petals, which they were to strew under the sovereign's chariot; and the six Radogks, clad in chomins and pectorals fringed with diamonds, with the hollow pearls of Karamy-yega around the neck, were waiting for Aracknai's signal in order to go in search of the sovereign in great pomp.

But the priest of Issoura did not appear. Already, the crowd massed in the courtyard of the palace was becoming restless.

Soulabakta detached himself from the group of the great Radogks in order to go and interrogate the Brahmin and ask him to hurry. Around the royal chamber everything was silent. The doors remained closed, without it being possible to make them yield.

"In the name of Brahma-Vishnu-Shiva, open up!" shouted the Radogk, impatiently.

And with his fist he hammered on the sacred ornaments of the first partition. Nothing moved behind the barriers of gold, jade, ivory, iron, silver, bronze and crystal.

"Open up!" shouted Soulabatka, more loudly, beginning to fear some new black magic; and, as no voice replied to his exhortations, he went to fetch the other husbands.

While they conferred, anxiously, Prismama, beside the Beloved, had forgotten everything that was not amour.

By means of a few drops of a voluptuous poison, poured over the sovereign's lips, he had prolonged her sleep beyond life. She was no longer suffering; her visage had resumed an ineffable serenity; her charming body, purified and adorned, reposed on new flowers, caused to bloom by the prestigious power of mantras and the will of the pitris.

The mystical lover, the passionate disciple, as if intoxicated by opium, was also falling into eternal slumber; but life was ebbing away from his being slowly, in warm gusts and ardent frissons, and that agony had the infinite delights of the act of amour. Every gasp that rose from his bosom was like a joyful plaint; he was succumbing in the renaissance of his intoxication, recklessly.

Outside, furious blows were breaking down the precious doors. Two had yielded already. The third, the ivory door, would not rest for long, but the iron door, which was next in the sequence, appeared inviolable.

Over the icy lips of the sovereign, Prismama sighed the last strophes of the sacred canticle.

"O Nahamam!

"You are as fragile and strong as the prayer that an ardent soul exhales, the perfume to which the flower gives birth, the kiss that expires on the lips of lovers! You are the sacred Ganges, honey and amrita, the essence of Zyaus, the mother of the Vedas and Brahmins! It is from your womb that everything that exists emerged!

"O Nahamam!"

On that sacred name, sweeter than the bagicha in which bees swoon, the iron door was broken down with an almighty din; the bronze door made lugubrious sonorities heard under the furious blows of the assailants.

Prismama felt death penetrate into him more delectably. In an extraordinary spasm, he let himself fall on to the corpse of the sovereign, while the bronze barrier and the silver door ceded in their turn, causing the glass shards of the final partition to fly all the way to the royal couch.

But the soul of Syta, ineffably bound to the soul of Prismama, had escaped through the mysterious door that arrests all human intelligence, and separates our wicked world from the ideal light of amour and justice.

PHARAOH'S LOVER

PART ONE

I
The Shadow of Osiris

The Egyptians, who imagined that they were primarily governed by the gods, retained for a long time the almost exclusive worship of the great mysteries contained in their sacred books, the love of ceremonies accompanied by music, processions and religious dances. Under the first pharaohs the priests still dictated commandments to the people, which they said they had received from occult powers of Good and Evil. Papyruses reproducing hieroglyphic fragments of the *Book of the Dead* are found in all sarcophagi, sometimes with occult and hermetic mottoes under the symbol of Osiris, which signifies "Hidden fire."

The esotericism contained in these formulae initiates us into the passage of the soul through the fields of Aaru. The soul of the deceased, in the course of its peregrinations, is initially only a perispirit, or astral body, but when it arrives at the end of its journey it is reintegrated with its carnal envelope. Embalming thus has the goal of preparing the body for that sort of resurrection: a new flower of flesh has to emerge from the hardened matrix of cadavers like a shoot from a desiccated seed. Nothing is lost, everything resuscitates and is transformed, infinitely . . .

It was thought that the initiate into the divine mysteries had singular powers over the forces of nature; he was a sort of demiurge or creator god who reigned over the human mind. Five thousand years before our era, the warrior and feudal influence mingled with the worship of sacred things, and Menes, the first king, dared to combat the influence of the priests.[1]

---

1 The mythical Menes, credited in ancient Egyptian records with unifying

The Nile was already channeled, agriculture affirmed in full productive force, and architecture displayed its immense, fantastic, superhuman monuments; the great Sphinx fixed its granite gaze on the clouds, and the prodigious temples of the ancient Shesou-Hor caused the people to marvel.[1]

Menes founded the city of Memphis and dedicated it to the god Ptah, who later became Aegyptos. The descendants of Menes were the Pharaohs, sons of God and the Sun. Among them, power was even transmitted to women. Most of the time, in order not to lose caste, the heir to the throne married his sister, but when a king died without male progeniture, the chief of a new dynasty married a princess of the former family in order that the adorable blood of the gods would be transmitted from generation to generation.

The first two or three dynasties only left faint traces in history, but the third, and especially the fourth, marked the apogee of the divine Empire that constructed the Pyramids and made the glory of Memphis.

Cheops, Chephren and Mykerinos accomplished those extraordinary endeavors, which will represent eternally the grandeur and the annihilation of those who edified them, because—the supreme irony of time!—those indestructible monuments, which neither revolutions nor terrestrial cataclysms could corrode, were the tombs of their creators.

Egypt and founding the First Dynasty, is nowadays usually identified with a king named Narmer. Widely different speculations were offered by various nineteenth-century Egyptologists as to the date of the foundation of the First Dynasty, the earliest of which, offered by Jean-Francois Champollion, was the beginning of the sixth millennium B.C. More recent calculations, assisted by radiocarbon dating, attribute Narmer's reign to the end of the fourth millennium B.C.

1 Shesou-Hor [followers of Horus] was the name given by several French Egyptologists, most prominently François Chabas in the 1870s and Étienne Brosse in the 1890s, to hypothetical Asiatic emigrants whom they credited with causing a significant rupture in the development of ancient Egyptian civilization. English sources usually render it Shesu-Hor or Hor-Shesu.

But, although implacable destiny has scattered the ashes of those great monarchs, their names remain engraved in stone, and perhaps their sacred phantoms are still wandering in the profound solitudes and the infinite sadness of dead cities.

Nitocris, the svelte princess "with the starry eyes and flowery cheeks" belonged to the sixth dynasty.[1] She germinated an epoch of strange splendor that lasted eight hundred years.

The queen, proud and charming, became the heroine of many legends because, Herodotus affirms: "In order to avenge her husband and brother, who had been murdered, she had an immense subterranean hall built and invited to a great feast a large number of the Egyptians whom she knew to have been the instigators of the crime. In the midst of the feast she caused the waters of the Nile to enter through a channel that she had kept hidden, and threw herself into a redoubt filled with ash, in order to avoid the punishment reserved for the culpable."

For a long time the phantom of the gracious sovereign wandered around the pyramid of Mykerinos, where her embalmed body reposed, and more than one traveler contemplated that radiant image escaped from the tomb with amour.

The specter of Queen Nitocris with the starry eyes remains resplendent above a lugubrious and mysterious interval of five centuries. Four dynasties filled it, but nothing has remained to us of their obscure reign.

Three thousand years before our era, a new capital of splendor and glory dethroned the ancient Memphis. Thebes, the city of a hundred gates, had conquered the world.

---

1 The phrase that the author places in quotation marks is not a traceable quote, but Nitocris was best-known in nineteenth-century France because she is briefly featured in Victor Hugo's *La Légende des siècles* (1862), the poet having presumably found her in Herodotus, in the quoted anecdote. The allegation that Nitocris was buried in the third pyramid was made by the Egyptian writer Manetho, who seems to have confused her "throne name" Menkara with that of the pharaoh Menkaure (called Mykerinos by Herodotus), the actual constructor of the pyramid.

The gods worshiped by the Shesou-Hor, Ammon and Osiris, replaced the august Ptah and Ra of the first dynasties. Amenemhat I and his son Senusret established Egyptian colonies, exploited copper and turquoise mines, constructed fortresses and subjugated Ethiopia. All the arts and métiers exercised in our day were cultivated successfully; caravans went to Asia in quest of golden and silver fabrics, delicately sculpted or enameled vases, cedar wood, hitherto unknown gems with lunar and solar reflections, rare perfumes of roses, tuberoses and jasmines, and slaves of amour with long eyes blurred by kohl. The Libyan chain was enlarged and gradually formed an oasis named the Fayoum, into which the floodwaters of the Nile were diverted.

In the center of that reservoir, dominating the surrounding area, stood two granite colossi: Amenemhat III next to the queen, his wife, and the subjugated waters came in forming waves to caress the feet of the sovereigns who had subjugated them.[1]

It was not until 2000 B.C. that the invasion of the Hyksos, or "herdsmen," devastated Egypt, and only Thebes served the tradition of grandeur and independence of the first Pharaohs. The struggle lasted nearly a hundred and fifty years; then Ahmose I took possession of power and defeated the Hyksos, who retreated in disorder beyond the isthmus of Suez. A fecund era opened for Egypt, and the Third Empire went forth, like a new sun, to project its light over the dazzled world.

II
The Marriage of Thutmose

That day, Thutmose I, the grandson of Ahmose, united his son, in accordance with the custom of the Pharaohs, with his sister

---

1 Modern chronology dates the reign of the Twelfth Dynasty pharaoh Amenemhat III to 1860-1814 B.C., long after the origin of the Faiyun Oasis in 3000 B.C or thereabouts, but Egyptian chronology was still very speculative when the present novel was written.

Atasu.[1] The old king, between two victories, employed himself with the welfare of his children. Immediately after the ceremony, however, he had to return to Asia to make war there, for the assimilation of the conquered peoples was proving difficult, and military intervention was incessant. As soon as the yoke seemed to lighten, the submissive kings raised the standard of revolt and refused the tribute. Thutmose I drew his subjects once again to the Asiatic conquest, and, the large number of petty peoples who lived in the lands of Canaan and Syria facilitating his bellicose projects singularly, he advanced as a conqueror all the way to the banks of the Euphrates.

Certainly, the union of his son and his beloved daughter caused him some anxieties, for the young prince, at the age of seventeen, seemed fifteen at the most and scarcely ready to fulfill his role as a husband, but the princess, beneath her cheerful appearance, seemed sage and shrewd, so he could be confident of the regency of the State. As for the royal groom, he only experienced respectful sentiments for the princess his sister, who was older than him, but he nevertheless accomplished the divine and paternal will zealously.

Atasu, exquisite in her gold-spangled veils embroidered with precious stones, smiled at the people, of whom she was, she thought, the veritable sovereign. She was more troubling and more adorned than the goddess Nut, more adorable than the mysterious Isis, and her entire being tended toward amour ineffably. In spite of her desire of obedience, she sometimes darted a pitying glance at the frail adolescent with the long nostalgic gaze, charged with ennui, and the pure profile whose delicate ridges were outlined too curtly in the poverty of flesh.

Atasu desired the kisses of a husband with all the passion of her blooming beauty, while the hereditary prince was only nourished as yet on mystical dreams.

---

1 I have retained La Vaudère's rendering of Atasu rather than substituting the now-conventional Hatshepsut. She became much more famous than her brother and husband Thutmose II, and is nowadays thought to have succeeded him as Pharaoh.

Thutmose, meanwhile, possessed a harem composed of the prettiest daughters of the Nile, but he hardly went there except to soothe himself with the vague harmonies of old songs and to go to sleep on the virgin breast of the evening's companion.

Atasu, in her hieratic robe decorated with flames, had the troubling attitude of a sphinx, and her forehead stood up proudly under the sacred Uraeus. Since the regency would be confided to her following her father's departure, she wanted to render herself worthy of the confidence that was being placed in her.

Officers guarded the doors of the palace, superb young men whose calanticas of metal leaves hung over their shoulders, and the Mashaous outside, carrying a spear in one hand and a buckler in the other, held the people in respect.

An animated, jovial, colorful crowd acclaimed the newlyweds on the streets of Thebes. The women, especially, with their sparkling smiles, their large eyes darkened with make-up and their pale bronze upper bodies with firm breasts, appeared very agitated and nervous. Atasu had, they said, promised to distribute fruits and jewels to them after the feast that was to unite all the members of the royal family, and the daughter of Pharaohs was generally adored.

In order to go to the palace, all the young woman had sheathed themselves in the while sarrau with red stripes of feast days, having slid bracelets of glass and silver over their arms, which clinked at every gesture. Bursts of sistra and tympani arrived from doorways, but when the reed flute, or mum made the melodies of the "Perfect Union" heard, everyone fell silent in order to listen to the amorous poem.

The pure voice of a singer delighted hearts to the accompaniment of psalterions. That voice had a timbre so crystalline and so surprising that no one had heard its like, and the name of the virtuoso was whispered: Zelinis, the lover and fiancée of the chief of the Royal Guard, Hary-Thé.

Behind a clump of myrtle and rose bushes, Zelinis was singing in order to obey the desire of young Prince Thutmose, who never wearied of hearing her. After the stanzas of the "Perfect Union" she intoned those of the "Path of Souls" and the "Abyss of Amour."

Egyptian music fully justified the description given by Quintilian: "It was the knowledge of all that is beautiful and decent in the body and in movement." It insinuated itself into the mind as a wave insinuates itself in hollows in the rocks; it flowed gently and blissfully, enlacing people with its limpid currents. A chorus composed of twelve hundred young women took up Zelinis' strophes, and all those voices had an angelic savor, rising toward the empty vault of the immense hall as if to delight the stars.

Atasu, meanwhile, had drawn closer to her young husband, whom she caressed with a tender and fraternal gaze.

"Would you not like dances to succeed these sacred songs, O my Master? The virgins of the temple of Ammon-Ra are only waiting for a signal to make known the new steps of Lunus, who rejuvenates and celebrate amour, those of Anta, the warrior goddess, and those of Anubis, who presides over embalmings. It is said that those sacred dances are marvelous." [1]

Thutmose did not reply, but with a sign, he imposed silence on the feminine choir. The little siol and mum flutes exhaled a final pearly note, and Zelinis' psalterion fell asleep, as if regretfully, with a melancholy sigh. Immediately, the tympani and the sistra beat time to the entrance of the virgins of Ammon-Ra, long and slender statuettes of pale gold, whose torso and hips were imprisoned in a network of pearls. Shaking the short curls of their hair, they glided gracefully, swayed and embraced one another in order to render the complicated figures of the pantomime. Tapering legs rattled silver anklets, and a fine sparkling mist fell from bodies rubbed with aromatics.

---

1 The insertion in the text of the name Lunus is eccentric, as it is usually employed in connection with a Phrygian god, lunar deities being far more commonly envisaged as female, but Helena Blavatsky refers in *The Secret Doctrine* (1893), which La Vaudère had certainly read, and in various other works, to "the god Lunus" being confounded with Thoth and Ptah. Even so, it is odd to see him characterized as the god of *volupté* [sensual pleasure].

They wrapped one another in garlands of roses, kissed one another on the lips and seemed to swoon in infinite ecstasy in order to celebrate the god of sensuality. Then the poem of Anta imposed warrior attitudes upon them under helmets and bucklers. They threatened one another, spears in hand, inflicting imaginary wounds, and, after a bellicose hand-to-hand struggle, became the cadavers of the vanquished, strewing the ground, uttering their great victory cry.

Lastly, Anubis was celebrated by mourners, whose veiled troops ran around the hall with sighs and sobs. The scene of the embalming was mimed artfully, but the resurrection soon followed, with joy and laughter, and the union of faithful lovers for eternal possession.

The young women glided, twirled and pursued one another, their hands full of shredded roses and jasmine petals. After the sobs, the laughter burst forth in the joy of the renewal of tenderness, the infinity of amour promised to the elect.

However, before the temptation of that young flesh, offered in adornment and perfumes, under the magnetism of those long eyes of velvet and nacre, no desire stirred in the nostalgic soul of the young king. Only the song of Zelinis had delighted his being, and, involuntarily, his gaze sought the suave apparition of the artiste beneath the bouquet of myrtles and roses.

Zelinis was separated from the crowd, chatting to her beloved lover Hary-Thé.

"Oh," she sighed, "how good you are to want to marry me, a mere singer from the temple of Hapi."

"You are the most beautiful and adorable of creatures. You are the one I have chosen among all to share the pleasures and the pains of the terrestrial voyage."

"But you're rich, adulated, and the brilliant and glorious future offered to you might be compromised by such a modest marriage."

"Shut up," he said, pressing her to his heart. "I love you."

"You love her!" sighed Outaya, Hary-Thé's former favorite, who passed close to them. "May you never regret that imprudent speech! Your life and that of your mistress are in my hands!"

Outaya while still a child, had been bought by Hary-Thé in the great slave market of Karnak. She was an Ethiopian whose parents had been massacred in the recent conquests. She came from a small village situated between Berber and Khartoum, and knew nothing of life, in spite of her exceedingly lively intelligence and her prodigious facility of assimilation. Mysterious and disquieting, with her heavy frizzy hair, her thick lips, slightly drawn back as if in a desire to bite or kiss, her broad nostrils, her eyebrows connected by an ebony streak, and her immense dark eyes, through which wild and feline gleams passed, she had charmed the officer.[1]

Her slim waist swayed over her hips, her proud breasts already protruded, although she was only ten years old. Immediately, the young man had made her his mistress, and she had loved him with all the ardor of her virgin flesh and all the fervor of her savage nature. He was like a part of herself, and she shivered with anguish at the thought of losing him.

"Be careful!" she repeated.

The young man frowned. "What are you daring to say?"

Outaya fixed her strange gaze on the man she loved wildly. "I'm only a humble slave, docile to the will of a man, and you know very well that what I say has no importance . . ." An ironic smile creased her lips, but Hary-Thé paid no heed to it, and, turning away from her insouciantly, he squeezed Zelinis' little hand more tenderly.

"Forget that woman's threats," he said. "What do you have to fear, since you possess all my tenderness?"

---

1 The reader might assume from this description that Outaya is black; Charles Atamian, the illustrator of the Tallandier text, certainly did. Subsequently, however, it is stated that she is not, and that her skin is pale; the author might have changed her mind, for some reason.

"Oh," she sighed, delightedly, "I feel safe against your bosom; I'm happy and desire nothing more on earth. Everything that is not your love does not exist for me. I only want to live for the pleasure of a husband and master. You know that my existence is more fragile, between your fingers, than the calyx of a flower, and that you can break it at your whim."

"Soon, my Zelinis, we'll be married, and you'll be respected by all. Even Outaya will bow down before your infinite grace. She will be the foremost of your slaves, and you can get rid of her if her conduct is not entirely submissive to your caprice. I'm giving you that woman, who was my lover. For what greater pledge of my tenderness could you be ambitious?"

"I'm not ambitious for anything, O my Master! I shall dissolve in your strength, ineffably."

While the lovers forgot themselves in their projects for the future, the young sovereign's gaze was still fixed on Zelinis with an infinite sadness, and it was in vain that his wife and sister Atasu ordered further celebrations, in order to please him, and figured in a ballet on a throne of flowers borne by twelve virgins clad in veils woven with gold.

The young queen raised her brunette head, circled by the sacred Uraeus, in a challenging manner, and her royal mantle, covered in diamonds, trailed behind the flowery throne like the sparkling tail of a comet. A golden belt with enormous cabochons of emeralds and rubies sustained her small firm breasts with pointed nipples, crossed over her loins and descended in front, molding over her charming body a transparent fabric spangled with precious stones. Ivory sheaths lined with down and encrusted with turquoises shod her delicate feet.

She was not jealous of Thutmose, who had shared her games, and whom she could not consider yet as anything but a child. However, she tested the darts of her coquetry on him, curious to see the expansion of the masculine strength that she did not know as yet.

The king was at the age of dreams misted with melancholy, of vague desires and fugitive chimeras with rapid wings. He was still ignorant, pursuing a bizarre ideal of superhuman beauty and morbid tenderness. The priests had made a troubled adolescent of him, pale and timid, blasé before the initiation, disdainful of joys that he had not savored.

His childhood had been spent in temples darkened by fear, spells and curses. Over the black veil of his terror passed indistinct forms clad in white: long processions of phantoms clinging to corners full of shadow, vanishing as they had come. Any voice whispering nearby filled him with anguish, while a dolorous sensuality impelled him to plunge further into his dream. He had ended up searching therein for the strange spasm of his heart, quivering in his breast like a different being awakening in the depths of his self.

The impoverished race of Pharaohs, which no new element invigorated, seemed likely to become extinct with the little prince with the nostalgic gaze. Only music made him shiver with pleasure. It was, for him, a bewitchment of intoxication, which soothed and attracted him, a subtle and rare phantasmagoria that transported his soul. A singular charm took hold of him, a soothing and seductive charm that he no longer resisted.

Zelinis, the priestess of the temple of Hapi, incarnated his dream suavely; she was the melodious enchantress of his solitary vigils, and he loved her for her charming voice, her eyes with the glaucous gleams of the sacred pool and the indifference that she showed toward him, while other women plunged into the adoration of his splendor.

Immobile under the royal awning, the fringes of which brushed his forehead, the pale Pharaoh remained silent, preoccupied or weary, the lover of a distant fiction of grace and beauty.

A whisper extracted him from his dream. The High Priest of the palace spoke to him in a low voice, as if ashamed of the mission he had to fulfill.

"Omnipotent Master, King of the World, a woman is imploring the grace of being heard by you."

"Who is she?" asked Thutmose, with ennui.

"She belongs to the household of Hary-Thé, the chief of the Royal Guard."

"Ah! Have her come in, then; I'm ready to hear her."

Outaya, dragging herself on her knees, kissed the Pharaoh's divine mantle. Then, without getting up—with the consequence that she remained invisible to those not surrounding the throne—she murmured: "I can give you the woman you love, O adorable Prince."

"The woman I love? But I don't love anyone."

Young Thutmose dared not interrogate his heart, however; he was afraid of understanding . . .

"The woman you love, Invincible Power of all that exists, is a singer in the temple of Hapi. I can deliver her to you, if you desire . . ."

The royal prince did not reply, but a tremor agitated his lips. After a long silence, he asked: "Do you know her intimately, then?"

"Yes, I live with her and she has no secrets from me."

"Does she love me?"

"She loves you . . . but she is not free, and it will be necessary for her to simulate death in order to belong to you."

Again, the prince meditated profoundly. That singular amour, which went as far was braving death, pleased him by its very audacity. However, he recalled that not once had the little singer's gaze fixed upon him, that he had believed her to be completely indifferent. That contrast also flattered his taste for the romantic and the strange.

"What are your orders?" murmured Outaya. "I am ready, O Splendor of the World, to obey you blindly. Dispose of your humble servant!"

The Pharaoh raised his frail hand, charged with rings, in order to dismiss the young woman.

"So be it," he said, wearily. "Deliver me Zelinis, and may the peace of the gods be with you."

III
The Spells of Harraouth

Princess Atasu was still reposing on her bed of flowers, surrounded by the sacred dancers; she was radiant at the center of the ballet, like an admirable star, and the virgins, who had carried her on their shoulders, were now shaking golden amschirs of intoxicating perfumes before her.

The High Priests of the temples of Hapi, Sebek and Anubis were standing alongside the prince, as if to protect him from excessive temptations, and when the dancers rested between figures, they sang, by turns, the praises of the gods and kings.

The immense halls, with ceiling supported by columns of marble and silver, were radiant with the fire of thousands of lamps, disposed like flowers in the bosom of translucent foliage. Perforated balustrades ran at a certain distance from the walls, isolating people of distinction from the crowd of performers. The floor under the feet of the latter was formed of a paste of glass striped with old and precious stones, illuminated by an internal fire that gave the diamantine ankle-bracelets and toe-rings a dazzling glitter.

Outaya, enveloped in her veils, had traversed the immense halls of the palace furtively, where the guards were asleep; on the terraces, domesticated lions and panthers had come to rub against her legs, and she had felt their warm breath on her hands; she had stopped, her heart hammering, to contemplate the magically-illuminated gardens in which enlaced couples were twirling to the exasperated sounds of sistra and tympani.

In the direction of the Nile, imposing edifices rose up into the transparent azure of the sky. There was a magical flight of terraces, pylons and porticos supporting hanging gardens, and obelisks covered with fateful inscriptions loomed up like arrows threatening the stars.

The wild and peppery scent of that night of amour was accentuated; the golden and coral sand of the pathways seemed to be smoking like volcanic ash. At those lascivious exhalations, Outaya's nostrils quivered, and her strong lips curled back in hateful desire.

She traversed another peristyle, decked with silk and silver draperies, and found herself in the women's apartments.

The empty harem displayed a sequence of rooms illuminated by lamps placed in niches on the edge of minuscule basins in which blue lotuses languished, and where iridescent little fish were asleep. Divans, encumbered by furs, fans and silky fabrics had light ivory tables in front of them supporting beauty creams, bottles of prestigious balms, gold and coral powders, aphrodisiac elixirs, black and red sticks, and a thousand delicate instruments for depilation, softening, polishing and rendering even more desirable all the flowers of flesh offered to the fantasy of the excessively young sovereign.

The heat was oppressive; it was one of those Egyptian nights when the air seems to be ferrying sparks, when the Nile is confounded with the earth, similarly immobile under a bloody moon. Acrid perfumes were exhaled more forcefully by the gardens, troubled waters, languid corollas, the joyful crowd and sleeping wild beasts.

Strangely anxious, her hands feverish, Outaya sometimes lifted a curtain in order to breathe more easily. Terraces succeeded one another after the chambers of amour. The moon illuminated the sad regions of the Dait, displayed on the edge of the silver fan of the shores of Arabia, which no breeze stirred, under the slender shadows of palm trees.

The young woman interrogated the area, her somber gaze charged with an even greater hatred. Around her, sacred cats were mewling at the stars, and she saw their phosphorescent eyes shining in the night like fireflies. Baboons were weeping, with almost human voices, and granite colossi and sphinxes loomed up more terribly.

On the ramparts of citadels, soldiers were coming and going; the rumor of the fête was exasperated down below, in the halls of the palace; it was the apotheosis, the supreme prayer of a people in delirium for the happiness of the Pharaohs.

Outaya resumed her uncertain course through the rooms of the gynaeceum, sometimes going astray and retracing her steps, ignorant as she was of the interior disposition of the palace.

A narrow stairway, however, took her to the gardens through an intermediate door. Innumerable torches were blazing around basins; the populace, pushing back the guards, had invaded the pathways of coral sand. Cries, songs and invocations of Mercury, the god of the Nile, rose up in all directions, and women holding their little lamps, provided with moringa oil and papyrus wicks, were demanding Atasu, the good princess.

Outaya, hiding behind clumps of mimosas and tamarinds, left the palace and went into the public square. There, fires were lit in front of colossal statues of Ammon, Thoth and Osiris for sacrifices agreeable to the gods. Semi-naked virgins with wide eyes burning with fever, were shaking amschirs charged with perfumes and intoning prayers. Outaya collected a few drops of blood from a goat sacrificed in honor of Ammon-Ra and plunged into the low quarters of the city.

She had decided to interrogate Harraouth, an initiate of the sacred Orgyes,[1] and to beg her to come to her aid. In spite of her commerce with the gods, Harraouth was not insensible to presents, so the young woman intended to offer her, in exchange for good advice, all the jewels that she was wearing. It was to the house of the prophetess and magician that young women went who were desirous of getting rid of the fruit of their sin, for she knew all the virtues of the herbs of life and death; she knew how to suppress over-demanding husbands and infidel lovers, and informed amorous women of means to make themselves loved.

---

1 This spelling of "orgies" was usually only used with reference to the cult of Orpheus, but some contemporary sources alleged that the cult in question, or analogues thereof, did exist in Egypt.

Outaya marched rapidly between the low, square houses with walls painted bright red a meter from the ground. At the height of the terraces that crowned those sordid constructions women showed themselves, their breasts naked under necklaces of turquoises and glass beads, their hair short, displayed in stiff locks around the cheeks. Under clumps of carobs, tamarisks and mimosas, couples were embracing while the shrill sounds of mum flutes overlapped.

The peel of figs and lemon was crushed underfoot; a spicy, acrid, bestial perfume gripped the nostrils: the reek of musk and corruption, withered flowers and rotten fruits, swimming in the middle of streets in black water.

Outaya stopped outside a hut daubed with symbolic figures under the protection of a gilded phallus.

The Ethiopian, in her narrow and scintillating gauze sheath, shivered from head to toe; the pearls of her necklaces, clasps and amulets rattled over her breasts and hips. Precipitately, she seized a cornelian fetish that hung down over her cleavage and kissed it feverishly; then she rapped on the prophetess' door with her index finger.

Harraouth, enveloped in the fateful veil of a magicienne, appeared on the threshold.

"I was expecting you," she said, simply. "Come in, and may the god Sebek protect you."

"Salutations, priestess of the sacred Orgyes."

"I know what brings you here, for we're in the month of Thoth and I've consulted the star Sothis in order to know the destiny of Thebes. You're watching over the amours of the hereditary prince, and you also want to slake your vengeance."

Outaya knelt down before Harraouth, her arms forming a cross. "By the gods of Good and Evil, what you say is true. I await from you the philter that will fulfill the Pharaoh's desire and deliver me from a rival . . ." In a low voice, she added: "What I want above all, as you well know, is the amour of Hary-Thé."

Harraouth had prostrated herself before a kind of altar on which incense and aromatics were burning, as well as Kyphi, a paste from the land of Punt composed of sixteen perfumes agreeable to the gods. She pronounced vague incantations and struck her breast violently.

Flames sprang forth from sacred vases all the way to the roof of the building, becoming entangled, like a golden fleece.

A red heart sustained by flamboyant sheaves appeared above the altar, and the priestess pricked it with the point of a fetish in the form of a dagger, which the Ethiopian wore between her breasts.

Drops of blood flowed in abundance, while a sort of groan escaped from the wounded viscera, rising and falling slowly, like an agonized plaint.

Harraouth showed Outaya the reddened fetish.

"This blood," she said, "is that of the Pharaoh. It will madden the heart of Zelinis. And here is the poison that will plunge your rival into an invincible and durable sleep." Swiftly, she dipped the silver point into a viscous brown liquid with a bitter scent.

"When Hary-Thé and his lover are asleep in one another's arms, you will approach softly, like a cat stalking a prey. You will glide through the shadow, invisible and silent, reach the lovers' couch, and prick Zelinis without troubling her repose."

"I'll prick her," murmured Outaya, breathlessly. "But what if she wakes up?"

"She won't wake up," Harraouth continued, with a sinister laugh, "and when her master wants to hug her in his arms, he'll only embrace an inert and cold body presenting all the appearances of death."

"Death! I don't want to kill her!"

"Wait . . . Zelinis won't die, and you'll have her taken to the house of Thutmose, while a slave of the same stature and appearance as the singer takes her place in the crypt of the embalmer priests. The Colchites and the Taricheutes will plunge the body into the natron, making a precious mummy of it, of which Hary-Thé will cherish the vain appearance."

"And Zelinis?"

"Zelinis will cause the soul of Thutmose to flourish; she will be his companion of election, and we will have accomplished the finest of good deeds!"

Outaya, however, remained pensive. "And you swear to me, Harraouth, that my action won't displease the man I love?"

"No, because he won't know about your crime."

"Might he, once again, accept my tenderness?"

"That depends on you."

"Oh, then I'm joyful and reassured, for my amour is as profound as the sea and as resplendent as starry Nut. Give it to me, quickly."

She put the weapon of life and death in her bosom and gave the prophetess her necklaces, her bracelets and her rings.

"I'm leaving, Harraouth. May the gods be with you."

The priestess of the sacred Orgyes, standing on the threshold of her dwelling, followed Outaya's progress along the muddy road with a somber gaze.

"Ah!" she murmured. "The folly of loving dooms women eternally, but it enriches sorcerers and priests. One lover more in the arms of a Pharaoh won't change the face of the world, and the amour that one pursues always slips away!"

IV
The Royal Couch

From the height of his throne, fulgurant with gold, ivory and nacre, under the sumptuous awning fringed with emeralds and rubies, Thutmose was dreaming, while the last figures of the ballet unfurled. Egyptian geese depicted in translucent enamel extended fantastic wings over him, and semi-naked women, moist under their networks of pearls, drew closer and closer, offering their beauty in flower.

"My royal spouse doesn't see me," said Atasu, laughing. "He isn't thinking about his wedding night, and nothing that makes the happiness of other men can move him. Is it necessary, O Master of the World, that the occult initiation of things comes to you in your sleep?"

She did not raise her voice, in order that only her brother would hear her, but the prince, his gaze lost in the mystical profundities of the dream he was pursuing, did not appear to understand.

"Ah!" murmured Atasu, chagrined. "You're still only a child; I'll initiate you in spite of yourself, and tomorrow, you'll no longer be ignorant of the joy of loving."

She uttered a final, slightly ironic, burst of laughter, which died away in thin notes and broke like light crystal; then, surrendering herself to her women, she quit the hall of festivities.

Sovereigns did not attend the banquet that followed their wedding, so Thutmose drew away from the sumptuous tables around which slaves were already hastening.

Zelenis, the little singer, was about to depart, abandoning her lover Hary-Thé, who could not quit the palace before the end of the meal. Seductive and anxious, she did not hurry, multiplying recommendations, imploring a final kiss from the man who was everything to her, and whom she never wanted to quit.

"Hurry," she begged. "Is there a torture comparable to that of waiting? I'll torment myself cruelly, while you'll forget me in your unconscious intoxication."

But he reassured her. "Have no fear, my adored, nothing will be able to retain me when you're far from me. I'll see you again soon, and our kisses will be all the sweeter after this short absence."

"I'm afraid, my love!"

"Afraid of what?"

"Everything and nothing. Outaya hates me!"

"She wouldn't dare attack that which makes my happiness and my life. In any case, if the woman importunes you, I'll get rid of her."

Zelinis pressed her lover more tightly against her bosom.

"I don't wish her any harm, but her gaze troubles me frightfully. She loves you, Hary-Thé. One last kiss, and I'll run away!"

They were in the garden, and Thutmose, immobile behind a column, watched them with his heart hammering. Was that envy, anger or desire? He could not have said. He had never experienced anything similar, and it appeared to him that before this cruel night he had not lived.

In her royal apartments, Atasu had abandoned herself to the hands of her women, who were adorning her for the great mystery, the initiation to the only human joys.

Delicately, the expert fingers of the servants ran over the charming body of the sovereign, strewing it with gold powder, marking, with a thin streak of azure, the delicate veins of the breasts, which they crowned with the double flower of a little carmine paint.

Lying back on the cushions, Atasu laughed like a little girl, amused by the tickling of the skillful little hands, while a table laden with choice dishes was brought closer. There were shells of jellied fish, strongly aromatized cooked meats, pastes of fruits and flowers, iced preserves and wines with reflections of precious stones in sculpted ewers of the same hue. There were green liquids with shades of chrysoberyl, peridot and olivine, and roseate liquids of amaldine, uvarovite and cymophane, sprarkling in cups, rising to the head in a swirl of flame.

Atasu drank the wine of amour, and her eyes gleamed strangely while she concluded her voluptuous toilette. Beside her was spread her robe of silver mesh dotted with pearls, under the weight of the enormous diamantine scarab that had fastened it to her shoulder a little while before. The sacred Uraeus from her forehead lay among the clasps, bracelets and rings, and, with a joyful kick, she had sent her little ivory slipper to the other side of the room, where it broke into three pieces.

Into her thick and rebellious hair, like a bush of darkness, the slaves had slid rose petals, and a light crown knotted around her temples replaced the hieratic symbol.

Among the ewers of aphrodisiac liquids, the essences were revealed of myrrh and oliban, mystical effluences, extracts of lemon, cloves, camphor and cassia, bitter and vehement, waters of spikenard, sandalwood, neroli, vanilla and tuberose, with voluptuous fragrances. Pots were accumulated containing bright lacquers, inks the color of dragonflies' wings and cantharides, and various creams, serkis, emulsions and lotions. And a hundred instruments in nacre and gold were glinting on tablets: forceps, scissors, strigils, stamps, tufts, crepons and files.

The toilette of a high-ranking woman lasted two hours every morning, and her bath, in the milk of almond, aveline and rose-water, was the most exquisite period of feminine life.

Atasu, a great flower saturated with perfumes, allowed herself to be carried to the royal bed, laughing and slightly drunk on vehement liquors. Everything was spinning delightfully before her eyes: the bas-reliefs on the walls, the pillars circled with gold and silver, the minuscule water jets that refreshed the air at intervals, and the large crouching sphinxes that guarded the four corners of the bed.

Negresses with hair braided with coral and turquoises fanned her gently, and the breeze of the flabella caused the pearly fringes of the royal awning, crowned by a golden goose with spread wings, to undulate.

Perfumes crackled in amschirs, while a rain of petals began to fall from the ceiling.

Between the great silver sphinxes, which stood to her right and her left, Atasu raised herself up on the royal couch, awaiting the advent of her royal husband.

Naked beneath a network of peals with cabochons of sapphires, she had spread her perfumed hair, mingled with diamantine powder, over her shoulders. Streaks of antimony further enlarged her admirable eyes; touches of carmine emphasized her delicately rounded lips and the narrow openings of her nostrils.

She resembled her brother somewhat; he possessed the same pure and elongated profile, the same blazing eyes and the same charming mouth, swollen and puerile. They were the same height, with slender, harmonious limbs, a relaxed and proud gait, and a broad sentiment of domination. The fraternal couple seemed made to reign, for beauty is the true conqueror of the world: invincible, like every divine gift, supernatural, mysterious and disquieting.

The women had withdrawn behind the curtains and had commenced the voluptuous chorus. Only the voice of Zelinis was missing from that soft, languid concert, seemingly coming from somewhere beyond terrestrial sensations.

Her eyelids closed, Atasu waited without impatience, knowing that it would be necessary for her to vanquish fraternal timidities, to become the passionate lover after having been the turbulent, malicious, sometimes slightly cruel little sister.

The dainty princess was not astonished at having to initiate the little boy that had lived alongside her, had shared her games and felt the same august blood flowing in his veins. All the Pharaohs married thus; sometimes mothers even married their sons in order that no strange principle would come to disturb their illustrious descendancy.

Atasu had placed her slender hands behind her nape, causing the curt tip of her breasts to protrude; a slight smile parted her lips; she was confident and she was happy.

"My Brother, my King, my Very Beloved," she said, when the young prince appeared under the gold and silver drapery sustained by a eunuch, "I am your faithful subject!"

"My Sister, my Wife, my Queen, I am the most fervent of your slaves."

She recoiled on the huge bed, encumbered by cushions, furs, and sparkling and precious gauzes. He slid next to her, and immediately she made him a necklace with her supple arms, drew him against her heart in the light of little lamps in the form of pink lotuses that ran everywhere amid the foliage and flowers.

He was trembling slightly, because, in spite of the gynaeceum that he had already possessed for several years, no woman had yet brushed his flesh. At the contact of the firm, soft skin, and the small hard breasts erect against his chest, he almost fainted, but authoritative lips stifled in his mouth the anguished exclamation of his ignorance.

More forcefully, Atasu held him against her.

"Don't you want, O Radiance of the Sun and the Stars, to know the supreme felicity of lovers who give themselves to one another? Don't you see the more ardent gleam in my gaze, which is seeking yours? Don't you hear the more emotional intonation of my voice, which speaks of amour? And don't you feel my kisses penetrating you with an indescribable ecstasy? I am the woman who loves and wants to give the joy of loving. I am the woman whose embrace causes the sadness and suffering of life to be forgotten. I am the dispenser of human and divine sensualities. I am your lover, and through us, the royal race will continue, for its greater glory and the happiness of the world!"

Thutmose, held tight against Atasu, did not respond, but the ardent speech descended within him, and he allowed himself to be caressed ineffably.

The princess went on: "To conquer you, O my Master, I shall find new kisses, new embraces, irresistible words that will throw you, swooning, against me. Do you not love me as I love you?"

And the ensorcelling music resumed, more irritating, gripping the nerves and shaking them vertiginously.

"*I give myself, frail and burning . . . like the embalmed breeze . . . on the wings of starry Nut . . . I am dying of unslaked amour!*

"*I give myself frail and burning!*

"*Take me, my beloved Master . . . as the bee takes the flower . . . I am the rose with the lascivious heart . . . who wants to imprison the sting!*

"*Take me, my beloved Master!*"

The broken rhythms sounded like sobs during the possession. There were morbid stretchings and wild surges, caresses of fingernails on fine and silkily grating skin, bites and burns. The emotion of extraordinary ardor contracted throats, and then the voices descended, like a corrosive liquid, all the way to the torn and hoarse notes of unbridled passion.

"Take me, my beloved Master!"

And it was Atasu, the expert virgin, who educated the timorous lover in the lascivious secrets at which her intuitive nature of a beautiful lover marveled. The words hardly mattered, for the inflamed notes of the canticle slid effortlessly, penetrating the utmost profundities of being.

Thutmose experienced an unsuspected ardor while his heartbeat accelerated forcefully. He experienced the vivacity of his sensations, the extraordinary emotion in which he found himself . . .

By means of gentle pressures, rapid frictions and more profound kisses, Atasu guided his inexperience, exciting his desire and suppressing the rebellions of his juvenile timidity.

He remained a stranger to everything that was not that young flesh quivering against his own, and burned to prove to her in a precise fashion that he was no longer the child of yesterday, the melancholy and feeble child, but a man avid for possession, a male like the others.

And she sighed: "Ah! You finally understand me! Your body is stirring under my kisses. I sense your desire vibrating in unison with mine, and I divine the confessions that you'd like to make to me . . . no, stay like this, forget yourself in my being, divinely, and let everything that is not the supreme felicity of the moment sink into darkness!

"Take me, my beloved Master!"

She had enlaced his slim legs with hers, retaining them recklessly.

Atasu was no longer talking, but, behind the high curtains, the nerves of the choir of women jangled to the chords of psalterions and lyres, their voices exasperated all the way to the final outpouring of the glorious hymn . . .

V

The People Are Satisfied

In the banqueting hall, the laughter was now flowing without constraint. Through the large bays open over the gardens, porticos could be seen lined up above illuminated and florid terraces. At intervals, in the golden and coral sand of the pathways, basins illuminated by large lotuses of pink and blue glass made their singing jets of water spring forth. The palm trees, mimosas and tamarisks formed discreet arbors where couples went astray amid the alarm of monkeys and squirrels disturbed in their sleep.

Felines with metallic eyes followed the amorous frolics; they sometimes drew nearer, purring an arching their backs, in a vague desire for caresses.

The officers that Hary-Thé commanded were drinking and laughing with the princes and aristocrats of the realm. The scribes were keeping somewhat apart. Outside, orators were haranguing the crowd, which was rather turbulent, for Thutmose and Atasu, in accordance with custom, had to show themselves after the initiation.

Spiced wines were circulating in precious ewers, tables were covered in amber, silver and jade trays bearing golden jellies, red mincemeat, huge fish swimming in thick sauces, birds in their plumage seemingly ready to fly away, glazed fruits, insects cooked in honey and vinegar, fritters, pâtés of acacia or roses. Sheets of hyssus cotton traversed by flowery garlands bore a thousand delicacies in milk or snow, meatballs rolled in spices, whose vehement taste would produce an invincible thirst.

And to the resonance of tympanons there were invocations of Ammon, the lord of eternity, to Ptah, to Thoth, to the particular triads of Nomes. The sphinxes on the edges of temples crouched in eternal mystery, the sacred ibises perched on one foot, the baboons, the wild beasts and the reptiles also seemed to be animated by a particular intoxication.

Egypt quivered, monumental and somber, with its obelisks, its pyramids, and its labyrinth. The heavy pylons, bearing globes of the Earth at their summit between two wings, guarded the entry to temples less jealously; the avenues populated by monsters on the borders of tombs conveyed a new life. Arranged along the walls, the dead, in their gilded and painted coffins, were certainly not insensible to the union of little prince Thutmose with his sister Atasu.

The frightful monuments of the valley of the Nile were filled with the hope of the people. Divine fire was translated there by grandiose symbols, by admirable forms of a unique and creative genius that radiated in the mystery of hypogea and in the fervor of sanctuaries.

Simultaneously gigantic and disconcerting, Egyptian endeavor expanded in the amour of a child-king and an exquisite princess with long eyes of nacre and velvet.

But the solemn hour has sounded. Here come the High Priests in linen mantles, carrying a mystical gondola ornamented with flowers, shaking a red-tinted veil. They display it on the terrace of the august chamber; the people acclaim them frenetically, and then demand the newlyweds again.

Mute, holding one another by the hand, the royal children, still shivering from kisses and hugs, finally appear, while triumphant prayers of thanks rise up and women embrace one another, weeping.

Hary-Thé had quietly risen to his feet in order to make his way to the entrance to the gardens. The crowd, recognizing the chief of the Royal Guard, parted before him, and he drew away avidly, praying to the goddess Hathor, queen of light, beauty and amour, to be favorable to him.

But a shadow was always elongated to his left, which was a sign of death, and he shivered in anguish for tomorrow, all the way to his heart.

Death, however, did not present itself to his mind with its cortege of dolor and fear. Like all men of his caste he was scornful of life. The inert mummy, stiff under its bandages, with the fixity of its enamel gaze in its golden mask, did not awaken any repulsion in him. He loved the solemnity of sarcophagi, the mystery of stone chambers in which the souls of the dead sleep.

All Egyptian architecture, in any case, in the image of human thought, only inspires a funereal dream. Pyramids, obelisks, pylons and immense columns represent a vague human form: that of the corpse wrapped in bandages. The Egyptian only thinks about the resurrection and only labors for eternity.

Thus, Hary-Thé was not anxious about the fatal presage; what he feared was separation, the departure of a beloved being for a distant country. And he trembled more forcefully in thinking that Zelinis, during his absence, might have run some danger, that her frail existence might have vanished like the final vibration of a crystal flute.

He was running now through the dark streets, bumping into rare passers-by, who examined him suspiciously, thinking that they were seeing a madman.

In front of a building higher than the others, painted bright red and ocher, he stopped, out of breath. A slave, who was watching out for him, immediately presented himself, with a torch in his hand, and guided him through the corridors to Zelinis' chamber.

On the threshold, Hary-Thé tottered, but two arms were already making him a necklace of sensuality, while burning lips were posed on his own.

VI
The Joy of the Kiss

"Finally! I was dying of impatience!"

"Oh, Zelinis, I made a journey at a run in order to see you again more rapidly. No danger has threatened you?"

"No," she said, smiling. "The house is silent. Outaya and the slaves must have been asleep for some time."

He uttered a long sigh of deliverance, and hugged the young woman to his breast recklessly.

"Today, alone, I've sensed how much I love you."

"And me, I believe that I can't love you any more. The human heart would break of too much love! In any case, when you're not there, everything becomes blurred and obscured, all of nature is in mourning!"

Hary-Thé imprisoned Zelinis' waist; she arched her back under the embrace, and stiffened herself against her lover's tumultuous breast. He drew her toward the cushions of a very low bed that occupied the center of the room, and their kiss sang softly, like the cooing of doves.

In the quivering of silks and gauzes, their nerves vibrated divinely. They were not the hasty lovers of an evening of desire but the fervent devotees of an almost divine cult, those who, knowing one another already, savor love in all its plentitude, delectably.

Zelinis, the little singer of the temple of Hapi, without asking for anything, had given herself to the officer, and he, in the dread of one day losing the one who, henceforth, was everything in his life, had resolved to take her for a wife.

What other, in any case, was more worthy of that choice? What other could have responded more closely to the mysterious ideal that he had created? Hary-Thé did not think that he had anything serious to fear from the rancor of Outaya, and he promised himself to get rid of the Ethiopian soon, the sight of whom now importuned him.

"Little Zelinis, you know kisses sweeter than honey! Under my lips your red-tipped breasts stand forth, quivering, and you are reborn more beautiful with every caress!"

And Zelinis, swooning, murmured: "I would, like, Master of my days, to repeat the words that fly from your mouth like moths of flame! I would like, O my Adored, to have your eloquence, in order to express my happiness to you. But perhaps my ecstasy speaks to you more passionately than I could do with well-turned phrases . . ."

"Yes, don't say anything, remain thus, like a pale idol under the lips of kneeling devotees. I want to animate your slender arms, shoulders and breasts; after the divine frisson. I want to inform you of other frissons, until the amorous annihilation into which we are both sinking deliciously."

For a long time still, Hary-Thé strung for his lover the golden pearls of his amorous science; then, finally, their eyelids veiled the intoxication of the dream, and they went to sleep in one another's arms, perhaps pursuing beyond the real world the sweetness of embraces and kisses . . .

Outaya, who had been hidden behind a curtain, waiting for the lovers to go to sleep, slid all the way to the couch ransacked by their intoxications and, faint with hatred, contemplated her rival.

Zelinis, her lips parted by a happy smile, was leaning on Hary-Thé's breast and resting tenderly against the heart that only beat for her. A papyrus wick in an opaline bowl illuminated the faces of the sleepers, rendered even more charming by a voluptuous fatigue. They were still smiling, confident in the amour that protects sincere lovers, drunk on embraces and caresses, worn out, blissful beyond human strength.

Outaya searched Zelinis' body for the place of her revenge. It would be sufficient to prick her lightly, the prophetess had said, and the poison would do its work invincibly.

Into the firm and polished bulb of the young woman's breast the trembling former slave plunged the point of the fetish. Zelinis immediately opened her eyes, shuddered, uttered a profound sigh and became motionless, almost as if the blood had suddenly been withdrawn from her veins.

Hary-Thé, overwhelmed by a voluptuous fatigue, had not budged. Everything was thus accomplished as Harraouth had predicted, and the criminal was amazed by such a complete success.

The little singer, her nostrils pinched and her eyeballs seeming suddenly having withdrawn into the depths of their orbits, had all the appearances of death. Gradually, her flesh was chilled and her limbs lost their suppleness.

Crouching at the foot of the bed, Outaya followed the effects of the poison anxiously running a tremulous hand over the delicate body of the young woman.

Silence enveloped people and things; only the regular respiration of Hary-Thé revealed an existence in the funereal calm of the room. Dead forever were the passionate exaltations and the bounding impetuosities, dead the intoxications that racked the nerves, elevated beings and transporting them to a mysterious paradise! The voice of the adored woman would never make her lover shiver to the bone again, would no longer fill his soul with an infinity of suddenly-revealed joys. He still retained on his lips the perfume of exquisite and troubling kisses; nervous tears rose to his eyes in the continued ecstasy of sleep.

Collapsed beside the couch, Outaya listened to the laments of her conscience, a sob that dug into her entrails, something like a departure beneath a stormy sky. She had thought that the death would be less rapid; the devastating effect of the poison plunged her into a kind of terror. She was overwhelmed by bitterness and regret, felt abandoned, floored by distress, the surprising intensity of which excluded any consolation, any pity and any repose.

What would Hary-Thé say when he awoke?

Already she could hear his cries of despair and revolt. Would he ever be able to forget the crime committed? The crime? There could be no question of that, since no criminal trace appeared on Zelinis' body. Hary-Thé, like everyone else would believe it a natural death, a death doubtless occasioned by an excess of pleasure—a folly of amour pushed as far as a mortal spasm, the human organism being unable to support certain paroxysms.

Those reflections did not calm Outaya, whom a morbid anxiety rendered immobile next to the large bed. She ended up by abandoning herself to the flow, carried away by the torrent of anguish that submerged her mind, and the clappers of bells seemed to be hammering her temples dolorously.

But the house began to wake up; slaves were coming and going in the garden. The young woman rose to her feet, painfully, and went back to the apartment reserved for her. Her ears attentive, she listened then to all the familiar sounds, waiting for the lover's wild cry, the frightful plaint of the wounded animal that would soon resound in the chamber of amour.

Her fingernails digging into the palms of her hands, she was breathing deeply, and her heart was rising tumultuously, as if it wanted to break through the partition of her flesh.

The hours passed, and the torture of the wait became intolerable. On the tips of her bare feet, she retracted her route, had the strength to raise the curtain that veiled the voluptuous retreat, and dared to look in.

VII
The Death of Amour

Hary-Thé was weeping recklessly on the edge of the bed.

At first, on feeling the icy body of his mistress beside him, he had thought that he was still asleep, unconsciously pursuing a frightful nightmare. He had palpated the cold flesh and the rigid limbs with a sort of incredulous curiosity . . .

Certainly, he was dreaming dolorously, and reality would soon surge forth from the anguishing mists, with its joy of amour, its hope of happiness son realized. Zelinis, the tender lover, was about to open her somber pupils and extend the vermilion fruit of her lips to him . . . He was once again about to know the savor of the delicious kiss, and draw from that morning communion the energy necessary for the quotidian labor.

"Zelinis," he murmured, in a whisper, "don't continue this game, which is frightening me. Quickly, smile at me, speak to me, tell me that you love me and that your first thought belongs to me . . . Zelinis . . ."

Several times, he repeated his lover's name, still wanting to doubt, and perhaps, prolonging his error in the fear of a real misfortune.

Cruelly, he bit his arm. But no, he was no longer asleep; he was really conscious and alive, alive beside his dead mistress.

The emotion was so great that he did not even have the strength to proclaim his grief and raise the alarm. Like a feeble child he fell down at the foot of the bed and wept in long sobs. He closed his eyes in order no longer to perceive the strangely fixed pupils of the corpse. But even through his closed eyelids he sensed the gaze of that supreme distress searching his soul, and, very quietly, like something inevitable, a logical consequence of his pain, he searched for something that could give him death in his turn.

Outaya understood his desire.

"Master . . ." she said, letting the curtain fall behind her.

"You were there? You were watching us?"

A frightful suspicion had just traversed the young man's mind. Brutally, he seized the woman's wrist and twisted it.

Stifling a dolorous cry, she spoke, in a hoarse but assured voice. "What has happened, Master? Why is Zelinis there, motionless, when she fills the house every morning with her joyful songs and adorns herself in order to please you?"

"Zelinis is dead," he said, abruptly, "and perhaps you know the cause of her death?"

"Me?" Heroically, she sustained the gaze of her former lover.

In a halting voice, he went on: "What other would have been able to conceive such an abominable crime? Were you not jealous of my mistress, and did you not desire to prevent our imminent union?"

Outaya sensed that her happiness, her future and her life were at stake; she made a superhuman effort and pronounced, in a low but calm voice: "By the gods that judge me, by the sun and the dead that we venerate, I swear that I do not merit these accusations. In any case, if I had struck Zelinis, her body would bear the wounds. The traces of a poison would be discovered as easily by the physicians and the embalmer priests. But you haven't quit your mistress; when could I have accomplished my crime?"

"That's true. When I found her, after returning from the palace, she was happy and well."

"You see?"

"Her amour was affirmed in all its plenitude. Never had she loved me as much!"

Outaya shuddered, her eyes clouded. "Oh!" she said, her throat tight and her voice hateful. "She died of the excess of her intoxication. Her heart broke, as a fragile vase breaks under the action of fire. She was unable to support the ardor of her sensations. It's your passion that has killed her!"

Hary-Thé, plunged in his dolor, made no further reply.

Meanwhile, the news spread through the house.

After having washed and perfumed the dead woman, the women covered their heads with thick veils, folded the upper parts of their robes to the waist, and, bare-breasted and beating their chests, they went through the streets of Thebes proclaiming the Master's chagrin. They implored the aid of public prayers for the deceased before confiding her to the embalmer priests.

The mourners uttered moans as they went, and the passersby gazed at the slaves with interest, whose folded sayons were overflowing with religious offerings.

"It's Zelinis who is dead!"

"Zelinis, the little dancer of the temple of Hapi!"

"Her master will give her a fine funeral."

"May her soul be glorious in the divine abode!"

The tears shed were only a testimony of sympathy for Hary-Thé, a mark of respect accorded to the woman who, by virtue of her omnipotent grace, had sown a little joy around her. Veritable grief was excluded from those demonstrations because for the Egyptians, the passage from life to death did not awaken any terror. The confident imagination of that people ornamented with flowers, perfumes and dreams the frightful mystery of the tomb. The mummies, with enamel eyes, golden masks and embalmed bodies swathed in bandages, often remained among the living; they were visited, they were consulted and grave decisions were made in their presence.

Does one not still see, on the ancient monuments, admirably conserved, funerary bas-reliefs that have nothing sinister about them? The paintings of crypts represent worldly receptions, dances, games and a hundred subjects of rejoicing. Around well-served tables, women bring the attractions of their grace and their beauty, for, in Egypt, everywhere that men are found, their companions are found. Couples profoundly united by marriage traversed life without ever being apart. And always, the idea of the end was placidly associated with thoughts and actions.

Independently of the bas-reliefs and paintings that ornament-ed sepulchral chambers, one saw wooden dolls there, sumptu-ously adorned, representing the wife of the deceased. They held amphorae and caskets laden with presents, sailed in precious gondolas to transport the mummy to the abode of eternal felic-ity. A few boats ornamented with baldaquins had already received the much-desired passenger, and the oarsmen were preparing to conduct him to the Amenti, traversing the lake of darkness.

The sarcophagi contained the deceased's favorite trinkets: golden caskets decorated with gems, ivory and jade figurines, pastes of rose and acacia and aromatics in sculpted bottles. A few mummies conserved writing equipment and tablets within arm's reach, with a verse from the *Book of the Dead* containing a prayer to Thoth, the god of writing.

And before the glorious dead man, Set's serpent Aker,[1] the demonic temptation of ancient beliefs, fled.

---

1 The author might be misremembering a passage from Madame Blavatsky's *Secret Doctrine*, which reports the myth that Set's evil serpent, named Apap [more often rendered Apep or Apophis], was slain by the chthonic deity Aker. However, the Egyptologist Karl Lepsius had previously referred to Aker as a serpent, even though he is more often represented as a pair of lions serving as guardians, so there was room for confusion.

Every Egyptian sepulcher had an exterior chapel, and the Pyramids possessed sumptuous temples in which the family gathered on certain anniversaries. Sphinxes, in their fateful pose, watched over the defunct. They expressed the four symbols of existence: knowledge, will, daring and discretion. They showed themselves, disquieting and proud, along desolate avenues, with the heads and breasts of a woman, the body of a bull and the claws of a lion.

But the deceased knew what they had to say on presenting themselves at the tribunal of Osiris, because they had been preparing themselves for death throughout their life.

"In the feasts held in the house of the rich," says Herodotus, "after the meal, people carried a coffin around the room, with a wooden face so expertly carved and painted that it appeared to represent the dead man perfectly; it was only a cubit long, or two at the most. It was shown to all the guests in turn, saying to them; 'Cast your eyes upon this man; you will resemble him after death, so drink now and amuse yourself!'"

VIII
The Voluptuous Rose

Hary-Thé, however, mourned his beautiful dream of amour, so quickly vanished, and he threw perfumes and flowers over the remains of his lover. It was necessary to restrain him forcibly in order to permit the embalmers to take the body of Zelinis away.

Outaya had slipped into the crowd of mourners and priests, intent on stopping the sinister work, for the little singer was undoubtedly going to wake up from her lethargy, and it was important to put her in a safe place.

The Taricheutes were to receive the deceased first; it was, therefore, on the guardian of the "waiting room" that it was necessary to act.

The former slave penetrated into the crypt where dead people of quality were preserved, in order that the embalmers did not attempt to outrage those whose beauty still awoke desires.

It was a long room, with a low ceiling, containing a large number of slabs on which women lay, covered in their veils and jewels.

Zelinis was deposited on a bed of rose petals, with a small cushion embroidered with pearls beneath her head. In that funereal assembly she was like a freshly-cut lily in the midst of a flower-bed of somber immortelles. Under the action of the atmosphere, her face had recovered the colors of life, and Outaya contemplated her, shivering, fearing an abrupt reawakening, so she decided to speak to the Taricheute guardian immediately.

"Venerated," she murmured, as soon as the crowd of guests and mourners had disperses, "I have a great secret to tell you, and I am putting my fate in your hands."

The man, accustomed to such speeches, did not blink. "I'm listening," he said.

"This woman is only asleep."

"I suspected as much, for her skin is warm, and her eyeballs still moist. Her lips will soon open to inhale a new life. What do you want me to do, then? Is it a crime that you desire?"

"Oh, no, Venerated! On the contrary, I want this flower of amour to open herself to the kisses of a glorious existence. I want to deliver her to the Pharaoh, who loves her . . ."

"And it's on his behalf that you've come to see me?"

"It's on his behalf . . . Except," she added, "I need another corpse."

"I can't dispose of the bodies that are confided to me . . ."

She trembled. "You can't dispose of those that will be reclaimed, but it's easy for you to choose among the host of other dead women."

The priest shook his head. "No," he said, "I dare not commit such a sacrilege."

"Who would know?"

"My conscience."

"I have jewels, precious objects, weapons, caskets, cups, statuettes . . ."

"What will you do with another mummy?"

"I'll give it to Hary-Thé, the chief of the Royal Guard."

"This young woman was perhaps his fiancée?"

"Yes, holy man, and it's necessary that he doesn't suspect that she's alive."

"I understand."

"You'll save me, won't you? Remember that I'm obeying an order from Prince Thutmose, and that a refusal would be ruinous for you. What are you risking, since the secret would remain between us eternally? Take me into the room of the people, and we'll choose among the other dead a young woman similar to this one."

"Look," said the Taricheute.

On the marble couch, Zelinis had made a movement. Outaya uttered a cry.

"It's necessary that she doesn't wake up!"

"Then take charge of having her transported to a safe place, and for the rest, rely on my zeal."

Two men were waiting outside. They wrapped the young woman in her veils and laid her in the bottom of a flower-basket. Guided by Outaya, the little troop set forth, balancing the immense sheaf on their shoulders, the corollas of which sometimes shed heir petals, letting an ardent perfumed rain fall on the passers-by.

Curious women, shaking the bracelets on their arms and ankles, ran behind the porters, begging them to give them a rose or a carnation; children gamboled around the gallant trophy, trying to leap up as far as the most accessible flowers.

Zelinis, a rose of amour in the midst of the roses, traversed the city swayed by the arms of the slaves, and slowly, the blood began to flow in her arteries again.

The sun was shining almost at the zenith, pouring its perpendicular rays into the valley of the Nile. In that blaze, the immense works carried out by the recent Pharaohs were affirmed in all their splendor. Temples with multiple columns displayed the finesse of their bas-reliefs and the majesty of their enormous walls. Under the porticos priests were lining up wicks of dried papyrus steeped in vases filled with moringa oil. The faithful would light their lamps there at the evening offices, for the processions before the venerated statues of the gods.

To the right and the left there was an agglomeration of narrow side-streets, whose houses seemed to lean over at the top as a welcoming salutation. Streamers floated from one window to another, brightly colored rags that attenuated the dazzling blue of the sky.

Sometimes, the porters paused to rest under the clumps of tamarisks and mimosas, and Outaya, parting the flowers in the basket, gazed at Zelinis, whose lips were parted in an unconscious smile.

At the entrance to the prostitutes' quarter, five whores were absolutely determined to ransack the basket. They suspended themselves from the porters' arms, stifling their insults beneath kisses, and the men, laughing, ended up giving them flowers in order to have peace.

They reached the palace, a superb city-within-the-city surrounded by broad and deep canals. A wall of granite formed a majestic quadrilateral behind the bridges, and the central gate was flanked by four pink marble obelisks.

On the platform of the walls, which were terminated by high towers, sentinels patrolled day and night, and the loud sound of the sambuca signaled their renewal at regular hours. Sistra and tympani announced the various phases of the interior life; soldiers clad in leopard-skin barred the main door.

The King's personal guard was composed of two thousand men, changed every year. The soldiers in question, like those outside, were divided into two groups, the calasiries and the hermotybies. It was not permitted to them to exercise any other métier than the one that retained them captive in the palace. The army was composed of infantry and very few cavalry, but in that era, men only fought in chariots armed for war. The invincible phalanges of the infantry were provided with spears and heavy shields. Under Thutmose I, the Egyptian warriors already constituted a powerful mass, whose helmets, breastplates, bucklers, spears, swords, javelins, bows, clubs and slings were displayed in a bellicose fashion under the blazing sun.

Before the royal regiment, the insignia of its chief, Hary-Thé, was carried at the end of a pole. It was a standing lion confronting the enemy. It was embroidered and heightened in gold on a crimson background, and bore for a motto: *Never vanquished!*

Outaya therefore represented herself as having come on her master's behalf, announcing that she was bringing flowers for the harem. She was allowed to pass and she traversed the main courtyard, preceded by the immense basket, whose sheaves undulated gently. In front of her the terraces succeeded one another, sustained by porticos of pink marble; stout, heavy eunuchs with flaccid hair, whose calanticas were ornamented by enamel eyes, were guarding the women's apartments.

"On behalf of Hary-Thé," the former slave repeated. "I'm bringing flowers."

But it was not easy to penetrate into the royal prince's gynaeceum when His Majesty was there. The priests around him kept a vigilant watch, for in religious Egypt the veritable authority and the real strength emanated from the silent and redoubtable sanctuary. The Pharaohs, haloed with gold like the sun, and glorious descendants of the stars, still had to incline before the first divine legislators and their representatives. Outaya was therefore conducted into the Mammisium of the palace, where the Sam, the great pontiff, received her and interrogated her.

The priest, in his white schenti—a sort of loincloth of extreme delicacy, attached to the hips by a cord—was imposing in his stature, and his dark gaze with steely glints searched souls.

He had thrown back the panther-skin that covered his shoulder, displaying pectoral ornaments in the form of little naos, containing sacred scarabs, or bari, symbolic gold and silver boats, represented with the figures of animals that were particularly venerated. Immense rings parted his fingers, and precious bracelets attached by small chains were stacked on his arms, usually hidden beneath the calasiris, a long tunic that passed over the schenti. His feet were molded in papyrus tatebs, terminated by long curved-back points, spangled with a dust of diamonds with cabochons of amethyst.

The Sam was the Grand Master of the palace, and nothing was accomplished without his assent. He welcomed Outaya, of whose projects he was aware, with a mysterious smile.

"Pontiff of Souls, Prophet of Days and Nights, I humiliate myself in your light," murmured the former slave, not without her heart beating rapidly.

The Sam pointed at the flower-basket with an accusing finger. "What is the crime that you are hiding in those flowers?"

"It's not a crime, it's a gift of amour."

"An amour that simulates death . . ."

"It was the only means . . ."

Outaya dared not lift her gaze to meet that of her judge. She trembled more forcefully, fearing a disgrace.

But the Great Pontiff went on, in a benevolent tone. "I forgive you, woman, for having troubled the mystery of Osiris and borrowed its redoubtable form in the accomplishment of your projects. Zelinis, by her omnipotent grace, will charm the leisure of a prince. She will dissipate the fog of the melancholy dream that obscures the Pharaoh's divine forehead. She will be a little melodious cicada in the silence of the Temple."

For a few minutes, he spoke into her ear in a low voice and then, smiling, made a sign to the porters and preceded them into the presence of young Thutmose.

"Here," he said, "is the present that you desired from your faithful servant. May these roses embalm your life and your heart."

"Prince," said Outaya, prostrating herself, "I bring you joy."

At that moment, Zelinis emerged from the bosom of the corollas, a flower of flesh and blood worthy of a king's kiss, and Thutmose, dazzled, uttered a feeble exclamation.

The little singer, kneeling amid the roses, whose petals caressed her breasts, paraded a surprised gaze around her. How did she come to be in the palace, almost naked under the Pharaoh's gaze?

Her mind, still clouded, floated indecisively; a vague dolor gripped her temples. She remained still, in a charming confusion mingled with terror, wondering whether what she saw might be the continuation of a dream, and whether everything might vanish like a magical invocation.

Outaya had disappeared, and Thutmose had drawn nearer, muted and delighted. With a finger placed on his lips he implored the silence of the strange flower of sensuality, radiant amid the roses.

PART TWO

I
The Embalming of the Courtesan

Meanwhile, Hary-Thé had wanted to see the body of his lover again, and the Taricheute had shown him the body of a young woman, hermetically veiled, which he had just purified and prepared for embalming.

The Taricheutes gave the dead their initial cares and conserved them for two or three days in special crypts. They were old men devoid of desires, who remained all day in the somber redoubt with the marble slabs covered in cadavers and the granite walls hollowed out with hieroglyphs. They murmured verses dedicated to Anubis, the god of Darkness, and kept, in onyx vases, oils, myrrh, honey, lotus and palm wines, balms, crushed aromatics and tablets of cassia.

Young priests being too frequently tempted to violate the bodies of particularly beautiful virgins or wives, they were only employed for the latter tasks.

"Let me see her face," Hary-Thé begged, raising a sacrilegious hand to the dead woman's veil.

But the Taricheute was inflexible. "I want to fix her immortal beauty, and you will find her again as she was at the sweetest moments of sensuality; but permit science to perfect its work."

"Let me place my lips on that icy flesh."

"No," said the old man. "You would not recognize her. What is the point of troubling the divine mystery of her last sleep? It is not permitted for me to obey you."

"Adieu, then," murmured the young man. "But you'll return her to me in all the splendor of her adorable youth?"

"I'll return her to you sweeter than Hathor, the goddess of celestial space, and more resplendent than Tewnout,[1] the queen and daughter of the sun. Go, my son, and have no fear for the future."

Hary-Thé, his throat full of sobs, had fled, and the Taricheute, engrossed in his prayers, had asked the gods to show him clemency.

The substitution of a body was a grave matter, which was severely punished in the sacerdotal class. That fraud, however, was accomplished quite frequently, thanks to the mystery that surrounded the practices of embalming. Because the deceased were only shown to families covered by a mask and enveloped in bandages, it was easy to make a body disappear, and obscure corpses sometimes occupied princely sarcophagi.

The priestly class, which had originally been the absolute sovereign of government, still conserved a profound influence, and its territorial wealth was immense. The priests did not pay any taxes, but they received taxes of wheat, metals, wine and forage, not to mention the fortune that was conceded to them by the dead for the rights of embalming and shelter in the catacombs. No one suspected them, no one attempted to remove the gold or ivory masks, or to unwrap the bandages of bodies confided to their care; thus, it sometimes happened that an important individual, enveloped in coarse, poorly-stitched fabric, after a more or less prolonged sojourn in the natron, came to take his anonymous place in the public crypts. Young dead women violated by the embalmers were delivered to the sacred crocodiles.

However, the Taricheute who had replaced the pretended cadaver of Zelinis with that of a courtesan named Nara, found in the prostitutes' quarter, handed the body of that woman over to the Paraschites who were to extract the viscera and the intestines, cleaving the abdomen with an Ethiopian stone.

---

1 The name of this goddess is usually rendered as Sekhmet; the name employed by the author seems to have been taken from Ernest Bosc's 1881 *Dictionnaire générale de l'archéologie et des antiquités*, and is otherwise very rare.

Nara, transported into the crypt of operations, was laid out on a wooden bench whose back represented the head of a lion. Scrupulously, the Paraschites depilated the body, and washed it in several solutions, violently aromatized, before submitting it to the action of chemical salts, of which the principal one was nitre, or natron.

They did the work urgently, knowing that they would be generously recompensed by the chief of the Royal Guard, Hary-Thé. Nara, moreover, seemed charming and still very young. Her pure, regular features had not been outraged by death, and her hair, which she wore cut above the shoulders, like that of all courtesans, was curly and seemed to make her an aureole of plumage. Her small teeth were shining like so many grains of rice between lips coated with a tenacious rouge, marvelously red in the pale face.

The skin of the corpse seemed so delicate that it had a satiny sheen, and the priests, before proceeding with the habitual preparations, could not resist offering Nara's beauty a direct homage. By turns, they took pleasure in that gilded flesh, steeped in balms, which seemed still to be alive and to be caressing them. The courtesan fulfilled her mission of amour beyond death, giving her kiss to its solicitors with the same smile of her painted lips and the same obedience of her supple arms, her breasts, her loins and all of her voluptuous body.

Extended on the wooden bench with the lion's head, she was certainly pleased by those last desires that her sovereign grace inspired, and her astral form took on a more vivid radiance. But, death having done its work in spite of everything, it was necessary to abandon those amorous games.

Then, by means of curved tongs and sharp irons, the Paraschites removed the brain via the nostrils, liquefying it as much as possible with special injections. After that they made a profound incision in the left flank by means of the obsidian stone and withdrew the heart, the lungs and the liver. The priest charged with that responsibility had put on the symbolic costume of his

employment; his head, coiffed with that of a jackal, the emblem
of Anubis, the guardian of the inferior hemisphere, was completely shaved, and he wore a scarlet schenti fixed over his hip by
a golden belt.

He plunged his right arm, rubbed with cedar oil, into the
lower abdomen and the chest, and then, after having raised the
bloody remains of the woman toward the vault of the crypt, he
placed them in the first canopic jar in order to consecrate them
to the Sun.

"O Sun!" he cried, "I deliver to you that culpable part of the
woman who is no more. She has sinned by desire, by greed and by
lust. May her entrails alone bear the weight of her remembrance,
since her purified body is separated from them in death!"

With fateful gestures he introduced myrrh and cinnamon,
mingled with cassia, into the cavities of the abdomen and the
stomach. The cranial cavity received liquid bitumen, which
hardened as it cooled; then Nara was plunged into a bath of natron and remained there for seventy days under the guard of the
Tarischeutes, in the company of other dead women of distinction
destined for superior embalming.

During that lapse of time, no one penetrated into the
halls of immersion and dessication. The family, praying in the
Mammisium of the temple, evoked the soul of the deceased,
begging it to accept their gifts and prayers, to put them in communication with the omnipotent spirit whose name—Osiris—it
was not permitted to pronounce.

Embalming was not only employed for the remains of human beings, but also applied to the cadavers of sacred animals
such as the cat and the crocodile. Beneath the Egypt irrigated by
the Nile there is a subterranean Egypt composed of innumerable
mummies, accumulated there by the singular piety of a people.
Monkeys, jackals and dogs sleep in thousands alongside kings,
and the sepulchral grottoes of the double chain that is prolonged
from the pyramids of Giza to beyond Philae are filled with cadavers. At the gates of the Libyan chain there is a mysterious city

whose pathways are bordered by urns, caskets and vases containing myriads of birds, with their eggs, and, above all, cats with enamel eyes and phosphorescent fur, and snakes with gilded coils painted in ocher and cinnabar.

The vast plain that departs from the foot of the Great Pyramid and extends to the north, the west and the south, is occupied by the catacombs of ancient Egypt, and everywhere, death rubs shoulders with life, the grandiose dream of the past mingling with the spring-like promises of the future.

After having sojourned for seventy days in a solution of natron, Nara was coated in liquid bitumen in order to be able to support the variations of temperature and humidity of the crypts. The Colchites then commenced the placement of the bandages.

Those final preparers wore blue schenti, and amulets of Al and Oannes clinked on their torsos. They worked in broad daylight in spacious courtyards, for they delivered themselves to veritable works of art and were considered as prestigious workmen.

They passed bandages between Nara's fingers and toes, not without having reddened the nails with henna and placed little golden sheaths at the extremity of the phalanges. The arms, legs and thighs were then carefully wrapped in strips of hyssus coated with Judean bitumen. Those thin pieces of fabric, rolled and tightened, measured hundreds of meters in length. They modeled the arms, more or less desiccated, the hardened flesh of the legs, the hollow chest and the absent abdomen. Their delicate and expert disposition reestablished the forms of the bodies abolished by desiccation.

Some mummies had masks enriched with precious stones, and pectorals of goffered leather in the breast, with gold cabochons. There, gemmed designs represented scenes of the adoration of the god Khem, an ithyphallic deity that was also named Ammon Generator. Theban mummies were the most sumptuous and the most successful. They contained hard stone fetishes on which chapters of the *Book of the Dead* were engraved, fateful jewels in the bezels of rings, necklaces, headdresses and clasps, and, in the place of the heart, an immense scarab was displayed, in gold or enamel, amethyst or jade. The scarab was the symbol of transformation, and represented, in hieroglyphic writing, the word kheper, to become, or to take form. The ancient Egyptians believed firmly in that emblem of resurrection, and death, for them, was only a passage: the somber repose of the chrysalid before the emergence of the moth of flame.

In the marble enclosure where the Colchites worked, the mummies, fully prepared, were aligned along the wall, upright, in their stiffened pose. What was most striking about them was their masks of agglutinated fabric, wax, metal or painted wood, with eyes of glass set in golden eyelids. All those eyes seemed to be alive, following the visitor with a strange and curious gaze.

The faces of certain women were covered with a fine linen fabric stuck to the skin itself; a little padding reinforced the cheeks, the chin and the ridge of the nose, reconstituting the former modeling of the flesh. The men wore a woven beard, more or less long in accordance with their quality. Men and women displayed their countless jewels and almost always wore the protective scarab on the breast, the image of reincarnation.

Young women, virgins, extended their arms along the abdomen with the hands crossed in a modest gesture; wives had their arms crossed over their breast, men and children allowed them to dangle along their sides. The lips were sometimes parted as if for a prayer, the hands were closed on amulets.

The Colchites, who had received orders to prepare the fake Zelinis with great magnificence and then recall her incomparable beauty by means of a mask, therefore delivered themselves to the most prestigious fantasies upon the body.

The slender body of Nara, in spite of the bandages, was sheathed in a robe of silver, embroidered with large hieratic flowers decorated with gems; an enamel mask, imitating the amber tones of skin was applied to her face, scarcely deformed by death, and mystical onyx irises were set in eyelids with black lashes, elongated and partly closed, as if weighed down by the ecstasy of a dream. Her lightly curled hair, sewn with pearls, was raised by a headband attaching and dissimulating the mask; two gold plaques linked by small chains fell over her ears.

Nara was thus the faithful image of Zelinis, an immortal and troubling Zelinis, a divine receptacle of hidden sensualities, an inviolable Zelinis purified of terrestrial sin.

However, she inspired mysterious desires, a lascivious dread, and a delicious emotion; she was a great flower desiccated in balms, a calyx of gold and silk, artificial, sumptuous and disquieting.

II
Hary-Thé's Preparations

"I desire," said Hary-Thé, "that the head of the funereal box that contains the beloved body should be very high and decked in plumes. It's necessary that the lid, simply fixed with the aid of a golden cord, can be lifted without difficulty, for, at any moment of the day of the night, I might communicate with the adorable soul, the double of my lover."

"It shall be done in accordance with your wishes," said the artist charged with the precious sheath. He had already gilded the plaster-lined papyrus of the lid, and was preparing to trace thereon symbolic figures of divinities and scenes of adoration in the fields of the Amenti, enhanced with hieroglyphic inscriptions.

Terracotta statuettes enameled in pale green and pink waited on tablets arranged along the wall above mummies. Some, of large dimension, bore fragments of the *Book of the Dead*. There were also amulets of turquoise, amber and jade, and sheaths of green feldspar in the form of stems, supporting lotus flowers.

Meanwhile the Colchite praised the virtue of the talismans, the prices of which were always very high.

"Don't you want, my son, to make a gift to your beloved of that sheath of translucent feldspar offered by Thoth to his worshipers? It's the color of spring florescence and brings good luck to anyone who buys it. Look how delicately tinted it is! The lotus blooming at its extremity is made of a single sapphire; no other jewel is as perfect!"

"No," said Hary-Thé.

"Would you prefer this boat in solid gold, or this jade chariot with ruby wheels?"

"What's the point? Zelinis was only a little singer at the temple of Hapi."

"Then it's necessary to give her this psalterion, or the flute of Osiris, whose sounds will appear enchanting to you. I also have a harp with thirteen strings, which one plays with two hands while turning it toward the sun. Would you like this lyre mounted on a tortoiseshell? All these Tebuni are very valuable, and will rejoice your friend's soul."

In spite of the solicitations of the embalmer priest, Hary-Thé remained indecisive.

It was necessary, however, to make a choice of the canopic jars destined to receive the heart, the liver, the lungs and the other parts of the mummy's body. Those vases, four in number, usually placed at the corners of the sarcophagus, were made of alabaster, limestone, Oriental onyx, enameled earthenware, porphyry or silver. Their lids represented the head of a sphinx, a jackal, a hawk, a lion or a baboon.

"My son," said the Colchite, "I engage you to take these jade canopic jars with incrustations of aquamarines. That's the stone of lovers, and the heart, in those precious cups, quivers with pleasure as if it were still beating next to a beloved heart."

"So be it," said the young man. "I'll take these canopic jars enriched with green stones. Their execution is delicate and savant. I'll also take that golden boat, the emblem of resurrection. As for the figurines you've offered me, I don't care about them, for in my dwelling Zelinis will have all the baubles and dolls that once charmed her."

"You're going to keep these remains at home?"

"Yes, she will be my constant companion, and her double will respond to my evocations."

"That is a legitimate desire."

"In any case, is Zelinis not as pretty as she was in her ephemeral existence?"

"She has the eternal beauty that, alone, ought to move men."

"Her lips are smiling at me, and she still seems to be speaking to me. I understand her hidden designs."

"This precious sheath suits you, then?"

"You've worked well, and I declare myself satisfied."

The chief of the militia leaned over the enamel mask, which he brushed with a kiss. Then he made a final recommendation.

"You will write, in diamantine signs, the name of Zelinis," he said, "and I desire that the coffin that contains the papyrus box should be as large as a bed, in order that my body can also be placed in it when I cease to live."

"The coffin will be in cedar wood or sycamore, as you choose, and it will be able to contain both of you."

Calmer, Hary-Thé resumed the road to his dwelling, in order to hasten the final preparations, for he wanted to receive the charming remains of his lover worthily. Already, he had had a room furnished, next to his own, in which all the objects of which she had been fond were gathered: her little bottles of enamel, her cassolettes, her amschirs, her metal mirrors with sculpted handles, her dolls of ivory and jade, and fresh flowers of persea: the tree consecrated to Isis, the fruit of which is shaped like a heart and its leaf like a tongue; the tree of all wisdom and all science.

That is because death, in the lover's belief, was not redoubtable. The funereal retreat of his mistress was as cheerful, and as full of futile and familiar ornaments, as their former love-nest.

In delicate bottles of enamel, and in ivory and nacre caskets, among the perfumes, balms, flowers and precious stones, the double of the voluptuous dead woman, her tender, light, vibrant and passionate astral form would reside. Her divine essence, her wandering phantom, would savor the former intoxications and the old preferences in the calm of the sanctuary.

Perhaps all the vanished souls of old Egypt also come back to visit the somber profundities of their hypogea, which modern science does not hesitate to profane.

Human being, the Egyptians thought, was quadruple in nature. The body had within it its double, its astral form, which kept it company in the tomb so long as it did not decompose. The astral form contained the soul, like a luminous kernel that was detached from the fruit after death and wandered in celestial space for centuries, subject to a thousand proofs. The intelligence inhabited the soul and tormented it incessantly, reproaching it for its weaknesses and faults.

Hary-Thé believed, therefore, that his lover could still comprehend and love him, if not with her body, at least with her invisible form, ardently and passionately. And what felicity might he not expect from her divine intelligence?

Ancient Egypt, with its own mores and its particular genius, revered woman. In the ancient bas-reliefs and writings, the maternal ancestor took precedence over all the other members of the family. A man called himself "my mother's son" rather than "my father's son." He honored his legitimate wife and courtesans. Queens governed the country and received more homage than kings. Daughters were charged with subsidizing the needs of their aged parents, while sons who had neither possessed nor inherited were not held to any such obligation. The rights of the wife to the wealth of the husband took precedence over those of the Treasury. Woman enchained with bonds of flowers the great bearded slave who lived in constant adoration of her science, her grace and her splendor.

Hary-Thé ornamented his lover's dwelling in order that she would be honored, fêted and pampered as in the feast days of her triumph.

Little Nara, therefore, was to rediscover all of Zelinis' delightful puppets, and also her ivory harp with oblique strings, which accompanied her sacred improvisations so well.

Outaya followed the preparations of the infatuated lover with a singular gaze, and even aided him with her advice and her memories.

"Here," she said, "we'll put flowers; there, that golden work-frame, on which Zelinis loved to embroider dream-like fabrics more delicate than a spider-web. Above her bed, with the sacred inscriptions, we'll hang the crown of roses that she wore at the Pharaoh's wedding, and in order for her to make herself beautiful, we'll slip into her papyrus box make-up, unguents, lotions, red sticks, powders and essences."

"You're good, Outaya, and I thank you for your eagerness."

The Ethiopian woman shivered with pleasure. "You no longer want to get rid of me?"

"No, for no one else would surround me with such tender care."

"I'm doing my duty, Master; it isn't because you've ceased to love me that I'll cease to serve you. One day, you'll render me justice, perhaps you'll accord a little pity to the woman who adores you on her knees."

Outaya's large dark eyes shone feverishly; her hot hands, as if by mistake, brushed the young man's. But he seemed unaware of their contact, entirely devoted to his funereal fantasy.

"Osiris, the divine genius of silence, will watch over our tenderness," he said, with a sigh. "The beloved's coffin will reopen for me; every day I shall enclose myself with her for long hours; I shall repose against her breast, as in the past."

"She is no more, Master, than a cold doll, motionless and without a heart. Why not seek to console yourself? Certainly, one can live with the thought of former felicities, but voluptuous reality is much preferable. Oh, Master, Master . . . if you wished . . ."

Hary-Thé did not deign to listen to Outaya's passionate intonations. He smiled, vaguely soothed by the amorous canticle, the ardent words of which he applied to the other, to the little lover who was waiting out there in her sheath of gilded papyrus.

III
The Mummy's Repast

Finally, the precious box was brought to him, so heavy, so laden with ornaments, that it required several slaves to install it in the officer's dwelling, under the silver awning that was set up for her.

It took up a considerable space in the room, scarcely different, in its sumptuousness, from the lovers' former bed.

The lifted lid allowed the sight of Nara's golden sheath, which fit easily into the interior, amid the amulets, scarabs and flowers.

Beneath the golden sheath the mummy appeared, with its floral robe constellated with precious stones over the bandages. The enamel mask with the resemblance of Zelinis smiled, the eyes filtering ecstatic gazes between their heavy eyelids. As it was, the funereal doll had nothing terrifying about it; the false face, cleverly colored, with its pure and delicate features, did not allow anything to be divined of the sinister face of the cadaver.

Hary-Thé wanted to celebrate the return of his beloved with a great feast, and set her before it, in the place of honor, in order that he could contemplate her endlessly.

"Zelinis," he sometimes asked, "would you like some of this dish? You were very fond of it during your life. I've had it made in accordance with your taste."

And the guests drank to the dead woman, whose fixed eyes and rosy lips smiled immutably.

In front of her, among the lotus flowers, the symbolic boat had been placed, whose oarsmen were onyx and its hull solid gold. In the center stood a tiny figure armed with a hatchet and a curved stick. A helmsman was steering the boat by means of a tiller, and at the prow, a young singer resembling the deceased was regulating the cadence of the oars.

That emblem was to symbolize the voyage the Zelinis was about to accomplish, by water, in the other world. It bore the mystical formula: *Magnification of the Osiris N.*

In the precious vessel Hary-Thé deposited honey-cakes, bon-bons and fruits, inviting Zelinis to accept those offerings. In his mind, the young woman's double was tasting those things, or, at least, inhaling the perfume and delighting therein.

Nara, very straight, maintained by means of ropes of flowers between the arms of a high-backed chair, was prestigiously radiant. The jewels of her forehead, and the fabric of her robe, florid with gems, threw off sparks; her enamel eyes shone in the pale mask. Hary-Thé even tried to put a glazed fruit to her lips, and persuaded himself that the motionless mouth had opened slightly.

The guests were joyful, for it sometimes happened that gala dinners were presided over by particularly dear mummies, and the fantasy was not particularly surprising for the ancient Egyptians, worshipers of Anubis.

The voices became more vibrant and the spiced wines went to people's heads

"I drink to your lover and your imminent embraces," cried an officer, bursting into laughter.

Outaya, her gaze somber and her hands feverish, circulated around the young men. She filled cups, naked beneath a transparent gauze that idealized her form, and gazes followed her ardently, with undissimulated desire; but she suffered from the indifference of her former lover. Was Zelinis dead, then, going to be more redoubtable than Zelinis alive?

What would she not have given to reconquer the tenderness of Hary-Thé, who alone occupied her heart? Continually, she drew close to him and tried to attract his attention by means of lascivious poses and cajoling gestures. Her flanks brushed the officer's shoulder; she lingered nonchalantly over that contact, slowly filling his golden cup, rearranging the crown of roses that had slipped over his forehead, but he, seeing nothing, hearing nothing, had no inkling of the amorous suffering that was palpitating next to him.

The guests, completely drunk, drew the disarmed woman toward them, plastering kisses upon her flesh at hazard. One of them had snatched away the diaphanous cloth that veiled her body, and she remained as motionless as a superb idol of lust.

"Would you like to sell me your slave?" asked Amoun-Zari, a newly-promoted lieutenant in the militia.

"Outaya is no longer my slave," said Hary-Thé. "She's free to go with you, if such is her pleasure."

But the young woman had looked the impudent fellow up and down disdainfully.

"My pleasure is to serve the Master I love."

Amoun-Zari shrugged his shoulders. "The master you serve and love cares little about you."

"By means of patience, one can attain anything."

"Well, be patient while giving yourself to me. Beauty doesn't flourish twice for women, and the time you're squandering in futile waiting is the best of your life."

Outaya smiled proudly. "My lord will weary of the presence of his cold doll; he will soon want other kisses, other embraces than those of his impossible dream. He will want to press a vibrant and passionate creature in his arms, and receive all the real marks of human tenderness. It's not at his age that one forgets only true joys of existence, those for which the Master of Hours has given us a body and a soul. I have no fear for the future."

"What do you think of that speech?" Amoun-Zari asked the distracted officer, who was scarcely listening.

The latter smiled indulgently. "It's necessary not to attach any importance to what Outaya says. She was very jealous of my mistress, and I even resolved to do without her services, but since the death of Zelinis, her humor has changed considerably. With time, she'll forget, become more reasonable . . ."

"Never," said the Ethiopian, dully.

"Get away! Within a week I want you to be Amoun-Zari's lover."

"Never!" repeated Outaya, and, taking her master's head in her hands, she kissed him fervently on the lips.

He pushed her away, with ennui. "Zelinis is watching us," he said. "She seems somber and angry."

"Zelinis? Oh, yes, I'd forgotten her!"

The Ethiopian laughed silently as she passed behind the sparkling doll, very straight in her sheath the color of the moon and the sun.

But they had drawn away from the table, and dancers, as at every good Egyptian meal, slipped in quietly and came to bow before the idol. They were all wearing floral sprays which they shredded as they passed. Two little boys, to either side of the cathedra, shook silver amschirs whose odorous fumes enveloped Nara with a cloud.

Singers from the temple of Hapi recited the dead woman's favorite verses, and addressed fervent prayers to Tewnout, goddess and daughter of the Sun, for the reunion of souls in the abode of glory.

Through large bays open over the gardens, the ardent breath of mimosas and tuberoses came; the sky, dotted with stars, seemed to be dissolving under a rain of fire.

The breasts and haunches of the dancers had voluptuous frissons; they undulated, bent down as if to seize the butterfly of dreams, and opened their hands, the fingers gilded with the pollen of wings. And butterflies were indeed fluttering around them, retained by light threads. The azure, emerald and crimson insects made multicolored aureoles for them, and nothing was as pretty as those flower-women brushed by the desires of a multiple and charming amour.

After the game of the butterflies came the game of flames. Dancers juggled with lighted torches, and, by virtue of the rapidity of their movements, seemed to be agitating amid arabesques, diamond-shapes and interlacing circles of fire. The woman could no longer be seen in an ardent halo. She had removed all veils; only the gems of her arms and her ankles swarmed like golden insects, reptiles with fiery coils. The dance accelerated, and was

eventually nothing but a fantastic farandole of breathless, feverish, extraordinary demons.

The eyes of the mummy also shone strangely in the middle
of that furnace. Her equivocal smile was accentuated, and she
became the redoubtable idol of a round of delirious bacchantes.

Again, Outaya took her master's lips against her own, but
he pushed her away harshly, almost angered, this time, by her
importunate caress.

"Take her away, Amoun-Zari," he said. "I give her to you."

The officer advanced and attempted to draw the young
woman away, who slid between his arms and took refuge behind
the mummy's high cathedra. Amoun-Zari, thinking that it was
a game, caught up with her, laughing kissed her brutally, and
in a hectic embrace, crushed her hard breasts against his chest.
Foaming with rage, she looked around for a weapon; but she was
naked, defenseless against the vehement desire of a man.

"Take her away," repeated Hary-Thé. "Her refusal isn't serious, and your kiss will cure her of her impossible amour."

"Master!" the Ethiopian implored. "What have I done? My
only crime is to cherish you! Don't send me away!"

The guests encouraged Amoun-Zari in the struggle,

"Are you going to let yourself be defeated by a woman?"

"In your place, I'd already have reduced her to silence!"

"Your kisses will stifle her cries!"

"Possess her immediately, then; she'll go with you afterwards
without resistance."

The officer knocked Outaya down, but she slid between his
legs like a snake, stood up, and, seizing one of the long pins
that fixed the mummy's mask, she plunged it entirely into her
aggressor's chest.

Her criminal action was accomplished so rapidly that none of
the witnesses was able to intervene.

Amoun-Zari, struck directly in the heart, vomited blood in
great gouts, tottered, took two or three steps, and then collapsed
with a hoarse cry.

196

The guests threw themselves upon Outaya who, upright, her lips drawn back in a disdainful rictus, allowed her hands to be tied.

"Is it necessary to deliver her to the law?" one of the guests asked.

"Yes," said Hary-Thé. "She merits punishment, and I want her to expiate her crime."

"I prefer to die," sobbed the young woman, "since you scorn me enough to sacrifice me to the whim of your companions. What have I done, though? I only solicited the favor of remaining with you as a humble slave. Could you not let me live in your shadow, accord me a place in your house? Why did you deliver me to that man?"

"Because your caresses importuned me. I only love, and will only love henceforth, the one whose body is immobile, but whose double palpitates around me like a bird of fire."

"Is that your last wish, Hary-Thé?"

"My last."

Outaya burst out laughing. "Well, then, cherish that doll with corrupted flesh and a hideous face beneath its enamel mask. Clasp in your arms that formless body with tones of ocher and bitumen, that rigid cadaver, that lamentable skeleton . . . be the lover of a lying mannequin, and I shall know the joys of vengeance!"

"Take that woman away!" said the chief of the Royal Guard, trembling with anger, while the former slave's laughter broke in a sob.

IV
The Pharaoh's Fantasies

Kings, like poets and simple children of the people, consecrate their existence to the pursuit of an ideal of goodness and justice, to the realization of a dream. Everyone down here is consoled because he looks beyond life, counting in a providential intervention in order to enjoy glory, wealth, gratitude, enlightenment and amour. Everyone extends his arms to seize the chimera of his desire, to clasp it to his heart, and to intoxicate himself with its deceptive smile until death.

That universal aspiration, which perhaps proves better than any reasoning the divine essence of man, is encountered to a higher degree among civilized peoples, among elite minds, ever unquiet and suffering.

Individuals of genius, who have often been the arbiters of human destinies, have only had to collect, explain and incarnate the ideal of their race and their time.

Little Thutmose, weary of religious ceremonies, sacrifices, facile amours and power, was seeking to distract his nostalgic soul, extended toward a fiction of mildness, justice and benevolence.

The kisses of his sister, Queen Atasu, had not been able to chase away his melancholy; he loved his young wife with more respect than passion, and the caresses of the creatures of sensuality that populated his harem could only stir his senses.

He was, moreover, still only a timid adolescent with a slender body, and a misty, incisive, melancholy gaze. The exhausted scions of an unmixed race take longer than others to develop. They only arrive at their definitive self after a host of gropings and metamorphoses. Elite minds, often contained in a debilitated body, are excessively impressionable, and, in consequence, more inclined to vary and be transformed in the wake of a keen emotion, or a mental or physical shock.

Thutmose, raised by priests in the study of the sacred mysteries, had paled over the books of the Trismegistus—the thrice great—for, of all the writers of ancient Egypt, Thoth was the most fecund. The priestly caste in its entirety wrote under that collective name, composed hymns in honor of the gods, rules of conduct for kings, treatises on astrology and religious compilations.

The little prince had studied those hermetic books conscientiously. Twice a day he went to the temple, preceded by the Cantor, carrying the musical symbol, the Horoscope, who held an

hour-glass and a green palm, and the Hierogrammat, recogniz-
able by the ostrich plumes that ornamented his head, the scroll
of papyrus and the calami—reeds—from which he was never
separated. Under the direction of those initiators, Thutmose had
learned geography, the phases of the sun and the moon, those of
the five planets, the chorography of Egypt, that of the Nile and
its phenomena. The Stolist, the Prophets and the Pastophores
had taught him philosophy, occultism and the art of healing.
His petty intelligence, exhausted by so much science, had folded
back upon itself; his mind became anxious under the weight of
the strange problems that weighed upon him.

The priests of Thebes had their laboratories, in fact, in the
dependencies of the temples, where they occupied themselves,
above all, with alchemy. They were astrologers, hermeticists or
occultists, commonly designated under the generic name of
philosophers. They were surrounded by great respect and only
operated in profound mystery, enclosed with their young pupil
in order to initiate him into the redoubtable symbols. Thutmose
possessed the art of transmuting metals, of making gold; but he
remained somber and taciturn, awaiting a beloved presence that,
better than all the hermetic secrets, would have filled his heart.
The philosophers preached, Atasu laughed, and the days passed
without leading to the blossoming of amour.

The young prince was charmed to discover Zelinis, who,
for months, had incarnated his dream. She was not, like other
women, a futile doll of lust. A little of the divine flame shone in
her face, and her voice had the melodious freshness of nocturnal
breezes passing through reeds.

The prince's vague and troubling desire took on substance.
The frail singer, lying under the flowers, flattered the imagination
and the sentiment, the two great springs of very young men. She
was better than a woman, she was a vision of amour and grace, a
chastely providential apparition.

Thutmose watched Zelinis' charming torso surge forth from
the roses heaped up in the basket. Finally, he approached, took

the young woman by the hand, parted the corollas around her, and helped her to step out of her narrow prison.

"You've come, and I'm glad," he said.

But she did not understand; her ideas were confused, her head heavy. She had gone to sleep next to Hary-Thé, in the intimate retreat in the low quarters. How did she find herself, now, in the company of the Prince in the palace of the kings?

"Let me go," she begged. "Doubtless I'm still dreaming?"

"No, you belong to me, and henceforth, you're going to live with me."

"I'm going to live with you? What about my fiancé? You know very well that it's him I love!" She was weeping, her face in her hands.

"Your fiancé," said the Prince, "has made the sacrifice of his love, for it's him who sent you to me."

"It's him who sent me?"

"Certainly."

"He no longer wants me?"

"He is effacing himself before my tenderness."

"That's impossible!"

Thutmose pointed at the basket. "You can see clearly that he really has made me the gift of your person. And, rose of sensuality, he has wrapped you in roses."

Zelinis opened her incredulous eyes wide. "He had me brought here?"

"Yes."

"Naked, in that basket?"

"Naked. But I shall give orders for your beauty to be given attire worthy of it. You shall be the purest jewel of the sacred temple, the most admired and the most precious."

Slaves hastened around Zelinis, eunuchs with drained flesh and atonal eyes. They were carrying ornaments of enameled gold, necklaces and bracelets, and fabrics steaming with precious stones, which glittered on the crystal of the floor-tiles.

Zelinis looked at the sumptuous room in which she found herself, with its silver basins and the chrome-plated mosaics on the walls. A throne stood at the back beneath squat columns enameled with polychromatic bricks, encrusted with lapis, opals and aquamarines. Feather cushions, tiger-skins and leopard-skins were strewn in disorder on the steps, which were also covered with abandoned musical instruments, perfume-burners in the form of monsters whose mouths, nostrils and eyelids disgorged clouds of aphrodisiac vapors.

In the perverse odor of aromatics, in the moist warmth of the room, Zelinis felt faint. She was also hungry, but she did not want to accept the fruits and delicacies that the eunuchs offered to her. Her chagrin was too great; she wanted to remain hungry and to die of it.

Concentrated now, her eyes fixed, she resembled a mysterious sleepwalker, overcome by grief.

"I beg you to live for me!" murmured the young prince. "You will only have to appear to give me joy."

"That's beyond my strength," said Zelinis. "I'm in love, in love in spite of everything, and nothing can cure me of that love."

"I'm only asking you for a little tender affection. You'll sing to charm my ennui, and your thoughts can remain faithful to another."

"What's the point, since that other disdains me and rejects me . . ."

"Look, choose."

She trembled before all that magnificence, which she had not dared to suspect. A crimson door-curtain attached to a golden rail veiled the entrance to the sanctuary where the amorous couch of the Pharaohs was displayed. But Thutmose, the sad child, hardly did more than pass through his gynaeceum. He liked the songs and dances of his women, in order to relax him after his sacerdotal studies, but he did not desire their voluptuous bodies.

"Choose," he repeated, pointing at the clothes heaped at the singer's feet.

She plunged her slender fingers into prodigious scintillation of velvets and silks, materials woven with gold and translucent minerals.

A slave put a pearl gorgerin around her upper torso, attached between the breasts by an emerald, and slid a gauze skirt around her pelvis with a fringe and pendants steaming with carbuncles, topazes and sapphires. The stones were alive, kissing her admirable womanly body, dotting her neck, legs and arms with multicolored flames.

When she was ready, Thutmose presented her with a harp with thirteen golden stings. "Sing now," he said.

But she closed her eyes, extended her arms and let herself fall amid the gems and fabrics. The ordeal had been too hard, and in any case, she was faint from hunger, having taken nothing during her singular slumber.

In small doses, the palace physicians slid extracts of meat and milk between her pale lips; mages pronounced incantations in order to protect her from evil spirits, because all malady, for Egyptian physicians, was submissive to malign influences and the best remedies consisted above all of the application of exorcisms.

The Pastophores interrogated the moon, which renders immortality; Mercury, which procures impassivity; the Sun, which grants the strength to support the glare of divine splendors without fainting; Venus, which clothes innocence; Jupiter, which takes possession of the treasures of intelligence; and Saturn, which enlightens everything with its immutable beauty.

Zelinis, having been born on the twenty-first of Thoth, ought to die in favor; had she been born on the twentieth, a particularly inauspicious date, she would not have been able to live, and any care would have been futile. But the wandering and visible stars were favorable to her; the moon and the sun, in their conjunctions, protected her amours. However, in spite of the exorcisms, the evocations and the prayers, she remained plunged in a kind of semi-slumber. The women lavished cares upon her, obedient to the orders of their master; even Atasu deigned to sit next to her couch for long minutes, fixing her soft and enigmatic gaze upon her.

The little queen was not at all jealous of her rivals in the gynaeceum of amour. She alone commanded the palace and directed her royal spouse as she pleased; she alone shared the prince's bed every evening, and solicited of his tenderness all that it could give. He was a friend and a submissive servant. What did the caprice of an hour next to a voluptuous love-slave matter? All men of distinction had their harem, and legitimate wives supported the sharing with serenity. Thus, it is true that sentiments and mores change in accordance with countries, religions and climates, with the consequence that nothing can be perfectly good or perfectly bad. In any case, the little queen had an idea.

Zelinis scarcely saw what was happening around her, and remained in the smoky catacombs of a dream in which she wanted to die. She felt a sort of vertigo, a torpid intoxication that prevented her from suffering too cruelly.

Hary-Thé no longer loved her. That thought alone remained acquired by her troubled mind, and that thought alone augmented her woe.

What was the point of so much effort, trouble and struggle, she said to herself, since life suddenly metamorphoses, without any reason; happiness vanishes, the dearest beliefs go up in smoke, and it is no longer permissible to expect a renewal of amour? However, she still hoped for a possible recall, the return of the former tenderness. The fiancé could not be lost to her; the man she had cherished uniquely, and who had sworn to embellish her existence, would certainly come to search for her. She had lived with him in one of those magical palaces that emerge from the ground to lodge illusions. Her ear had heard new melodies, her lips had quivered in the breath of infinite kisses, and even in sleep, her heart, next to the beloved lover, was moved delectably. She was mourning her charming error today, but she nevertheless wished for, and had a presentiment of, its resurrection.

Gradually, however, the notion of things returned to her more clearly. Again, then, fever burned her limbs and ideas of suicide haunted her. By virtue of an abrupt reversal, all confidence was abolished in her, in spite of the exhortations of the Pastophores who visited her. It seemed to her that an icy veil had been thrown over her shoulders, which imprisoned her more dolorously than after her first awakening.

Oh, how she regretted the sweet moments spent with the cherished lover, when a future of tranquil happiness had smiled upon her and she had allowed herself to be conquered delectably by the penetrating voice of amour and hope! She saw the Beloved again, leaning over her in the mystery of the closed room, lavishing the most tender caresses upon her, teaching her all the secrets of sensuality with the unique ambition of making her happy!

So, it was that passionate friend who had sacrificed her to the royal fantasy, and had separated from her forever? Was that possible?

She would have liked to be one of the stone sphinxes that decorated the entrance of the little house in the low quarter, in order always to watch over the house of the ingrate, and to see him a few times a day, to pass in his shadow.

The flood of thoughts collided within her; then, after having examined and debated the surprising facts of her life for a long time, she sensed everything in her mind becoming confused again, and renounced understanding, a human rag carried away by the fatality of things.

After a long slumber, a sharper pain bit into her skull, a ripping sensation that made her put her closed fists to her forehead. She opened her eyes, looked around her with anguish, and was astonished to see that she was still in the luxury of the royal gynaeceum, surrounded by silky cushions, flowers, eunuchs and smiling slaves with long painted eyelids.

She pretended then to fall back into lethargy, remaining motionless and apparently insensible to the cares with which she was surrounded and the exhortations that the temple servants lavished upon her.

V

Queen Atasu

"Little Zelinis, it's necessary to distract Thutmose by means of the songs he prefers."

"I can't sing; I'm infinitely sad . . ."

"The melodies can be gay or sad, at the whim of the artiste, and provided that there is a little of her soul therein, their power is magical. Take your harp with the thirteen golden strings and reawaken your Master's dormant spirit!"

Thus speaks Atasu, who has cradled her young husband in her supple arms, but has not been able, in spite of her amorous science, to bring back the ecstatic smile for which she was ambitious.

Thutmose allows himself to be loved, but he remains the troubled and nostalgic adolescent of the first days, the timid young man whom an excessively illustrious blood, with no admixture, had been unable to endow with energy or will.

"Sing!" Atasu repeats, arching her slender waist beneath the broad belt that terminated in front with three emerald tears. And she presents Zelinis with an ivory psalterion.

Thutmose, his eyes closed, very pale and shivering after his tumultuous night, is lying on a silver bed encrusted with opals and turquoises. The insignia of the divinity, the whip and the hook, have slid from his hand, and his feverish breast is rising with difficulty.

"Sing!" orders the little queen, whose large onyx eyes have redoubtable sparks.

But she soon softens, puts her arm around Zelinis' neck and kisses her gently.

That royal caress reminds Zelinis of the kisses of her ingrate lover; she does not push away the supple and charming body leaning over her, and offers her mouth to the fresh lips. Without resistance, now, she savors the charm of soothing frictions, and admires the passionate science of the sovereign, who, from time to time, raises her head to smile at Thutmose, her royal and timid husband.

"You see, I'm not jealous. I'll give you joy with Zelinis, since it's her that you desire. The two of us will be able to vanquish your ennui and initiate you into marvelous ecstasies."

The dancer is clad in a tunic of silver gauze and her hair is steeped in perfumes; she is adorable in her ardent pallor, with the circle of bistre that surrounds her immense eyes of somber velvet. Atasu kisses her curly eyelashes, her forehead and her little ears, slowly, as one savors a long-coveted delicacy. She speaks in a voice that is sometimes grave, like the murmur of waves, and sometimes light, like the trill of a crystal flute.

The singer, penetrated by a new languor, listens without interrupting her, glad to feel loved again, and in a fashion that cannot tarnish her saddened memories, for the amour of a woman is so different from that of a man. The caprice that she inspires is not the whim of a master nor the trembling ambition of a slave. She feels that she is the friend of the woman caressing her, and the consciousness of her reconquered pride renders her more loving.

And then, she has been a Pallacide in the temple of Hapi; as a child, she has known the frictions and the perverse disquiet of little girls, sequestered like her, and who, weary of mystical invocations, wanted sensations more directly troubling and sweet. Like her companions, she has shivered in the breath of magnetic kisses, the puerile and feverish kisses of little virgins consecrated to the gods. One of them has visited her by night, teaching her the charm of the confession, the haunting of desire and the final intoxication of possession. She has woken up, stunned by caresses, in the friend's arms, and her smoky eyelids, her bruised lips and her indolent gait have revealed the burn of the embrace.

It was only having become old that persevering priestesses, initiated into the ultimate mysteries, shaved their heads like men,

learned to observe the stars, resented incense and funerary offerings to the gods, studied the astrological books of Thoth and
prepared those of their companions who wanted to know the
hidden science.

Atasu, turned toward Thutmose, cradled Zelinis on her
breast, feeling her shoulders quiver. The warmth of her body,
rubbed with aromatics, invaded her, caused her to swoon delectably, exasperated her desire to possess her more fully, to make
her irresistibly hers. Perhaps the pride of appearing more learned
and more adroit than her husband entered into the actions of the
little sovereign to some degree. She followed, on the prince's face,
the astonishment and admiration that her boldness provoked,
and a satisfied smile spread over her lips.

She took off the necklaces and removed the fabrics that veiled
the singer's loins, her fingers avid and trembling, irritated by the
obstacles.

The young woman was no longer resisting; languid and feverish, all her fears disappeared in the passionate expectation that
rendered her defenseless, desirous of complete abandonment.

The two women, still girls, admired one another, marveling,
bewildered by new sensations, their breasts erect in the expectation of the struggle. Their firm flesh rebounded under lips, they
covered one another with light caresses, surprised by that perfection of forms, the pure softness of the epidermis that ensures
feminine triumph.

Zelinis closed her eyelids over the intoxication of the dream,
for which she had not dared to be ambitious, allowing herself
to be plundered like a dainty flower blooming for the felicity of
the bees of amour. She abandoned herself, joyfully, to the viola-
tion of her fragile corolla, proud of the extraordinary adoration
that made her, like her companion, a mistress and queen of
sensuality . . .

The Bewitchment of Caresses

"You no longer want to leave?" asked Atasu, readjusting the sacred Uraeus on her forehead.

The little dancer shook her head.

"I want to remain in the radiance of your tenderness, to be your slave and your lover. Nothing of what you have offered me has troubled my soul, and I can conserve the image of the Beloved in my heart. I had a tender friend; now I possess a passionate sister; I'm ready to satisfy the slightest of her caprices."

Thutmose gazed at Atasu thoughtfully. He remained surprised and slightly alarmed by that amorous science, which nevertheless stimulated his nerves, enveloping him with an infinitely sweet occult caress. His virile strength was affirmed by that game. Desires came to him that he had never felt. It seemed to him that he was subject to a transformation, that his melancholies of a frail adolescent had disappeared, to give way to an ardor that he would not have suspected.

His malady had a latent sadness that nothing could vanquish, the vague dread of an occult danger that was manifest in a host of extranatural sensations. He suffered from a sort of acute morbidity of the senses; the precious stones on his flesh bruised him, as did the embroideries of his garments; the odors of certain flowers suffocated him, and even light plunged him into a temporary hypnotism. He would have liked to remain in the midst of beings and things without touching anything; all the secret fibers of his being contracted at the idea that everything in nature was alive, and languishing like him.

Atasu, more developed, and already amorous like a true woman, was afflicted by the nostalgic sadness of her husband and brother. She knew that every impression reverberated on the young man's nerves in long dolorous vibrations, that his languid days mingled bitter joys with inexplicable enthusiasms. The little prince, initiated too soon into the practices of the temples, to the emotions of power, to dissolving amour, to the corrosive emotions of the flesh, retreated into secret meditations, imagining that he was living in the midst of strange, hostile beings full of a cruel animality, whom he could neither hear nor comprehend.

Atasu, with her feline gestures, her charming body, her laughing kisses and her embraces, frightened him a little. Zelinis, a creature of dream, an ideal artiste, was closer to his soul. He found, in the chords of her ivory harp and in her pure voice, the unavowed sentiment that made him feel faint, the vague aspiration, the mystical delectation that satisfied his fragile nature. She was the languid lotus of the temples, the elect corolla of divine felicities.

But the little queen wanted to awaken more precise sensations in him, and she imagined initiating the singer in to her caprice, of winning her to her cause by means of the omnipotence of caresses. Zelinis, deeply troubled, almost unconscious, her soul and body in pain, only opposed a feeble resistance to the projects of the initiatrix. Was she not free, in any case, to follow her fantasy? Who could criticize her for it? Devoid of relatives, devoid of friends, forsaken by the man who ought to have defended her, she found in the royal affection a consolation, a support, a reason to live. Sometimes, she wondered whether she was really awake.

The suddenness of her fall left her incredulous. She did not understand that she had yielded to the folly of the flesh; then, she extended her fingers, her breasts and her lips to kisses, she obeyed the august caprice, her temples hammering, her eyes burning and her breast heaving, surrendered herself entirely like an amorous slave.

The gynaeceum, with its silky drapes and its low furniture was an irresistible dispenser of lascivious dreams. From everywhere, the perfumes of swooning flowers arrived, the gentle whisper of fountains and the caresses of light. The joy of loving burst forth in the precious sanctuaries, and rose toward the perforated vaults, with laughter, sighs and sobs.

A dread came to Zelinis. Alone in the world, she feared being abandoned by the person who was now her reason for living.

She threw herself into her arms, begging her to love her forever, to guide her, to protect her, to calm her like the inexperienced girl that she still was. With sincere transports she embraced the magicienne, proved to her that she was ardently cherished. And, in fact, she surrendered herself to the bewitchment of those singular embraces, desired the pepper of febrile kisses, waited impatiently for the shock that they imprinted on her nerves. She affirmed herself as an adorable instrument of amour, always vibrant, whom the little queen never wearied of causing to moan, in order to reawaken the torpid senses of her timid husband.

"Sing!" she said, again, to the former Pallacide of the temple of Hapi.

And after the song of the lips came the song of desire, whose sighs were as melodious as those of the ivory psalterion.

"Ah," murmured Zelinis, arching her supple and ardent young body, "I feel that I have an entirely new soul, a soul that vibrates divinely under the melody that your lips spell out. Have I existed before now? I want to forget, and only to think about my new mission!"

And she sang these words, which Atasu had composed, to a soothing and seductive tune:

> *The liana enlaces the liana,*
> *Giving the example of amour!*
> *One and the other bathe in the azure,*
> *They feel an ardent sap*
> *Circulate in their united branches,*
> *And embrace one another more tightly.*
>
> *They murmur, caressing one another,*
> *Swooning under the kiss of the breeze!*
> *And their undulating corollas,*
> *Are mouths of sensuality!*
> *The liana enlaces the liana,*
> *Giving the example of amour!*

The ardent sun reddened, suspending a vermilion radiance on the cushions indurated with silver and gold, and the precious furniture; and through the large bay overlooking the city, beyond the swarming streets and the sordid suburbs, plateaux of sand were perceptible, unfurling infinitely. Here and there, palm trees extended their somber hands around monuments. The mountains of the left bank were filled with tombs, subterranean palaces hollowed out in the rock and serving as sepulchers for kings. At that distance, the immense bas-reliefs of temples could be seen, between crouching sphinxes. The stone had amber hues and glittering scintillations; the obelisks were clad in a crimson sheath that darkened toward the base. On the columns, the staircases and the domes of the nearest pylons, the radiance suspended multicolored gems.

When Zelinis was alone, she leaned in the corner of the terrace, gazing at the city where she had lived, and from which she was separated by the insurmountable walls of the royal gynaeceum. She was now agitating in a tale of enchantment, but a great lassitude prevented her from thinking about the distant things of her former existence.

Thutmose, having emerged from the sacerdotal shadow, having escaped the monsters of Set, the murderer of Osiris, hermetic labors and the mysteries of Isis, believed that he was disentangling his new self in the stammering of puerile ecstasies, in the troubling freshness of adoring voices that rose up for his pleasure.

He had never inspired anything but a kind of commiseration with the saddened languor of his face, in which only the immense eyes with the feverish gleam were alive, and the debility of his nonchalant body.

He was ashamed of himself, desiring, for the first time, to dominate and curb heads under an irresistible influence. He remembered that, once, in his harem, when a woman had kissed his lips, he had shivered, as if struck by the fear of a bewildered animal that is only thinking of fleeing. Now, he was amused by his terrors, feeling that he was sufficiently master of himself to kiss the eyes of the dainty princess, his wife, in spite of all her amorous intrepidity.

And he pleased himself with the two women, listened to their light babble, between the caresses and the lascivious games, associating himself with their puerile joy. Thutmose no longer wanted to die. He no longer loved to fathom the mystery of pyramids consecrated to royal sepulchers, to dream beside hypogea in the light of opaline lamps, in the incense of gently swung amschirs, or to survey the pharaonic endeavors. His sole ambition, henceforth, was to ensure his descendancy, and it was with an unprecedented ardor, on emerging from the gynaeceum, that he clasped Queen Atasu to his heart.

VII
The Mysteries of Isis

The first period of the New Empire, which began about eighteen centuries before our era, was the warrior and conquering era of Egypt. After the submission of Ethiopia, Thutmose I, the father of the young Prince and Princess Atasu, whose amorous history we are narrating, drew his subjects into Asiatic conquests. He advanced as a conqueror all the way to the banks of the Euphrates, where commemorative steles celebrate his expedition. Every season saw booty flood into the city of Thebes. Troops of slaves, carts loaded with weapons, precious fabrics, vases, perfumes and barbaric jewelry filed incessantly through the flag-decked streets; unknown animals arrived from Asia. It was under Thutmose I that the horse was seen for the first time, and all the princes wanted to try to mount the ardent and docile stallions, adorned with precious stones like divinities. Pigs, plump and pink, provoked inextinguishable laughter, and certain edible dogs were served at the tables of the rich.

Thutmose I, covered in glory, announced his imminent return, and the young spouses wanted to summon the blessings of the gods upon the Chief by means of a solemn ceremony.

Already, the valley of the Nile was beginning to be covered with monuments that bore the conqueror's cartouche and recalled his exploits. Every city had a temple for the particular divinity that was venerated there. In Nubia, colossi twenty meters high guarded the entrances to subterranean palaces; in Syria, steles with the name of Thutmose perpetuated his glory.

The valley of the Nile saw gigantic Pyramids rise up, which a hundred thousand men carved in stone brought from the Arabic chain. Those monuments enclosed several sepulchral chambers and corridors that had complicated directions in order to thwart the culpable calculations of those who might have been tempted to violate the sepulchers.

The entrance of a Pyramid was concealed under the external decoration of the monument, generally in polished stone. The passages that went from one room to another were interrupted in their course by profound shafts hollowed out in the rock. Enormous monoliths in the form of obelisks loomed up on the banks of the sacred river, mysterious witnesses to the first civilizations of the world, and the solidity of their granite defied the outrages of the centuries.

That day, Atasu had to choose the placement of an obelisk erected to her glory and that of Thutmose I, for she was already taking an active and preponderant part in the government, her brother being too young as yet to act. Her regency, history tells us, was glorious. She sent an expedition to the coasts of the land of Punt, which then represented the southern shores of the Red Sea, as well as to Araby and Africa, and the conquerors came back loaded with booty. Later, her troops crushed the Syrian people, in coalition, crossed the Euphrates, reached the Tigris and went upstream as far as Nineveh. The kings offered her their submission, and she proved herself a truly great queen.

That day, however, under the warm effluvia of the embalmed morning, when the blue lotuses of the banks of the Nile opened their mystical eyes, Atasu was only thinking about amour. She desired to offer her voluptuous body to the gods in the temple of Hapi, in order to be fecundated in joy, for her young husband, accomplishing the divine will, was to deposit the sacred seed in her—at least, she hoped so.

Zelinis, the former Pallicide of the temple, accompanied the royal couple, for she participated in all the ceremonies, scarcely quitting the queen, who loved to lean on her shoulder and to draw the courage for great decisions from her gaze.

In front of the temple, young women were shredding roses. Small boys carrying on their shoulders gilded statuettes of Anta, the warrior goddess, Anubis, the supreme god of Egypt, Hathor the goddess of celestial space, and various other important figurines, arranged themselves around the dancers. The latter, clad in foliage and flowers, drew the chariot of Isis, primordial nature, the universal womb, who tamed the serpent, the hideous Apophis. So, the mime charged with filling that august role had charmed reptiles around her wrists and ankles, whose ocher and cinnabar coils undulated slowly. Her symbolic headdress was a disk with two small cow's horns; attached to her arms were wings that extended to cover the mummy of Osiris at the moment of the mystical operation that was to return him to life.

Religious festivals in honor of the goddess were very numerous. They were renewed every month, from the month of Thoth, when the image of Ammon-Ra emerged processionally from the sanctuary, accompanied by the king and queen, to the months of Paophi and Athyr, the days of the principal panegyrics.

Sacred crocodiles were brought to the banks of the Nile, where heifers were immolated in their honor. The gigantic amphibians, charged with the prayers, plaints and recommendations of the people, plunged into the river, which they rendered favorable to harvests, and which they caused to overflow at an opportune time for the greater fertility of Egypt. Baboons consecrated to Thoth-Lunus because their eyes were veiled during the conjunction of the moon and the sun, witnessed the rejoicing, crowned with roses, and their yellow eyes gleamed strangely when the priest-esses, shaking their odorant amschirs, inclined toward them.

Isis was veiled with an arachnean gauze spangled with silver; she remained seated in the adoration of the prostrate faithful. The pure voices of virgins celebrated her glory, recounting in ardent strophes her amours with her brother Osiris, whom she resuscitated by means of her incantations.

"You are the mother of all things, you are that which has been, is and will be; and no mortal has lifted your veil!"

It was customary, in each ceremony, to beg the goddess to preside over the inundations of the Nile, the source of all fertility, to inspire the winds, to protect navigators, to tighten sails and inflate them with her vital breath. The festivals, or Mysteries, of Isis were celebrated in particular at the winter solstice, and had a funereal character then, in order to recall her union with her brother Osiris and the death of her beloved.

Thutmose and Atasu had prostrated themselves before the mother of the world, and implored her to bless the act that they were about to accomplish, to deposit in the womb of the queen the seed of another glorious life, in order to perpetuate the reign of the Pharaohs.

The dance of the young women circled round the august lovers, and voices rose up in a triumphant hymn of hope and tenderness.

VIII
The Temple of Hapi

The temple had just opened its doors, and the spinning dancers were engulfed within it, preceding the statue of the goddess Isis and the royal couple.

The priests, arranged to either side of the entrance, were clad in linen and wearing the schenti. The servants of Osiris had panther-skins on their shoulders, the insignia of their rank. Many wore a calasiris embroidered with gold and a few displayed a pectoral in the form of a small naos, which enclosed the sacred scarab; their fingers were laden with rings with enormous bezels; their breasts seemed to buckle under the weight of necklaces with large beads engraved with fateful inscriptions. On their feet they wore papyrus tatebs terminating in long curved points.

The dancers scattered roses, and the songs, under the high vaults, acquired graver sonorities.

The Sam, the high priest of the palace, was officiating. Under his sparkling calasiris he made slow gestures of benediction. He was holding an emerald scepter, the insignia of his high functions, and he ordered the release of four doves, saying: "Give flight to the four lives, Amset, Sis, Soumants and Kebhsniv. Steer toward the South, the North, the Occident and the Orient, in order to reveal to the divine powers that Horus, the son of Isis and Osiris, is coiffed in the royal crown and that King Thutmose is going to cover himself in glory."

The Her-sesheta, the primary initiate, the Ker-heb, the master of ceremonies, and the Sotem, the auditor, assisted the Sam, surrounded by the guardians of the temple, Prophets, Hierogrammats, Horoscope Priests and Hieracophores.

The Sam exhorted Thutmose to patience, calm fervor and hope in the decisive act that he was about to accomplish for the Pharaonic descendancy. The little prince trembled slightly, but Atasu smiled, sure of herself and her sovereign power.

A ram was immolated, and the horoscopes, each holding a clepsydra in one hand and a palm leaf in the other, announced that the work of amour would be effectuated for the good of all, and that the prince who would be born of the embrace would be Egypt's greatest conqueror.

The priestesses and prophetesses then took possession of the queen in order to prepare her for her divine mission. They took her into the crypt of the temple, undressed her and rubbed her with magical balms. Those priestesses, or Pallacides, were the young virgins who had once initiated Zelinis into the sweetness of love, but since her flight with the officer, the singer could no longer penetrate the labyrinth, nor mingle her voice with the choruses of the sacred hymns.

Atasu relaxed, crouching on an onyx step, with her arms dangling between her legs. She laughed, gently tickled by the fingers of the young women, who proceeded with the ablutions, methodically, in accordance with the religious rites. The principal Pallicide, or Grandmistress of the Order, had unfastened her necklaces, her bracelets and her royal robe, which lay at her feet in a prodigious scintillation. She had shaken the princess' thick hair over her shoulders, and Atasu, docile but still laughing, repeated the solemn words.

She abandoned herself while the young women passed layers of balms with subtle and rare effluences over her breasts and loins. The delicious perfumes floated around her, like an aura, evaporating from her flesh in ardent gusts.

She was naked, supple, slender, adorably feline, her breasts erect in amorous battle, circled around the nipple with a line of gold. Her pelvis was harmoniously rounded like a sacred amphora, and her legs, exquisitely modeled, were elongated in a nonchalant stretch.

The Pallacide anointed all the mysterious shelters of her body with unknown balms, and finally offered her a vermilion liquor, mingled with gold powder, which was intended to augment her desires and render her apt for procreation.

In the temple, the songs continued, while young Thutmose, confided to the priests, received cares as attentive as those that the Pallacides were lavishing on his sister.

Both of them emerged from the crypt and, unescorted, went into the royal Pyramid, where the blessed union of the gods was to be accomplished.

IX
The Pyramids

The Great Pyramid, or Royal Pyramid, had an immense square base two hundred and twenty-seven meters on each side, and was a hundred and forty-six meters in height. It contained several chambers leading to the sepulchral chamber of the mummy. The ceiling and lateral walls of that hypogeum were covered with colored and gilded sculptures and hieroglyphic inscriptions. The figures concluded, at the place where the body lay, with a representation of the sun and the reincarnated soul of the deceased passing from one hemisphere to the other.

In its triple coffin with precious ornaments, the mummy of Amenhotep, the son of Ahmose, reposed in the gigantic Pyramid. That king had pacified Asia to the north-east and Ethiopia to the south, had conquered the latter country, as vast as Egypt herself, pushed the frontier back as far as the fourth cataract, and established on the banks of the Blue Nile the laws, customs, language and religion of the Pharaohs.

In the dwelling of the glorious ancestor, Atasu and Thutmose, enlaced, had prostrated themselves for a fervent prayer. No sound from outside reached them. Only Zelinis' psalterion resonated softly under the singer's trembling fingers. The friend and confidante of the little queen addressed her passionate prayer to the gods in a pious hymn. She too desired the complete union of the royal children for the continuation of the race, the happiness of the Egyptian people and the future of the land. She only had her charming body to offer, and she gave it generously, wishing that her kisses might be as soft as flowers, in order to envelop the august embrace.

Thutmose and Atasu were lying on a bed covered with lion skins, without disuniting. The oblong flames of torches trembled around them, magnifying the characters of the bas-reliefs, which seemed to be agitating fantastically. The smoke of amschirs, filled with odorous powders, rose under the vaults with the chords of the ivory harp, now exhaled quietly and delicately, as if animated by a lascivious breath. Lines of shredded roses, jasmines and tuberoses described long parabolas on the floor, emitting honeyed and peppery gusts.

Atasu's thin nostrils palpitated; she twisted her slender fingers, parted by the bezels of rings. The heavy coils of her hair spread out over the tawny fur; her veils, raised all the way to her breasts, fell to either side of the bed, leaving the rest of her body naked. On the edge of the couch, her fingernails and toenails, tinted and polished, gleamed like amaldines.

The double of the dead man was watching over the creature of sensuality, and a lamp in the form of a galley illuminated a golden statue, the image of Amenhotep, standing over his tomb. Onyx gems mounted in the hollow orbits caused the eyes to live, which seemed to be scintillating with a malicious joy.

Thutmose, however, enervated by the religious ceremonies or the solemnity of the place, clasped the little queen against himself but did not hasten to give her more precise marks of tenderness. A veil extended over his thoughts; he felt an extreme lassitude throughout his body. In his covered eyes, as cloudy as a low sky, nothing could be read but an infinite tenderness.

Atasu placed the fiery corolla of her mouth on his eyes and cheeks, lightly.

"Don't you want," she sighed, "to drink from the cups of my breasts and know the honey of my lips? Don't you want to consult the astral gems of my eyes, while accomplishing the act that I expect? I only ask, however, for your caress and I'll submit to your will, whatever it might be. Are you not the ring-dove moaning in the olive grove, the lion-cub already appealing for nostalgic lionesses? Think of your divine mission, and don't disappoint the hope of your people!"

Atasu, now weeping softly, summoned Zelinis in an ardent transport, incapable of resisting any longer the suggestion of her senses.

The singer obeyed, and the two women soon fell back on the tawny fur.

The gods and goddesses on the walls became increasingly animated under the capricious flames of the torches. In the center of one panel, an effigy of a human figure stood, scarcely emerged from the block of stone, the only image that was not perfectly carved; it represented the supreme Organizer of the world, left unfinished because the human hand ought not to pretend to the real representation of the divine features. And the bizarre figure rose up directly facing Thutmose, the pale child with the uncertain desires . . .

Droplets of sweat ran down the hollow cheeks of the prince, in his futile torment, exasperated by the musky odor exhaled from the bodies of the two lovers. He gazed at the charming group, and felt his fingers tremble and his heart contract with desire. A mad desire gripped him to seize Atasu, his lover, his wife, and possess her irresistibly; and he ran his groping and limp hands over her.

The young women, languid and feverish, closed their eyes; all their hesitations vanished in the passionate expectation that delivered them defenseless to all caprices, desirous of extreme sensations.

Marveling, Thutmose admired that perfection of forms developed in movement. The firm flesh rebounded under the caress; he pecked them here and here like great flowers blooming for the felicity of butterflies. They abandoned themselves, proud of their magical power, glad of the supreme adoration that was about to make them women, mistresses and queens of enchantments.

The words that they whispered had their echo in the tumultuous heart of the prince; he felt a more vivid blood circulating in his veins; frissons passed over his skin, almost dolorous in its sensitivity

"Speak again," he begged, "stay like this. The hour that is passing, ardent and marvelous, will never be found again, and everything is united to charm my dream!"

He rolled his burning forehead over the small rigid breasts, which rose up toward him, and the perfume of moist flesh reminded him of the flavor of the persea fruit, which gives the supreme science.

Atasu had seized him passionately and clasped him against her. He rendered her caress for caress, and she had the ecstatic pleasure of accomplishing the wishes of her people . . .

For a long time the young man remained motionless in the pride of his triumph; then he got up, lit seven lamps before the golden statue, and began to pray.

Certainly, the double of the glorious ancestor, the Ka, or mysterious inhabitant of the sepulcher, had witnessed that act of amour and had approved of it. The fragile phantom, the astral body or perispirit, detached from the mummy, had associated itself with the ecstasy of Atasu and Thutmose, the two royal children, divinely united to perpetuate the race. The dead man, ripened in the profound well of the mastaba, had blessed the ephemeral embrace in his eternal dwelling.

Atasu and Zelinis, panting, intoxicated and stunned, now experienced a sudden weakness. They lay down, each with one arm folded beneath her fine little head, helmed in darkness, and went to sleep ineffably under the malicious gaze of the Pharaonic mask.

X
The Return of the Conqueror

Thebes, already full of marvelous monuments and pompous edifices, almost frightening in their massive solidity, wanted to perpetuate the memory of that memorable day by erecting two statues to the glory of young Thutmose and his wife Atasu. The famous colossus of Memnon, which rendered harmonious sounds at sunrise, was less venerated subsequently than the images of the two royal children, whose smiling grace time has spared.

The little queen rejoiced infinitely, for she was able, when the old monarch returned to his Estates, to announce to him that the gods had blessed their union, and that the sacred race of Pharaohs would be made illustrious once again by the reign of a great king and a great conqueror. Such, at least, had been the prediction of the Horologues, or Horoscope Priests. Thus, the august descendancy of the Sons of the Sun would follow an admirable progression, in accordance with the mysterious law that regulates all things: the gods, the worlds, empires and humans.

The bas-reliefs of times gone by illustrate, by their sculptures, which have remained intact, the text written on the stone, and enable the physiognomy to live again of those ancient races, which had our tastes, our desires, our anxieties and our tendernesses. Humans merely expressed their intimate sentiments and passions more freely. They did not blush to show themselves as nature had made them, in their amours and their hatreds; sensuality was not shameful, and proved to be omnipotent among gods and human alike. In religious ceremonies, the priestesses of the temples uncovered the most secret parts of their bodies. Their robe was cleft in front, throughout its length, and when they danced before the altars, kneeling down and standing up again, their beauty had nothing hidden.

Cheops, wanting to construct his Pyramids and lacking resources, demanded that his daughter prostitute herself and thus procure him the necessary millions. The young woman obeyed the parental will, and demanded of each of those with whom she had commerce a commemorative stone. It was with the exclusive aid of those stones, the legend adds, that one of the three Pyramids was built. But it was not uniquely to finish Pharaonic constructions that kings sent their daughters into houses of prostitution; they sacrificed them for infinitely less important reasons.

Herodotus tells us that one prince, waning to discover the thief of a treasure, sent his pretty and gracious child to deliver herself to the voluptuous caprice of the men of the city in order to extract from those temporary lovers the secret of the larceny. The young woman, having seen all the men of the capital without discovering the guilty party, offered herself to the men of neighboring cities and the fields, even including vagabonds and criminals.

A woman who had not deceived her husband was scarcely ever encountered, if we believe another legend, according to which the son of Sesostris, having lost his sight, consulted a horologue who advised him to rub his eyes with the saliva of a faithful woman. But no Egyptian woman fulfilled the desired condition, and the prince's wife less than any other. Desperate, the royal blind man was able to populate a city with the women with whose virtue he had experimented fruitlessly, and, in order to offer himself a slight consolation, the legend tells us, he set fire to the impure city, which burned along with all its inhabitants. That gigantic blaze of joy did not return the Pharaoh's sight, but it doubtless warmed his desiccated heart and enabled him to experience a few agreeable sensations . . .

The history written on the granite, in revealing to us what we call "the unconsciousness of ancient peoples," teaches us, however, that the Pharaohs were great kings and that the Egyptian civilization was the oldest in the world. The Nile, of the mysterious and sacred waters, has seen more kings born and die than have passed over all the European thrones in nineteen hundred years. Egypt was really our mother and our initiatrix; her thought still animates us, her arts dazzle us, and the voices of her dead speak to us across the centuries in the gigantic tombs of the Pyramids.

Thus, Old Thutmose returned to his good city of Thebes, covered in laurels, followed by his warriors, his Calasiries and his Hermotybies. Carts containing the severed ears and hands of the vanquished accompanied the conqueror for the edification of his people.

Cavalry scarcely existed, for the horse was of recent importation into Egypt, but the strength of the army resided in its invincible phalanges of infantry, armed with spears and large shields, javelins, swords, bows, arrows, clubs and slings. At the head of each regiment, on a pole, the insignia of its chief was carried, a sumptuous standard confided to the bravest. The flamboyant fabric depicted a sacred animal, a lioness, jackal, ram or baboon. Those images, in reality represented Sekhmet, Thoth, Anubis, etc., which is to say, one of the parts of the divinity of the unique god.

On his ivory chariot with gilded wheels, which gave him a little moving sun to either side of his person, Thutmose advanced, to the acclamations of the crowd. The explosive sound of trumpets, sistra, cymbals and tympani covered all other sounds, and that army on the march resembled a rutilant river, a galactic streak against the implacable azure of the sky. The banners of precious stones borne by the princes of the blood scintillated behind the chariot, with ostrich-plume flabella on the end of long reeds. Incense-bearers, sacred musicians, singers, the corporation of cultivators, and scribes, or hierogranmats, arranged themselves to either side of the royal cortege. The open temples were decked with flowers, and perfumes, in golden and silver vases, were burning on the steps. The statues of gods, before the pylons, seemed to be associating themselves with that glorious passage; the horoscope priests cast invocations to the sun, to the stars, to the waves, to water and fire, summoning the birds of good augury, which described rapid parabolas above Thutmose.

Here is the royal city, the Eternal Temple, illuminated from the base to the summit, in spite of the rays of a radiant sun. Embroidered drapes with cabochons of precious stones hang from terraces, trailing under the wheels of chariots; gigantic triumphal arches representing fabulous animals ride up in clumps of verdure, supporting flowery interlacements next to hypetre altars on which sacrifices were ablaze.

The entire palace guard was waiting, under the surveillance of Hary-Thé, the melancholy chief who was still mourning his dead dream. If the young man had been able to penetrate the walls of the harem and see his beloved, whom he believed to be dead, in her amorous glory and the prestige of royal luxury, he would certainly have fainted with emotion, but Outaya, a prisoner, was keeping her secret.

Before receiving the offerings of the princes of the State, who had come in great pomp, the old king clasped his son Thutmose and his daughter Atasu to his heart. The latter, kneeling, handed the monarch the insignia of power of which she had made very reasonable use in his absence.

Thanks to her, young Thutmose had raised his desires as far as the scepter and accomplished his sacred duties. She felt, moreover, an appetite for domination, and that natural tendency had rendered her task facile. The adorable charms of her person were equaled by the finesse of her mind and the decisiveness of her character. She had made a prompt habit of the métier of queen, taking the entire administration of the country into her charge, substituting, by her wise resolution, for the timorous indecision of her husband and brother, scolding the ministers and even the clergy, previously omnipotent, making herself its head in reality and disarming rancor with her pretty smile.

While young Thutmose was dreaming, while smoking, on one of the terraces of the palace, Atasu presided over the Council of Ministers, spoke, obtained information, negotiated and acted. She extended her restless need for information and surveillance over everything. She was equally instructed regarding her father's bellicose operations, encouraged him by means of numerous messages, and advised him, trying to obtain financial and military advantages of which he had not thought.

Matters of amour held in her heart the place occupied in her mind by affairs of State; so she confided to Thutmose the great event of her life. She announced to him that her womb was quivering with delight, for the horologues had predicted that she would give birth to a child as beautiful as the moon, who would astonish the world by his magnificence and his conquests.

XI
Pharaonic Rejoicing

For five days the celebrations continued at the palace, in the immense halls and garden with shady shelters, chattering fountains and transparent lakes florid with lotuses. Divine melodies departed from terraces in embalmed breezes. Between the columns, the embroidered royal banners, decorated with precious cabochons, alternated with standards captured from the enemy. The tables were covered with flowers, fruits, wines and delicious dishes.

Atasu was sitting next to her father, enthroned under the awning adorned with geese with extended wings; she was truly the heroine of the day, resplendent among the three hundred women with perfect forms amber and pale bronze faces, who surrounded the august platform.

The melancholy Zelinis remained immobile in the sovereign's wake. For some time she had sensed her favor decreasing, and her shivering soul was interrogating the future.

Deprived of her two affections, abandoned once again to the banality of days, there was nothing left for her to do but disappear. Happiness, it appeared, was not made for her, since all her beautiful dreams vanished as soon as they were realized.

The slaves of amour, the dancers and the eunuchs seemed to be casting ironic glances at her as they passed. They were certainly conscious of her disgrace, and were rejoicing in it.

In hours of doubt and sadness, Zelinis evoked more forcefully the specter of her first amour. Hary-Thé, whom she believed to be unworthy and a perjurer, no longer appeared to her in a hateful, indifferent or disdainful form; on the contrary, he showed her a smiling face, imprinted with a serene pity and a generous contentment. In thinking of the affection that he had had for her, the young woman felt infinitely tender. She would have liked to see him again, to obtain explanations dear to her heart, for a secret voice told her that he was not guilty, that a conspiracy woven against their tenderness had separated them, and that a few words would suffice to dissipate the misunderstanding,

The officer in the Royal Guard and the little queen had been her only veritable amities; she could not imagine any other, not desiring any other felicity on earth. Her action in the palace remained beneficent, for she had contributed to the blossoming of the august amour and had witnessed, charmed, the honeymoon that had relegated her to the background.

Alas, the beautiful dreams of old were agonizing with the caprice of the sovereign, entirely devoted henceforth to her husband and the little being she bore in her womb. Deprived of air and sunlight, the singer's tenderness shook its last vine-branches over the almost-extinct fire of her heart. She absorbed herself in memory, recklessly and dolorously, the energy of her thought being still too active, the need to soothe herself with a human sympathy still being too ardent in her heart.

Sometimes, she seemed to be duplicated, to escape herself, and while her body was hypnotized by virtue of the force of its desire in the adoration of sacred power, her rebellious mind analyzed itself and lamented with a bitter compassion, stimulated to the point of revolt.

In spite of her determination to be calm and resigned, she emerged from those struggles tottering, bruised, wounded in the utmost depths of her being, and all the torments of passion were unleashed within her.

Zelinis was etiolated. Her pure face elongated, no longer having anything living but her large luminous eyes, so tender and so profound.

Crouched on the steps of the throne, she watched the dancers, naked under arachnean gauzes, whirling like great dragonflies with metallic wings. There were women there from the harem of Thutmose I and that of the young prince. All displayed perfect forms, languid smiles and a great science of voluptuous mimicry. Flowers ornamented their temples; their loincloths descended between their legs in light garlands, which the dance shredded. They juggled with glass balls or caused green and blue scarabs to glide over huge fans whose thousand spangles scattered the light. Their feet agitated incessantly, their torsos undulated, swaying, and when they flexed their knees, their hair, cut to shoulder-length, rose up like an ebony hoop and haloed them in darkness. Then they leapt up, under flying veils, pivoted on the tip of one foot, making their breast and bellies move, their arms opened as if appealing for the embrace, their eyelids closed in an extraordinary intensity of desire.

The little mum flutes, siols and psalterions slowed the rhythm with amorous motifs, and finally, sistra, sesceks and tympani accentuated bravura passages, unleashed in their ensemble; then all the dancers agitated madly for the tragic and murderous scenes of the pantomime. Songs in honor of the gods formed an essential part of the festivities, for it was important to thank the divinities for their beneficent collaboration in the Pharaoh's victories.

These were the principal myths that were celebrated, and the idols that filed past pompously, carried by the libanophore, Kerheb and Sotem priests:

The god Lunus, who presided over renewal, rejuvenation and rebirth, was surrounded by young women, ideally beautiful, their hair crowned with roses, their limbs naked under light garlands to which captive butterflies were attached.

The goddess Anta was presented seated on a golden throne, her head coiffed with a white miter ornamented with red plumes;

her right hand held a spear and her left a club. She was the warrior goddess, who was only brought out for great royal ceremonies. She was escorted by a guard of honor recruited from among the bravest and most handsome officers of the army.

The god Anhur, whose name signified "he who leads the sky," had the form of the solar divinity Shu. He was represented standing, clad in a long crimson robe constellated with carbuncles; an immense wig surmounted by the Uraeus and four peacock plumes gave him a majestic air. Women danced backwards in front of him, shaking amschirs with vehement vapors.

Apophis-Apap, in Egyptian "the great serpent who personifies the darkness," was sustained by twenty children clad in metallic scales. He undulated in a sinister fashion, agitating his long body, striped with ocher and cinnabar, making a frightful hissing heard.

The goddess Bast, with the head of a cat, was surrounded by a flying battalion of little girls, naked under a tight feline skin whose head, with metallic eyes, extended between the breasts. The children leapt and ran around comically, to the sound of little flutes whose agile stridulations concluded in mewls.

Horammon, the androgynous god, who had the faculty of engendering by himself, was surrounded by Prophets in white robes, who had to know by heart the ten sacerdotal books treating the duties of religion and the *Book of the Dead*.

Khem, the ithyphallic deity who is "the husband of his mother" symbolized generative force, principles of birth and rebirth. He was represented standing, his right arm raised in the attitude of a sower, while the left arm remained, like the rest of the body, enveloped in bandages. Enlaced young couples, lips pressed to lips, circled slowly around the silver throne that supported the god; a sparkling gauze enveloped the narrowly united bodies of the couples, whose eyes were closed in a profound ecstasy.

Then came Ma, the goddess who "introduced Death." She was crouching, her body enveloped in a silver sheath and her head surmounted by a solar disk, or the hieroglyph formed by a palm leaf. Mourners and priestesses enveloped her with incense and addressed soft supplications to her.

Maut was coiffed by the pschent, or double diadem; a vulture, the symbol of maternity, showed its head on the forehead of the goddess, spreading its wings to either side of her temples. Maut was clad in a golden sheath, and her right hand held the sign of life.

Seb, the personification of the earth, was lying on a bed of jasmine and tuberose, and the divinity of the celestial vault was curved above her like an acrobat, touching the ground with her feet and hands. Selk was clutching canopic jars against her breasts, with a scorpion in her hair. Shu, the god of light, was presented at the same time as the goddess Tewnout, forming with her the lion couple.

All those divinities, and many others, with their corteges, finally surrounded the mysterious Isis under the sign of eternal life: the ansate cross or phallus-cross, which, in the Menat, symbolizes generative force. The figures of the divinities were made of clay, wax, wood, enameled or varnished earthenware, porcelain, soft or hard pastes, precious stones, ivory, silver and gold. The sacred individuals bore in their hand the sign of life, the pedum, a curved staff or scepter surmounted by the head of a cucupha. The men had woven beards, the women sometimes held a lotus stem.

Isis, on her chariot drawn by twelve lions, was crushing the head of the serpent. The priestesses of the good goddess were clad in gauze spangled with silver, and wore, like her, a disk on the head adorned with two small cows' horns. Wings made of long white plumes were attached to their shoulders. They displayed an air of purity and chastity, which contrasted with the lascivious mimicry of the dancers, always in movement. Finally, an immense sheaf of flaming roses bore the boat, or bari, sacred to Isis, drawn by twelve more lions with enormous heads and powerful muscles.

Luminous roses rose into the blue of the sky to a great height, and then fell back gently in a rain of fire. The divine animals, the jackal of Anubis, the cat of Bast, the lapwing of Osiris, the scarab, the vulture and the uraeus passed in radiant streaks like strange constellations. For a moment, the gigantic animals ran through the azure, seeming to pursue one another for a ferocious combat; then their inflated bodies dilated further, burst, and were suddenly extinguished, and new flowers of flame rose toward the conquest of the stars. Winged serpents also traversed the horizon in fulgurant zigzags, like flashes of lightning, and mountains of fire crumbled into the floods of lava that seemed to invade the pathways of the royal garden.

The guests having had the pleasure of the eyes and ears, slaves brought tables, fully prepared, circled heads with fresh flowers, and threw carpets and soft cushions on to the lawns for other less ideal occupations.

From the height of the terraces, the soldiers drew a loud blast from their bronze trumpets, and the feast commenced.

Under the sequence of porticos lined up near foundations with light cascades, in the midst of sheets covered with foliage and flowers, dishes strongly seasoned with honey and spices passed on large trays of enameled faience, silver, amber, glass, jasper and lapis lazuli. Rice, maize, sorghum and barley formed the basis, with mincemeat and aquatic plants, leaves and flowers. Cooked papyrus stems, pâtés of freshwater oysters and the species of lotus that provides the fruit known as Egyptian beans surrounded birds stuffed with glazed and jellied conserves. Fish from canals and lakes, cooked in transparent jellies, the various species of the Nile delta, seemed still to be swimming in the midst of yellow and brown sauces with vehement flavors. A thousand delicacies fell over roses, pomegranates and Libyan jujubes, bunches of grapes and figs; large creams trembled in cups, and slaves passed by continually carrying bottles of viscous wines the color of amethyst, emerald and topaz, and ewers containing jasmine water, almond milk and avelines, for frequent ablutions.

Atasu, her husband and old King Thutmose had taken their places at the table of honor, placed on a platform hung with crimson velvet and sustained by four silver leopards. Nearby, fountains of artificially colored water maintained a delightful coolness. Women and young boys were lying on carpets and furs, couples charming in strength and beauty. Their nudity, with reflections of pale bronze and amber, was already mingled, in the expectation of a more complete pleasure. The orgy was in preparation, sighing in the great garden with the blue and pink pathways.

For the royal table, solid gold platters supported delicate pâtés, little birds with delicate and firm flesh, cooked fish-eggs surrounded by pomegranate, plum and olive seeds, marmalades and snowy sorbets, honeyed, peppered and vanilla-flavored creams, fritters of persea, acacia and roses. Each guest had several cups before him, sculpted in precious stones of great value, for palm wines, and wines from Ethiopia and Arabia, with a perfume of bitter almond, and the sacred persea wine that was drunk from amethyst cornets.

Children circulated, presenting small warm loaves of bread in silver baking-dishes; young women agitated immense flabella in order to drive away flies and refresh the air.

The peppered and honeyed delicacy of the meats and the vehemence of the wines stimulated eloquence. Everyone was speaking at the same time, and hands were enlaced softly. New dancers penetrated mysteriously into the arbors then, gliding like apparitions. A silvery light bathed them magically; they approached and drew away rapidly, disappearing into the foliage. Men had risen to their feet, trying to seize them. Soon, cries and groans departed from the somber thickets where couples were embracing. All the men went pale simultaneously, and an immense orgy reigned in the Pharaoh's house and the city of a hundred gates.

Thutmose had detached Atasu's belt and, in front of everyone, kissed her on the lips. When he had taken her into the amorous refuge of the palace and the old Pharaoh had withdrawn himself, the naked young slaves who had been displayed in the corteges lay down on florid couches and surrendered themselves to the desires of the guests.

Couples enlaced, parted and reformed among the flower petals, the songs and the dying chords of psalterions. Young women circulated carrying jars filled with ice-water, essences of rose, nard, myrrh and vervain; others offered cups of new wines and unknown liquors. Red lips adhered to erect breasts in the intoxication of caresses, enlaced virgins offered themselves together for initiation.

On days of triumph, sexual intercourse reigned as master; after the rain of blood the rain of roses; after the intoxication of the battlefield, the intoxication of the field of joy; after the homicidal struggle, the voluptuous struggle! The Egyptians, in any case, loved pleasure above anything else, and in truth they only had two cults: that of amour and that of death.

XII
The Magicienne's Revelations

Zelinis had drawn away, seeking a little calm and fresh air. Having arrived at the end of the garden she crossed the path of a woman walking with a long stride. It was Harraouth, the initiate of the Sacred Orgyes, who had come to offer her science to lovesick couples and read their destiny in the stars. She never failed to go to the annual feasts, the Panegyrics and royal celebrations. She was consulted eagerly, for her reputation as a seeress was great.

After a momentary hesitation, the singer called to her and interrogated her. Although she did not expect anything of the future, a final curiosity impelled her to approach the woman, whose occult science she feared.

"Harraouth," she said, "tell me my destiny. "You doubtless know me and can read my name in my face."

The old woman's eyes gleamed. "Yes, I know that you were

brought to the young Pharaoh in a basket of roses, and that Queen Atasu heaps you with her favors. I also divine that she is weary of your caresses and that she is neglecting you, because your humor is eccentric . . ."

"I've been abandoned by everyone."

"Perhaps . . ."

"What do you mean?"

Harraouth put a finger over her lips, and the wrinkles of her cheeks creased in an equivocal grimace. "Do you have valuable jewels, and is your soul generous?"

"I will give you my bracelets and necklaces . . ."

". . . And also your clasps, your pins, your anklets and the rings on your fingers and toes?"

"You have grave things to reveal to me, then?"

"Your life depends on my secret."

"My life?"

"Better still, your happiness."

"Speak, then, speak quickly!"

"Give me your jewels first."

Disdainfully, Zelinis unfastened her necklaces, removed the brilliant plaques from her veils, and the precious stones from her hair, pricking her fingers in her haste.

Placidly, Harraouth stuffed the jewels into a bag that never quit her.

"Do you know Outaya?"

"Outaya, the former slave of Hary-Thé? Yes."

"Well, it's by the will of that woman that you're here. Your lover has not ceased to cherish you; he believes that you're dead, and is mourning you . . ."

Zelinis had braced herself against a tree in order not to fall over. Those extraordinary revelations filled her with stupor.

"Hary-Thé believes me to be dead?"

"For more than a year he has kept the mummy of the courtesan Nara beside him, which he mistakes for you."

"How could these events have come about?"

"Think . . ."

"But I don't know; no memory remains to me . . ."

"Did you not wake up from a deep slumber?"

"Yes, in the royal gynaeceun, and I was told that my lover had given me to the Pharaoh . . ."

"It was not Hary-Thé who sacrificed you but Outaya, after plunging you into a profound lethargy having all the appearances of death."

"Outaya, being jealous, wanted to get rid of me?"

"Exactly."

Zelinis felt a flood of flame set her veins ablaze, and her heart beat tumultuously.

"Oh, how happy I am! How can I thank you, Harrouth, for what you have just done for me!"

She dragged herself, laughing and weeping, to the feet of the prophetess, and kissed her garments. The latter pushed her away gently.

"Perhaps you will have need of my good offices again. I will see you again soon, and for new presents, I will be your servant. In the meantime, go in peace. Events will be propitious for you, without your having to provoke them. Too much haste will compromise the future. It is necessary that everyone's destiny is accomplished, in accordance with the mysterious orders of the god who governs us. Go, Zelinis, floral bonds are unfastened softly, and the queen, who was your tender friend, will also become your benefactress. When the time has come, I will guide you to the light . . ."

Suddenly magnified, Harraouth took on an august and majestic appearance in the eyes of the tremulous singer. A kind of astral light seemed to envelop her, and she drew away toward other anxieties and other desires.

XIII
The Queen Amuses Herself

"Sing," said Atasu, presenting Zelinis with the harp with thirteen golden strings.

But Zelinis shook her head. "Other virtuosos will soothe your ennui, O my Queen."

"You know very well that it's you I prefer."

"You preferred me yesterday, but today your caprice has followed the flight of the migratory bird and the errant breezes of the Nile. I cannot delude myself any longer, for your gaze is distracted when it poses upon me, your thought accompanying a charming maternal dream. You are right, O Light, to allow that new sentiment to develop within you, and I cannot have any chagrin in consequence."

"Truly?"

"Don't be wounded by my words, I beg you. They prove to you all the interested amour and all the gratitude that inflames me."

"You can resign yourself so easily?"

"I am not resigning myself, I am forgetting that a great Queen has deigned to descend as far as me, and I only want to surround her, henceforth, with a pious and boundless respect."

"Very good, little Zelinis; it's because another amour possesses you!"

"You know my entire life."

"I know that you cherished a handsome officer in the Royal Guard."

"Alas."

"Confess that the memory of the ingrate still makes you ardent with tenderness when the breeze brings the embalmed soul of flowers."

The troubled singer stammered, not knowing how to respond.

"You see that I've divined correctly!" And Atasu menaced the young woman maliciously with her slender finger,

"I'm in love, it's true," confessed the former Pallacide of the temple of Hapi.

The Queen clapped her hands. "That's it!"

"I'm in love," Zelinis went on, more firmly, "but it isn't, in fact, a new love; it's the love that I thought dead, which has been adorably resuscitated."

"Explain yourself."

"Oh, it's quite simple, and since you have the generosity of interrogating me, dear Star of my life, I'll tell you everything."

Atasu put her elbow on the arm of her tall ivory chair encrusted with turquoises, and put her little brunette head, circled by the sacred Uraeus and adored above the ears with two rosy plumes, in the palm of her hand. The necklaces spread out over her long neck and her corselet, dotted with pearls and rubies, pushed up her pretty round breasts with gilded nipples.

"I'm listening."

"You know that I was brought to the palace in a basket of roses for the pleasure of young Prince Thutmose?"

"Your lover Hary-Thé offered you to the Pharaoh, who had manifested sympathy for your person and your talents. That was flattering for the Price, but a little humiliating for you . . . for Hary-Thé, if I remember rightly, had promised you marriage?"

"All that is in conformity with what was said, but it isn't the truth."

"What are you saying, child?"

"I'm saying, august Queen, that the officer of the Royal Guard has not ceased to cherish me, that he has remained faithful to me, and that I was betrayed by a slave, an Ethiopian woman who had been his mistress."

"But that's a magical tale! What is the name of this jealous woman?"

"It would tell you nothing."

"Tell me anyway."

"Outaya."

"The name is, in fact, unknown to me."

"I'm not boring you, I hope?"

"You're interesting me infinitely. Continue, lovely friend."

"Outaya, then, in order to get closer to Hary-Thé and reconquer his tenderness, plunged me into a profound lethargy that gave me all the appearances of death."

"But that's frightful!"

"You're laughing, my beloved Queen?"

"I'm laughing because I can see you very much alive in front of me, in spite of the rings around your excessively bright eyes. I'm laughing because I'm joyful at the idea that we'll be able to avenge ourselves, in our turn, and punish this Outaya for such a black crime."

"What! You want . . . ?"

"I want to return you to the man who adores you."

"Oh! How good you are . . . !" Zelinis wept with joy, kissing the Queen's hands and feet recklessly and rolling her forehead on her knees like a wheedling cat. "I'll see Hary-Thé again?"

"You'll see him again."

"Soon?"

"As soon as possible. But I'll need other information. I desire to know how Hary-Thé has conducted himself since . . . your funeral, for I suppose that he had you decently embalmed? In fact I can scarcely divine the end of the adventure, unless that execrable Outaya substituted a real dead woman for the very much alive Zelinis."

"I hadn't thought of that."

"How can we find out?"

"Consult Harraouth, the prophetess, who told me what I know about it."

"Send for Harraouth, the old screech-owl from the temple of Hapi."

The little queen was not very respectful of magicians, diviners, sorcerers, prophets, horologues and hierogrammats. In fact, she laughed at everything, but nevertheless remained very sensate and very adept in matters of government.

XIV
A Pallacide

In her witch's den, Harraouth accomplished miracles. It was said—an incredible thing!—that thanks to her philters, wives remained faithful to their husbands and husbands to their wives, that the elegant folk of Thebes paid their debts, that merchants no longer cheated people in regard to the quality of their merchandise and that no one lied without necessity.

It is true that the magicienne also exercised her power in the contrary direction, and did as much evil the next day as the good she had done the day before . . . everything depended on the price.

When she was before Atasu's throne she prostrated herself in a profound adoration, and then declared that times were hard, and that a few generous presents would relieve her poverty.

"Speak," said Atasu, "and you will be recompensed."

Attracted by curiosity, the sovereign's women gathered on either side of the throne. They contemplated the old woman, who traced fateful signs in the air with her staff, delivering herself to a hectic and bizarre mime.

In the hope of an honest remuneration, Harraouth, without having to be asked again, gave up Outaya's secret, recounting that she had bought a dead courtesan from the Taricheutes, similar in stature and appearance to Zelinis, that the mummy, in its bandages and beneath its enamel mask, had been delivered to the officer, who conserved that macabre mannequin piously in his intimacy.

Atasu then declared, fixing her sharp gaze upon the tremulous prophetess, that that theft and substitution merited punishment.

"There is in Thebes, as you know, a tribunal composed of thirty white-haired magistrates, with a president who wears on a golden chain the image of the goddess Sate, Truth. There are secondary judges taken from the nomes, all hierogrammats of distinction, who know the sacred writing, cosmography, astrology, geography and topography. Those magistrates know many things, which cause them to be a trifle scornful of men and their paltry faults. We shall therefore seek ourselves, and without the help of the laws, the punishment that it is appropriate to impose on the guilty. To begin with, you, Harraouth, will be imprisoned in the temple of Hapi."

"Me, imprisoned!" cried the terrified magicienne.

"Such is our will. Although you have passed the age of initiation, you will instruct the Pallacides in the sacred sciences; you will shave your head, you will only eat dried fruits and you will only drink Nile water, boiled and mixed with salt. Thus, your days will end in prayer and you will be respected by everyone."

"Oh!" sobbed the prophetess. "What have I done to the gods to merit that cruel punishment?"

"Don't blaspheme!"

"Have pity, divine Radiance of starry Nut!"

But Atasu, always inflexible, extended a menacing finger toward the old woman. "I have spoken. Now, rid me of your presence."

Harraouth bounded like a wounded lioness, and as the servants approached her she whirled her staff, howling frightful imprecations. It was necessary to summon the guards, who dragged her out of the room in the midst of the laughter of the women and the gurgles of the swooning eunuchs.

Zelinis was trembling slightly.

"Don't you fear the magicienne's vengeance, silver Star?"

"I'm making her great, among all, I'm informing her of the means of penitence and I'm permitting her to distinguish herself by means of her sacred virtues. What more do you want, Zelinis?"

"You're right, as always; I admire your wisdom, my adorable Queen! And for me, what have you decided?"

"An inspiration has occurred to me that I believe to be marvelous. Tomorrow, Hary-Thé will be summoned by the Pharaoh. His service at the palace will oblige him to absent himself early in the morning, and his lodgings will be without surveillance. I want to send an intelligent and devoted man there, who will inform me regarding people and things. Have confidence, amorous child, happiness is imminent!"

PART THREE

I
New Danger

Outaya, thin, almost fleshless, but with a gleam of hope in her eye, made her way toward Hary-Thé's house. The Pharaoh, in order to celebrate his return, had granted mercy to all the criminals, and the prison had just opened its doors to the officer's former slave. For a year she had been groaning in a narrow cell, wishing for and asking for an end to her torture. Her crime merited the supreme punishment, so every morning she had expected the arrival of the executioner. Not once, during those long days of solitude, had she received a visit from Hary-Thé, and she had no news of him. However, the memory of the officer imposed itself despotically on her imagination as the sweet refuge, the last oasis that consoles all miseries.

The young woman sincerely regretted the murder she had committed in a moment of madness, and all that was within her, even the day before, was desperation, doubt and remorse, without the relief of tears, which would not rise as far as her eyelids. Life dragged on, heavy and dolorous, full of sinister visions, and yet she had made no attempt to render Zelinis the happiness that she had stolen from her. That woman remained the detested rival, the sole and veritable enemy.

What would she say to the Beloved when she presented herself before him? How would he receive her? Those questions belabored her weakened head. She felt a cruel hammering in her temples; her dry throat was contracted, and she often stopped in order to recover her breath.

Hary-Thé's house was a long way from the prison, so the journey was arduous and painful for the Ethiopian woman. Almost naked, her hair tangled and her feet bloodied by the burning sand, she sat down by a public fountain in order to make her ablutions there and refresh her painful limbs.

Around her, servants were hastening, going into dwellings with elegant peristyles formed by slender wooden colonnettes, expanding at the summit like stems crowned with foliage. She no longer recognized those porticos covered with interlacements and meanders, those walls painted in bright colors, those alabaster and porphyry plaques, those verandas protected by floating drapes, those courtyards, those terraces with dangling flowers, those mosaic floor-tiles and the jets of water that covered them incessantly with glittering droplets.

Outaya felt more at ease in the poor quarters. There, the dwellings were made of four walls of cob, a few small yards in which fruits and vegetables were drying, a rectangular space where the family slept in the open, with the celestial vault for a ceiling with its innumerable golden nails.

Even in the poor districts, however, women were sheathed coquettishly in a blue sarreau with broad yellow or white stripes, and bracelets of glass or metal clinking on their arms. Tall, thin men drove donkeys before them. On either side of the street, workmen toiled, fabricating long curved shoes and papyrus boots. Troops of children with large fearful eyes ran past, their hair flying in the sunlight, similar in their svelte forms to statuettes of ivory or jade. Merchants opened their shops, closed during the night by planks that slid between grooves, one at the height of the lintel and the other at ground level. Pyramids of fruits were piled up next to displays of barbaric jewelry, razors, little knives and large mirrors. Gold and silver were beginning to serve as means of exchange, but they circulated in the form of ingots or powder, and their value was assessed by weight.

Jewelry was sold in the greatest abundance, after the fruits and vegetables necessary for alimentation. Such was the Egyptian's love for brilliant adornments that even the poorest wore necklaces of glass beads, imitating by means of clever metallic oxidations rubies, emeralds, sapphires and amethysts. False pearls found in sarcophagi are still perfectly conserved.

Outaya gazed, enviously, at young women covered in copper amulets, enameled plaques, bracelets and anklets, draped in scarlet loincloths. In the midst of the scornful laughter of vendors they touched, on the shelves displayed in the open air, headbands, rings, belts with enormous cabochons mounted in silver, scarves of arachnean gauze, and heavy embroideries with the glaucous glimmer of stained glass.

Many Egyptian men and women wore wigs, with the result that shops selling false hairpieces were numerous. On tall mushrooms, heavy capillary edifices were set, woven, curled, wavy or twisted, retained by bands of gems. The women of the people had folded cloths falling vertically over the ears, the ordinary coiffure of sphinxes, or little bonnets espousing the form of the head exactly. Artificial beards, always square and straight, ornamented male chins.

Outaya sighed before the magnificence of the displays, and her nudity filled her with bitterness. Doubtless the officer would show himself all the more implacable because she was less seductive. She was walking now with a feverish haste between low houses partly painted in vermilion. It was the quarter of amour, and laugher departed in bursts from the clumps of carobs and tamarisks that separated the terraces. The peel of figs and lemons crunched underfoot; an acrid perfume gripped the nostrils. The former slave went past the dwelling of Harraouth, full of shadow and mystery. She hesitated momentarily, and called to the prophetess in a low voice; then, not having received any response, she continued her route.

She was horribly weary; at every moment, life seemed to abandon her, objects spun round her fantastically, and the sound of cataracts filled her ears. She tottered, staggering like a drunken woman. For hours she dragged herself along like that, with the sole thought of finding the Beloved. She had forgotten the way, but her instinct guided her, and she only collapsed in front of the adored threshold, the redoubtable threshold, between the two granite sphinxes.

II
The Abyss

Hary-Thé returned from the palace, where he accomplished his functions mechanically, without seeing anything around him, without speaking to anyone, so intense was his pain, still.

The phantom of Zelinis, her double, assuredly, accompanied him in all his missions. He saw the dear smile of the dead woman, he heard her harmonious voice sighing in the nocturnal breeze, and his bewildered thought was hypnotized by the obsession. Sometimes, he felt the mysterious hammer of dementia beating inside his head in order to warn him, and his brilliant eyes, his hollowed orbits, frightened him when he looked into a mirror; long frissons ran along his limbs.

On his return, he found Nara's mummy, with its enamel mask, its adornments and its sheaths of gems hiding the body swathed in bandages. That macabre presence, which he sought and feared, influenced his soul more dolorously. At times, he imagined that an icy garment fell upon his shoulders. He sensed himself marching in fatality, in a desolate illusory flight, no misery. At the slightest hitch, the slightest object, bloody lights passed before his eyes and murderous desires haunted his mind.

Those crises of dementia became more frequent. With an effort, he pulled himself together again, in the vague fear of the constant menace that now hung over him. He sensed the abyss close at hand, vertigo gripped him in the frightful attraction of the void, and he stiffened himself, clinging on to anything that could offer itself as a support.

There was a tragic melancholy in the frequency of those struggles, unknown to the indifferent. He came and went, thought and acted, with a semblance of reason, but in the depths of his being, the evil was alert, and he suffered from the futility of his desires. He was affirmed as his own obstacle, and all his past sacrifices only served to push him further into his torment.

If he shut himself away with the glittering and sinister mummy, it was in order to speak to her, to inform her of his projects, of his hope for an imminent reunion, to interrogate her and ask her for advice. She was good, since she had loved him; she was kind, because she had suffered. Each of her pities was made of a caress, each of her consolations of a drop of blood. He would have liked to press himself in her merciful arms, which had opened recklessly for him in dreams, giving him the illusion of a greater happiness.

But all those vain aspirations, all those desires, never realized, troubled his mind more and more every day. He began weeping for the dead woman and himself, knowing that he would never succeed in reanimating her, that he could do nothing, that she no longer existed for him or for anyone, and that nothing in the world could bring her back to life.

The fear of madness progressed in his soul, and yet, perversely, he sought the morbid intoxication, plunging deeper into his malaise.

Symptoms that he had already felt appeared at certain moments. In the presence of a deserted place, a plain or a watercourse, he was suddenly seized by the idea that he could not cross the void yawning before him, and a desolation overcame him, a boundless despair, accompanied by palpitations, oppressions, frissons and surges of heat. His strength drained away, his legs buckled, and he remained annihilated for hours.

His suffering was comparable to that of Zelinis; their independent and perspicacious souls were appealing to one another and searching for one another.

Since the fatal evening, Nara had received the officer's homages. She was present at his meals, remained behind him while he worked, watched over his sleep. Mechanically, the servants pushed the mummy's box into the rooms of the house in the young man's wake, unconcerned by that singular fantasy. Everything connected with the cult of the dead was sacred for the Egyptians, who sometimes lived for months with the remains of a beloved wife or child. The enamel mask was wiped, or the adornments renewed, and the macabre doll continued to give the illusion of youth and beauty.

The officer of the Royal Guard had been present at the celebrations given in honor of Thutmose I, but he had only paid distracted attention to the procession of the gods, the dances and all the rejoicing that had followed. Zelinis, hidden among the other women, had remained as invisible to him as he had remained to her. In any case, believing herself forgotten and betrayed, no desire had come to the young woman to show herself to her former friend. The sight of her would certainly have been dolorous to him, so she had hidden herself obstinately in the shadow of the throne.

Thus, the two lovers, still madly infatuated with one another, could almost have touched one another without recognizing one another, suffering cruelly from a separation that only existed in their demented souls.

III
The Eternal City

"Outaya!"

The Ethiopian woman, on the threshold of the dwelling, had stood up in front of the young man, immobile with shock.

"As you see, I've obtained my mercy, and I've come . . ."

"Oh, yes! The triumphant King has been generous." He frowned, trembling slightly

"I no longer have anyone but you in the world. If you abandon me, I'll commit a new crime in order to return to prison."

"You merited the punishment."

"Do you not believe that, in a year, I haven't expiated it? It isn't my fault that the executioners didn't want me."

"People less guilty than you have been executed."

"I didn't ask for my mercy . . ."

"And what do you want, now?"

"I told you; I have no resources, no relatives, and no friends."

"You imagine that I will take pity on your misery?"

"Yes, for your heart is good."

Hary-Thé was, in fact, hesitant. Outaya's conduct horrified him, but he recalled that she had loved him, and that, in sum, she had only been criminal by virtue of amour.

"Come in," he said. "My slaves will give you some clothes and something to eat."

She fell at his feet and hugged his knees.

"Oh, how I thank you! I knew, Hary-Thé, that you wouldn't reject me."

Without replying, he obliged her to get to her feet, and made her go into the house ahead of him. But she was overflowing with gratitude; a thousand protestations and a thousand inflamed oaths spilled from her lips.

"I love you! I love you, even more than in the past! You can't know what I'd do for you!"

"Go on, and moderate your transports."

"You forgive me?"

"Yes," he said, wearily. "Let everything be forgotten . . ."

After further tears and outbursts of joy, she allowed herself to be taken away, and Hary-Thé remained alone with his dolorous chimera.

After that emotion, life became uniform, gray, enervating and aimless again.

He wanted to consult his sad companion, and went into the room where Nara was waiting for him, sumptuously sheathed in gold and silver. Fervently, he knelt before her and kissed the hem of her robe. He was even sadder and more discouraged than usual. Between that of which he had once dreamed and what had been realized, there was the distance that separates illusion from experience, enthusiasm from disenchantment.

The arteries in his temples were beating more feverishly; it seemed to him that a danger was threatening him in the profound peace outside. Closing his eyes against the sun's rays that were filtering through the curtains, full of dancing dust, he sank into a melancholy meditation, without seeking to react against the obsession that possessed him despotically. The morbid fit became painful, to the extent of malaise, and became overwhelming.

Finally weary of that constant vague torture, he resolved to create a more real emotion. Having obtained news of Outaya, he went out and traversed Thebes, seeking the placement of the sepulcher where he intended to bury his Beloved's remains definitively.

A special enclosure, a sort of arena reserved by Nature on the left bank of the Nile, was consecrated to royal sepulchers. It was in one of the eternal houses of that place that Thutmose and Atasu had loved one another and Zelinis had received the caresses of the little queen.

The funereal palaces, newly constructed, were hollowed out more deeply in the bosom of the mountain. Chambers, corridors and cellars covered with bas-reliefs and paintings retraced the life of the deceased and embellished the abode of the ever-present double. The ornamentation of the hypogeum also followed the soul in its long peregrinations through the infernal or celestial regions, and finally retraced its final judgment before the tribunal of Osiris. Representing death triumphant and justified seemed to the Egyptians to be an equitable measure, at the same time as a safeguard against the fatal events of the afterlife. As soon as the sarcophagus was put in place, the opening of the sepulcher was carefully sealed, and no human being ought ever to penetrate it again.

Doubting his courage, Hary-Thé attempted to affirm himself in the idea of separation by choosing a dwelling for the eternal repose of Zelinis. He was yielding to the advice and exhortations of his comrades, whom his excessively long dalliance with his lover's remains was beginning to disquiet.

To tell the truth, his excursions remained purely platonic, and he returned from them even more anxious and even more discouraged.

All the tombs of Thebes did not resemble the eternal houses of the kings. Sometimes, the sepulcher consisted uniquely of a small chapel covering a well. Often, the mummy was simply placed in the middle of an edifice of pyramidal form into which a walled cavity had been fitted. The simplest sepulchers were limited to a hole dug to a depth of a few meters, to the bottom of which the coffin was lowered, and it was then covered with earth and stones.

Hary-Thé walked slowly through the city of the dead. Pathways bordered by sphinxes, terminated by two obelisks flanking a monumental pylon at the entrance to a temple sometimes opened before him. He stopped, pensively, near gigantic monuments of granite, and pronounced vague words whose magnified echo reverberated in the distance, for it was not permitted to penetrate into the isolated profundities of the sanctuaries. Only the Sam, the great pontiff, and the sovereigns came at certain dates to offer prayers there, and the sacred niche, or naos, that contained the divine image, was only opened to the Pharaoh.

It was, however, into the sacred enclosure that Queen Atasu had penetrated, by special favor, with her retinue; but that was a matter of giving the throne an heir, and the dead, in that case, were able to do something for the living.

Hary-Thé wandered along the galleries and peristyles, and between the columns of the hypostyles. At that hour the pathways were deserted, and the young man felt even sadder and more fragile next to the granite colossi backed up against the walls and the obelisks looming up before the pylons, which the last rays of the sun tinted pink.

A fearful admiration filled him before the mysterious bas-reliefs and the immense sphinxes with empty eyelids. The light was dying, decreasing between the pylon and the sanctuary. After the bright daylight and the turquoise sky outside, the heavy columns of the hypostyle hall loomed up in a blue-tinted shadow that changed into darkness in the narrow redoubts in the depths.

Having come in search of the placement of a sepulcher, Hary-Thé lost himself again in his reveries, forgetting the purpose of his visit. Large aquatic birds passed over the edifices in the dazzling azure, seemingly swimming in dormant water, an infinitely soft dead sea. Other, distant birds mingled their plaints and their voluptuous and melancholy songs, and a great desire for amour made the young man feel faint. The sensation was prolonged within him with a disquieting intensity; he forgot himself therein and caressed himself with long evocations.

At that moment he wanted to bury himself in an ocean of languid and perverse joys, in which the mind fused with the flesh. He would have liked to exhaust the violence of his tortuous intoxication, to savor the quiver of reckless tenderness, to enchain a woman with an endless series of kisses, and then melt gently into her for a new joy . . .

The moment passed; he sensed an occult presence floating in the air, a form striving to appear, to drag itself into a space that had become indefinable, and he stood still, delectably, his eyes dilated and his heart hammering.

The stone colossi and the crouching sphinxes protected him against the attacks of the living; they were benevolent beings full of strength and silence. He awaited their sovereign justice, the support of which he had need. Oh, if only he had been able to live for a long time thus in the grandiose calm of this granite desert!

When he decided to go back to his house, night had fallen and the eyes of the stars were blinking between the joints of the stones. He had not decided anything, and he went away slowly, as if regretfully. In the distance, the Nile was a great murmur, the languid perfume of lotuses rose into the air like the respiration of their slumber.

He no longer found, in the midst of the walls, anything but funerary statuettes representing the masters and the inhabitants of the sepulchers, the majority seated, hands on knees in calm and majestic attitudes; their imposing and mild faces, in the astral light, seemed to be alive; their stone eyes had amicable gazes. Hary-Thé spoke to them, convinced that the errant souls, the doubles, of the dead remained in the vicinity of their images. But jackals and hyena-like dogs began to howl lugubriously behind him, and, finally recalled to reality, he returned to the city of the living.

IV
Outaya

Outaya was waiting for him on the threshold of his house. Her hair was smoothed, impregnated with perfumes. A silver headband circled her head and barbaric jewels were clinking on her shoulders.

She was beautiful thus, in spite of the somber fire of her large feverish eyes and the thinness of her body, devoured by passion.

"It's you again!" he said, annoyed.

"I wanted to thank you again, to offer you my adoration, in exchange for what you've done for me."

"Forget it."

"Never!"

"You need to rest now, try to get better and recover your strength."

Outaya nodded her head, smiling. The heat was overpowering. No breath of wind stirred the heavy branches of the mimosas and pomegranate trees lined up against the wall. Hary-Thé went into the house first, faintly illuminated by a small lamp hanging from the wall, and they found themselves very close to one another, hand in hand.

The acrid and musky odor emitted by the body of the former slave intoxicated the young man, so long starved of caresses. Several times, the thick hair had brushed his face, and the hard breasts had sought his chest with an offer of caresses. He did not say anything, stunned and unconscious. His fingers quivered in the fingers that held them captive forcefully, and his throat tightened with sudden desire.

She drew him against her, willful and feline, divining that such a moment might not be found again, and that it was necessary, in an audacious coup, to overcome the young man's final hesitations. Passionately, with a great sigh, a sort of swooning coo, she placed her lips on his and enveloped him with her arms.

He did not resist, blinded, transported, succumbing under the sudden maddening of his senses. She knew the profound kisses that unchain energies, carrying will away in the bewildering vertigo. She enchained the body with her supple and strong limbs, and stuck herself to him more lasciviously. He felt her knees, her legs, her loins and her breasts burning his flesh. Her breath, which he drank, ran through him like a jet of flame

She perceived that she was about to vanquish. Then she played submission, abandoning herself, allowing herself to be carried irresistibly toward the couch in the great dark room . . .

❋

Hary-Thé, suddenly returning to himself, wondered whether he was really awake. The suddenness of his fall left him incredulous. He could not understand how he had yielded to the banal temptation; his weakness made him indignant, and horrified him. With his entire body, he was still holding Outaya crushed against him. She lifted her mouth for his kiss, but he pushed her away in a surge of hatred. Then she shivered, her eyes misted by tears.

"Forgive me," she said, in a humble voice. "I couldn't help it, I love you so much! Why push me away? I'll make myself so obedient, so small, that you'll forget me . . ."

As he did not reply, she became bolder, and hid her forehead against his breast again.

"In any case, are you not free? Let's stay together, as before, when you raised me up as far as your amour. You weren't cruel then. Let's try to resume that former existence, so tender, so sweet. I want to deliver myself to you, entirely, forever, I owe you that, since you're my lover and my master again, the man I swear to adore on my knees! I only came out of prison to remain at your feet, like a submissive animal. Since you've liberated me, since I've given myself to you, in the coolness of your house, I've had you at the end of all my thoughts. Keep me, dear Beloved, since no obstacle exists any longer between us."

She extended her arms, her breasts and her lips to his kisses, her eyes burning, enlarged by lust, for she thought that she had vanquished him and held him at her mercy, weaker than a child. After the tortures, the exile and the danger, she was finally triumphant, and her entire horrible calvary was forgotten.

She experienced an immense joy in feeling the body of her reconquered lover against her; she had ecstatic gazes for him, and a reckless pride in possession. Within her there was the certainty of an accomplished law, the serenity of a logically attained goal.

They were lying on the big bed in the darkness of the chamber of amour. But a slave, hearing noises, brought lamps.

Immediately, the young man sat up, with terror.

The enamel eyes of the mummy, forgotten, were shining strangely at the back of the room, and the mummy seemed to be standing up straight, rigid and menacing in her sumptuous sheath.

He extended a convulsive finger toward her

"She can see us!"

Outaya laughed scornfully. "That doll!"

"Oh, what have we done?"

She tried to take him against her again, to close his mouth with her kisses, but he shoved her away brutally.

"I hate you! Get out!"

All his fears, all his anguish, returned. Madness gripped his forehead again; he measured all the horror of his action, shivering.

"Return to yourself!" begged the Ethiopian. "I swear to you that we haven't been criminal! If you knew . . . if you knew . . . later, I'll tell you . . ."

He raised his hand against her, wanting to throw her out, but he fell back on the couch, stunned. At present he experienced an impression of height, swinging above the void. Everything around him was spinning: the curtains, the weapons, the chairs, Outaya and the mummy herself. He saw her agitating hectically, her mask fell, and she appeared to him with her black orbits, empty of gaze, her desiccated flesh, and her lips twisted in a frightful rictus.

He spoke, and he heard himself speak, with a distant voice moist with tears. There was a being within him who was gesticulating, imploring and threatening, and a mute, gagged, reasonable being who was watching the folly of the other, but could not help him. Then he fell back upon the couch; now he had lead in his skull, molten lead, whose weight he felt vertiginously. After the amour, the anguish, the terror and the despair, he arrived at oblivion.

"It's only a doll!" Outaya repeated.

And as he remained motionless in front of her, she burst into irresistible, frenetic, inextinguishable laughter . . .

V

Between the Sphinxes

That day, Hary-Thé lingered in the eternal city, where he had finally chosen a placement for the inhumation of his mistress. For long hours he had wandered between the sphinxes of the funerary pathways, examining with a distracted eye the works that were being carried out for the tomb of Thutmose I, for it was customary to prepare the last dwellings of Pharaohs while they were alive, and then embellish them during their reign, in accordance with their taste and their esthetic inspiration.

The gigantic statue of the King stood on the bank of the Nile near the images of his children, young Thutmose and Princess Atasu. At the time of the maximum flood, the waves came to bathe the feet of the three colossi; subjugated, the river rolled at the feet of the conquerors like a submissive monster, docile and affectionate.

The names of Thutmose and Atasu, like those of Amenemhat and Senruset, were to be written in history in luminous traits. The ancestors of the old king had, like him, associated with their power while they were alive the son who was to succeed them, and that custom had permitted authority to pass, by degrees, from the father to the son without any diminution of paternal and filial affection.

Hary-Thé dreamed of establishing Zelinis' sepulcher near the granite colossi. The tomb would be developed in depth, with chambers decorated with bas-reliefs representing the life of the little singer. The corridors would extend beneath the sacred mountain to end at the last room, where the dear remains would be deposited. Independently of the serdab and the crypt, there would be a small chapel, adorned with a life-sized silver statue of the deceased, who would be represented seated, playing the harp with thirteen strings.

Although he was not rich, the officer desired that the hypogeum be constructed with great magnificence. He heaped himself with reproaches at the memory of his unworthy weakness; his conduct filled him with desolation. That woman who, by means of the omnipotence of the flesh, had suddenly imposed herself, seemed redoubtable to him. He cursed the influence that she had had upon him, in spite of his resolutions and his disgusts. And he was irritated further, because an incomprehensible phenomenon was occurring within him. While his mind analyzed scornfully, his senses were ardent in voluptuous evocations of recent embraces, and he arrived at such a nervous tension in consequence that he ground his teeth. Since the morning, he had been suffering, incapable of any occupation, even unable to fulfill his duties at the palace; and it was incredible, that exasperated furnace suddenly blazing in the snow of his imagination!

He drew away along the profound pathways, pushing pebbles in the warm sand, and the brightness of the sky, after the penumbra of the gray walls, dazzled him singularly. He felt very weak, hypnotized in the contemplation of a sumptuous hypogeum that was being constructed for an important person. Artists were sculpting joyful or sad scenes on the walls. The proprietor, who was still alive, was represented in the crypts in his endeavors, his pleasures, his hunts and his feasts; then, one saw his internment, one saw the long cortege of mourners, friends and relatives unfurl; even the mummy was laid in its papyrus coffins and prepared by pious ceremonies for the glorious reincarnation.

Cheerfully, the fortunate possessor of those marvels was directing the work personally, criticizing and encouraging.

Hary-Thé saw the walls, the stones, the columns and the statues with stiff gestures spinning, and his ears were ringing lugubriously. Suddenly, he shivered: the Ethiopian woman was coming toward him, smiling, undulating and feline under the bracelets and plaques of her barbaric jewelry.

"Outaya! You, always you!"

"I followed you, Master, frightened by your demented gestures. Put your arm on my shoulder, and I'll sustain you."

He uttered a groan and drew away from her.

"Why are you resisting? I know full well that you covet my body in spite of yourself. Your entire being is turned toward woman; why reject again the felicity that is offered to you? I'll envelop you with so much care, so much sweetness, that you'll forget the death of . . . the other and the desolation in which you're languishing."

"Never!"

"Oh, you say that, but I know you too well, I know you'll succumb this evening as you did yesterday evening. You'll always find me beside you henceforth; you'll only have to reach out our hand to encounter my caress. My Beloved, my Master! Think, then what existence would be in the solitude and annihilation of the heart! Living without amour, tearing your flesh away from her flesh, no longer having the one who has reconquered you, agonizing far from the one who has resuscitated you with her blood, her bones and her nerves! Is that possible? You'll extend your arms and close them on the void; you'll seek consoling joys, holy intoxications, and you'll only find emptiness in the depths of our soul! The gods don't want men to reject the affection of a tender and devoted companion, they favor lovers and spouses. You'll love me because henceforth, I'll be a part of you. You'll protect me, because your amour has rendered me criminal and I've expiated my crime in dolor! Don't reject me, my adored Master!"

The young man felt all his courage abandoning him again. They stood there facing one another between the sphinxes with empty eyelids, in the fiery calm of nature, in the eternal mystery of life and death . . .

VI
The Occult Influence

Outaya searched for a further argument by which she might convince her Beloved. All of her flesh was burning; her feverish eyes launched flames.

"Come," she said.

And she plunged between the crumbling stones of ancient sepulchers, in search of a shelter. She marched at a nervous pace, without stopping; then, thinking that he was hesitating, she stayed by his side, gradually becoming somber, seized by frissons, like him. Their footprints were effaced in the sand; musky and troubling odors passed in heavy gusts, coming from the Nile.

They sat down on a fallen pylon in the hollow of a shelter carved in the rock.

"Outaya," he said, "I'm weak, but I don't love you. I sense that I will never be able to love you. Perhaps my senses will succumb again, but my soul, hostile and haughty, will condemn my fall; I will hate you for having vanquished me . . ."

"How can you pronounce such horrible words?"

"My intention is not to cause you pain; I only to want to bring you to resignation, to forgetfulness . . ."

"But you can't remain without amour!"

"I don't know what the future has in store for me, but of what I am certain is that my heart is dead for you."

He closed his eyes in order not to see her any longer; and yet, he sensed her there, vibrant with passion, burning with dolorous covetousness. She was beautiful enough thus, to break all oaths. Through his narrowed eyelids he saw her breasts erect, he saw her shoulders, her loins, her legs, and he was gripped, in spite of everything, by the desire to possess her again. Fumes of amour exasperated his flesh; as on the previous evening, vertigo impelled him.

"Go away!" he cried. "Go away!"

"No, I'll stay beside you; you won't have the strength to chase me away. There isn't one place in my body that I haven't surrendered to you, don't you remember? My forehead, my eyes, my mouth, my breasts, everything is yours."

"You've intoxicated me, maddened me, doomed me, and I want you to go away forever. I'll ensure your fate, and see that you're happy."

Outaya took him in her arms again, and stuck herself against him more narrowly.

"You can't quit me yet. You can't say, with that certainty, that all hope is lost for me. Today you think that, but the future is omnipotent; it knots bonds between people, binding them so tightly that only death can succeed in parting them. Do you believe that you won't experience anything in your conscience, in the depths of your intelligent and virtuous being, for the mother of your child?"

"I have no child."

"I can become a mother. That long year of imprisonment has given me the desire for infantile smiles and kisses. I've been so close to death that it would be sweet for me now to give life, to attach myself, henceforth, to something fragile and tender."

He contemplated her with a consternated expression.

She was kneeling in the sand before him; her pale bronze body seemed to be gleaming between the rocks. Her emaciated pelvis was broad, her breasts only demanded to flourish again under the dew of lactation, and over her cheeks the flavorsome maturity of the flesh returned in warm tones. The young man, penetrated by the heady, acrid and strong perfume that was like the passionate respiration of her body, sensed once again the intoxication that flowed from her setting his senses ablaze and killing his reason.

"Go away!" he said, in an imploring voice.

"No, no, think of the child that will be born of us, the feeble little being who will seek our caresses and find your name in its babbling." After a pause she went on: "I thought you were cured of your folly, that you would forgive me, and that we would stay together in an adorable intimacy. What will become of me if you take away my entire soul?"

She had taken him in her arms again, cradling him against her breast, like a sad child that one is consoling.

The sun was setting in an immense red glow that seemed to be extending curtains between the temples of death. The south wind, the terrible and burning Khamsin, began to blow, bringing its dancing dust, which penetrated the nostrils and dried the throat. The earth was cracking and rising up everywhere in the fields, after having been fecundated by the Nile flood and yielded their admirable harvest. The enormous monoliths appeared to be emerging from a bath of blood; the impassive face of the pyramids received the ardent caress, which crowned them with pink flames and descended over the sphinxes of the pathways in long fulgurant jets.

Outaya was haloed herself by crimson rays. Her slightly thick lips and the warm color of her skin revealed in her the union of the dark African race and the pure Asiatic race.

Hary-Thé, a descendant of the Shesu-Hor, the ancestors who, according to ancient belief, knew the Golden Age and the reign of the gods, was submissive to the ascendancy of the Ethiopian woman, as the piled-up blocks of granite, the megalithic monuments, were submissive to the kiss of the sun. His energy gradually melted under the magnetism of that devouring flesh; for a second time, he was about to succumb, when a shrill stridulation extracted him from his ecstasy.

Twenty mourners, their foreheads covered in ashes, the top of their robes folded over the belt, advanced in disorder, preceding a funeral convoy: the canopic vases enclosing the entrails, the boat, mounted on wheels, in which the coffin of the mummy reposed. Behind the boat marched the sacrificers, leading a heifer and a calf, the latter symbolizing the new birth that ought to confer eternal life in the deceased. Eight priests, wearing above the schenti the linen calasiris and the pectorals in the form of the naos, followed with the guests, who were not very numerous.

The entire convoy stopped, not far from the enlaced couple, and the sacrificers immolated the symbolic animals in honor of the gods, while the witnesses recited passages from the *Book of the Dead.*

Recalled to reality by that spectacle, Hary-Thé got to his feet, disturbing the frantic troop of dancers, whose epileptic gestures, cries and lamentations were to close the ceremony on the threshold of the dead person's hypogeum.

"Who is being buried?" asked the officer of one of the mourners.

"A woman of great beauty, who inspired as many amours as there are stones in her tomb."

Hary-Thé drew away, still followed by the Ethiopian. In front of the temple of Hapi, they encountered another cortege: that of Harraouth, the new priestess of the Pallacides. Hermetically draped in yellow, representing the solar goddess who bears the title of "the Vegetation of the Two Lands," the magicienne was holding a sistrum in her right hand and a cornelian aegis in the form of an usekh, or symbolic collar, in her left. Over her arm was passed a bucket of lustral water; her head, newly shaved, was coiffed by a wig of angular curls falling over her shoulders. And, in a clownish contrast, next to the old witch with the blinking eyes and the wrinkled flesh stood the god of Eternal Youth, crowned with roses, with a finger over his lips.

The immaculate troop of Pallacides surrounded Harraouth's chariot, and the priests, directed by the Sam, who were to carry out the final consecration, were already disappearing into the sanctuary.

At the sight of Outaya and Hary-Thé, a wild gleam lit up in the magicienne's gaze

"Ah, dainty couple, beautiful lovers," she said sniggering, "hurry home, quickly! The roads are not safe this evening, and jealousy is on watch! Ha ha ha!"

Her laughter died away under the vaults of the temple, the doors of which closed upon her forever.

VII
Justice is Done

It was shivering that the officer returned home, and slipped into the obscure bedroom, into which the Ethiopian followed him. The servants were not in the house, the lamps were extinct, and the table was not laid for the evening meal.

Astonished and slightly anxious, Hary-Thé went through the different rooms, lit a few papyrus wicks dipped in oil along the walls, and asked Outaya to procure aliments.

Nothing, however, seemed to have changed in the habitual order of things. The furniture was in place, fresh flowers were displayed in vases next to the bed—but a new perfume, which the young man respired with disturbance, reigned in the room.

A small table was rapidly brought for the meal, prepared by the Ethiopian: maize soup, rice, freshwater fish, olives and dates.

Hary-Thé thought that he was hungry; a sort of anguish, however, gripped his throat, and the dishes that he bore to his lips immediately became repugnant.

"Is what I have served you not to your taste?" asked Outaya, shivering. "Would you like me to bring you other aliments?"

"No."

"Have I displeased you again?"

He did not reply, and she was further desolated by his dejected expression.

"It's necessary that you listen to me; I've decided to make revelations to you that will fill you with surprise."

He shrugged his shoulders. What could that woman tell him that he did not know already?

"Oh, you don't suspect my secret. When you know it, your entire existence will be turned upside down. Perhaps you'll throw me out, and then I'll have nothing more to do than die . . . Oh, if you knew . . . !"

Distracted, he was scarcely listening to that voice, quavering with amour and dread. He only expected the evocation of some voluptuous scene, a mendacious tale destined to trouble his senses.

She had taken the forehead of the Beloved and placed it against her breasts, the tortuous and feverish emotion of which he could feel.

"Why are you forgetting our former tenderness, our desires, our lust? You cherished me, however! The other day, again, you were less cruel . . ."

He had stood up, determined to send the Ethiopian away, but she had taken his mouth beneath her palpitating lips, and knotted the kiss, irresistibly. He pushed her away with so much force that her head bumped a table, and a few red drops pearled on the skin. She reared up like a serpent then.

"You don't want me any more?"

"No, everything is finished."

"And you'll never take me back?"

"Never."

"Well, then," she said, "I'll go to finish with life, but before then, you'll know what I did. I put Zelinis to sleep in order to give her to the Pharaoh."

Hary-Thé fixed her with a wild, uncomprehending stare.

"Zelinis isn't dead—she belongs to another . . ."

He uttered a hoarse cry, threw himself upon the woman and clenched his fists around her throat.

"You're lying! You're lying!"

She gasped. And for him, it was a veritable joy to kill her. An intoxication rose to his brain, a terrible trepidation shook him from head to toe. He saw fire; his breast heaved.

The Ethiopian agitated her arms, and tried to speak, but the sounds were stifled and indistinct; her eyes were bulging out of their orbits. Hary-Thé opened his hands and let her head fall back, which made a dull sound on the floor. A little pity returned to him, however; he gave his cares to Outaya, who was already recovering consciousness.

In the mind of the unfortunate man there was a deafening sound of bells, a heavy hammering of bronze that beat the rhythm of his madness. Something like the moist wings of nocturnal birds passed over his forehead; as in a nightmare, he listened to the vengeful voice of the former slave.

"I put Zelinis to sleep with a fetish that the magicienne Harraouth gave me, and I had her taken to the Pharaoh . . ."

"Why? But why?"

"Because I wanted to have you all to myself."

"You have accomplished that infamous action?"

"I have accomplished it."

"Without remorse?"

"Without remorse! Zelinis is in the royal gyneaceum, the favorite of young Thutmose."

"But that dead woman that I keep beside me . . . ?"

Outaya turned toward the mummy and said, with a convulsive burst of laughter: "That dead woman you cherish so profoundly is the courtesan Nara, who died suddenly after a night of debauchery!"

Hary-Thé felt a sharp pain at the base of his skull. The lamps, which he had lit, made faint vacillating fireflies around him; then those fireflies began to whirl, the floor rose up, undulating like a tumultuous sea. In a sudden spasm, all his fibers overturning, he saw Outaya swallow something in an opaline capsule from her necklace and let herself fall with a hoarse cry. Mechanically, he lifted her up and laid her down on the cushions. Then, with a grateful sigh, she took his hand, placed it on her lips, and her soul passed between the open fingers of her very Beloved.

VIII
Amour and Death

All was calm again in the tragic chamber in which the two women reposed who had died of amour. Hary-Thé, maddened and incredulous, went from one to the other, wondering if he was not the victim of a frightful dream. What new hallucination was torturing his mind?

All of it was so strange that he stood there with his eyes wide open, with a sensation of absolute emptiness. The consciousness of the present moment escaped him; he remained bewildered, devoid of thought and will. Then, suddenly, the idea that dementia was covering him with its shadow germinated within him and made him tremble.

Outaya, the Ethiopian, was already allowing a dull and vitreous gaze to escape through her eyelids; Nara, the courtesan, with the luminous gaze of her enamel mask, seemed to be smiling ironically. But that was not Nara, it was Zelinis; the former slave had lied.

How little it needs to trouble the human brain, thought Hary-Thé. *It's certain that Zelinis is dead, and that it's her desiccated body that I keep beside me under the bandages and the precious sheaths. But why did Outaya make me those criminal confidences? Has Outaya really killed herself? Perhaps she's only asleep, and my morbid imagination has created all these things?*

He remained immobile now, buried in the deliria of his dream. Meanwhile, the flight of the minutes was slow and dolorous for him; a weight remained on his breast; a kind of anxiety and curiosity possessed him dully.

It seemed to him that he saw the drapes over the doors agitating, and the little lamps resumed their fantastic round dance again. Nocturnal birds passed above the walls, screeching; the Khamsin was blowing more forcefully, raising whirlwinds of sand that were covering the streets with a gray layer.

Hary-Thé was avoiding sounding the depths of the room when a slight rustle made him shudder. He turned round fearfully; it was a slave who had come from who knows where, and who was advancing, with a confused and mysterious expression. The officer made him a sign to bring light, for the lamps were burning low, frightfully. Momentarily, he had the idea of retaining the man and demanding explanations from him; his nerves were vibrating terribly, and solitude was becoming intolerable to him, but a sort of shame, an inexplicable malaise, stopped him.

Unexpected events acquire or lose their gravity in accordance with mental dispositions or the more or less singular circumstances in which they are produced. Hary-Thé, who had been living in the company of a mummy for a year, had never, until that day, shivered with the slightest superstitious dread. He was watching over a dear person, and that duty, although dolorous, had nothing terrifying about it. Suddenly, however, an entire dramatic and criminal past had been revealed to him, sinister presentiments enveloped him, and everything appeared fantastic and terrible to him.

The pale phantom of fear extended its long tremulous arms over him; menacing eyes were mounted in the walls and vague forms wandering in the corners; it was like a swarm of larvae, an entire tenebrous life revealing itself in the darkness.

The feeblest creature—a lamb, his favorite dog or a songbird—would have been a support for his troubled mind, but for a year, he had been living alone, incapable of attaching himself to any affection, and he remained motionless, the sweat of fear on his brow.

Footsteps sometimes resounded outside, and at that noise, although so natural, he clung to his bed with an inexpressible anguish. A hairy form traversed the ceiling, a moth flew heavily above the lamps, and he stared, not daring to turn his eyes away from the point on which they were fixed, in the fear that they might encounter some cause of real amazement.

Then he was ashamed of his weakness and, getting to his feet, he passed a damp cloth over his forehead, and carried Outaya into a neighboring room, for her presence had become intolerable to him. She was already cold, and he had to admit that she really had ceased to live.

When he returned to his place, it seemed to him—pure illusion, certainly—that the mummy had changed its position in its papyrus box. The body, which had been slightly tilted to the left a little while ago, had suddenly straightened up.

Hary-Thé did not know what time it was, but it seemed to him that he had been there for centuries.

He thought about the hypogeum he had chosen, which was all ready to receive the body of his lover. The next day, he would occupy himself with the definitive funeral arrangements. As for the Ethiopian, he would deliver her to the Taricheutes, who could do with her whatever they wished. That was not his concern.

Certainly, it was time to flee the too-beloved specter, for madness, by ungraspable gradations, was possessing him more every day. After the great dolor of the early days, there had been a permanent sadness, a sentiment of fatigue, of oppression, dejection and anxiety. The wellspring of energy seemed to dry up within him; it was impossible for him to act, or even to make any kind of decision. With regard to the external world, he appeared to be living in a constant hallucination, and sometimes did not even recognize his most intimate friends. His step was hesitant; he lurched like a drunkard, only seeing objects through an opaque fog, and he no longer found the sound of his own voice, which seemed to him to be coming from afar, or losing itself in space, without being able to reach the ears of those to whom it was addressed distinctly.

All those symptoms indicated that it was necessary to act as quickly as possible, and the young man, in his moments of clarity, was truly frightened. Very often, during the morbid dream in which he was vegetating, he had endured indefinable malaises, sharp disturbances, and he had told himself that a great generous goal, passionately pursued through obstacles, would doubtless cure him. He had therefore made the resolution to request enrolment in the active army, for, if it was a great honor to command the Royal Guard, it was even more glorious to fight alongside the King. Hary-Thé would be able to distinguish himself in the warrior phalanx; he would accomplish splendid actions and would come back appeased, if not consoled.

That line of conduct was assuredly the best one for a man desirous of protecting himself against the morbid obsession of memory. Until then he had considered his madness as a kind of intoxication, comparable to that caused by opium, and he had humored himself therein ardently, thinking that he would always be able to emerge from it easily when the moment for action came. Today, the faculty of will-power was beginning to escape him; he truly felt the monster's redoubtable claws entering into his flesh.

"Tomorrow," he said, aloud, "I shall separate myself from you, dear lover, adorable phantom of my happiness!"

Suddenly, a sort of very low, very faint groan struck his ear. He wanted to doubt, to persuade himself that his senses, once again, were abused. However, he could hear the beating of his heart distinctly.

He touched the cold mask of the mummy. The contact made him feel ill, but he maintained it resolutely, his attention riveted to the enamel features and the body lying in its sheath of precious stones. A few minutes went by in profound anguish. Then it became evident that the breasts were swelling and that an imperceptible tremor was agitating the limbs.

Under the pressure of an inexpressible horror and terror, Hary-Thé recoiled all the way to the door, with the intention of fleeing, escaping the torture of his imagination bewildered by terror.

This time, he had certainly seen and heard; the vision had imposed itself as an indisputable reality. Outside, the wind was blowing tempestuously; the flames of the lamps were oscillating and taking on blue or green tints; every object had become as mobile as the uncertain light that animated it. The drapes shuddered and swayed, and long rapid shadows passed over the ceiling.

Incapable of supporting his torture any longer, the officer advanced toward the funeral doll, raised his hand to his face, and, with a disturbance that was close to a faint, snatched away the enamel mask.

He had closed his eyes in the apprehension of the deformed, desiccated, hideous object that was about to appear, but a slight sigh caused him to open them again, and he saw—*he saw*, with an extraordinary delight—the young and smiling face of his mistress, whose gaze enveloped him with amour.

"Zelinis!"

He rolled his forehead on the warm breast, turgid with life, still fearful of an awakening a hundred times more desolate than previous ones, after the inexpressible inebriation of hope.

"Zelinis!"

Then she sat up, and threw her charming arms around his neck.

"Here I am!"

"Alive!"

He stammered, unable to find words to express his delight. "It's really true, then?"

"It's true. Atasu, the good Queen, has enabled me to take the place of the deceptive doll, which has been buried today. I breathe, I exist, in order to love you, in order to enable you to forget the former suffering, to give you all the joy that life contains."

She had rejected her sheath, florid with gems, displaying a naked body, slender and polished, with elastic flesh and harmonious forms created for the eternal desire of the kiss.

With a kick, the young man sent the papyrus box flying to the far side of the room, where it broke, and, picking up his lover, with a great cry of triumph, he carried her to the bed where he had groaned so much, and wept so much, for months . . .

Epilogue

Queen Atasu brought into the world a son more handsome than Ammon-Ra, the god of the sun who created the moon, the planets, the sky and the earth.[1] That son received the insignia of future power—which it was the custom to place on the swaddling-clothes of newborn royals—from the hand of Hary-Thé. That was a great honor for the officer of the Guard, but the sovereign had insisted that it be offered to him, because, she affirmed, exceptional services had motivated the choice. Then, smiling, she had murmured in Zelinis' ear: "Isn't it just that your husband should have his part in our happiness? You seconded me so powerfully in the initial work!"

Doubtless Hary-Thé was unaware of that feminine collaboration in the amorous education of young Thutmose. Atasu, always very eloquent, praised the talents of the pretty singer, who, during her sojourn in the palace "had been able to charm the royal leisure," and that attestation appeared to everyone to be a rare and virtuous eulogy.

Things therefore concluded to general satisfaction, since the officer married his Very Beloved, and the Nation acclaimed the birth of a prince who, according to the astrologers, would be a great king. Who could have asked any more of ironic destiny?

----

1 It is now believed that Thutmose II only fathered a daughter, Neferure, with Hatshepsut, and that his son, Thutmose III, was the son of a subsidiary wife, but La Vaudère could not have known that. Thutmose III was, however, a great conqueror and builder when he became Pharaoh after Hatshepsut's death.

A PARTIAL LIST OF SNUGGLY BOOKS

G. ALBERT AURIER *Elsewhere and Other Stories*

CHARLES BARBARA *My Lunatic Asylum*

S. HENRY BERTHOUD *Misanthropic Tales*

LÉON BLOY *The Tarantulas' Parlor and Other Unkind Tales*

ÉLÉMIR BOURGES *The Twilight of the Gods*

JAMES CHAMPAGNE *Harlem Smoke*

FÉLICIEN CHAMPSAUR *The Latin Orgy*

FÉLICIEN CHAMPSAUR
The Emerald Princess and Other Decadent Fantasies

BRENDAN CONNELL *Unofficial History of Pi Wei*

BRENDAN CONNELL *The Metapheromenoi*

RAFAELA CONTRERAS *The Turquoise Ring and Other Stories*

ADOLFO COUVE *When I Think of My Missing Head*

QUENTIN S. CRISP *Aiaigasa*

QUENTIN S. CRISP *Graves*

LADY DILKE *The Outcast Spirit and Other Stories*

CATHERINE DOUSTEYSSIER-KHOZE *The Beauty of the Death Cap*

ÉDOUARD DUJARDIN *Hauntings*

BERIT ELLINGSEN *Now We Can See the Moon*

BERIT ELLINGSEN *Vessel and Solsvart*

ERCKMANN-CHATRIAN *A Malediction*

ENRIQUE GÓMEZ CARRILLO *Sentimental Stories*

EDMOND AND JULES DE GONCOURT *Manette Salomon*

REMY DE GOURMONT *From a Faraway Land*

GUIDO GOZZANO *Alcina and Other Stories*

EDWARD HERON-ALLEN *The Complete Shorter Fiction*

EDWARD HERON-ALLEN *Three Ghost-Written Novels*

RHYS HUGHES *Cloud Farming in Wales*

J.-K. HUYSMANS *The Crowds of Lourdes*

J.-K. HUYSMANS *Knapsacks*

COLIN INSOLE *Valerie and Other Stories*

JUSTIN ISIS *Pleasant Tales II*

JUSTIN ISIS AND DANIEL CORRICK (editors)
Drowning in Beauty: The Neo-Decadent Anthology

VICTOR JOLY *The Unknown Collaborator and Other Legendary Tales*

MARIE KRYSINSKA *The Path of Amour*

BERNARD LAZARE *The Mirror of Legends*

BERNARD LAZARE *The Torch-Bearers*

MAURICE LEVEL *The Shadow*

JEAN LORRAIN *Errant Vice*

JEAN LORRAIN *Fards and Poisons*

JEAN LORRAIN *Masks in the Tapestry*

JEAN LORRAIN *Monsieur de Bougrelon and Other Stories*

JEAN LORRAIN *Nightmares of an Ether-Drinker*

JEAN LORRAIN *The Soul-Drinker and Other Decadent Fantasies*

ARTHUR MACHEN *N*

ARTHUR MACHEN *Ornaments in Jade*

CAMILLE MAUCLAIR *The Frail Soul and Other Stories*

CATULLE MENDÈS *Bluebirds*

CATULLE MENDÈS *For Reading in the Bath*

CATULLE MENDÈS *Mephistophela*

ÉPHRAÏM MIKHAËL *Halyartes and Other Poems in Prose*

LUIS DE MIRANDA *Who Killed the Poet?*

OCTAVE MIRBEAU *The Death of Balzac*

CHARLES MORICE *Babels, Balloons and Innocent Eyes*

GABRIEL MOUREY *Monada*

DAMIAN MURPHY *Daughters of Apostasy*

DAMIAN MURPHY *The Star of Gnosia*

KRISTINE ONG MUSLIM *Butterfly Dream*

PHILOTHÉE O'NEDDY *The Enchanted Ring*

YARROW PAISLEY *Mendicant City*

URSULA PFLUG *Down From*

JEREMY REED *When a Girl Loves a Girl*

JEREMY REED *Bad Boys*

ADOLPHE RETTÉ *Misty Thule*

JEAN RICHEPIN *The Bull-Man and the Grasshopper*

DAVID RIX *A Blast of Hunters*

DAVID RIX *A Suite in Four Windows*

FREDERICK ROLFE (Baron Corvo) *Amico di Sandro*

FREDERICK ROLFE (Baron Corvo)
An Ossuary of the North Lagoon and Other Stories

JASON ROLFE *An Archive of Human Nonsense*

www.ingramcontent.com/pod-product-compliance
Lightning Source LLC
Chambersburg PA
CBHW050228110726
47898CB00007B/2068